TALES OF PAIN
& Wonder

TALES OF PAIN & Wonder

Caitlín R. Kiernan

INTRODUCTION
Douglas E. Winter

AFTERWORD
Peter Straub

Design & Layout by Michael Smith
Printed and bound in England by T. J. Books

PS PUBLISHING LTD
Grosvenor House, 1 New Road, Hornsea,
HU18 1PG, England

e-mail: editor@pspublishing.co.uk
website: www.pspublishing.co.uk

Publication History

"Anamorphosis" Copyright © 1996 by Caitlín R. Kiernan. First published in *Lethal Kisses*, edited by Ellen Datlow, Orion Books Ltd.

"To This Water (Johnstown, Pennsylvania 1889)" Copyright © 1996 by Caitlín R. Kiernan. First published in *Dark Terrors 2*, edited by Stephen Jones and David Sutton, Victor Gollancz Ltd.

"Bela's Plot" Copyright © 1997 by Caitlín R. Kiernan. First published in *Love In Vein II*, edited by Poppy Z. Brite, HarperPrism.

"Tears Seven Times Salt" Copyright © 1996 by Caitlín R. Kiernan. First published in *Darkside: Horror for the Next Millennium*, edited by John Pelan, Darkside Press.

"Superheroes" Copyright © 1997 by Caitlín R. Kiernan. First published in *Brothers of the Night*, edited by Michael Rowe and Thomas S. Roche, Cleis Press.

"Glass Coffin" Copyright © 1999 by Caitlín R. Kiernan. First published in *Silver Birch, Blood Moon*, edited by Ellen Datlow and Terri Windling, Avon Books.

"Breakfast in the House of the Rising Sun" Copyright © 1997 by Caitlín R. Kiernan. First published in *Noirotica 2*, edited by Thomas S. Roche, Masquerade Books.

"Estate" Copyright © 1997 by Caitlín R. Kiernan. First published in *Dark Terrors 3*, edited by Stephen Jones and David Sutton, Victor Gollancz Ltd.

"The Last Child of Lir" Copyright © 1997 by Caitlín R. Kiernan. First published in *The Urbanite* #8, edited by Mark McLaughlin, Urban Legend Press.

"A Story for Edward Gorey" Copyright © 1997 by Caitlín R. Kiernan. First published in *Wetbones* #2, edited by Paula Guran. Reprinted in *Candles for Elizabeth* (1998, Meisha Merlin Publishing).

The author wishes to note that the text for each of these stories, as it appears in this collection, will differ, often significantly, from the originally published texts. In some cases, stories were revised for each reprinting (and some have been reprinted numerous times). No story is ever finished. There's only the moment when I force myself to stop and provisionally type THE END.

CONTENTS

CONTENTS (CONT...)

Introduction:
Pain, Wonder, and Caitlín R. Kiernan

SHADOWPLAY: A GLIMPSE, NO, LESS THAN A GLIMPSE, this black blurring the corner of my eye as Ian Curtis, center stage, spasms back into the microphone, *I did everything, everything they wanted to,* and the black sharpens and I feel the razor touch kiss burn the flesh of my cheek and ear and the black blurs, the black fades, the black vanishes into the kohl cool ghoul goth that swarms the dance floor, leathered punks and baby dykes and paintfaced poseurs, black on black into black, through the smoke and the sweat and the sound, *I let them use you for their own ends,* but I'm hearing blood and I'm seeing blood and I stumble away from the stage, tripping, nearly falling, hands righting me, fighting me, and then I'm past them and I'm fading with the black, fleeing flowing following him through the fringes of the crowd, down the spiral of stairs and into the basement of the club, down and down until I'm out the fire door and into the alleyway, into the night.

Streetside, she is waiting: charred hair, charred eyes, charred lips. The one with the name, the impossible name, taken from a tin of chocolates: salmonella, Salman Rushdie, no, wait… Salmagundi. Her face, milkpale, curves to me with a wasted smile and she offers those carnation lips and then her hand, the pad of her thumb sliced and seeping. Blood trickles to the pavement at her feet.

The pavement. At her feet.

Where the black has left his offering.

Between her scuffed Doc Martens is a knapsack, cast aside as the black escaped into the place he always escapes—the night—which offered him what night always offers: more darkness.

Salmagundi steals from the shadows, offers her wet hand to the slashed skin of my neck; wound on wound. Her touch is cool and fleeting, gone as she descends upon the knapsack like a starved predator. Behind us in the darkness, Ian Curtis, the hanged man, dead now for some twenty years, beckons me: *This is the way...* or is it Salmagundi who asks: *Step inside...*

She inverts the backpack, its insides scattering on the concrete to form a mosaic of detritus and death, pain and wonder. A jumble of compact discs—Fields of the Nephilim, Daisy Chainsaw, PJ Harvey, Crimson Stain Mystery, TranSister, Seven Deadlies. An aged engraving of boats with tall sails and, in the distance, Pollepel Island. A vial containing pills and powder and three .45-caliber ACP cartridges. A print of Magaud's *A Kiss in the Glass*. Rat-eared paperbacks—*The House at Pooh Corner*, Flaubert's *Salammbô*, Fort's *The Book of the Damned*, and something called *The Hellfire Club*. A tarot card, the King of Pentacles. A glass jar, sealed and shrouding something wet. And a video-cassette, its spine labeled, in a barely legible scrawl: *...Between the Gargoyle Trees*.

Who? I ask her.

Jimmy D, she answers. Jimmy fucking DeSade.

Her fingers dance into the backpack, plunge into a hidden pocket, find the only thing left in this stained canvas reliquary. She reaches the envelope out and offers it to me.

It's a manuscript.

Hatchet for the Honeymoon: In the lost white-bread dream of the 1950s, Niagara Falls was nirvana for newlyweds. Although this crashing and chaotic divide seems an ironic attraction for couples intent on consummating vows of lifelong bliss, resorts and restaurants and even a fine Ripley's "Believe It or Not" Museum thrived there on the tourist trade while Joe McCarthy rooted out communists, networks fixed game shows, and that likable Ike chipped and putted his way through eight years in the oval office.

Today the falls are unchanged, thundering on with the sublime indifference of the centuries-old; but stateside, the town of Niagara Falls is a gray ghost, another dreary testament to the post-industrial. Honeymooners and vacation crowds prefer brighter and more exotic realms—or the façade of man-made volcanoes (and yes, even waterfalls) in Las Vegas and Atlantic City. There is nothing new to be seen here; the only recent attraction has been there all along: the nearby childhood home of local-boy-made-bad, Oklahoma City bomber Timothy McVeigh.

The enthusiasts who scheduled the 1997 World Horror Convention in Niagara Falls failed to see past the dire locale to another painful irony: the genre that the convention was meant to celebrate had taken its own fall, into an abyss from whose depths some writers and publishers could not seem to surface. And the increasingly cheap feel of genre horror was only underscored by the venue, a Days Inn Hotel whose Lovecraftian squalor, leprous wallpaper and damp carpet were tainted with the smell of something dying.

Many of the events that took place that weekend seemed as desperate as the surroundings. At one memorable panel on short fiction, a well-meaning writer asked how he could get his work published in one of Stephen Jones's anthologies; Steve replied, without missing a beat: "Write better stories."

But the lesson seemed lost. For too many of the writers, editors, publishers, and readers who wandered those ill-lit corridors, the notion of "better" had devolved into a curious belief that a writer could succeed through familiarity and froth: that repetition and sensation were all that mattered, and that what readers really wanted was the literary equivalent of *Friday the 13th Part XX.*

Down the hall, the convention held a shameless hour of readings—the equivalent of open-mike night—devoted to a singular premise: the gross-out. A vote would honor the work that proved the most vile and disgusting. Nothing else mattered—not style, not substance, not characters, and certainly not story. The event was far more well-attended than the short fiction panel.

With each hour the adventure grew more surreal. Poppy Z. Brite was being stalked. Pete Atkins was, in turn, suffering the uninvited attentions of a woman who suddenly, and without invitation, demonstrated the art of guzzling beer from a bottle stuffed between her breasts. And Ramsey Campbell, ostensibly a guest of honor, looked alternately bemused and in need of several drinks of his own.

So far as I could tell, only Christa Faust was having fun, unwinding videos of Japanese women wrestlers and disappearing at odd intervals only to emerge in a new incarnation: riotgrrl, forties femme fatale, Catholic schoolgirl, gothette. When she insisted that I attend her panel of readings, I glanced longingly towards the bar but relented.

It was then that the vise of despair that had gripped my head for most of the weekend loosened. Christa's friend Caitlín Kiernan offered a story, but much to my surprise, it was not her own; instead she read something that had influenced her prose, and her desire to write. Even more surprising was her choice. Dressed in goth finery—black lace and fishnets and Doc Martens—Caitlín seemed likely to favor something vampiric, Le Fanu or Stoker or even Anne Rice; but instead she presented a dimly remembered classic that was dear to me: "The Fog Horn" by Ray Bradbury.

An abundance of writers acknowledge Bradbury as a literary godfather, but most of them were born a decade or two earlier than Caitlín Kiernan; and they tend to favor his more famous fiction—*The October Country* or *The Martian Chronicles* or *Fahrenheit 451*. That Caitlín should embrace this particular story was impressive, not only because she chose to honor Bradbury at a time when many of her peers reject fifties-vintage fiction (if they know it at all), but also because she insisted upon the power of a text that was purely a construct of atmosphere and emotion, in which language was used with the intensity of magic—to invoke, not to tell; to disturb, not to shock; to purify, not to pander.

I knew then that Caitlín Kiernan was a person whom Steve Jones would never have to tell to write better stories; that this, in fact, was what she was intent on doing. And that one day, when another young writer would have the chance to read the short story that had influenced him or her, it might well be a story that was written by Caitlín Kiernan.

Who's Killed Poetry? This question, voiced in the concluding pages of *Tales of Pain and Wonder*, haunts much of Caitlín R. Kiernan's fiction; in a sad sense, it parallels the question unspoken but inescapable in that grim convocation at Niagara Falls: *Who's killed horror*? (Not that poetry is horror; but horror, on occasion, rises to the poetic, in the finest sense of the word.)

An answer, in either instance, may be found in the angry retort of Caitlín's avatar Salmagundi Desvernine, who condemns those who have "made emotion almost completely inaccessible through language." She overstates her case - and, of course, neither poetry nor horror is dead—but her purpose is one of caution: When words are devalued—when the literature of horror is reduced to people spouting gross-outs into a microphone—then writers have no one to blame save themselves. Voices that the marketplace has silenced in what some foolishly call the "death of horror" are, more often than not, those of the imitators, the exploiters, the hollow, the inane; in other words, the very voices that deserved silence. The only tragedy is that their downfall took so many conscientious writers with them.

On occasion we read and write and ruminate about the elements of great fiction, as if writing could be reduced to the fulfillment of a recipe. But it is difficult to find agreement, even among thoughtful writers and critics, about what makes for a good short story. Poorly written texts sometimes linger in the memory and the marketplace, particularly those that touch something deeply human or deliver a certain frisson. The most elegant prose, on the other hand, may gather dust, unread or forgotten. The reasons are usually intricate, and often transcend the texts themselves; but in reading these *Tales of Pain and Wonder*, there is an intense and obvious reason why Caitlín Kiernan's stories stand, like Caitlín herself, head and shoulders above most of the rest of the current crowd: She writes stories that are about something more than being stories.

If that observation seems troubling or confusing, then I urge you to step over to the bookshelves, yes, there, to the ones marked "Horror" or "Fantasy and Science Fiction," and consider the contents of one of those anthologies—and they are legion—packaged around some ostensibly clever and marketable theme, often linked to the word "dark" or "night" and, if possible, to the "surprising" notion that this fiction can be written by women or gays or lapsed Methodists or Yankees fans. Thus, perhaps, *Dark Declinations*, a collection of horror stories, preferably penned by inhabitants of some niche, about those who have just said no. The stories presented in these books seem to have been written about nothing but being part of the anthology; they are, to be blunt, stories written to fill space. This is not a problem for commercial writers, who, like journalists, exist for this very reason; but it is a problem for a creative writer, one concerned with emotion and other troubling things inside them that demand expression, since the space that is being filled belongs to someone else.

Caitlín Kiernan's stories, even when appearing in theme anthologies, fill a space that is genuinely hers—thematically and stylistically. Rarely do her texts offer the punch line ending of a campfire tale, or even a tidy denouement. Instead they present a fine mingling of attitude and atmosphere, expressed with delightful idiosyncrasy—like Bradbury, but only in the fierce impulse to use words as magic.

If there is truly a New Gothic (and not merely a Gothic that has insistently evolved), then Caitlín Kiernan is an icon of the form. Her narratives modernize the Gothic and Romantic at their most fragile and forlorn, an aching aesthetic that offers W. B. Yeats as the new front man for The Sisters of Mercy. In these pages we experience, literally and figuratively, Andrew Eldritch's "Black Planet"—a world where "the sun makes no difference whatsoever"; and, indeed, a world that has ended, even though no one has noticed.

Life, like death, is about atrophy and decay; and the long slow slide towards oblivion is viewed through fogged and cracked and leaking glass that seems to face down, down, always down. Consider, if you will, an epitaph from these pages—"He wanted everything terrible for himself"—which efficiently summarizes her ensemble of characters. These marginalized fringe-dwellers—more distant from the cast of *Friends* than the Donner Party—are aimless children of a no-deposit no-return reality, forming an uneasy collective of lost boys and girls whose Peter (and Great God) Pan is known as Jimmy DeSade—one righteous piece of scum who survives and thrives because, like a writer of good fiction, he "*knows* dead; the difference between metaphor and a corpse."

Caitlín Kiernan has succeeded in the profound task of making that time-honored indulgence of the Gothic and Romantic, malaise, into something animated, alive, worthy of experience for its withered wisdom. With pain, she reminds us, there is sometimes healing; and with wonder, there is often loss. But without pain and wonder, there may well be nothing meaningful to life.

—Douglas E. Winter
Oakton, Virginia
October 1999

"I tell you only what I know—not what I believe or imagine—and the human is sometimes as inscrutable, as inexplicable, as the supernatural."

—Ellen Glasgow (1916)

"I don't mean that kind of ghost. I mean a ghost from the   world today, with the soot of the factories on its face and the   pounding of machinery in its soul."

—Fritz Leiber (1941)

AUTHOR'S PREFACE
TO THE THIRD EDITION

IT HAS BEEN EIGHT YEARS SINCE THE ORIGINAL PUBLICATION of *Tales of Pain and Wonder,* and it has been more than thirteen years since the earliest story in the collection was written. Therefore, it should go without saying that I am not now the woman I was then, and so it should also go without saying that my feelings towards each of these stories, and towards the collection as a whole, have changed substantially over these years. Editing this edition, I often felt as though I were reading another author's fiction, and I suppose that I was, after a fashion. I have changed, in ways both subtle and profound, and so my writing has changed, as well. Reading a piece like "Anamorphosis," written in May 1994, I am confronted by the voice of a much younger writer, and one who was enamored with the voices of any number of literary anarchists and outlaws, from James Joyce to William Faulkner, Kathy Acker to Kathe Koja, William Burroughs to Nick Cave to Gertrude Stein. Many things shape the writers we become, and one of these is the writers whom we love, the writers who have come before.

Anyone who has been following my work over the last decade and a half cannot help but note a gradual and marked stylistic shift, from the fractured sentences, sentence fragments, unconventional punctuation, and portmanteaux to something at least approximating a more "conventional" style (simply compare "Anamorphosis" to "Salammbô Redux"). The process was, by and large, a natural and unconscious one. By the time I was aware it was happening—probably sometime around 2002—I saw no point in trying to prevent the shift. Indeed, I think that would have been the worst thing I *could* have done. As I have said elsewhere, a writer who stops evolving is, in a sense, dead. Certainly, her art dies when she ceases to evolve.

However, none of this invalidates what I was doing in 1994 or 1998 or 2001. Am I a *better* writer than I was when I wrote "Anamorphosis"? I certainly hope so. And I certainly hope that in another thirteen years, I'll look back at the stories I'm writing now and feel the same dissatisfaction and unease that much of *Tales of Pain and Wonder* now evokes in me. There would be something very, very wrong, I believe, if I had read these stories and still loved them as much or in the same way as I did when they were written. That said, I do still care greatly for these tales, and I care even more for the characters still trapped within them, if only because they are all minute bits of me frozen in the clumsy, aging framework of narrative.

And now, having said *that*, I must also admit that I have allowed myself to indulge in a certain degree of revision during the two months I spent editing this edition of the collection. I still am not sure whether or not this was the "right" thing to do, but I simply saw no point in not revising when I felt that something no longer rang true and that revising would improve a given sentence or a paragraph or an entire story. I see no particular value in preserving these stories in their original state merely for the sake of maintaining a literary artifact. The older versions of the stories are still out there, in the magazines and anthologies where they were first published and in the two earlier incarnations of this book (and in some cases, no two published versions of a story are the same, as I must *also* admit that I have been revising all along).

As with previous editions, these stories appear here according to the date that they were written, not the date of their original publication. There are two exceptions: "...Between The

Gargoyle Trees," was actually written shortly before "Lafayette," and "Mercury" was written in October 2003, long after the first and second editions of *Tales of Pain and Wonder* were printed. This third edition includes one new story, "Salammbô Redux" (*née* "Little Conversations"); I'd always intended the collection to include another story about Salammbô Desvernine, but wasn't able to find it for many years after the book's initial release. Finally, one story, "Angels You Can See Through," has been excised from the text, as it was the only piece that I no longer felt comfortable reprinting.

In the original preface to *Tales of Pain and Wonder,* I wrote: "And if, by the fourth or fifth piece, you've begun to perceive a ragged sort of narrative, it isn't your imagination. But, be warned: this narration is as much one of theme as of plot, and the most significant connections may be little more than tonal (or atonal) resonances, so don't get carried away. (Those wishing to read these stories in their 'narrative' order are referred to the Alternative Table of Contents at the end of the book.)" This is still true, and the Alternative Table of Contents has been amended to reflect the deletion of one story and the insertion of the two not heretofore included.

—Caitlín R. Kiernan

Ah, love, let us be true
To one another! For the world, which seems
To lie before us like a land of dreams,
So various, so beautiful, so new,
Hath really neither joy, nor love, nor light,
Nor certitude, nor peace, nor help for pain;
And we are here as on a darkling plain
Swept with confused alarms of struggle and flight,
Where ignorant armies clash by night.

—Matthew Arnold (ca. 1851)

Tales of Pain
& Wonder

For Kathryn (at last)

In Memory of Elizabeth Tillman Aldridge
(1970-1995)

ANAMORPHOSIS

DEACON WAS WALKING, RAGGED BOOTS SLAPPING concrete, not even noticing cracks or a quarter someone dropped. *Just keep walking,* marching, letting the red shit behind his eyes bleed off with the Atlanta April heat, *and what's that Mr. Eliot? Sorry, man, no lilacs,* just bus-fart diesel and the shitty, sweet stink of kudzu. In the east, the sky had bruised down to dull indigo, and there was still orange towards downtown, and Deacon, pressed in twilight.

He didn't want to go back to his apartment, one sweaty room and a thrift-store Zenith, always the same snowy channel because the knob broke off. Didn't want to stop walking and have a beer, two beers, even though he still had the twenty Hammond had shoved into his hand when no one was looking. No way he wanted to eat. Might never want to eat again.

"Yeah, well, Lieutenant Hammond says this one's different," the greasy cop with the neck like a dead chicken had said as they climbed the fire stairs, seven flights because the elevator was busted. And the stairwell choking black because the lights must have been busted, too, and Deacon had just kept his hand on the rail and followed the cop's voice and the tattoo of his shiny policeman shoes.

This one's different, and he almost stepped in front of a big ugly Pontiac, Bondo and some paint on its shark snout the

5

color of pus. The horn blared, and behind the wheel the driver jabbed one brown finger at heaven. And Deacon stepped back up onto the curb, *This one's different, Deke, okay?*

They had stood in the long hall, yellowy incandescence and scrubby green carpet, Hammond looking old and sick, hatchet-faced and yesterday's stubble sandpapering his cheeks. Deacon had shaken his head, *yeah, man, whatever,* didn't know what else he was supposed to do, what he was supposed to say, but Hammond really looked like cold turds, and he'd said, almost whispered, *Just be cool, man, it's real rough in there, but just be cool.*

Deacon watched the Pontiac until it turned and headed down Edgewood. The streetlights along Hilliard buzzed like giant bugs and faded on.

Hammond had opened the door, and then there'd been other voices inside, other cops, muttering navy shapes past the detective's wide shoulders. The air that spilled out into the hall had been cool and smelled the way hands do after handling pennies or old keys, meat and metal, and Deacon had known that there weren't going to be any handkerchiefs or dog-eared snapshots this time, no pacing back and forth over a weedy, glass-crunchy vacant lot where someone had said the missing husband or girlfriend or daughter had last been seen. Once Hammond had even made him hold a tongue some old lady had found in her garbage can, a dried, shriveled tongue like beef jerky or some Viet Cong's misplaced trophy, and *Aren't you getting anything, Deke?*

but this one was going to be different.

Just stay cool, Deke,

He was alone on the street now, except for the sound of cars on other roads, and low voices through the opened door of a bar with its rusty sign that read Parliament Club, Ladies Always Welcome. Deacon walked on past the bar, dark in there with little pools of neon, and someone laughed, deep and threatening enough that he didn't turn his head to look.

Hammond had looked at him one more time, apologetic, before they'd stepped through the unnumbered door, and

Deacon had slipped, skidded and would have gone down on his ass if chicken neck hadn't been back there, caught him under the arms. *Christ, man, what the*—but by then he could see for himself. The carpet had ended at the threshold, and the floor was just hardwood and something on it that looked like Karo syrup. Except that it wasn't, and *what the hell, Hammond. I don't need this kind of shit.* But the door had clicked shut behind them, safety bar snug down across his lap and the rickety little train was already rattling into the fun house.

The apartment had been bigger than his, cavernous studio and a kitchen off to one side, a hallway that probably led to a bedroom. One wall entirely of dirty awning windows, hand-cranked open, like that was gonna help the smell. He'd wanted to cross the room and stand there, stare out at the city rooftops and catch mouthfuls of clean air, not look at the syrupy maroon floors or the brighter smears down the plaster walls. But instead he had just stood, staring, tasting the acid ghost of the diner eggs and hash browns from breakfast hanging at the back of his throat and waiting for Hammond to say something, anything that would make sense of this.

You okay, Deke? I know, Christ I know, man, but

Deacon had done his hangover morning counting trick, backwards from twenty-five, and the room, impossible Jackson Pollock nightmare, shreds and things hanging, draped from furniture and lampshades. Disemboweled sofa cushions and crisp slivers of shattered glass.

just tell me if you feel anything, anything at all.

I feel sick. And he'd gagged, covering his mouth with the back of his hand.

Hammond's frown had deepened, careless thumb gouges in wet clay, and to chicken neck—*Cummins, why don't you see if you can find Mr. Silvey a glass of water?* But Deacon had raised one hand and shook his head to stop Cummins, hadn't dared open his mouth again to speak. Breakfast and bitter bile tang and the room, getting in past clenched lips, slipping through his nostrils.

Deacon had closed his eyes, swallowed, and when he opened them it had all still been there, and Hammond, running fingers through his thinning hair.

He looked up from the sidewalk, disoriented, no street signs in sight and for a moment the buildings, the billboards, meant nothing. And the unreliable certainty that if this amnesia could be generalized, made complete, but then the world tilted back; vicious recognition, a derelict beauty salon, windows and door plywood scabbed and bandaged with movie ads and election bullshit. Almost full dark, and there were better neighborhoods.

What do you want me to do? as he'd taken one step towards the center of the room, the gutted sofa and belly-up coffee table, shoes smacking like cola-sticky theater floors.

Anything you got, Deke, as he'd lit a cigarette, one of his stinking menthol Kools, exhaled gray-white smoke, but even that hadn't disguised the red smell. *Do that voodoo you do,* and to chicken-necked Cummins, lingering somewhere too close, *I want to know the second forensics shows up down there. You understand? The absolute second.*

Deacon had looked up at the high ceilings, just bare concrete and exposed plumbing, hovering fluorescent fixtures on taut chains. Jagged butt-ends of shattered tubes. And ropy garland loops dripping thick blood and shit spatterings below. The video tape, glossy brown in the morning sun and shadows, had reached down to the floor like streamers.

Who was this, Hammond?

He hadn't felt the breeze through the open windows, but the lights had swayed a little, rust creak and whine, and the tape had rustled like dead leaves.

Small-time porn operator, and the detective had sucked at his cigarette, *guy named Grambs.* Pause as the smoke whistled out of him, and Hammond had inhaled loudly, chewed at his lower lip; eyes cloudy with the familiar indecision that Deacon knew meant he was weighing how much to say.

Anyway, looks like Mr. Grambs had bigger enemies than us, so that was all he was getting today, but really Deacon hadn't given a crap. His head had begun to throb, rubber band winding itself up at the base of his skull and dull sinus burn. And hadn't he read something somewhere about poison fumes from broken fluorescent bulbs? Mercury gas. Neurotoxins. Mad as a fucking hatter.

Deacon sat down on the metal bench inside the plexiglas bus-stop shelter, alone, and here the tubes were shielded behind dirty plastic and hummed like a drowsy memory of wasps, electrons danced, and he blinked in the ugly greenish light.

I don't want this one, he'd said to the detective, but that had been later, after he'd stepped over or around crimson rags and the expensive-looking chair toppled over on its side, after he'd noticed all the mean little gouges in the dark wood. And there behind the sofa, hiding in plain sight, such perfect circumference, an architect's anal-retentive circle traced in tattletale gray and argent feathers, eggshell, sharp teeth, and the pencil shafts of small, bleached bones. And the mushroom clumps, fish-belly toadstools and fleshy orange caps, sprouting from the varnished floor. Maybe five feet across, and nothing inside except the fat pinkish slug of the penis, the scrotal lump, a crinkly bit of blonde pubic hair.

Slow seconds had passed, time seep, and no sound but a garbage truck loud down on the street and the cellophane crackle of a police walkie-talkie.

I don't want this one, Hammond. Go find yourself another skull monkey, but maybe he hadn't said the words aloud, because no one had seemed to hear, and his mouth had been so dry, tongue and palate snagging at each other like worn-out velcro.

In the bus stop, Deacon closed his eyes, shut out the shitty light and the translucent reflection of himself in the plexiglas, tried to swallow, and his throat felt twice as dry as it had in the dead man's apartment. But, hey kiddies, we got a cure for that, yes sir, that's something we can most definitely fix.

Hammond had been suddenly swearing at everyone then, for not having seen, for not being able to find their assholes with a flashlight and a roll of Charmin, and Deacon had sat down on the edge of the sofa, not minding the stains, the wet that had soaked right through his threadbare jeans.

Nobody fuckin' touch it! Hammond had growled, *Don't even fuckin' breathe on it!* He'd shouted for Cummins, but Cummins had already been talking, had stopped and started over again. *Forensics is downstairs, sir. They're probably already on their way...*

But Hammond had interrupted, *Take Mr. Silvey out the way you brought him in.* And then, *If I need to talk, Deke, I want to be able to find you.* He hadn't taken his eyes off the thing on the floor, the thing within a thing. And he'd pushed the sweaty, crumpled bill into Deacon's hand.

And try to stay halfway sober.

Then Cummins had led him back across the room to the door, ride over, this way, please, and watch your step, hadn't said a word as they'd followed the darkened spiral of the stairwell back down to the sun-bright street.

Deacon had the job at the laundromat thanks to Hammond, and Tuesdays and Thursdays and weekends he sat on the wobbly bar stool behind the counter, watched street lunatics and traffic through the flyspecked windows. Read the paperbacks he picked up at the Salvation Army or Goodwill for a quarter apiece and tried to ignore the incessant drone of washers and dryers. Just make sure no one steals anything or writes on the walls or craps on the floor. Sometimes, the machine that sold detergent and bleach would break down, or one of the Maytags would stop running and he'd have to make an out-of-order sign, red Magic Marker on ripped-up Tide boxes or pages torn from the phone book.

Late Saturday morning, and the hangover had faded to the dimmest brown pulse of pain in his head, but things could be worse, he thought, the handy credo of the damned, but true, nonetheless. The laundromat could have been full of the fat ladies in their dust-stained pink house shoes, every dryer roaring, tumbling loads of towels and boxer shorts like cotton-blend agates. The hangover could have had a little more backbone, could have done the dead soldiers proud.

There was a Ben Bova space opera beneath the counter, and a coverless collection of Faulkner short stories, but the eleven-thirty sun hurt his eyes too much for reading. Deacon pushed his sunglasses tight against his face and sipped at a warming can of 7-Up.

When the pay phone began to ring, he moaned, glared through his tinted drugstore lenses at the shrill metal box stuck up below the sign that read "The Management Assumes No Responsibility..." Thought about slipping out until it stopped, maybe going across the street for a fresh soda. Or perhaps he could just stay put and stare the fucker down.

Fifth ring, and the only customer in the laundromat, a Cuban girl in overalls and a Braves cap, looked at him. "You gonna get your phone," she said, not quite a question and before he could answer it rang again. She shook her head and went back to her magazine.

Deacon lifted the receiver halfway through the next ring, held the cool plastic to his ear. "Yeah," he said, and realized that he was actually sweating, had all but crossed his fingers.

"Jesus, Deke. Does Hennessey know you answer his phone like that?" The detective's voice was too big, too friendly; behind Hammond, Deacon could hear the station-house mutter, the clatter of tongues and typewriter keys.

"Hey," and Deacon wanted to sit down, but knew that the cord wasn't long enough for him to reach his stool. He leaned against the wall, trying not to notice that the Cuban girl was watching him.

"We gotta talk, bubba," Hammond said, and Deacon could hear him lighting a cigarette, hear the smoke exhaled and hanging thick around the detective's head.

"I think," pause, and so quick then that the words seemed to come from someone else, "I think I'm gonna sit this one out. Yeah, man, I think I'd rather sit this one out."

Heavy silence pushing through the phone and a woman's faint laughter, Deacon's heart and sweat and the dark eyes of the girl across the laundromat. And when Hammond spoke again, his voice had lost its big, crayonyellow sun cheeriness.

"I thought we had an understanding, Deke," then more silence, skillfully measured and strung like glinting loops of razor wire against his resolve. And he wanted to ask when there'd ever been an understanding, what Hammond could possibly think he understood, how much understanding you could buy for the odd twenty bucks and this shitty job.

Instead, he stared back at the Cuban girl, and waited for the silence to end.

"Well look. I don't want to get into this over the phone, bubba, so how about we meet up after your shift, somewhere we can talk."

The girl looked away and Deacon closed his eyes, focused on the not-quite dark, the afterimages swimming there like phosphorescent fish.

"Yeah, sure," he said, finally, "whatever," imagined the cautious edges of Hammond's smile slinking back. "I'm here until six, unless Wendel's late again." And of course, the first bar he named was okay with the cop, and certainly, six-thirty was perfectly fine, calculated concessions now that any pretense at resistance had been put down.

Deacon set the receiver back in its cradle, and when he opened his eyes the girl was gone.

He wanted more than the beer he'd nursed since six thirty-five, wanted more than anything else, even the amber burn of the scotch and crystal clarity of the vodka lined up pretty behind the bar, to just get up and walk out. Almost half an hour and no sign of Hammond, and he was still sitting in the smoky gloom, obedient, sober. He sipped at his flat beer and watched the glowing Budweiser clock over the door, tiny Clydesdales poised forever in mid trot, and promised himself that at seven he was out of there.

Just what exactly is it that's got you so fucking spooked anyway, Deke? the purling, sexless voice inside his head asked again, something he pictured from a cartoon, angel-white wings and a barracuda grin perched on his shoulder. *A little goo and a couple of 'shrooms? Afraid whatever chewed up poor ol' Mr. Grambs and sprayed him back out is gonna come lookin' for you?* Deacon watched the clock and the door, and concentrated on tearing his cocktail napkin into soggy confetti.

Think the boogeyman wants your balls, too, Deke?

And the door opened, still so much brighter out there, and for a moment the street sounds were louder than the jukebox disco, for a moment Hammond stood framed in the fading day, silhouetted absurdly like some Hollywood bad ass. Then the door eased itself so slowly shut behind him, and Deacon was blinking past the light trapped inside his eyes, the detective moving through the murmuring happy-hour crowd towards the corner booth.

"I'm late," he said, like Deacon wouldn't have noticed on his own. And the waitress, swooping in like a harpy with a tray and a soppy bar rag; Hammond pointed at Deacon's almost empty mug, held up two fingers for her to see. She took the mug away, left Deacon staring at the ring of condensation on the table between them, the wet rim raised around something scratched into the wood.

"Look, before you even say a word, I gotta apologize for dragging you up there the other day," and he fished the green pack of cigarettes from his coat pocket, tapped it hard against his wrist, and a single filtered-tip slid smoothly out; the Kools made Deacon think of burning cough drops, and he wondered if there was a word for that, for being reminded of an odor you'd never actually smelled.

"Sick fuckin' shit, Deke, but I just wanted you to see it, you know. I needed you to be there, stand there and—"

"It's all right," but he didn't look up, didn't dare meet Hammond's eyes when he said that. "I'm all right."

"Yeah, well, you had me worried, bubba. On the phone, you

had me thinking I'd scared you off." And before Deacon could respond, the big kraft envelope was lying in front of him, nothing on the outside but a coffee stain, and he really didn't want to know what might be inside.

"There's some stuff in there I need you to take a look at, Deke," and then the waitress was back with their beers, set them roughly down and was gone again. "Just tell me if you get anything. And then we'll talk."

Deacon picked up the envelope, carefully folded back the brass-colored clasps, reached inside and pulled out several sheets of heavy paper; a child's drawings in colored pencils, one done in the sort of pastels that smear and stain your fingers if you touch the finished page. Stiffer, slick paper underneath, and he knew without looking that those would be glossy black and whites. He put it all back on the table, took a long swallow from the fresh beer, dry cold, and Hammond sipped at his own, watching every move.

"Just the drawings for now," the detective said, "and then we'll go over the photographs, afterwards."

Deacon studied each piece, each as unremarkable as the last, depthless stick figures outside stick houses, an animal that might have been a horse or a brown dragon, another that he was pretty sure was supposed to be a giraffe. Simple green and blue and red, violet, and everything traced in heavy black lines that bracketed the primaries. The last was actually a page torn from a coloring book, and he recognized Winnie-the-Pooh and Eeyore. Lots of messy smudges, as if someone had handled these with dirty hands, but even the smudges held inside dark borders.

He chose the giraffe, random pick or maybe it seemed like the one that must have taken the most work, the most time, each brown spot divided from yellow with that bold black. Deacon followed the outlining with his fingertips and waited for the gentle vertigo, for the taste like licorice, and the first twinge of the migraine that would swell and dog him for days. Index finger past indistinct shoulders and up the long neck, and here was another of the smudges, hovering to the left of the giraffe's head.

Glasses clinked loud behind the bar, and stitched into the din of voices, an old Rolling Stones song blaring from the jukebox, people talking louder to be heard. Deacon tried to shut it out, tried to focus on the rough grain of the paper beneath the whorl of his fingerprint. He lingered a moment longer on the head, goblin parody of a giraffe's head, both eyes on the same side and the knobby little horns looking more like a television antenna, rabbit ears. Long tongue lolling from the corner of its mouth.

But like sitting on the john, five days and no BM, or the maddening name or word or thought just out of reach, tip of your tongue but nothing, grasping at shadows at the corner of your vision. Nothing.

Almost ten minutes spent staring before, finally, "I'm sorry," although Deacon didn't *feel* sorry, felt vague relief and reluctant embarrassment, a need to escape the smell of stale beer and the detective's smoke, the pounding mesh of conversation and rock and roll. To escape this thing that was being asked and the memories of that eighth-floor abattoir, fungus and copper, the growing certainty that Thursday morning had only been window dressing.

"Shit," and Hammond crushed out his cigarette, gray wisp curling from the ashtray, and drained his glass. "Then that's all she wrote, hmmm?"

"Maybe if I knew something, man, if I knew *anything,* maybe then—"

"Maybe then you could just tell me what I want to hear, right, Deke? Maybe then you could be wrong, and I'd go the fuck away, get out of your face and let you get back to the booze, right?"

Deacon didn't answer, stared at the giraffe, the smudge carefully bordered. Waited for Hammond to be finished.

"Look, you think I like getting messed up in all this hocus-pocus? Christ, Deacon, you know how much flak I caught over the Broder case? And if IA finds out I had you up there the other day, my ass is gonna sizzle for a month."

The waitress rushed past, balancing empty mugs and cocktail glasses, stopped long enough to ask them if there'd be anything else.

"No ma'am, I think we're finished," cold, slamming finality in the statement, words like fishhooks, and Hammond took out his wallet, laid down money for them both, and a fat tip, besides.

Deacon returned the giraffe drawing to the stack, pulled the photos from underneath. On top, surprise, not crime-scene *noir,* but a color portrait of a small girl, seven or maybe eight, cheesy K-Mart pose in front of a flat winter backdrop. Red and spruce-green dress, and she'd smiled for the camera, wide and gap-toothed, plastic holly in her gingery hair.

"Did she do the drawings?"

"Yeah, she did them."

"And Grambs, he was into children."

"Yeah, Kreskin, Mr. Freddie Grambs was a grade-A, first-class sicko," exhaustion, exasperation thinning his voice, sharpening its edges. "And he liked to take dirty pictures of little girls. Made a lot of money selling them to other sickos."

"And she's missing, isn't she." *Or dead,* and he knew, more than ever, that he didn't want any part of this, but the hot barbs, Hammond's twisting guilt needles, were in his flesh now. Flensing resolve, backing him into submission, lightless cul-de-sac, and the barracuda jaws laughed and yammered, *So close, Deke, so goddamned close, and you don't even give a shit, just too fucking yellow to say no.*

The detective said nothing out loud, nodded slowly.

Deacon laid the smiling child on top of the giraffe, her giraffe, and there was the thing from behind the couch, the methodical arrangement of bone and feather, and the corpulent fungi, spongy organs from ruptured floorboards, *but, something's different, what?* And *yes,* the next shot, wider angle this time, and it wasn't Grambs' apartment at all, someplace smaller, seedier, one room and no evidence of a window. Ruined walls that might have been papered, pinstripe ghosts of darker and lighter grays within the splatter.

"Those were taken the day before, over in Midtown," a pause, then "Grambs had a partner."

Deacon didn't look at the lump inside the ring, been there, seen that shit. He rubbed his smokesore eyes, began to put the drawings, the photos, back the way he'd found them, stuffing it all back into the envelope.

"Look, bubba, do you see now? Do you see *why* I'm going outside the department for help on this?" Hammond was speaking quietly, calmly measuring his words, his tone, making Deacon feel like a fish straining at the end of an invisible line, the big one, easy does it, a little slack, don't let him get away.

"*Two* of these, and we're stumping around with our thumbs up our butts. Forensics has been over both scenes with tweezers and goddamned microscopes, and they don't have a fuckin' clue what happened to those SOBs."

Deacon closed his eyes, smoothing the envelope flat with the palms of both hands.

"What do you want from me?" he asked, and that was the white flag, wasn't it, "I tried, honestly. I tried, and I didn't get anything."

"Those things on the floor, the circles, is that some sort of cult symbol or what?"

"I don't have any idea," and the basement smell, musty cloy, rushed suddenly back at him. "Sometimes mushrooms grow like that, you know,   toadstools, in the woods. Fairy rings."

Hammond sighed, rapped the table once with his knuckles.

"Well, hang onto the pictures, Deke. Keep trying. Maybe something will come to you later."

Deacon opened his eyes and Hammond was standing now, straightening his tie, rubbing at wrinkles in his white shirt.

"You think she might still be alive, don't you, the girl who did the drawings."

"Hell, bubba, I can hope, right?" and he laid a twenty and a crumpled ten on the table. "Eat something, okay. Call if you come up with anything."

After the detective had gone, Deacon signaled the waitress, ordered a pitcher and a double shot of oily bar-brand vodka. When she brought the drinks, he gave her the ten, pretty much wasted the bill, crammed his change and the twenty into the front pocket of his jeans. And then he sat for a while, breathing other people's cigarettes, and watched the yellow- brown envelope.

Deacon woke up, dragged slowly, by degrees, back to fuzzy consciousness by the noise next door, men shouting and the hot smack of flesh against flesh. He'd dozed off sitting on the old army hospital bed, his back against the cast-iron headboard and wall, sheetrock washed the blue of swimming-pool concrete. Rumpled blanket and the lost girl's art scattered carelessly across his lap like fallen leaves. His bladder ached and his back hurt, a dull drum between his shoulder blades, neck stiff and slime on his lips, his stubbled chin, coagulating slug trail of his own saliva. Dark outside, eleven-fourteen by the clock radio on the floor, still playing public radio jazz.

Through the thin plasterboard, androgynous weeping, and "You suck dick like a woman, sissy," the man said. "You suck dick just like a goddamned lousy fish." Deacon brushed the drawings aside and stood, waited out the vertigo before risking the long walk across the room to the toilet.

His urine was dark, the color of apple juice or rum, and after he'd flushed it away, he went back to sit on the squeaky edge of the bed. His mouth still tasted like stale beer and the greasy fried egg and sausage sandwich he'd picked up on his way home from the bar, keeping promises. He briefly considered another trip to the bathroom to brush his teeth, but picked up the envelope, instead, and dumped its contents across the foot of the bed.

And there was the girl, Sarah M. in black felt tip on the back, and so she had a name, and a birthday beneath, 2/23/87, so it was eight after all.

"Sarah," he said, and turned the Kodak paper back over. Next door, something hit the wall and shattered, and the crying faded down to ragged sobs. A door slammed, and Deacon listened to heavy footsteps pass his door.

And then she came, no effort, swept inside him in a choking swirl of orange peels and dirty river water, and Deacon dug his fingers into the mattress, gripping cotton-swathed springs like a lover's flesh,

and Sarah's on another bed, green pencil in her hand making grass for a giraffe that floats in construction-paper nothingness until she lays her streaky lawn beneath its bulbous feet

the scalding chills and nausea, the sinking, folding himself into her, into himself; Deacon held onto the bedding, held onto her.

the pencil scratches the paper like a claw, and something moves, flutters past her face and she smiles, more teeth than in the portrait, swats it playfully away, but it's right back, a whirlwind around her head, whipping curls and shimmering strands of blackness, glimpses of mockingbird-gray wings and a dry clatter like jackstraws falling

"Oh," that single, empty syllable drawn out of him again and again, "*Oh*," and Deacon knew better, knew to stay put and ride it out, but the pain at the base of his skull leapfrogged past migraine, past anything he'd ever imagined, and he tried to stand, panic and legs like taffy, blind to everything now but Sarah, Sarah M. and her goddamned mutant giraffe and the whirlwind racing itself around her red hair.

As he fell, feet tangling in lamp cord and old magazines, as gravity sucked him towards the floor, his perspective shifted, falling past the girl, past the edge of her bed and its gaudy pink Barbie bedspread

and the whirling thing settles on her shoulder, snuggles itself into her hair, and from this fleeting vantage the blur solidifies, light curdling into substance, as Deacon landed hard, hard enough to knock the wind out of him, leave him gasping, tasting blood,

wings spread wide, kite-boned and iridescent butterfly scales, gristle twigs,

clinging madly to the floor, sensing there was farther to fall. He opened his mouth to scream and felt the warm rise, the indisputable acid gush from his lips,

leering jaws, lipless, eyes like indigo berries sunk deep in puckered skin, and it sees him, then hides its impossible face in her hair.

Sarah laughs. And the sunlight through her window, the tempera sky, goes out, and here it is cold, slime dank, and beneath his fingers, bare stone. A dark past the simple absence of light, can't see, but he can hear, metal clink and scrape and her breath, labored; the sweet-sour ammonia stink of piss, shitty-rich pungence, mold. Distant traffic and the steady drip of water from somewhere high overhead. Wet hiss, air drawn hard across clenched teeth, or escaping steam, and

she was gone, and nothing left under him but the floor of his own apartment, his face cushioned in cooling vomit and umber shag. He did not open his eyes, already strained painfully wide, but the darkness had begun to pale, thinning itself to a pasty, transparent charcoal as the world faded leisurely in, neat Polaroid trick.

Deacon blinked at the huge and somber dust bunnies massed beneath his bed, an old Schlitz can back there just out of reach. And then the straggling headache caught him, slammed home, and he turned over onto his back and stared helplessly into the electric white sun screwed inside its bug-filled globe, crisped little Icaruses; he knew that feeling, passing too fucking close to something hot enough, black enough, to boil your blood and brains and leave behind a hollow parchment husk.

Deacon Silvey lay very still, hands fisted, and waited for the pain to ease off enough that he could move without puking again or passing out, until the phantom smells faded and finally there was only the vomit reek, the kinder mustiness of his room. And then he crawled the five feet to the telephone and dialed Hammond's number.

Hammond had sent a car for him, and the two officers had complained about the Olympics while Deacon stared silently out at the lighted, empty streets, at the bright cluster of office towers and high-rise real estate like a talisman against the night sky. If there'd been stars out, they'd been hidden safely behind the soft Dreamsicle-orange curtain, the combined glow of ten thousand sodium-vapor bulbs. The envelope with Sarah M.'s drawings and the photos had ridden on the seat next to him.

Now it sat marooned in the wild clutter of the detective's desk, concealing the art history textbook he'd spent fifteen minutes rummaging for in cardboard boxes and on the sagging shelves he'd built out of alley-found boards and concrete blocks. Deacon sipped scalding, sugary coffee from a styrofoam cup and waited for Hammond, waited to say words that sounded just as insane no matter how many times he pulled them apart and stuck them back together, polished absurdities, arranged and rearranged in his head like worn and finger-worried Scrabble tiles.

Just show him everything, let him connect the dots for himself. If he can see this on his own—

The office door slammed open, banged loud against the wall, and Hammond seemed pulled through by the slipstream, threaded into the disorder. More than exhaustion on his face, haggard; around his guarded eyes not sleep, but sleep forestalled, sleep purposefully misplaced. The eyes of someone who might not want to sleep ever again. For a moment, Hammond stared at him, as if he hadn't expected to find Deacon sitting there, anyone else, either; as if he'd been escaping, fleeing into this sanctuary of manila folders and overflowing ashtrays and had encountered an obstacle, had been caught.

"Deacon," he said, shutting the door more carefully behind him, but the *way* he said it, Deacon hardly recognized his own name. "So what you got for me, bubba," and the words sighed out, hushed of their intended tone, sieved raw. Deacon chewed at his lower lip, toying with a ragged piece of skin there, his eyes drawn past the impatient envelope to the dusty gray streaking the detective's suit, unwashed hands stained with rust and dirt.

"C'mon Deke. You even look sober, man. Something's up," and still that brittleness, picture-perfect likeness of Hammond's bluster, but cold porcelain cast and maybe already broken. Sharp and scattered edges waiting to slice. Deacon set down his coffee cup, no clear spot on the desk, so he put it on the floor a safe distance from his feet. And then he slid the big green book from beneath the envelope, *Art Through The Ages* and Matisse's five dancing maidens on the cover, imperfect ring, left hand to right to left; began to flip through dog-eared pages as he spoke fast, nearly stuttering, before he lost his nerve.

"Remember when you said that it didn't matter whether or not you believed, if *I* even believed, that the only thing that mattered to you was whether or not it worked? You said that, the first time—"

"I remember what I said, Deacon."

"It's important this time," and he wandered past Hieronymus Bosch and the St. Anne altarpiece and into pages of baroque architecture; couldn't recall the page number, but this was certainly too far, and so he began to search more slowly backwards. "It's important, or else you're gonna throw me out on my ass before I'm finished."

And there, the top two-thirds of page 691, and he turned the book around so Hammond could see, bent across the desk; caught the fusty smell clinging to the detective beneath ubiquitous stale menthol, faint dampness, mold and iron rot.

"This was done by a Sixteenth-Century German painter named Hans Holbein," and he pointed at the two men in the painting, standing, neat-trimmed beards and somber faces, be-

fore an emerald curtain, arms resting on the tall side table between them.

"They were ambassadors to England. You have to understand,
this thing is fucking meticulous. Look at the stuff on the table,"
and he jabbed his finger, first at a globe, then a compass,
astronomical and navigational instruments he knew no names
for. "The realism is incredible. He got every detail, the numbers
on the sundial, the broken string on the lute, and the perspective is flawless. But here," and Deacon moved his finger down
towards the men's shadowed feet. "There," and the gray-black
slash across the bottom of the painting. "What do you see
there?" Hammond took the book from him, shrugged, stared a
moment longer before shaking his head. "Now," Deacon said,
"Move your face a little closer to the book, and look *across* the
painting from an angle, towards the upper right-hand corner."

Hammond hesitated, mouth drawn taut and sincerest I-have-
no-intention-of-humoring-you-much-longer cast in his eyes,
but then he obeyed, leaned close and tilted his head, stared at
The French Ambassadors, eyes narrowed, almost squinting.

"Do you see it?" Deacon said, nearly a whisper.

Hammond shook his head again, his cheek almost touching
the paper now. "Yeah, okay, it's a skull," he said, "but it's still
distorted, all stretched out."

"That's because Holbein meant it to be viewed through a special cylinder-shaped mirror. Now," and he reached for the envelope, noticed how his hands had begun to tremble, "look at
this." Deacon pulled out the giraffe drawing and laid it inside
the open book. "The smudge up next to the head. Try the same
thing, except this time, look out of the corner of your eye,
straight down from the top edge of the paper."

Hammond paused, then set aside the textbook and lifted the
drawing, flat across both palms, to eye level. He turned his head
away so that he seemed to be watching a row of file cabinets
across the office, instead. Then, lips parted slightly and not exactly a sigh, but lungs emptying, breath across ivory-yellowed
teeth and nothing drawn in to replace the expelled air.

"It's there on every one of them, more than once on some," Deacon said, and waited for a response. Hammond said nothing, laid the drawing on the desk and continued to stare at the file cabinets.

But Deacon knew what he'd seen, knew what Sarah M. had carefully scrawled there in the same deliberate hand as she'd decorated the giraffe. Knobby arc of wings and the ridiculous, needle-toothed grin, the spidery arms and legs, too many joints, ending in the stiletto intimation of claws. Pupiless eyes like poisonous blue-black berries.

"Okay, bubba," Hammond said quietly, sometime later, after he'd finally returned the giraffe to the envelope and closed *Art Through The Ages,* "now it's my turn."

Deacon and the detective sat alone in the darkened conference room, their faces lit by a shifting salt-and-pepper blizzard of electronic snow; Hammond had hit the mute button even before the tape began, and now, past the three and a half minutes salvaged from Gramb's apartment, the voiceless storm raged across the screen.

"The optics guys thought maybe it was a flaw in the camera lens," Hammond said; he made no move to turn the lights back up or shut off the television.

Deacon concentrated furiously on the writhing static, but saw nothing past the last seconds, the last scratched frames of tape. Final, brutal close-up of Sarah's face, harsh light and tears and something indistinct moving rapidly across the shot. And then the VCR had clicked itself off, rewind whir, and this, white and gray and black and him talking, the things he'd seen in his apartment when he'd held the giraffe, the darting blur and the piss-stinking place. Playing the proper psychic and describing every sound, the traffic, the dripping water, every vague, half-assed excuse for an impression he could recall.

And Hammond nodded, took out a Kool, but didn't light it, held the cigarette tight between his fingers and stared down at the dull glimmer from the television reflected in his s hoes.

"Yeah, bubba," he said. "Well, we've been there. We tracked down a realtor friend of Mr. Grambs this evening, and he was nice enough to show us a basement over on Butler," and Hammond coughed, clearing his throat, too loud in the dark room. "Shit, Deke, those guys had their own little Hollywood crammed into a hole about the size of the men's crapper down the hall."

"No," Deacon said. "The place I saw was nothing like that."

"They were keeping her in a subbasement, Deke. Christ, there are old cellars and tunnels down there that go all the way back to the friggin' Civil War. Nobody has any fucking idea..." and Deacon turned, his chair grating on the tile; the detective looked like an old man, timesick, every line, every wrinkle deepened, and bleeding shadow.

"We found the trapdoor under a throw rug, right there in the middle of the basement. Brand new Yale padlock on it, big enough to choke a goddamn horse," and he held up his fist to demonstrate.

"I climbed down first, this rickety-shit ladder, you know. Guess it went down twenty or twenty-five feet, and the floor was just cobblestones. It was like crawling into the sewers, man, the smell..." Deacon looked away, didn't care for the sudden age masking Hammond's face, clouding his eyes.

"That kid's been missing since *February*, Deke."

"She was dead?"

"Dead? Hell, she wasn't even *there*. I stepped off that ladder right into a bunch of those goddamn mushrooms, *huge* things, high as my ankle and big around as dinner plates. I shined a flashlight around, hardly ten feet square, and it was just like before. Not a soul, just this perfect circle of those things. And the bones, pokin' up out of all those toadstools. And this."

Hammond removed something from the pocket of his jacket, handed it to Deacon. Slippery, cool plastic, an evidence bag, already numbered, and inside, something he had to hold up into the flickering light to see clearly. Four, maybe five ginger strands of hair.

"Listen, bubba. I'm telling you this because if I don't tell someone...but it doesn't leave this room. Do you understand?"

"Who would I tell, Hammond?"

"I picked those up right at the center, before anyone else came down the ladder. And I swear before the saints and angels and Holy Jesus, they weren't just lying there, Deke, they were sticking up *out* of those old cobbles. I had to *break* them off."

Deacon passed the bag back to the detective, and for a little while they sat, not speaking, only their breathing and footsteps coming and going in the hallway outside, muffled conversation from other rooms.

"I'm not going to be able to help you anymore," Deacon said, and he stood up. Hammond remained seated, had gone back to staring at his shoes.

"I'm sorry," he said. "I truly am sorry about that, bubba, but after this shit, I guess it's fair enough. You take care of yourself, Deacon Silvey."

"Yeah, you too," and then Deacon walked to the door, slow, stepping cautiously around other chairs, invisible in the dark and the flittering afterimages from the television screen. The doorknob was cold, almost as cold as the fluorescent light that flooded in through the open door, keen and sterile light that could cut like scalpel steel if you looked directly at it long enough.

He shut the door behind him.

> *Come away, O human child!*
> *To the waters and the wild*
> *With a faery, hand in hand,*
> *For the world's more full of weeping than you can*
> *understand.*
>
> —W. B. Yeats, "The Stolen Child" (1886)

TO THIS WATER
(JOHNSTOWN, PENNSYLVANIA 1889)

⇒ 1 ⇐

HARDLY DAWN, AND ALREADY MAGDA HAD MADE HER way through the forest into the glittering frost at the foot of the dam. When the sun climbed high enough, it would push aside the shadows and set the hollow on fire, sparkling crystal fire that would melt gently in the late spring sunrise and drip from hemlock and aspen branches, glaze the towering thickets of mountain laurel, later rise again as gauzy soft steam. Everything, ice-crisped ferns and everything else, crunched beneath her shoes, loud in the cold, still air; no sound but morning birds and the steady gush from the spillway into South Fork Creek, noisy and secretive, like careless whispers behind her back.

Winded, her breath puffing out white through chapped lips and a stitch nagging her side, she rested a moment against a potato-shaped boulder, and the moss there froststiffened too, icematted green fur and gray lichens like scabs. Back down the valley towards South Fork, night held on, a lazy thing curled in the lee of the mountain. Magda shivered and pulled her shawl tighter about her shoulders.

All the way from Johnstown since nightfall, fifteen miles or more since she'd slipped away from the darkened rows of company houses on Prospect Hill, following the railroad first and

later, after the sleeping streets of South Fork, game trails and finally the winding creek, yellow-brown and swollen with the
runoff of April thaw and heavy May rains. By now her family
would be awake, her father already gone to the mill and twelve
hours at the furnaces, her mother and sister neglecting chores,
and soon they would be asking from house to house, porches
and back doors.

But no one had seen her go, and there would be nothing but
concerned and shaking heads, shrugs and suspicion for their
questions and broken English. And when they'd gone, there would
be whispers, like the murmur and purl of mountain streams.

As the sky faded from soft violet, unbruising, Magda turned
and began to pick her way up the steep and rocky face of the dam.

This is not memory, this is a pricking new thing, time knotted,
cat's cradled or snarled like her sister's brown hair, and she is
always closing her eyes, always opening them again, and always
the narrow slit of sky is red, wound-red slash between the alley's
black walls and rooftops, pine and shingle jaws. And there is
nothing left of the men but callused, groping fingers, the scalding whiskey soursweetness of their breath. Sounds like laughter from dog throats and the whiskery lips of pigs, dogs and
pigs laughing if they could.

And Magda does not scream, because they have said that if
she screams, if she cries or even speaks they will cut her tongue
out, will cut her hunkie throat from ear to ear, and she knows
that much English. And the big Irishman has shown her his
knife; they will all show her their knives, and cut her whether
she screams or not.

The hands pushing and she turns her face away, better the
cool mud, the water puddled that flows into her mouth, fills her
nostrils, that tastes like earth and rot and the alcohol from
empty barrels and overflowing crates of bottles stacked high
behind the Washington Street saloon. She grinds her teeth,
crunching grit, sand sharp against her gums.

And before she shuts her eyes, last thing before there is only raw pain and the sounds she won't ever shut out, Magda catches the dapper man watching from the far-away end of the alley, surprised face peering down the well. Staring slack jawed, and light from somewhere safe glints coldly off his spectacles, moonlight on thin ice.

The demons growl, and he scuttles away, and they fold her open like a cockleshell.

By the wavering orange oil light, her mother's face had glowed warm, age and weariness softened almost away, and she had been speaking to them in Magyar, even though Papa said that they'd never learn that way. And she had leaned over them, brushing her sister Emilia's hair from her face. Her mother had set the lamp carefully down on the wobbly little table beside their bed, herself in the wobbly chair, and it had still been winter, then, still dirty snow on the ground outside, the wind around the pine-board corners of the house, howling for its own misfortunes. And them bundled safe beneath quilts and rag-swaddled bricks from the hearth at their feet.

Magda had watched the shadows thrown across the walls, walls bare save knotholes stuffed with old newspapers and the crucifix her mother had brought across from Budapest, blood-dark wood and tortured pewter. And the lamp light had danced as her mother had spoken, had seemed to follow the rise and fall of her words, measured steps in a pattern too subtle for Magda to follow.

So she had closed her eyes tightly, burying her face in pillows and Emilia's back, and listened to her mother's stories of child-hood in the mountain village of Tátra Lomnitz and the wild Carpathians, listening more to her soothing voice than the words themselves. She knew all the old stories of the house elves, the hairy little domovoy that had lived in the dust and sooty corner behind her grandmother's stove, and the river people, the Vodyaniyie and Rusalky; the comfort her sister drew from the fairy tales, she took directly from the music of timbre and tender intonation.

"And in the autumn," her mother had said, "when a fat gander was offered to the people who lived under the lake, we would first cut off its head and nail it to the barn door so that our domovoy would not know that one of his geese had been given away to another."

And then, sometime later, the lamp lifted from the wobbly table, and her mother had kissed them both, Magda pretending to sleep, and whispered, her voice softer than the bed, "Jó éjszakát," and her bare footsteps already moving away, sounding hollow on the floor, when Emilia had corrected her, "Good night, Mama."

"Good night, Emilia," her mother had answered, and then they had been alone with the night and the wind and the sky outside their window that was never quite black enough for stars, but always stained red from the belching foundry fires of Johnstown.

It was full morning by the time Magda reached the top, and her eyes stung with her own sweat, and when she licked her lips she tasted her own salt; not blood, but something close. Her dress clung wetly to her back, clammy, damp armpits, and she'd ripped her skirt and stockings in blackberry briars and creeper vines. Twice, she'd slipped on the loose stones, and there was a small gash on her left palm, purpling bruise below her thumb. Now, she stood a moment on the narrow road that stretched across the breast of the dam, listening to her heart, fleshpump beneath cotton and skin, muscle and bone. Watching the mist, milky wisps curling up from the green-gray water, burning away in the sun.

Up here, the morning smelled clean, pine and the silent lake, no hint of the valley's pall of coal dust or factory smoke. There were clouds drifting slowly in from the southwest, scowling, steelbellied thunderheads, and so the breeze smelled faintly of rain and ozone as well.

Magda stepped across the road, over deep buggy ruts, pressing her own shallow prints into the clay. The pockets of her skirt bulged with the rocks she'd gathered as she climbed, weather-smoothed shale and gritty sandstone cobbles the color of dried apricots. Four steps across, and on the other side, the bank dropped away sharply, steep, but only a few feet down to water, choked thick with cattails and weeds.

Quickest glance, then, back over her shoulder, not bothering to turn full and play Lot's wife proper. The fire burned *inside* her, scorching, righteous flame shining through her eyes, incapable of cleansing, scarring and salting her brain. And, carefully, Magda went down to the cold water.

And when they have all finished with her, each in his turn, when they have carved away at her insides and forced their fat tongues past her teeth and so filled her with their hot seed that it leaks like sea-salt pus from between her bloodied thighs, they slosh away through the mud and leave her; not for dead, not for anything but discarded, done with. For a long time, she lies still and watches the sky roiling above the alley, and the pain seems very, very far away, and the red clouds seem so close that if she raises her hand she might touch them, might break their blister-thin skins and feel the oily black rain hiding inside. Gazing up from the pit into the firelight her own Papa stokes so that the demons can walk the streets of Johnstown.

But the demons have kept their promises, and her throat is not sliced ear to ear, and she can still speak, knows this because she hears the animal sounds from her mouth, distant as the pain between her legs. She is not dead, even if she is no longer alive.

"Tell us about the Rusalky, Mama," her sister had said, and her mother had frowned, looked down at hands folded on her lap like broken wings.

"*Nem*, Emilia," her mother had answered firmly, gently, "Rusalky is not a good story for bedtime."

And as her sister pleaded, Magda had sat straightbacked on the edge of the bed, silent, watching the window, watching the red and starless sky, and already, that had been two weeks after the men with the buckboard and the white mare had brought her home, two weeks after her mother had cried and washed away the dirt and blood, the clinging semen. Two weeks since her father had stormed down from Prospect Hill with his deer rifle and had spent a night in jail, had been reminded by the grave-jowled constable that they were, after all, Hungarians, and what with all the talk of the Company taking on bohunkie contract workers, cheap labor depriving honest men with families of decent wages, well, it wouldn't do to look for more trouble, would it? and in the end, he'd said, it would have been the girl's word against anyone he might have brought in, anyway.

In that space of time, days stacked like broken dishes, not a word from Magda and no tears from her dark and empty eyes. When food was pressed to her lips, a spoonful of soup or gulyás, she'd eaten, and when the sun went down and the lamps were put out, she had lain with her eyes open, staring through the window at the seething sky.

"Please, Mama, *kérem*," her sister had whined, whined and Magda turned then, had turned on them so furiously that a slat cracked gunshot loud beneath the feather mattress. Emilia had cried out, reached for their startled mother. And Magda had pulled herself towards them, hands gone to claws, tetanus snarl and teeth bared like a starving dog. And all that furnace glow gathered, hoarded from the red nights, and spilling from her eyes.

"*Magda, stop this*," and her mother had pulled Emilia to her. "You're frightening your sister! You're frightening me!"

"No, Mama. She wants to hear a story about the Rusalky, then I will *tell* her about the Rusalky. I will *show* her about the Rusalky."

But her mother had stumbled to her feet, too-big Emilia

clutched awkwardly in her arms, and the wobbly chair tumbled over and kicked aside. Backing away from the sagging bed and Magda, burning Magda, Emilia's face hidden against her chest. Backing into the shadows crouched in the doorway.

"She wants to hear, Mama, she *wants* to hear my story."

Her mother had stepped backward into the hall gloom, had slammed the bedroom door shut behind her, and Magda had heard the key rattle in the lock, bone rattle, death rattle, and then she'd been alone. The oil lamp still bright on the wobbly table, and a train had wailed, passing down in the valley, and when the engineer's whistle and the rattle and throb of box-cars had faded away, there had been only her mother's sobs from the other side of the door and the distant clamor of the mills.

Magda had let the lamp burn, stared a while into its tiny flame haloed safe behind blackened chimney glass, and then she'd turned back to the window, the world outside framed safe within, and she'd held fingers to her mouth and between them, whispered her story to the sympathetic night.

All the lost and pretty suicides, all the girls in deep lakes and swirling rivers, still ponds, drowned or murdered and their bodies secreted in fish-silvered palaces. Souls committed to water instead of consecrated earth, and see her on Holy Thursday, on the flat rocks combing out her long hair, grown green and tangled with algae and eels? See her sitting in the low branches of this willow, bare legs hanging like pale fruit, toes drawing ripples in the stream, and be kind enough this sixth week past Easter to leave a scrap of linen, a patch or rag. Come back, stepping quietly through the tall grass, to find it washed clean and laid to dry beneath the bright May sky.

And there is more, after that, garlands for husbands and the sound of clapping hands from the fields, voices like ice melting, songs like the moment before a dropped stone strikes unseen well water.

Carry wormwood in your pockets, young man, and bathe with a cross around your neck.

Leave her wine and red eggs.

And when she dances under the summer moon, when the hay is tall and her sisters join hands, pray you keep yourself behind locked doors, or walk quickly past the waving wheat; stay on the road, watch your feet.

Or you'll wind up like poor Józef, remember Józef, Old Viktor's son? His lips were blue, grain woven in his hair, and how do you think his clothes got wet, so muddy, so far from the river?

And see her there, on the bank beneath the trees, her comb of stickly fish bones? Watch her, as she pulls the sharp teeth through her green hair, and watch the water rise.

This is what it's like to drown, Magda thought, *like stirring salt into water,* as she drifted, dissolving, just below the lake, sinking slowly into twilight the color of dead moss, the stones in her pockets only a little help. Her hair floated, wreathing her face, and the last silver bubbles rose from her open mouth, hurrying towards the surface. Just the faintest, dull pressure in her chest, behind her eyes, and a fleeting second's panic, and then there was a quiet more perfect than anything she had ever imagined. Peace folding itself thick around her, driving back the numbing cold and the useless sun filtering down from above, smothering doubt and fear and the crushing regret that had almost made her turn around, scramble back up the slippery bank when the water had closed like molasses around her ankles.

Magda flowed into the water, even as the water flowed into her, and by the time she reached the bottom, there was hardly any difference anymore.

⇝ 2 ⇜

Thursday, wet dregs of Memorial Day, and Mr. Tom Givens slipped quietly away from the talk and cigar smoke of the clubhouse front rooms. Talk of the parade down in Johnstown and the Grand Army Veterans and the Sons of Veterans, the amputees in their crutches and faded Union blues; twenty-four years past Appomattox, and Grant was dead, and Lee was dead, and those old men, marching clear from Main to Bedford Street despite the drizzling sky. He'd sat apart from the others, staring out across the darkening lake, the docks and the club fleet, the canoes and sailboats and Mr. Clarke's electric catamaran moored safe against the threat of a stormy night.

And then someone, maybe Mr. D.W.C. Bidwell, had brought up the girl, and faces, smoke shrouded, brandy flushed, had turned towards him, curious, and

Oh, yes, didn't you know? Why, Tom here saw her, saw the whole damnable thing,

and so he'd politely excused himself. Had left them mumbling before the crackle and glow of the big sandstone fireplace, and by the time he'd reached the landing and the lush path of burgundy carpet that would carry him back to his room, the conversation had turned inevitably to iron and coke, the new Navy ironclads for which Carnegie, Phipps, and Co. had been contracted to produce the steel plating. Another triumph for Pittsburgh, another blow to the Chicago competition.

Now, he shut the door behind him, and so the only light was dim gray through the windows; for a moment, he stood in the dark before reaching for the chain. Above the lake, the clouds were breaking apart, hints of stars and moonshine in the rifts, and the lake almost glimmered, seeming to ripple and swirl out towards in the middle.

It's only wind on the water, Tom Givens told himself as he pulled the lamp chain hard and warm yellow drenched the room, drove the blackness outside, and he could see nothing in the windows except the room mirrored and himself, tall and very much needing a shave. By the clock on his dresser, it was just past nine, and *At least,* he thought, *maybe there'll be no storms tonight.* But the wind still battered itself against the clubhouse, and he sat down in a chair, back to the lake, and poured amber whiskey. He drank it quickly and quickly refilled the glass, tried not to hear the gusting wind, the shutter rattle, the brush of pine boughs like old women wringing their bony hands.

By ten, the bottle was empty, and Tom Givens was asleep in the chair, his stocking feet propped on the bed.

An hour later, the rain began.

The storm was as alive as anything else, as alive as the ancient shale and sandstone mountains and the wind; as alive as the scorch and burn of the huge Bessemer converters and the slag-scabbed molten iron that rolled like God's blood across the slippery steel floors of the Cambria mills. And as perfectly mindless, as passionately indifferent. It had been born somewhere over Nebraska two days before, had swept across the plains and in Kansas spawned twister children who danced along the winding Cottonwood River and wiped away roads and farms. It had seduced Arctic air spilling off the Great Lakes and sired blizzards across Michigan and Indiana, had spoken its throaty poetry of gale and thunder throughout the Ohio River Valley, and finally, with its violent arms, would embrace the entire Mid-Atlantic seaboard.

As Tom Givens had listened distractedly to the pomp and chatter of the gentlemen of the club, the storm had already claimed western Pennsylvania, had snubbed the sprawling scar of Pittsburgh for greener lovers farther east. And as he'd slept, it had stroked bare ridges and stream-threaded valleys, rain-shrouding Blairsville and Bolivar, New Florence and Nineveh, had followed the snaky railroad through Conemaugh Gap into the deep and weathered folds of Sang Hollow.

And then, Johnstown, its patchwork cluster of boroughs crowded into the dark hole carved in the confluence of two rivers. The seething Cambria yards and the tall office buildings, the fine and handsome homes along Main Street. The storm drummed tin- and slate-shingled roofs, played for the handful of mill workers and miners drinking late inside California Tom's, for the whores in Lizzie Thompson's sporting house on Franks-town Hill. George and Mathilde Heiser, closing up for the night, paused in the mercantile clutter of their store to watch the downpour, and inside St. Joseph's parsonage, Reverend Chapman, who'd been having bad dreams lately, was awakened by his wife, Agnes, and they lay together and listened to the rain pounding Franklin Street.

Unsatisfied, insatiable, the storm had continued east, en-gulfing the narrow valley, Mineral Point and the high arch of the Pennsylvania Railroad viaduct, and, finally, sleeping South Fork.

As alive as anything it touched.

The girl on the dam doesn't know he's watching, of that much he's certain. He sits by open windows, and the early morning air smells like the lake, like fish and mud, and something sharper. He's been drunk more than he's been sober since the night down in Johnstown, the night he sat in the balcony of the Washington Street Opera House, *Zozo the Magic Queen* on stage, and some other fellows from the club talking among themselves more than watching the actors.

The girl from the dam is walking on the water.

He leans forward, head and shoulders out the window because he can't hear, Irwin braying like a goddamned mule from the seat behind, and he can't hear the words, the players' lines, can only hear Irwin repeating the idiotic joke over and over again. Beneath the window of his room, the audience is seated, and he stares down at men's heads and ladies' feathered hats, row after row on the front lawn of the South Fork Hunting and Fishing Club.

Somewhere, far away still but rushing like locomotive wheels, thunder, like applause and laughter and the footlights like lightning frozen on her face.

"Ask Tom," the usher says. "Tom saw the whole damnable thing," and Irwin howls.

And then she's gone, if she was ever really there, and the crowd is on its feet, flesh smacking flesh in frenzied approval; if she was ever there. Lake Conemaugh is as smooth as varnished wood, and he knows it's all done with trapdoors and mirrors, and that, in a moment, she'll rise straight up from the stage planks to take her bows. But the roses fall on the flat water and lie there, and now the curtains are sweeping closed, velvet the color of rain rippling across the sky.

"...saw the *whole* thing," Irwin echoes, so funny he wants to say it over and over, and they're all laughing, every one, when Tom gets up to go, when it's obvious that the show's over and everyone else is leaving their seats, the theater emptying into the front porch of the clubhouse.

Sidewalk boards creak loud beneath his shoes, thunk and mold-rotten creak; after the evening showers, the air smells cleaner at least, coal dust and factory soot washed from the angry industrial sky into the black gutters, but the low clouds hold in the blast-furnace glow from Cambria City and the sky is bloodier than ever.

Spring buggies and lacquered wagon wheels, satin skirts and petticoats held above the muddy street. The pungent musk of wet horse hair.

And he knows that he's only stepped out of his room, that he stands in the hall, second floor, and that if he walks straight on he'll pass three rooms, three numbered doors, and come to the stairs, the oak banister, winding down. But it's dark, the sputtering white-arc streetlights not reaching this narrow slit, inverted alley spine between Washington and Union, and the carpet feels more like muck and gravel, and he turns, *starts* to turn, when thunder rumbles like animal whispers and cloth tearing and

Why, Tom here saw her. Saw the whole damnable thing

the shadow things hunched, claws and grunts and breath exhaled from snot-wet nostrils, and she turns her head, hair mired in the filth and standing water, face minstrel smudged, but eyes bright, and she sees him, and he knows she's begging him to help, to stop this, to pull the shadows off her before there's nothing left to save.

But a shaggy head rises ox slow from the space between her breasts, and these eyes are nothing but the red sky, molten pools of stupid hunger, and Tom turns away, lost for a moment, feeling his way along the silken-papered walls, until his fumbling hands find the cool brass doorknob and the thunder splits apart that world. Splits the alley girl like an overripe peach, and he steps across the threshold, his bare feet sinking through the floor into the icy lake, and she's waiting, dead hand shackle tight around his ankle to pull him down into the fish slime and silting night.

Mr. Tom Givens woke up, sweat-soaked, eyes wide, still seeing white-knuckled hands clasped, sucking air in shuddering gulps, air that seemed as thick, as unbreathable, as dark lake water. The crystal-cut whiskey glass tumbled from his hands, rolled away beneath the bed. And still the pain, fire twisting his legs, and outside the thunder rumbled across the Allegheny night like artillery fire and Old Testament judgment.

Both legs were still propped up on the four poster and, as he shifted, the Charley horse began slowly, jealously, to relax its grip, and he realized there was no feeling at all in his left leg. Outside, furious rain pounded the windows, slammed the shutters against the clubhouse wall. Tom Givens cursed his stupidity, nodding off in the chair like a lousy drunkard, and carefully, he lowered his tortured legs onto the floor. Fresh pain in bright and nauseating waves as the blood rushed back into droughty capillaries; the room swam, lost its precious substance for a moment, and the dream, still so close, lingering like crows around the gray borders.

Lightning then, blinding sizzle that eclipsed the electric lamp, and the thunder clamored eager on its heels.

He sat in the chair, waiting for the last of the pin-and-needle stab to fade, listened to the storm. A wild night on the mountain, and that went a long way towards explaining the nightmare, that and the bourbon, that and the things he'd seen since he'd arrived at the lake two weeks before. He'd come out early, before the June crowds, hoping for rest and a little time to recover from the smoky bustle of Pittsburgh.

The loose shutters banged and rattled like the wind knocking to come inside, and he got up, cautious, legs still uncertain, but only two steps, three, to the window. And even as he reached for the latch, thumbed it back, even as he pushed against the driving rain, knowing that he'd be soaked before it was done, he heard the roar, not thunder, but something else, something almost alive. Immediate and stinging cold, and the sashes were ripped from his hands, slammed back and panes shattered against the palsied shutters.

And through the darkness and the downpour he saw the white and whirling thing, impossibly vast, moving past the docks, dragging itself across the lake. Silvered clockwise, and the deafening roar and boom, and Tom Givens forgot the broken windows, the frantic drapery flutter, the shutters, ignored the rain blowing in, soaking him through, drenching the room. He watched as the waterspout passed by, and the girl, the girl standing there, her long dark hair whipped in the gale, her body an alabaster slash in the black night. She raised her bare arms, worshipping, welcoming, granting passage, and turning, her white gown become a whirling echo of the thing, and her arms were opened to him now, and he knew the face.

The face that had turned to him, helpless, pleading, in the Johnstown alleyway, but changed, eyes swollen with bottomless fury and something that might be triumph, if triumph could be regret. And he knew as well that this was also the girl that he'd watched drown herself off South Fork Dam barely a week back.

Her lips moved, but the wind snatched the words away.

And then lightning splashed the docks in noonday brilliance, and she was gone, nothing but bobbing canoes and the waves, and the trees bending down almost to the ground.

～≈～

He passed the night downstairs, hours sobering into headache and listening to the storm from the huge main living room. He sat on pebble-grained calfskin and paced the Arabian carpeted floors, thumbed nervously through the new Mark Twain novel someone had left, finished or merely forgotten, on an end table. Occasionally, he glanced at the windows, towards the docks and the lake. And already the sensible Nineteenth-Century part of his mind had begun to convince itself that he'd only been dreaming, or near enough; drunk and dreaming.

Finally, others awake and moving, pot and pan noise and cooking smells from the kitchen, and the warm scents of coffee and bacon were enough to stall the argument; rational breakfast, a perfect syllogism against the fading night. He smoothed his hair, straightened his rumpled shirt and vest with hands that had almost stopped shaking and rose to take his morning meal with the others.

Then young Mr. Parke, resident engineer, shaved and dressed as smartly as ever, came quickly down the stairs, walked quickly to the porch door and let in the dawn, light like bad milk and the sky out there hardly a shade lighter than the night had been. And something roaring in the foggy distance.

John Parke stepped outside, and Tom Givens followed him, knowing that he was certainly better off heading straight for the dining room, but finding himself shivering on the long porch, anyway. Before them, the lawn was littered with branches and broken limbs, with unrecognizable debris, and the lake was rough and brown.

"It's up a ways, isn't it?" and Tom's voice seemed magnified in the soppy air.

John Parke nodded slowly, contemplative, then spoke without looking away from the water. "I'd say it's up at least two feet since yesterday evening."

"And that awful noise, what is that?"

Parke pointed southeast, towards the head of the lake, squinted as if by doing so he might actually see through the fog and drizzle.

"That awful noise, Mr. Givens, is most likely Muddy Run coming down to the lake from the mountains." A pause, and, "It must be a blessed torrent after so much rain."

"Doesn't sound very good, does it? Do you think that the dam is, ah, I mean, do you..."

"Let's see to our breakfasts, Mr. Givens," John Parke said, offering up a weak smile, a pale attempt at reassurance, "and then I'll see to the lake."

The door clanged shut, and he was alone on the porch, rubbing his hands together against the gnawing damp and chill. After breakfast, he would go upstairs and pack his bags, find a carriage into South Fork; from there, he could take the 9:15 back to Pittsburgh. More likely than not, there would be others leaving, and it would be enough to say he was sick of the weather, sick of this dismal excuse for a holiday.

Whatever else, that much certainly was true.

Tom Givens turned his back on the lake, on the mess the night had made of the club grounds, and as he reached for the door, he heard what might have been laughter or glass breaking or just the wind whistling across the water. Behind him, one loud and sudden splash, something heavy off the docks, but he kept his eyes on the walnutdark wood grain, gripped the brass handle and pulled himself inside.

A week drowned, and what was left of her, of her body, bloated flesh sponge like strawberry bruise and whitest cheese, pocked by nibbling, hungry black-bass mouths, this much lay knitted into the pine log tangle and underbrush jamming the big iron fish screens. The screens that strained the water, that kept the lake's expensive stock inside (one dollar apiece, the fathers and grandfathers of these fish, all the way from Lake Erie by special railroad car) and now sieved the cream-and-coffee brown soup before it surged, six feet deep, through the spillway; and the caretaker and his Italians, sewer diggers with their shovels and pickaxes, watched as the lake rose, ate away the mounds of dirt heaped all morning along the breast of the dam.

Blackened holes that were her eyes, grub-clogged sockets haloed in naked bone and meaty tatter, cribs for the blind and newborn maggots of water beetles and dragonflies.

Some minutes past gray noon, the lake spread itself into a wide and glassy sheet and spilled over the top, began its slice and carve, bit by bit, sand and clay and stone washed free and tumbled down the other side. And now the morning's load of cautious suggestions, desperate considerations and shaken heads, gambles passed on, the things that might have been done, didn't matter anymore; and the workmen and the by-standers huddled, the dutiful and the merely curious, all rain-drenched, on either hillside, bookends for a deluge.

Tom Givens sat alone, safe and almost drunk again within the shelter of the South Fork depot, sipping Scotch whiskey from his silver flask and trying not to watch the nervous faces, not to overhear the hushed exchanges between the ticket agent and the yardmaster. During the night, almost a quarter mile of track had washed out between South Fork and Johnstown, and so there had been no train to Pittsburgh or anywhere else that morning, and by afternoon the tracks were backed up; the Chicago Limited stretched across Lamb's Bridge like a rusty, fat copperhead, and a big freight from Derry, too common for names, steamed rain-slick and sullen just outside the station.

He'd come from the club in Bidwell's springboard, but had lost track of him around noon, shortly after John Parke had ridden down from the dam. Soaked through to the skin, quite a sorry sight, really, drowned rat of a man galloping in on a borrowed chestnut filly; Parke had gathered a small crowd out-side Stineman's supply store, had warned that there was water flowing across the dam, that, in fact, there was real danger of its giving way at any time.

Bidwell had snorted, practiced piggy snort of authority and money, had busied himself immediately, contradicting the dripping engineer, assuring everyone who'd listen (and everyone listens to the undespairing cut of those clothes, the calm voice that holds itself in such high esteem) that there was nothing for them to get excited about. Mr. Parke had shrugged, duty done, had known better than to argue. He'd sent two men across the street to wire Johnstown from the depot's telegraph tower, had climbed back onto the mud-spattered horse, and then he'd gone, clopping up the slippery road towards the lake.

Tom Givens' ass ached from the bench, torturous church-pew excuse for comfort, and the rain was coming down hard again, hammering at the tin roof. He closed his eyes and thought briefly about dozing off, opened them again and checked his watch, instead; twenty minutes past three, nearly three hours sitting, waiting. Tom Givens snapped the watch shut, slipped it back into his vest pocket. And he knew that the sensible thing to do was return to the club, return to its amenities and cloister, and he knew he'd sooner spend the night sleeping on this bench.

When he stood, his knees popped loud as firecrackers, and the yardmaster was yelling to someone out on the platform; the ticket agent looked up from his paper and offered a strained and weary smile. Tom Givens nodded and walked slowly across the room, pausing to warm his hands at the squat, pot-bellied stove before turning to stare out rain-streaked windows. Across the tracks, Railroad Street, its tidy row of storefronts, the planing mill and the station's coal tipple; farther along, the Little Conemaugh and South Fork Creek had twined in a yellow-brown ribbon swallowing the flats below the depot, had claimed the ground floors of several houses out there. Along the banks, oyster-barked aspens writhed and whipped in the wind and current.

There were people in the street, men and women standing

about like simple idiots in the downpour, shouting, some running, but not back indoors.

And he heard it, too, then, the rumbling thunder growl past thunder, past even the terrible whirl and roar from his nightmare, and the trembling earth beneath his feet, the floorboards and walls and window panes of the depot, resonating with sympathetic tremor.

Run, Thomas, run away.

One, two quickened heartbeats, and it rolled into view, very close, fifty feet high and filling in the valley from side to side, an advancing mountain of foam and churning rubbish. Every stump and living tree and fence post between the town and the dam, ripped free, oak and birch and pinewood teeth set in soil-frothy mad-dog gums, chewing up the world as it came.

Run, Thomas, run fast. She's coming.

But there was no looking away, even as he heard footsteps and someone grabbed, tugged roughly at his shoulder, even as he pissed himself and felt the warm spread at his crotch. He caught a fleeting glimpse of a barn roof thrown high on the crest before it toppled over and was crushed to splinters underneath.

She's here, Tom. She's here.

And then Lake Conemaugh and everything it had gathered in its rush down to South Fork slammed into the town, and in the last moment before the waters reached Railroad Street and the depot, Tom Givens shut   his eyes.

Beneath the red sky, he has no precise memory of the long walk down to this particular hell, slippery cantos blurred with shock and wet, does not even remember walking out onto the bridge. Only the dimmest recollection of lying on the depot floor, face down as it pitched and yawed, moored by telegraph-cable stitches; window shards and the live coals spilling from the fallen stove, steam and sizzle in the dirty water, gray-black soot shower from the dangling pendulum stove pipe; dimmer, the pell-mell stumble through the pitchy dark, leaf dripping, hemlock slap and claw of needled branches, and his left arm has stopped hurting, finally, and hangs useless and numb at his side; falling again and falling again, and unseen dogs howling like paid mourners, the Negro boy, then, sobbing and naked and painted with blood the sticky-slick color of melted tar, the two of them staring down together at the scrubbed raw gash where Mineral Point should have been,

Where is it? Tell me where it's gone.

Mister, the water just came and washed it off.

and his eyes follow the boy's finger and howling dogs like mourners and

Mister, your arm is broke, ain't it?

There is nothing else, simply nothing more, and above him the sky is furnace red, and he sits alone on the bridge. Sandstone and mortar arches clogged with the shattered bones of the newly dead, South Fork and Mineral Point, Woodvale and Franklin, Johnstown proper, the flood's jumbled vomit piled higher than the bridge itself. Boxcars and trees, hundreds of houses swept neatly off foundations and jammed together here, telegraph poles and furniture. Impossible miles of glinting barbed wire from the demolished Gautier wireworks, vicious garland strung with the corpses of cows and horses and human beings.

And the cries of the living trapped inside.

And everything burns.

Tar-black roil, oily exhalation from the flames, breathed crackling into the sky, choking breath that reeks of wood smoke and frying flesh. Embers spiral up, scalding orange and yellow white, into the dark and vanish overhead, spreading the fire like sparkling demon seeds.

Around him, men and women move, bodies bend and strain to wrestle the dead and dying and the barely bruised from the wreckage. And if anyone notices that he makes no move to help, no one stops to ask why.

From somewhere deep inside the pyre comes the hoarse groan of steel, lumber creak, wood and metal folded into a single shearing animal cry, rising ululation, and the wreckage shudders, shivering in its fevered dreams; and for this they stop, for *this* they spare fearful seconds and stare into the fuming night, afraid of what they'll see, that there might still be something worse left, held back for drama, for emphasis. But the stifling wind carries it away, muffles any chance of echo, and once again there are only the pain sounds and the burning sounds.

And he is the only one who sees her, the only one still watching, as she walks between the jutting timbers, steps across flaming pools of kerosene-scummed water. One moment, lost inside the smoke, and then she steps clear again. Her hair dances in the shimmering heat and her white gown is scorched and torn, hanging in linen tatters. And the stain blooming at her crotch, rust-brown carnation unfolding itself, blood-rich petals, blood shiny on the palms of the hands she holds out to him.

Dead eyes flecked with fire and dead lips that move, shaping soundless words, and *Oh, yes, didn't you know? Why, Tom here saw her,* and what isn't there for him to hear is plain enough to see; she spreads her arms, and in another moment there is only the blazing rubbish.

...saw the whole damnable thing.

He fights the clutching grip of their hands, hands pulling him roughly back from the edge, hands grown as hard as the iron and coke they've turned for five or ten or fifteen years, forcing him down onto the smooth and corpse-cold stones, pinning him, helpless, to the bridge.

Above him, the sky is red and filled with cinders that sail and twinkle and finally fall like stars.

If there were such a thing as ghosts, the night was full of them.
          —David McCullough, *The Johnstown Flood*

For Melanie Tem

BELA'S PLOT

*H*OLLYWOOD IS A VAMPIRE, MAGWITCH THINKS AGAIN and sips at his sweet iced coffee, coffee milkfaded the muddy color of rain water. He stares out at the heat shimmering up from the four-o'clock street, the asphalt that looks wet, that looks like a perfect stream of melted licorice beneath the too-blue sky. Stares out through his dime-store shades and the diner's smudge-tinted plate glass and wishes his nerves would stop jangling, humming livewire from the ecstasy he dropped with Lark and Crispin the night before.

A very bedraggled hooker crosses Vine, limping slow on a broken heel, squinting at the ripening afternoon. Magwitch watches her, and wonders that she doesn't simply burst into white flame, doesn't dance a fiery jig past the diner window until there's only a little ash and singed wig scraps floating on the liquid blacktop. He closes his eyes, but she's still there, along with all the wriggling electric lines of static from his head.

When he opens them again, Tam's walking towards him between the tangerine booths, her long-legged, confident stride and layers of lace and ragged fishnet beneath the black vinyl jacket she almost always wears. He smiles and stirs at his coffee, rearranging ice cubes, and Tam draws attention from the fat waitress and the two old men at the counter as she comes. She sits down across from him, and he smells sweat and roses.

"Where's Lark?" she asks, and he hears the impatience rising in her voice, the crackling restlessness she wears more often even than the jacket.

"I told Crispin they could meet us at Holy Cross later on," and he watches her eyes, her gray-green eyes painted in bold Egyptian strokes of mascara and shadow, looking for some hint of reproach that her instructions have not been followed, that anything is different than she planned.

But Tam only nods her head, drums nervous insect sounds against the table with her sharp black nails, and then the fat waitress sets a tumbler of ice water down in front of her and Tam orders nothing. They wait until the woman leaves them alone again, wait until the two old men stop looking and go back to their pie wedges and folded-newspaper browsing.

Tam takes a pink packet of saccharin, tears it open and pours the coke-fine powder into her water. It sifts down between the crushed ice, dissolves, and she stirs it hard with her spoon.

"*Well?*" and she tests the water with the tip of her tongue, then frowns and dumps in another packet of Sweet'N Low. "Am I supposed to fucking guess, Maggie?"

"These guys are bad," he says, and he looks away from her mossy eyes, looks back out at the street, into the glare and broil; the prostitute has gone, vaporized, or maybe just limped away towards Hollywood Boulevard.

"These guys are bad motherfuckers," but Magwitch knows there's nothing he can say, and no point in trying, now that she's made up her mind.

You might have lied. You might have tried telling her you never found them, or that they laughed at you and threatened to kick your skinny ass if you ever came poking around again.

"And you're beginning to sound like a goddamned pussy, Maggie." Tam raises the tumbler to her red lips, razored pout, and he watches her marble throat as she swallows. She leaves a lipstick crescent on the clear plastic.

Magwitch sighs and brushes his long, inky bangs back from his face.

You might have told her to go to hell this time.

"Friday night, they'll be at Stigmata," he says. "And they said to bring the money with us if we want to talk."

"Then we're in," she says, and of course it's not a question; the certainty in her voice, the guarded hint of satisfaction at the corners of her painted mouth, make him cringe, down inside where Tam won't see.

And if he feels like a pussy, it's only because he's the one that's done more than talk the talk; he's the one that sat very still and kept his eyes on the shit-stained men's room floor while Jimmy DeSade and the Gristle Twins laid down their gospel, the slippery rules that Tam had sent him off to learn.

"Did you drive?" she asks, and he knows that she's seen his cruddy, rusted-out car parked on the street, baking beneath the July sun and gathering parking tickets like bright paper flies. Proves the point by not bothering to wait for his answer. "Christ, Maggie, I hope to fuck you got your AC fixed. I need to make some stops on the way."

Magwitch finishes his coffee, swallows a mouthful of cream-slick ice, before he lays two dollars on the table and follows Tam out into the sun.

By the time they reach Slauson Avenue, twilight's gone and all the long shadows have run together into another sticky L.A. night. The gates of Holy Cross Cemetery are closed and locked, keeping the dead and living apart until dawn, but Tam slips the rent-a-cop at the gate twenty bucks, and he lets them through on foot. Tam doesn't climb fences or walls, doesn't squeeze herself through chain link or risk glass-studded masonry, and he's seen her talk and bribe and blow her way into every boneyard in the Valley.

Magwitch walks three steps behind her, and their Doc Marten boots clock softly against the paved drive, not quite in step with one another and keeping unsteady time with the fading traffic sounds. A little way more, and they leave the drive and start up the sloping lawn, the perfect grass muzzling their footsteps as they pass reflecting pools like mirrors in darkened rooms and the phony grotto and its marble virgin, the stone woman in her stone shawl who kneels forever before the virgin's downcast eyes.

The markers are laid out in tuxedo-neat rows of black and white, one after the next like fallen dominos, and they step past the Tin Man's grave, over the fallen Father of Dixieland Jazz and Mr. Bing Crosby, and here are Lark and Crispin, nervous eyesores, waiting alone with Bela.

They could be twins, Magwitch thinks, fingering this old and well-worn observation. And he remembers how much he loves them, beautiful and interchangeable brothers or sisters in their spider threads and white faces, realizes how afraid he is for them now.

Neither of them says anything, wait to hear in their silksilent anxiety, and Magwitch steps forward to stand beside Tam. The toes of her boots almost touch the flat headstone, and it's much too dark to read the few words cut deep into granite—"Beloved Father," dates of birth and death.

There should be candles, he thinks, because there have always been candles, cinnamon or rose or the warm scent of mystery spices and their faces in the soft amber flicker. Sometimes so many candles at once that he was afraid the cops would see and make the guards run them out. Enough candles that they could sit with Bela and read aloud, taking turns with Mary Shelley or Anne Rice or *The Lair of the White Worm*.

"It's all been arranged," Tam says, her voice big and cavalier in the dark. "Friday night we'll meet them at Stigmata and work out the details."

"Oh," Lark says, and this one syllable seems to drift from somewhere far away; Crispin breathes in loudly and stares down at his feet.

"Jesus, you're *all* a bunch of pussies, aren't you?"

Crispin does not raise his head, does not risk her eyes, and when he speaks, it's barely a hoarse whisper.

"Tam, how do you even know that Jimmy DeSade is telling the truth about the cape?"

And Magwitch feels her tense, then, feels the anger gathering itself inside her, sleek anger and insult taut as jungle-cat muscles, "She doesn't," he answers, and a heartbeat later, "Neither do I."

"Jesus Christ," Tam hisses and lights one of the pungent brown Indonesian cigarettes she smokes. For an instant, her high cheekbones and pouty lips are nailed in the glow of her lighter, and then the night rushes back over them.

"If you guys fuck this up..." but her voice trails away into a ghost cloud of smoke, and they stand together at the old man's grave, junkie old man cold and in his final casket almost twenty years before Magwitch was born. And there is no thunder and forked lightning, no wolf-howling wind, only sirens and the raw squeal of tires on cooling city streets.

Magwitch sits, smoking, on one rumpled corner of Tam's bed in the apartment he could never dream of affording, that she could never afford either if it was only her part-time at Retail Slut paying the rent. If it weren't for the checks from her mother and father that she pretends she doesn't get once a month, faithful as her period. The sun's coming up outside, the earth rolling around to burn again, and he can see the faintest graying blue rind around the edges of Tam's thick velvet drapes. The only other light comes from her big television, sleek black box and the sound down all the way, Catherine Deneuve and David Bowie at piano and cello.

"I wouldn't even have *thought* of suggesting it," she says, and it takes him a moment to find his place in the conversation, his place between her words. "Not if they weren't acting that way. If they weren't both scared totally shitless."

"It should be their call," he says softly and stubs out his cigarette. He doesn't want the twins along either, wants them clear of this so badly that he's almost willing to hurt them. But almost isn't ever enough, and no matter what Tam might say, he knows that she'll have them there, lovely china pawns by her side, lovelier for the fear just beneath their skin.

"Oh," she says. "Absolutely. I just won't have them going tharn and fucking everything up, Maggie. This is for real, not cemetery games, not trick or fucking treat."

Magwitch lies back on the cool sheets, satin like slippery midnight skin, and tries not to think about the twins or Jimmy DeSade. Watches Tam at her cluttered antique dressing table, the back of her head, hair blacker than the sheets and her face reflected stark in the Art Deco mirror. Knowing he could hate her if only he were a little bit stronger, if he'd never let himself love her. She selects a small brush and retraces the cupid's bow of her upper lip, her perfect pout, and he looks away, staring up at the ceiling, the dangling forest of dolls hanging there, dolls and parts of dolls, ripe and rotting Barbie fruit strung on wire and twine. The breeze from the air conditioner stirs them, makes them sway, some close enough to bump into others, a leg against an arm, an arm against a plastic torso.

And then Tam comes teasing slow to him, crosses the room in nothing but white, white skin and crimson panties. She crouches on the foot of the bed, just out of reach, a living gargoyle down from Notre Dame, stone made flesh by some unlikely and unforgiving alchemy. Her eyes sparkle in the TV's electric glare, more hungry than John and Miriam Blaylock ever imagined; as she speaks, her left hand drifts absently to the tattoo that entirely covers her heart, the maroon and ebony petals that hide her nipple and areola, thorns that twine themselves tightly around her breast and draw inky drops of blood.

"I'm sure Lark and Crispin won't disappoint me," she says and smiles like a wound. "They never do."

And of course she's holding the razor clutched in her right hand, the straight and silver razor with its mother of pearl handle, that bottomless green and blue iridescence.

"And you won't ever disappoint me, sweet Maggie."

He sits up, no need for her to have to ask, turns his back and grips the iron headboard, palms around cold metal like prison bars. The old springs creak and groan gentle protests as she slips across the bed to him, and Magwitch feels her fingertips, Braille reading the scars on his shoulders, down the length of his spine, one for every night he's spent with her.

"You love me," she says, and he closes his eyes and waits for the release of the blade.

Friday night, very nearly Saturday morning now, and Magwitch is waiting with Lark and Crispin at their wobbly corner table on one edge of the matte-black circus. Through the weave and writhe of dancers, he catches occasional half-glimpses of Tam at the bar, Tam talking excitedly with the two pretty boys in taffeta and shiny midnight latex, the boys who have posed for *Propaganda*, but whose names he can't remember. Lark sips uneasily at her second white Russian, and Crispin's eyes never leave the crimson door at the other end of the dance floor. The Sisters of Mercy song ends, bleeding almost imperceptibly into a crashing remix of Fields of the Nephilim's "Preacher Man."

It has been more than a year since the first rumors, the tangled bits of hearsay and contradiction that surfaced in the shell-shock still after the riots. A year since Tam sat across this same table and repeated every unlikely detail, her sage-green eyes sparking like flints, and she whispered to him, "They have the cape, Maggie. They have the fucking cape."

He doesn't remember exactly what he said, remembers her leaning close and the glinting scalpel of her voice.

"Hell, Maggie, there was so much going on they didn't even care if the cops saw them. They just walked right in and started digging. I mean, Christ, who's gonna give two shits if someone's out digging up dead guys when half the city's burning down?"

He didn't believe it then, still doesn't believe it, but Magwitch knows that playing these head games with the likes of Jimmy DeSade is worse than stupid or crazy. He fishes another Percodan from the inside pocket of his velvet frock coat and washes it down with a warm mouthful of bourbon.

"I don't think he's going to show," Crispin says, and there's just the faintest trace of relief, the slimmest wishful crust around his words. And then the crimson door opens on cue, opens wide, and Jimmy DeSade, black leather and silver chains from head to toe, steps into the throb and wail of Stigmata.

Even over the music, the sound of Lark's glass hitting the floor is very, very loud.

Together, they are herded out of the smoky, black-light pit of the club, up narrow stairs and down the long hall, past the husky old tattoo queen who checks IDs and halfheartedly searches everyone for dope and weapons, out into the night. Jimmy DeSade walks in front, and one of the Gristle Twins drives them from behind, and as they leave the sidewalk and slip between abandoned warehouses, an alley like an asphalt paper cut, Magwitch wants to run, tells himself he *would* run if it were only Tam. Would leave her to play out this pretty little horror show on her own; but he looks at Crispin and Lark, who hold whiteknuckled hands, and there's nothing but the purest silver terror in their eyes.

Jimmy DeSade's junkheap car waits for them in the alley, rumbling hulk of a Lincoln, rust bleeding from a thousand dents and scrapes in its puke-green skin, one eye blazing, the other dangling blind. Its front fender hangs crooked loose beneath shattered grille teeth, truculent chrome held on with duct tape and wire. Jimmy DeSade opens a door and shoves them all into the backseat. And the car smells like its own shitty exhaust and stale cigarettes and pot smoke and spilled alcohol, but more than anything else, the sweet, clinging perfume of rot. Magwitch gags, covers his mouth with a hand, and then Tam is screaming.

"Don't mind Fido," Jimmy DeSade says in the Brit accent that no one has ever for a minute believed is real, and then the twisted thing stuffed into the corner with Tam tips over, all bloodcrusty fur and legs bent in the wrong places, and lies stiff across their laps. Its ruined maroon coat is alive, maggot seethe, and parts that belong inside are slipping out between shattered ribs.

"Manny here ran into the poor thing the other day, and shit, man, I always wanted a doggy."

Tam screams again, and Crispin and Lark vomit in perfect, twinly unison, spray booze and the pork-flavored Ramen noodles they ate before leaving Magwitch's apartment onto the roadkill tangle. Magwitch swallows hard, turning his head to the window as Manny pulls out of the alley into traffic.

"You stupid, sick fuck..." he says, and the Gristle Twins laugh, and Jimmy DeSade grins his wide, yellow-toothed smile, and winks.

"Oh god," Tam whispers. "Oh god, oh god," and she dumps the mess into the floorboard, leaving their laps glazed with dog and vomit, velvet and satin and silk stained and goreslicked.

When Jimmy DeSade laughs, it sounds like bricks and broken bottles tumbling in a clothes dryer.

"Man, I love you prissy little goth-geek motherfuckers," he says and thumbs through the stack of twenty- and fifty-dollar bills Tam gave him back at Stigmata, three hundred dollars all together, and he sniffs at the money before it's tucked inside his leather jacket.

"You dumb buggers wear that funeral drag and paint your eyes and think you're fucking around with death. Think you're the Reaper's own harem, don't you?"

"Fuck you," Tam says, whimpers, and "Yeah," Jimmy DeSade says. "Yeah, well, we'll see, babe."

The city rushes past the Lincoln's windows, and Magwitch tries to keep track, but nothing out there looks familiar, and he doesn't know if they're driving west, towards the ocean, or east, towards the desert.

"You better have it," Tam says. "I paid you your goddamned money, and you better have it."

Jimmy DeSade watches her a moment silently, feral chalk-blue eyes, Nazi eyes, and he smiles again slow.

"You got yourself an unhealthy obsession there, little girl," he says, oozes the words across his lips like greasy pearls, and the middle Gristle Twin, the one whose name isn't Manny, snickers.

"We made a deal," Tam says, and Magwitch has to stop himself from laughing.

"Don't you worry, Tammy. I got it all right. And *oh*, Tammy, you should'a *seen 'im*, the shriveled old hunky fuck," and Jimmy DeSade's eyes sparkle, lightless shine, and he bites at his lower lip with one long canine. "Lying there so bloody peaceful in his penguin suit, the dirt just dribbling down into his face. And that cape, that cape still draped around his bony shoulders right where it was when they closed the casket on him."

Jimmy DeSade sniffles his cokehead's chronic sniffle and wipes his nose, grime-cracked nails and the one on his little finger elegant long and polished candy-apple red.

"Nineteen hundred and fifty-six," he purls. "Terrible long time to go without one sweet breath of night air. That was Elvis' big year, did you know that, Tammy dear? Too damn bad it wasn't poor old Bela's."

The nameless Gristle Twin pops a cassette into the Lincoln's tape deck and a speed metal blur screeches from the expensive, bass-heavy speakers behind their heads. Magwitch trying to ignore the music, tries desperately to concentrate on the buildings and street signs flashing past, as the car leaves Hollywood behind and rolls along through the hungry California night.

In the catacombs beneath downtown, the old tunnels dug a century before for smugglers and Chinese opium dens, and the air is not warm here and smells like mold and standing water. Magwitch sits on his bare ass on the stone floor; his black jeans are a shapeless wad nearby, but when he reaches for them it wakes up the pain in his ribs and shoulder and he gasps, slumps back against the seeping wall. There is light, row after row of the stark and soulless fluorescent bulbs, and so he can see Crispin and Lark, naked and filthy, huddled together on the other side of the chamber.

Tam, wrapped in muddy vinyl and torn pantyhose, stands with her back to them near the door.

There are chains like rusty intestine loops, chains that end in meat-hook claws, dangling worse things than the road dog in Jimmy DeSade's car.

And Jimmy DeSade sits on the high-backed wooden chair in the center of the room, smoking and watching them. The others have all gone, the Gristle Twins and the woman with teeth filed to sharp piranha points, the man without ears and only a pink, scar-puckered hole where his nose should be.

"Are you finished?" Tam says, "Are you satisfied?" And it frightens Magwitch how little her voice has changed, how ice calm she still sounds.

"Will you show me the Dracula cape now?"

Jimmy DeSade chuckles low, shakes his shaggy head, and Magwitch hears a whole laundromat full of dryers, each churning with its load of bricks and shattered soda bottles.

"I'd like to," he says and crushes his cigarette out on the floor, grinds the butt flat with the snakeskin toe of his boot. "I would, Tammy, I really would. But I'm afraid that's no longer something I can do."

Tam turns around slowly, arms crossed and the jacket pulled closed to hide her small breasts. Her face is streaked with blood and makeup smears and livid bite marks, the welts and clotting punctures, dapple her throat and the backs of her hands. The flesh around her left eye looks pulpy and is swollen almost shut.

"Yeah, well, you see, I let it go last week to a Lugosi freak from Mexico City. This crazy fucker paid me ten Gs for the thing, can you believe that shit?"

For a moment, Tam's old mask holds, indomitable frost and those eyes that betray nothing, show nothing more or less than she wishes. But the moment passes, and the mask splinters, falls away, revealing the roil beneath, the shifting kaleidoscope of bone and skin, tumbling bright flecks of rage and violation. And Magwitch is almost afraid for Jimmy DeSade.

"Hey, Tammy. It's just biz, right?" And he holds out his hand to her. "These things happen. No bad feelings?"

Her lips part, a wet salmon hint of her tongue between teeth before the cascade of emotion drains away and there's nothing left in its place, and she falls, collapsing into herself and gravity's will, crumples like ash to her knees and the uneven cobblestones.

"Sure," Jimmy DeSade says. "I understand," and he stands and pushes the chair aside. "When you guys are done in here, turn off the lights, okay, and close the door behind you?" He points to a switch plate rigged on one wall, a bundle of exposed red and yellow wires.

And they're alone, then, except for the things without eyes, the careless hanging sculptures of muscle and barbed wire, and Magwitch drags himself the seven or eight feet to Tam. The pain in his side strobes violet, and he has to stop twice, stop and wait for his head to clear, for the crooning promise of numb and quiet and cool oblivion pressing at his temples to fade.

They do not come here much anymore, visit the old man less and less as summer slips unnoticed into fall. Without Tam, the guards are less agreeable, and they've been caught once already sneaking in, have been warned and threatened with jail. Tonight, there's a cough dry wind, and Magwitch has heard on the radio that there are wildfires burning somewhere in the mountains.

Lark finishes the chapter, Mina's account of the sea captain's funeral and the terrified dog, somnambulant Lucy, and Crispin blows out the single votive candle he's held up to the pages while she read. Even such a small flame is a comfort and Magwitch knows they share the same sudden uneasiness when there's only its afterimage floating in their eyes, the baby-aspirin orange blot accenting the night.

Lark closes her paperback and lays it on the headstone, sets it neatly between the three white roses and the photocopied snapshot in its cheap drugstore frame. A dashing, impossibly young Lugosi, 1914 and the shadow of his fedora soft across eyes still clear with youth and ignorance of the future. In the morning, the groundskeeper will clear it all away, will grumble and hastily restore the sterile symmetry of his ghostless, modern cemetery.

"I saw Daniel Mosquera last night," Lark says, and it takes Magwitch a second to place the name with a face. "He said someone saw Tam in San Francisco last week, and she's dancing at the House of Usher now."

And then she pauses, and the traffic murmurs through the wordless space she's left; Magwitch imagines he can smell woodsmoke on the breeze.

"This is the last time I can come here, Maggie," Lark tells him.

"Yeah," he says, "I know," and Crispin nods and puts the stub end of his candle down with everything else.

"But we'll still see each other, right?" Lark asks. "At DDT, and next month Shadow Project's playing the Roxy, and we'll see you then."

"Sure," Magwitch says. He knows better, but is careful to sound like he doesn't.

"You sleep tight," Lark whispers and kisses her fingertips, then touches them to the grass.

When they've gone, Magwitch lights a cigarette and sits with Bela another hour more.

RICHARD
KIRK

Tears Seven Times Salt

Jenny Haniver sits with herself on the always damp mattress in the center of her concrete floor, damp cotton ticking mildewed dark, and no light comes through the matte-black painted windows of the basement apartment. Her books are scattered around her like paper bricks, warped covers and swollen pages. And the candlelight flicker and fluorescence steady from the dozens of aquariums bubbling contentedly, rheumy, omnipresent whisper of air through charcoal and peat and lavalit. She knows the words by heart, sacred interplay of Latin and English, holy pictures of scales and skin flayed back, ink glistening muscles and organs open across her lap.

If this knowledge were enough, she'd have gone down to them a long, long time ago.

Jenny's fingers follow the familiar, comforting lines, and her lips move, pronouncing soundlessly, bead counting each razor thin flare of cartilage and needle stab of bone, hyomandibular, interoperculum, supraoccipital crest.

Necessary, but utterly insufficient; dead end to salvation or evolution, transcendence, and when she finishes, Jenny closes the big book and sets it aside.

The apartment is too small, and her tanks line every inch of shelved wall; her long and cluttered tables, stolen doors laid across crumbling cinder blocks, take whatever space is left, uneven surfaces crowded with formalin-cloudy jars and wax-bottomed dissection trays, rusted pins and scalpels. The dumpster-scrounged mattress at the center and her at its soggy heart. She opens her eyes, irises the color of kelp, slick hazel brown and dead-star pupils eating the tiny pool of yellow candlelight and the greenwhite flood wrapped around. The air stinks like everything wet, fish and fish shit, mold and algae and the fleshy gray mushrooms that grow unmolested everywhere.

When Jenny Haniver stands, rises up air-bubble slow from her careless lotus, some of the layered bandages on her long legs tear, gauze crust clinging to the jealous old mattress fabric, tearing at the useless scabs underneath. She ignores the pain, not even an inconvenience anymore, just a distant murmuring taunt of failure.

Rumors of rumors reach even into her basement, and tonight Jenny Haniver has come out to see if there's any truth between the lines. She comes here less and less often now, this cavern of steel and cement, a warehouse once, and the tainted Hudson sighing past outside so the air tastes safe enough. She wears a dingy black and silver body suit to hide the marks, the bandages, sips at salty tequila and watches the dancers, bodies writhing seagrass and eel tangled in the invisible current of sound, alternating mix of industrial clatter and goth's sultry slur. Grease-paint vampires and boys with bee-stung lips the color of live gillflesh, ravestench reek of sweat and smoke and the fainter, briny tang of spilled beer and cum.

"Jenny," the girl says, shouts softly over the music and sits down in the booth across from her. Jenny looks up from her drink and waits until she remembers the face, puts a name with the hair bleached white and eyebrows shaved and penciled back in place.

"Hello," she says. "Hello, Maria."

"No one ever sees you anymore," the girl says, leaning in closer to be heard, and the black-light strobes catch on the silver stud in her tongue, the single tiny ring in her lower lip. "Someone said they saw you up in Chelsea last month. Pedro, yeah, he said that."

Jenny nods, neither yes nor no, faintest smile showing her teeth, sharp and plaque-yellowed triangles, incisors and canines filed piranha perfect. She lets her eyes drift back down to her glass, and the girl keeps talking.

"Jamie and Glitch got a new band together," she says. "And Jamie's singing, mostly, but Christ, Jenny, you know she can't sing like you."

"I heard that Ariadne came back," Jenny tells her, and the girl says nothing for a long time, a stretched, uneasy space filled up with the grind and wail from the speakers, calculated pandemonium and the background rumble of human voices.

"Jesus, where the hell'd you hear something like that? People don't come back from the tunnels. You get that low, and you don't come back."

Jenny Haniver doesn't argue, finishes her tequila and watches the dancers. The girl leans close again, and her breath smells like cloves and alcohol.

"I scored some X," she says. "You want to do some X with me, Jenny?"

"I have to go," Jenny says and stands, notices a glistening, oily patch on the candy-apple naugahyde where she's soaked through the bandages and the nylon body suit.

"Everyone misses you, Jenny. I'll tell Glitch you said hi, okay?"

She doesn't reply, turns quickly and leaves the girl without a word, pushes her way across the dance floor, moving between tattered lace and latex and hands that casually, desperately grope as she passes, that undertow of oblivion and need and at least a hundred different hungers.

Jenny Haniver's father never raped her, never laid her open like a live gray oyster and planted grains of sand for pearls and psychosis; none of that trendy talk-show trauma, nothing so horrible that it would have to be coaxed to the surface with hypnosis and regression therapy.

He was a longshoreman, and her mother had left him when Jenny was still a baby, had left him alone with their child and his senile old mother with her Polish accent as thick as chowder. Sometimes, when he was drunk, he hit them, and when he was sober he sometimes said he was sorry.

Once, after a layoff or a fight with his foreman, he backhanded Jenny so hard that he knocked out a front tooth, just a baby tooth and already loose anyhow, but afterwards he cried, and they rode the Q train together all the way out to Coney Island, to the New York Aquarium. He held her up high, and Jenny pressed her face flat against the thick glass, eyes wide and drowning in the mossy light filtering down from above, unbelieving, as weightless groupers and barracuda and sharks like the sleekest nightmares cruised silently past.

After the club and the long February-cold walk back to her apartment, Jenny stands before the mirror in her tiny bathroom, unframed looking glass taller than her by a head, and the walls papered with bright prints torn from library books. Millias' Ophelia and John Waterhouse's Shalott, *The Green Abyss* and a dozen nameless Victorian sirens. She has stripped off the body-suit rag, has wound away most of the leaking bandages. They lie in a sticky, loose pile at her feet, stained unforgiving shades of infection and a few bloody smears.

The air is so cold that it moves slow and heavy like arctic water around her naked body, gelid thick and redolent with the meaty, sweet perfume of rot that seeps from the incisions that don't heal, from the dark, red-rimmed patches down her thighs and legs, her belly. The most recent, only two days old, has already faded, silverblue shimmer traded for a color like sandwich grease through a brown paper bag. She touches it, and the cycloid scales flake away like dandruff, drifting dead and useless to the floor.

Jenny Haniver closes her eyes until the disappointment and nausea pass, and there's nothing left but the drip of the faucets, the bubbling murmur of her fish tanks from the other room. This time she will not break the mirror, won't give herself up to the despair. Instead, she opens her eyes and stares back at the gaunt thing watching her, metallic glint of desperation in that face, Auschwitz thin, the jut and hollow of bones just beneath death-pale skin.

You can't win, she thinks. *I won't die locked in here.*

Jenny Haniver turns her back on the mirror, turns to the shower stall, no bathtub here, and she pushes aside the mildew-blackened plastic curtain. She has to use the wrench lying on the little shelf intended for soap or shampoo to turn on the water, and it comes out numbing cold. She stands under the spray until she's stopped shivering, until she can't feel anything but the distant pressure of the water pounding itself futilely against her immutable flesh.

When Jenny Haniver was a child, Old Mama talked to the pipes, leaned over sinks and tubs, the toilet and storm culverts, and spoke slow and softly through the drains, microphones that would carry her raspy old woman's voice down into the bowels of the city, the city beneath the city. Jenny would sit and watch, listening, anxiously straining to hear the responses that her grandmother clearly heard.

"Why can't I ever hear anything?" Jenny finally asked one winter afternoon. After school, and she had been watching for almost an hour from the kitchen table as her grandmother had leaned, head and bony shoulders into the white sink, alternately placing an ear and then her lips against the drain. When she spoke, it almost seemed that she kissed the rust-stained rim of the hole.

Old Mama raised her head, impatient scowl, and Jenny knew she'd interrupted, was sorry, but afraid to say so. The late afternoon sunlight, dim through the dirty kitchen window, caught in the lines and creases of Old Mama's face, shadowing each wrinkle deeper, making her look even older than she was. Eyes like a pecking bird, dark and narrowed, regarding her impudent granddaughter.

"Not until you begin to bleed for the moon," Old Mama said, and she grabbed roughly at the crotch of her shapeless blue house dress. She grimaced and showed her gums. Jenny wasn't stupid; she knew about menstruation, knew that someday she would get her period, and that then she wouldn't be a child anymore.

"But then you won't have to wait for them talk to you, Jenny," Old Mama went on, "because *then* they will smell you, will smell you ripe in the water from your bath or when you wash your hands or flush the toilet. Then they will come to take you *back*."

Jenny was afraid, even though she knew that Old Mama wasn't well, wasn't right in the head, as her father sometimes said, drawing circles in the air around his ear.

"Back where?" she asked cautiously, not really wanting to know what Old Mama meant.

"Back down to the sewers, down there in the shit and dark where Old Papa found you."

Jenny's grandfather had worked under the streets, had told her stories about the alligators, the huge, blind sewer rats that never saw the sun, and the cats as big and strong as dogs that lived down there and fed on them. But he was dead, and he'd never said one word to her about having found her in the sewers.

"You were such a very ugly baby that even the fish people that live down there didn't want you. They left you under a big manhole, and Old Papa found you, naked and smeared in shit, and he had such a soft heart and brought you home."

Jenny opened her mouth, but she was suddenly too scared to say anything.

"Your Mama, *she* knew, Jenny. Yes, your Mama knew that you weren't really her baby, and that's why she went away."

Old Mama laughed, then, dry cackle, and waggled one arthritis-crooked finger at Jenny.

"And don't ask your Papa. He is too stupid and doesn't know that his little girl is not a real little girl. If he knew, he would be so angry he would put you back down there now, or he would kill you."

And then she put her head into the sink again, and Jenny sat staring at Old Mama's skinny rump, still unable to speak, pinned between the cold, solid knot settling in her stomach and the hot, salt sting of the tears gathering in her eyes. After a while, Old Mama got bored, or the fish people quit talking to her, and she went off to watch television, and left Jenny alone in the kitchen.

After the shower, after she dry swallows two of the green cephalexin capsules—antibiotics she buys cheap on the street—and puts clean bandages on her legs, Jenny falls asleep on her stinking mattress.

And she dreams of Ariadne Moreau and the hanging room and taut wires that hold her, suspended high above the slippery floor. A hundred stainless-steel barbs pierce the blood-dabbed flesh of her outstretched arms, shoulders and breasts and upturned face, matchless crucifixion. Ariadne holds her steady and draws the scalpel blade along the inside of her thighs, first one and then the other, down the length of each dangling leg.

"The old hag should have gone to jail for telling a kid crazy shit like that," Ariadne says.

Jenny doesn't take her eyes off the point far above where all the wires converge, the mad gyre of foam and salt spray eating up the ceiling, counterclockwise seethe of lath and plaster and rafters that snap like the ribs of dying giants.

"People like that," Ariadne says, "make me sorry I don't believe in Hell anymore."

And then she binds Jenny's ankles together with duct tape and begins to sew, sinks the needle in just above her right ankle, draws fine surgical silk through and across to the left.

Closing the wounds, stitching away the scalpel's track and the hateful cleft of her legs.

Jenny Haniver follows Forty-Eighth Street westward, black wraparound shades against the late morning sun that shows itself for brief moments at a time, slipping in and out of the shalegray clouds like a bashful, burning child. She walks with quick, determined steps, ignoring the sharp jolts of pain in her feet and legs that seem to rise from the sidewalk. Moves between and through the mindless jostle of shoulders and faces, avoids her reflection in the shop-front and office lobby panes of glass she passes. The chilling Hudson wind rips at her shabby pea coat, flutters her long, snarled hair.

The way down to the tunnels, the gully between Tenth and Eleventh avenues that Ariadne showed her months ago, has not moved and has not been sealed. From the edge of a garbage dumpster, Jenny climbs over the chain-link fence that the city has put up to keep the mole people out or in; clings to the steel tapestry, the diamond-shaped spaces like gar scales in between, with bare, wind-gnawed fingers and the worn toes of her tennis shoes. There is a single strand of barbed wire along the top that gives her a moment's trouble, but the solution costs only a few drops of her blood and a ragged, new tear in one arm of her coat.

Thirty feet down to the tracks, and she inches along the sheer granite walls, nothing but scraggly, winter-dry clumps of goldenrod and poison sumac for treacherous hand holds. Then she slips and drops the last eight feet to the gravel roadbed below, landing hard on her ass, heart pounding and blood in her mouth from a bitten tongue, table salt and pennies, but nothing broken.

In front and behind, the old railroad disappears into the rock, blasted away over a hundred years ago, and nothing comes through here anymore but the occasional freight train. She takes off her sunglasses, stuffs them into a coat pocket, and walks into the darkness on a welcoming carpet of clothing and shattered green Thunderbird bottles, empty crack vials and discarded syringes.

Inside, the stench of urine and human feces is as thick, as complete, as the dark; Jenny gags, acid-bitter taste of bile, and hides her mouth and nose in the crook of one arm. She knows that there are people watching her, can feel the wary or stark terrified track of their eyes, and sometimes she can hear faint whispering from the side tunnels. Something whooshes past, and a bottle smashes with a loud, wet pop against the tunnel wall, peppering her with glass shards and drops of soured wine or beer.

"*Who are you?!*" a hoarse and sexless voice demands. "*Who the hell are you?!*"

She does not answer it, stands perfectly still and stares back at the gloom, feigned defiance, pretending that she's not afraid, that her heart's not thumping crazy in her chest and her mouth isn't dry as the gravel ballast underfoot.

Not another word from the dark, only the far-off growl of cars and trucks on the street above, and Jenny starts walking again, thankful for the company of her own footsteps.

There are iron grates set into the roof of the tunnel at irregular intervals, dazzling, checkerboard sunlight from the unsuspecting world overhead that only makes the blackness that much more absolute. She walks around, not through them, but keeps careful count of the blinding, gaudy pools in her head; one, three, five, and at the seventh, she turns left. The basket-handle arch of the side tunnel is faintly visible, dim reflection off the measured stagger of brickwork, and spray painted sloppy white above and across the chunky keystone—JESUS SAVES and a tag like a preschooler's goldfish. Jenny looks over her shoulder once before she leaves the light behind and follows the gentle slope of the side tunnel west, down towards the river.

She learned to hear the voices in the pipes three years before her first period, hardly a month after her grandmother had told her about Old Papa finding her in the sewers.

Very late at night, when she was sure that everyone else was asleep—her father lost in his fitful dreams and Old Mama snoring like a jackhammer down the hall—Jenny would slip out of bed and tip-toe to the upstairs bathroom. Would bring a blanket because the tile floor and cast-iron tub were always freezing, and lie for hours, curled fetal, with her ear pressed tight against the drain.

And at first there was nothing but a far-off ocean hum like conch shells and the sounds of the building's old copper plumbing clearing its hundred throats, the gurgle or glug of water on its way up from the mains or back down to the sewers. The metal-hammered clank of pipes expanding or contracting. Sometimes, she would doze and dream in the muted greens and browns of the big Coney Island aquarium, lazy sway of sea plants and anemone tendrils and the strange shadows that moved like storm clouds overhead.

And then, three nights before Christmas and a fresh blanket of snow like vanilla icing, she heard their voices, so faint at first that it might have been anything else, trapped air or her straining imagination. And Jenny lay very still, suddenly wide awake and every muscle tensed, hearing and not believing that she was hearing, not wanting to believe that she was hearing.

The softest, sibilant mumble, and gooseflesh washed prickling cold across her skin.

Not words, at least not words that she could understand, a muffled weave of hisses and clicks and velvet sighs that rose and fell in overlapping, breathy waves. Jenny fought the fear, that slick red thing twisting inside, and her pounding heart, the urge to pull away, to run wailing to her father and tell him *everything*, everything that Old Mama had said that day in the kitchen and everything since. The urge to turn the tap on scalding hot and drown whatever was down there.

the fish people who live down there

But Jenny Haniver did not run. She squeezed her eyes shut

and ignored everything but the wet voices, fists clenched, knees braced against the side of the tub. Tried to wrestle something like meaning or sense from the gibbering. And afterwards, she would come back every night, would spend the house's dead hours listening patient and terrified until she began to understand.

The city beneath the city, accumulated labyrinth of pipe and tunnel extending skyscraper-deep beneath the asphalt and concrete Manhattan crust; sewer and rumbling subway and tens of thousands of miles of gas and steam and water mains. Electric and telephone cables like sizzling neurons buried in the city's flesh, copper dendrites wrapped safe inside neoprene and rubber and lead.

Jenny Haniver walks the anthill maze, walls of crumbling masonry and solid granite. She counts off each blind step, Ariadne's directions remembered like a combination lock's code; forty-five then right, seventy-one then left, deeper and deeper into the honeycombed earth beneath Hell's Kitchen. The air grows warmer by slow degrees, and the only sounds left are the nervous scritch and squeak of the rats, the faint drip and splash of water from the walls and ceilings as the musty air turns damp.

Her eyes do not adjust, register only the ever increasing absence of light, a thousand shades past pitch already; dark that can smother, that seeps up her nostrils and settles in her lungs like black pneumonia. She walks clumsy as a stumbling zombie, hands out Frankenstein-stiff in front of her, lifts her feet high to keep from tripping over garbage or stepping on a rat.

Fifty-seven, then right, and that's the last, and for all she knows she's lost, almost certain that she'll never be able to reverse the order and follow the numbers backwards to the surface. And when she catches the dimmest shimmer up ahead, she believes it can only be panic, a cruel will-o'-the-wisp tease dreamed up by the rods and cones of her light-starved eyes. But with every step the light seems to swell, become faint bluish glow now, and she can almost make out the tunnel walls, her own white hands somewhere in front of her face.

There are new sounds, too, parchment-dry susurrance and the moist smack and slap of skin against mud. The air smells like shit, and the cold rot of long-neglected refrigerators. The tunnel widens, then, abruptly opening out into a small cavern, low walls caked thick with niter and a scum of luminescent fungus, and she can see well enough to make out the forms huddled inside. Skin bleached colorless by the constant dark, stretched much too tight over kite-frame skeletons, razor shoulders, xylophone ribs. Bodies naked to the chill and damp or clothes that hang in tatters like a shedding second skin.

Jenny follows the narrow path between them, and they watch her pass with empty, hungry eyes, shark eyes, grab at her calves and ankles in halfhearted frenzy, hands no more than blue-veined claws, arms no more than twigs.

Ariadne Moreau sits by herself on a crooked metal folding chair at the far end of the chamber, lion's mane nimbus of tangled black hair and necklaces of rat bone draped like beads around her neck. She wears nothing else but her tall leather boots and vinyl jacket, both scabby with dried mud and mildew. Her thighs, the backs of her bony hands, are splotched with weeping track marks, and she smiles, sickly weak approval or relief, as Jenny approaches.

"I knew that you'd come," she says, and her voice sighs out of her, husky wheeze, and she extends one hand to Jenny, trembling fingers and nails chewed down to filthy nubs. "I never stopped believing that you'd come."

Jenny does not take her hand, hangs a few feet back.

"It isn't working," she says, and opens her pea coat, displays her own ruined flesh to prove the point. She's only wearing boxers underneath, and all the bandages are oozing, stains that look like sepia ink in the weird blue light of the cave. A few have come completely undone, revealing her clumsy sutures and the necrotic patchwork of grafts.

"I have to know if you've learned anything. If you've seen anything down here," she says, and closes her coat again.

Ariadne's smile fades, jerky, stop-motion dissolve, and she lets her arm drop limply again at her side. She laughs, an aching, broken sound, and shakes her shaggy head.

"*Anything*," Jenny says again. "*Please,*" and she takes the baggie of white powder from her coat pocket, holds it out to Ariadne. Behind Jenny, the mole people whisper nervously among themselves.

"Fuck you, Jenny," words spit softly out like melon seeds. "Fuck you, and fuck the voices in your sick head."

Jenny steps closer, sets the heroin gently on Ariadne's bare knee. "I'm sorry," she says. "I can't stay."

"Then at least let me kiss you, Jen," and Ariadne's arms strike like moray eels, locking firmly around Jenny's neck and pull her roughly down. Ariadne's mouth tastes like ashes and bad teeth, and her tongue probes quickly past the jagged reef of sharpened incisors. Jenny tries to pull away, pushes hard, and Ariadne bites the tip end of her tongue as their mouths part, bites hard, and Jenny stumbles backwards and almost falls among the restless mole people, pain and the deceitful copper warmth of her own blood on her lips.

Ariadne laughs again, vicious, hopeless chuckle, wipes her mouth with the back of one hand and snatches up the baggie of dope from her knee with the other.

"Get out of here, Jenny. Go back up there and slice yourself to fucking ribbons."

Eyes that are all pupil now, and the dark smudge of Jenny's blood on her chin.

Jenny Haniver runs back the way she came, dodging the forest of grasping hands that rises up around her.

In the dream, the dream that she's had again and again since the first night she heard their voices, Jenny Haniver drifts weightless in silent hues of malachite and ocher green. The sun filters into and through the world from somewhere else above, Bible storybook shafts in the perfect, silting murk. She moves her long tail slowly from side to side and sinks deeper, spreads her silver arms wide, accepting and inviting. And he rises from below, from the cold, still depths where the sun never reaches, the viperfish night, and folds her away in pelvic webs and stiletto spines. She gasps, and the salt water rushes into her throat through the crimson-feathered slits beneath her chin.

Jenny sinks her teeth, row after serrate row, into the tender meat of his shoulder, scrapes his smooth chest with the erect spurs of her nipples.

And the voices are all around, bathypelagic echoes, as tangible as the sweet taste of his blood in her mouth.

She has never felt this safe, has never felt half this whole.

Their bodies twine, a living braid of glimmering scales and iridescent scaleless flesh, and together they roll over and over and down, until the only light is the yellowish photophore glow of anglerfish lures and   jellyfish veils.

She wakes up again, stiff crammed into the dank cubby hole, more blind than in the last moment before she opened her eyes. There's no sense of time anymore, only the vague certainty that she's been wandering the tunnels for what must be days and days and days now, and the burning pain in her mouth and throat, Ariadne's infection gift rotting its way into her skull. She is drowning, mind and body, in the tunnels' incessant night tide and the sour fluids that drain from her wounded tongue.

Jenny Haniver coughs, fishhook barbs gouging her chest and throat, and spits something thick and hot into the dark. She tries to stand, braces herself, unsteady arms and shoulders against the slimeslick tunnel wall, but the knifing spasms in her feet and legs and the fever's vertigo force her to sit back down, quickly, before she falls.

The rats are still there, waiting with infinite carrion patience for her to die. She can hear their breath and the snick of their tiny claws on the stone floor. She doesn't know why they have not taken her in her sleep; she no longer has a voice to shout at them, so kicks hard at the soft, flea-seething bodies when they come too close.

Because she cannot walk, she crawls.

Here, past the merciful failure of punky concrete and steel-rod reinforcements, where one forgotten tunnel has collapsed, tumbled into the void of one much older, she lies at the bottom of the wide rubble scree. Face down in the commingled cement debris and shattered work of Colonial stonemasons, and the sluggish river of waste and filth-glazed water moves along inches from her face. The rats and the muttering ghosts of Old Mama and Old Papa and her father will not follow her down; they wait like a jury, like ribsy vultures, like the living (which they are not) keeping deathbed vigil.

There is wavering yellowgreen light beneath the water, the gaudy drab light of things which will never see the sun and have learned to make their own. So much light that it hurts her eyes, and she has to squint. The ancient sewer vibrates with their voices, their siren songs of clicks and trills and throaty bellows, but she can't answer, her ruined tongue so swollen that she can hardly even close her mouth or draw breath around it. Instead, she splashes weakly with the fingers of one straining, outstretched hand, smacking the surface with her palm.

Old Mama laughs again, and then her father and Old Papa try to call her back, and then promise her things she never had and never wanted. This only makes Old Mama laugh louder, and Jenny ignores them all, watches the long and sinuous shadows move lazily across the vaulted ceiling. Something big brushes her fingertips, silky roughness and fins like lace, unimaginable strength in the lateral flex of those muscles, and she wants to cry but the fever scorch has sealed her tear ducts.

With both hands, she digs deep into the froth and sludge that mark the boundary between worlds, stone and water, and pulls herself the last few feet. Dragging her useless legs behind her, Jenny Haniver slides into the piss-warm river, and lets the familiar currents carry her down to the sea.

"O that this too too solid flesh would melt..."
—William Shakespeare

SUPERHEROES

THE THIRD SATURDAY NIGHT OF JULY, SUNDAY MORNING now, and the air was rain cool and smelled like asphalt steam when Darby and Carter left the theater, stepped out of the artificial chill and popcorn-butter stink, Pinky walking in their footsteps. The third weekend of the month and the one weekend that Classic Cinema showed *The Rocky Horror Picture Show*, one screening only, midnight Saturday; this ritual as sacred to them as anything in a church had ever been, liturgy of noisemakers and squirt guns, toilet paper and melba-toast sacraments.

Stingy allotment, one night of glitz and sparkle a month for a Georgia town, and the only night when hardly anyone treated them like freaks, one night when Darby and Carter could wear lipstick and eyeliner in public. And something to do besides sit in their bedrooms, listening to their music and smoking, making out sometimes and Pinky prattling on about who she thought was the cutest member of the Cure this week, or what it would be like to sleep with Trent Reznor. Their costumes and makeup a little better every time, almost as good as the college kids who stood under the screen and acted out the film, scene by scene, Darby always going as one of the Transylvanian party guests and Carter in drag as Columbia. Pinky too fat to be Magenta, too fat for the French maid outfit, but it didn't stop her,

79

no matter how many hints they dropped, and they couldn't ever just come right out and tell her.

Darby stopped just outside the theater doors, running both hands through his black hair; a few grains of rice fell out and bounced around his feet. "You got any cigarettes left?" Carter asked him, and he fished the half-empty pack of Camels from the inside pocket of his tuxedo jacket, gave one to Carter, one to Pinky even though she was always bumming smokes, never had any to offer anyone else. And they stood watching the crowd as it squeezed through the doors and broke apart in the parking lot, at least half in costume, slackers and punks and townies, University students and a surly clump of frat boy lookie-looks. Some of the live cast came out, and the girl who played Columbia, a dead ringer for Little Nell, stopped and smiled wide at Carter.

"Nice outfit," she said, and "Thanks," he replied, and then she smiled even wider. "Shit, I thought you were a real girl," and she laughed, skipped away to catch up with the others. "Bitch," Pinky said, sneering after the girl. And Carter just shrugged. "It's a sort of a compliment," he said.

Quick *clack, clack, clack* on the concrete for them and a half spin, not real taps but beer bottle caps stuck to the soles of his shoes, tipped his gold-sequined top hat and the tails of his gold-sequined jacket flying out behind. Someone clapped for him, and it got a half-smile from Darby, hard not to smile for Carter.

"Are we gonna go back to your house, Darby?" Pinky asked, and then, whispered, like the world's biggest secret, like something dangerous. "I got three Darvon out of my mother's medicine cabinet this morning."

Darby looked across the parking lot, past the piss-yellow pools of light and the cars lined up in front of the theater, the people getting in and driving away, and he squinted, as if trying to see farther. "Look, Pinky, can you get another ride home tonight?" and he knew that she could, at least three or four others still hanging around the doors she could beg a ride off easy if she tried, or he wouldn't have asked.

"Sure, I guess I could," she said, "if you guys have other plans," sounding more hurt than she was, and Darby groaned inside, not even half up to Pinky's calculated self-pity tonight, not up to his own guilt, as involuntary as gagging. And Carter watching him, Cleopatra-eyes full of doubt, misgiving, and he knew Carter was hoping that he'd change his mind at the last minute, after all.

"Yeah, we do, kinda," he said, instead. "But I'll call you tomorrow, okay?"

Big Pinky frown, dramatic loud sigh. "That's okay," she said, dumpier, white-faced Eeyore. "I'll find a ride. But I'll hold on to the pills. Maybe tomorrow night?" and "Yeah," Darby said. "Maybe. We'll call you." And she hugged them both and walked away, trailing her own private cloud of cigarette smoke and dejection and patchouli fumes.

"You're being mean to her again," Carter said, and Darby looked back out at the parking lot. Fewer people now, easier to see all the way across. "Bullshit," he said and pushed his sunglasses down towards the tip of his nose, staring at Carter over the rims. "Look, you promised you'd do this with me. You didn't have to promise. If you'd rather be popping pain killers with a fag hag, that's your business." Words he knew would cut, would find their mark.

"Jesus, Darby. That's what I mean. There's no point talking about her like that. I said I'd fucking come."

Darby took a deep drag off his Camel and flicked the butt into the gutter, started walking, and he knew that Carter would follow, immediately heard the *clack, clack, clack* of his Columbia shoes on the blacktop. And he stopped so Carter could catch up. "Can't we at least go and change our clothes first?" and more sharply than was necessary, "There isn't time," too sharp, but the adrenaline was getting to him. "We have to be there at exactly 2:30. *Exactly* 2:30, Carter. He won't wait around if we're not."

And Carter followed him, silent except for his shoes, past the darkened A&P, the Chevron station closed up for the night and the row of dumpsters a little farther back, farthest edge of the parking lot from the theater, where the asphalt ended in sticky red mud and pine trees, pothole alley behind the shopping center. Much darker back there, tree shadows, whispering needles and dumpster shadows, wet garbage stink. The quarter moon slipped in and out of the clouds, too small and too cold and much too far away to be a comfort.

Darby looked at his wristwatch, tilted its face back towards the shopping-center glow to read the dial.

"Then, if he doesn't come by 2:35, we can go?"

"He's coming," Darby said, final word, and Carter held his hand tight and together they waited.

A rumor traded between the dark children and their computer screens, wishful thought gathering substance and momentum like a phosphor snowball as they passed their electronic notes around the world. Veiled hints and insinuation hidden between goth-band gossip and love letters to vampires, fishnet need and black-vinyl desire. Something that might have been real all along, or only a collective wet dream they'd forced into a deal with reality, or something else altogether.

And it had been seven months since Darby found that first mention of Jimmy DeSade on alt.gothic, rainy January and the three of them at Carter's house that night. Getting fucked up on Robitussin and Pinky hogging the stereo, playing the same Daisy Chainsaw CD over and over again while Darby and Carter sat at Carter's new Compaq Presario, blue-white monitor glare competing with the candlelight. That first message, hardly a whisper... *about as real as Jimmy DeSade, Shelley, dear. Get thee a fucking clue.* Prickling sick rush of excitement in Darby's stomach, then, inexplicable, but the same rising-sinking prickle as the first time Carter had offered to suck him off, and he'd followed that thread back as far as it went—*Re: Are cheetos gothick?! (Was: Poseur Alert from Brooklyn)*—following the original thread, and that was the only time the name came up. A simile, nothing more, but he'd scanned through every other message in the newsgroup anyway, stayed at the keyboard long after Carter had lost interest and gone off to talk Pinky into playing something else.

And when he hadn't found anything, had posted *Who's Jimmy DeSade?* and just four words to the message: *Well? Who is he?* No reply that night, no answer for days afterwards, bleak-slate skies and that name in his head, and Carter had started to complain about all the time he spent online. "My parents are gonna absolutely shit a cat when they get the AOL bill, Darby," and when he was about to turn loose, forget it, another mention: *Like the junk heap Jimmy DeSade drives, right?* and that time he'd e-mailed the poster who'd written the message, Salome@omniserv.com, and the response had said only, *shhhhhhh* and *Listen, babygoth...* Those words read over and over until he had a hard-on, and he'd written back, *Listen for what?! (And don't call me a babygoth, I'm 16)*, but there had never been an answer. And he'd found himself imagining, fantasizing Jimmy DeSade, making pretty pictures, awful pictures, in his head whenever he and Carter fucked around. A rattletrap car and the man behind the wheel, big scarecrow man and his face always lost in the thinner bits of the fantasy, but that car clear enough, bumping down a dark and dirt-paved road, the choking dust trailing out behind.

"I'm cold," Carter said, standing as close to Darby as he could. Thunder not far away, towards Normaltown or Bogart, and for the last five minutes a misting rain. They'd stepped back, a little shelter in the cover of the pines, wet needles crunching like soggy breakfast cereal under their shoes.

"Stop whining," Darby said, and he didn't take his eyes off the road, just an alley, really, running between the woods and the rear of the shopping center.

"Fuck you, Darby. It's raining, and I'm cold."

"Go home, then," more a threat than an alternative, and

Carter stepped back, one foot or two, and "I feel like Charlie Brown in drag, waiting with Linus for the stupid fucking Great Pumpkin, Darby. That's what this is like. Waiting for the goddamn Great Pumpkin."

"Then go *home*, Carter. I'm not forcing you to do anything, and I'm tired of your whining."

Instead, "What time is it?" Carter asked him, and Darby didn't want to look at his watch, didn't want to know how fast the minutes were creeping by, adding up, making a fool of him. "It's not time yet," he said.

And he took out the razor blade, the one he always kept with him now, stainless steel in his pocket since the first night he'd talked Carter into letting him cut and press his eager lips to the open wound. Catch the warmth, the warmth that spilled out into the world, into him, like light. Fingered it nervously like a coin or a good luck charm.

"What do you want?" Carter said, looking at the razor the nervous way he always looked at it.

"I just want to know," Darby said. "If he's real. I just want to know."

"Is it gonna hurt?" Carter had asked the night in February, first-time night. Thunderstorm night, and Darby had bought the pack of Schick blades at the drugstore that afternoon, when there had only been prologue black clouds building over the town and wind that smelled like spring.

"No," he'd said, not knowing but by then his dick so hard it ached, and when he closed his eyes he saw Jimmy DeSade coming, rolling along back roads and empty midnight interstate. Wanting to care if he hurt Carter, but not caring, anyway. Not caring about anything but the way it would feel when the blade traced a paper-cut line along Carter's shoulder, dividing cream skin; tear here, dotted line; not caring about anything but the face he couldn't see behind the dirty windshield.

Raging hard-on for a hearsay, gossip phantom or just a game

the netgoths hadn't let him in on; butt of their jokes, the way he'd begged for details, and every now and then a scrap or a crumb thrown his way or not hidden before he found it, just enough that he wouldn't forget and never any more. Ligeia@well.com and a signature line, *The children of the night can't sing for shit—Jimmy DeSade*. Or, taunting, infuriating uncertainty just for him: Nitejaw1@perfidia.co.uk and...*those lousy wankers haven't put out any new songs worth shit since Jimmy D. and Salmagundi were a thing.*

And Carter had only flinched, the cut an inch long but longer than he'd meant, longer and deeper, the thick blood welling like spilled ink in the candlelight and his heart skipping hard beats by the time he'd kissed it away. Soft moans from Carter that had only made him harder, and when Darby had reached around Carter's waist, he'd been hard, too.

Outside, the rain had turned to hail, and the thunder had sounded like judgment rattling at the windows.

"Just admit it, Carter. Admit you're scared and go the hell home while there's still time."

"Why won't you tell me what time it is, Darby? That's all I asked. If you're right, what's the big deal?"

But Darby kept his wrist where Carter couldn't see, where he wouldn't have to watch the hour hand and minute hand, rushing second hand; 2:38 last time he'd risked a glance, and he hadn't even told Carter that. It was raining harder now, first a steady drizzle, and then coming straight down, and they were both getting soaked, makeup running and both of them shivering soppy inside their costumes. Although Darby tried hard not to shiver, tried to reveal no sign of discomfort, to show no hint the cold was getting in, that he was anything but confident.

"I should leave you here, Darby. You'd have it coming, after the way you talked to Pinky. After the way you've been talking to me."

"Just shut up, Carter."

"You see what I mean? I really should leave you standing here alone in the fucking rain all night."

And Darby took something from the inside of his tux jacket, the rain soaked through and the paper wet, a wet page from Carter's printer, and he read the words there again. At least the ink hadn't started to run or smear, and it was all still there, still real.

"Just leave your snotty ass standing out here to get the flu or pneumonia. Christ, Darby, the rain is going to ruin my costume—"

And Darby turned on him, all the ripe and rotten frustration getting out through his eyes, green fire ringed with smeared mascara, and the razor clenched between his thumb and index finger. "Go the fuck home, Carter! *Now*, goddamn it!" and Carter just stood there, staring at him, disbelief and his scared face like a ruined watercolor. A big run in his hose from their scramble up the low and muddy bank to the shelter of the pines when he'd gotten tangled in some briars.

"If you can't shut up and stand there a few goddamn minutes without whining, I don't want you here."

Lower lip trembling and a tear distinct from the rain on Carter's cheeks, the kind of sniveling shit Pinky would pull, and Darby pushed him so hard he almost slipped and fell.

"He is coming," and the soggy printout held so Carter could see. "I didn't make *this* up. I didn't imagine *this*."

"No, but maybe you're being too stupid to know someone's just playing a joke on you," and Darby gritted his teeth, swung the razor blade and fabric *shrrriped* when it caught the lapels of Carter's jacket, wide gash through the dripping sequins and the fabric underneath.

"You crazy son of a bitch," and that was all before Carter was running, *clack, clack, clack, clack* across the wet road; Darby looked down at his hand, a traitorous, alien thing at the end of his arm and the wet glint of the razor there. He looked across the road, and saw that Carter had stopped on the other side, stood with his back to concrete walls painted the latex color of oatmeal, no shelter at all from the rain over there, but he stood very still and stared back at Darby.

"Jesus, Carter," rain muffled words, and *I'm sorry*, but apologizing just inside his head, because he was afraid it wouldn't matter, too late or just that Carter wouldn't hear. So he went back to waiting, and Carter waited with him, or apart from him, on the other side.

April, and Darby had been failing algebra again, his parents talking about summer school like it was the boogeyman and bitching about his hair, that he'd started wearing eyeliner to school. *It's no fucking wonder you're always getting your ass kicked*, said his father. And *Other boys your age have started dating*, said his mother. He'd taken blood from Carter's shoulder every chance he got, his lips to the breach and his hand around his penis, the warm salt-penny-chocolate taste and orgasm, the stain on his lips and cum on the sheets of their beds. The scars and fresher cuts lined up neatly on Carter's shoulder and thighs, like marks a prisoner might make on the wall of his cell to count the days.

And Carter refusing to take from him, no complaints, no resistance, but no reciprocation, either. "I just don't want to, that's all."

Sitting at Carter's computer when he could and finding next to nothing, when nothing might have been a blessing, better than the teasing bits and whispers he found instead.

Balzac45@angeleno.com and *That sOundz like sOmething Jimmy DeSade wOuld have dOne—befOre the riOtz—IMHO*. No one ever answering his questions straight, when they bothered to answer them at all.

And one night, middle of the month and his bedroom window open, cricket and cicada racket underneath This Mortal Coil, and Pinky had been whining, bored Pinky whine, and how she wished they had fake IDs and then they could get into a club or a bar, like there was anywhere in town worth sneaking into. Atlanta, then, she'd said. Atlanta has real clubs, but only Carter had a car, and his parents wouldn't ever let him drive that far. "You want to try something new, Pinky?" and Carter had looked at him, concern, confusion, and Darby had gone to the shelf where he kept his razor blades, hidden in the middle of a stack of comics and *Fangoria*, someplace his mother wouldn't look.

"Like what? A new drug?" she'd asked, and Carter hadn't said anything, just that look, *Are you sure, Darby? This might not be such a good idea.* And maybe betrayal, too, because hadn't he told Carter it was sex, enough *like* sex, even *better* than sex, maybe?

"No, it's not a drug. It's something else," and he'd shown her the silver and blue plastic dispenser of razor blades. "It's something different."

"Oh," she'd said. "You mean bloodletting, Darby? I've done that, with Jackie and her cousin, last year. She had a special little knife from India," and "Aren't you worried about getting AIDS?" before Carter had taken the dispenser from his open hand. "She doesn't want to do it," he'd said.

"She didn't say that, did you, Pinky?"

And she'd looked down at Carter's hand, fist squeezed tight around the blades, had shrugged, dim apprehension in her eyes, but she wasn't afraid, and it had pissed Darby off. "Never fucking mind," and he'd taken the razor blades away from Carter and put them back safe between magazine- slick covers.

"I'm sorry, Darby," shouted across the road, Carter's words getting to him through the downpour tattoo. "I am. I'm sorry." No reply, nothing he could have said, and he tried not to look at his watch, the wet crystal and hands like school-yard bullies. But he did. 2:57, it said, and he couldn't pretend it was fast, not *that* fast, anyway. Had checked it three times that afternoon against the time on the Weather Channel.

"Can I come back over there and stand with you, Darby?"

Lightning and thunder right away so he could make like he hadn't heard, wished he hadn't seen Carter so stark in the half-second flash of daylight: rusty streaks of the temporary orange color he'd put in his hair running down his cheeks, hair plastered flat and the puddle around his heels.

"I won't say anything else, Darby. I'll keep my mouth shut."

Darby was still holding the razor, stainless steel washed clean by the rain, and he didn't answer, imagined that he hadn't only cut Carter's jacket, had cut his throat and let all that blood out at once. Scalding, stickydark jet in time to Carter's heart, dark spray across the wet pine straw, bright and fading surprise and terror in Carter's eyes before he fell, sank slow-mo into Darby's waiting arms, Darby's waiting lips. Maybe that would have been enough, that one indelible act, offering, forfeiture, and maybe he wouldn't be standing here, afraid of his wristwatch. Carter yelling at him from behind the A&P. Maybe he hadn't understood, had done something wrong. Their ridiculous *Rocky Horror* clothes, maybe, or the fact that he hadn't come alone.

"Go home, Carter!" he screamed. "I don't want you here," and Carter shook his head and stood there in the rain.

In May, he'd had the dream, the only time, third Saturday of the month, and so there'd been *Rocky* with Carter and Pinky and whatever they'd found to do afterwards. No sleep until almost dawn, and Pinky had given him a Xanax she'd stolen from her older sister, so he'd passed out cold. And standing on the long dirt road under a swollen sun the color of a cardinal's feathers, heavy summer heat and sweat in his eyes as he watched the dust cloud coming towards him down the clay-red slash between the pines. Smell of turpentine and baking air, and the sun glinting mean off the hood of the old Lincoln. Hot, rustling breeze through the pine needles and the wild animal sound of the car's engine, the sound of bald tires on the road, and he stepped back, stood waiting in oven shade until the car rumbled to a stop, dust cloud catching up with it and sifting down around him. And the door, opening wide so the cool air washed out, wrapping itself around his ankles, slithering up the legs of his jeans. Asking him in, sanctuary (*never mind the smell, it grows on you, after a while*), refuge from the demon sun and this fucking town and his fucking parents. The hand before it retreated into air-conditioned shadows, bulky silver rings on every finger, nails like a mechanic's, oil grunge beneath those nails, except the one on his little finger, so long and sharp and gleaming perfect crimson.

"What you waitin' for, little boy?" Jimmy DeSade said, sexy smooth Brit accent, and the cold air worked its way through Darby's underwear and coiled tight around his dick. "You only get asked one time."

The cold, like a dead and loving tongue, and then the orgasm had awakened him, and Darby had lain in bed an hour longer, semen scabbing on his skin, staring at the afternoon sunlight through the curtains.

"Please, Darby. I'm freezing."

3:19 a.m., last time he looked at his watch before he'd taken it off and thrown it across the road at Carter. Faint smash when it hit the back wall of the grocery store, instead, and Carter had picked up what was left.

"Let's just go back to my house," he said, easy to hear him now because the rain had stopped. Dripped down around Carter from the limbs, from his hair and clothes. Dripped as loud and constant as the watch had ticked. "I'm gonna have to go soon, Darby, and I don't want to leave you out here by yourself."

"Go on, then," Darby said. "Run away home."

He stood out of sight, under the trees, had sliced the tip end of every finger with the razor blade, cut broad X's on the backs of both hands and smeared his face with the blood, tasted it, his *own* blood for once. And it tasted and felt no different in his mouth than Carter's, but meant nothing, except that he was bleeding.

"Please come home with me."

But Darby turned and walked deeper into the woods, briars and brambles tearing at his black clothes, his shoes sinking in pine straw and mud, and before long he couldn't hear Carter calling him anymore.

"It totally changes the whole movie," Pinky had said, muggy June night, still a week before *Rocky Horror*, and Carter had rented the video so they could practice the responses. Then back to his bedroom, Pinky and Carter talking while Darby sat at the computer.

"It's the song that shows us how Brad and Janet have been changed by everything that happened to them in the castle," she'd said. "And when it's not there, it changes everything."

"Well, I've called the theater three or four times now," Carter said, "and asked them to *please* get the British release instead, but I don't think they're ever gonna. They *always* show the British print in Atlanta."

And Darby had typed in Carter's password and waited, the wait that always seemed like a short forever while the modem dialed into the server. Pinky and Carter's conversation was nothing but annoying.

"You've got mail," the computer chimed and he'd clicked the mailbox, just one letter waiting, 101017.865@compu-serve.com and the subject line, one word, *DeSade*. And his heart had skipped and hammered.

"The verse Janet sings. That's how you *know* it's really a vampire story," Pinky said, "and that all the Frankenstein stuff is just superficial."

Even though Darby had stopped asking questions in April, had given up, and he'd almost called Carter to come, then, to see, before he moved the mouse, the pointer, and double-clicked again.

"And *that's* why Brad and Janet are so fucked up in *Shock Treatment*, because it's really making fun of all those old science-fiction movies where everything gets like magically okay and normal again as soon as the   monster's gone."

The message so short, lean sentences, rationed words, and he'd read it over and over again:... *an associate of Mr. DeSade...* and *He finds this perseverance endearing...* and, then... *meeting might be arranged, if you're interested. Yours Sincerely, V.* and Darby had told the computer to print, stared unblinking at the bright screen while the noisy dot-matrix printer put ink to paper, making it solid, substantial, before he'd moved the cursor over to the reply icon.

"Loss of innocence," Pinky had said, "and the illusion of morality. Nothing can ever be the same again. *That's* what 'Superheroes' is saying at the end of the movie," sounding pleased with herself, and then the wail of a train whistle through the open window, far away and coming closer.

And he moved faster and faster between the trees, caught his feet in creeper vines and deadfall tangles, fell and got up and kept moving, running finally. No thought to where, except that his feet would carry him away from Carter and his own shitty life, away from the town and school, away from everything. He came to a small creek strangling with the night's runoff, and lost a shoe on the silty bottom, pulled the other off, full of mud and water, anyway, flung it away into the dark and ran on in his sock feet. Sharp, jabbing sticks and rocks bruising his feet until the pain from the cuts on his hands seemed unimportant.

And then the trees ended, all at once, and the narrow cleft of a dirt road before they began again. Began again to go on that way forever, and Darby heard the rattle and grind of the car's old engine, deathrattle, oildry grind, before he saw the headlights. Nothing but the headlights, set far apart like reptile eyes or the space between him and morning. Moving so fast, bouncing over ruts and potholes, bearing down, and Darby waited in the trees, breathless, side stitch and feet bleeding through his socks. Until the car was almost on him, and he stepped across.

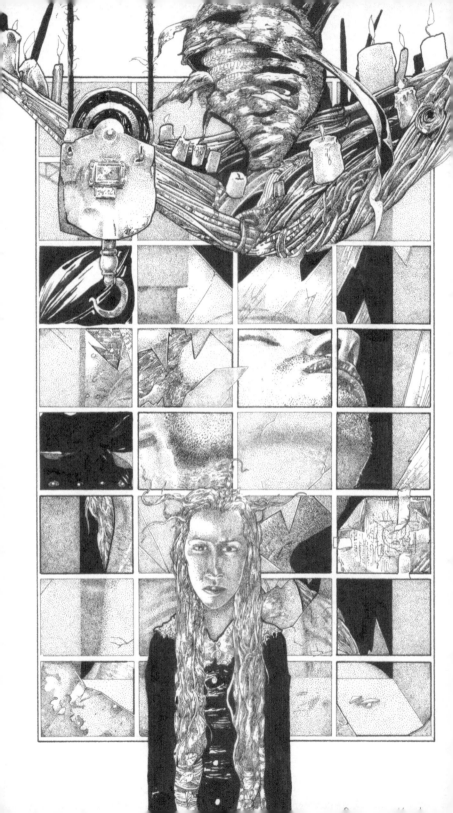

GLASS COFFIN

~ 1 ~

THEY BUILT SHIPS HERE. THIS FORGOTTEN PLACE ON the wide gray Hudson, past the sprawling rust crane- and brick-crumble wastes and quarry floods of Jersey. Manhattan like Heaven on the other side, and it might as well be a thousand miles away, misty unreal thing of steel and sparkling glass as insubstantial as a matte painting of the Emerald City. The yard, once upon a time Desvernine Consolidated Shipyard, just the yard for twenty-five years now. All her ironclad children gone to wars or bellies full of oil, the cold and crushing bottom of the sea. One building dock empty and another clogged with stillbirth scrap, unfinished tanker husk that will never be anything more, and the hammerhead cranes still standing speechless watch, counterbalanced midwives. Concrete and one hundred thousand shades of corrosion.

From one window of her room, once an office for engineers and blueprints, Salmagundi Desvernine watches the yard, has folded back the heavy plastic drape that keeps out the wind and snow and stares through broken panes across the corrugated rooftops towards front gates padlocked and chained against the world outside. Squints to see farther than she can, strains to steal a glimpse beyond the road that winds away

through other abandoned industries, disappearing, finally, between the high gneiss and granite bluffs, boulders pollution
scarred and spray-paint tagged, wrapped in fog the color of
rust.

"He'll be back soon," Ariadne Moreau whispers from the half
light and shadows behind Salmagundi, dust and the clutter of
antique furniture, and she turns to see the girl, oldest of the
seven, the children of the yard. The old wounds on her arms
faded now, needle kisses, and it's been almost two months since
the last time Ariadne came back herself; they all come back
sooner or later, no matter the demons or angels that draw them
away. Almost all the comfort left in the world, Salmagundi
thinks, and she manages an unfinished smile for Ariadne.

"He should have been back Friday," should have come
rumbling down that snaketwist road, all dust and exhaust in his
battered snot-green Lincoln Continental and the children
rushing out to meet him, Jesus and Rat with their jangling keys,
Wren and Joey anxious for the gifts he always brings, the emptiness where Glitch should be, and Jenny Haniver and Ariadne
hanging back, cautious handholders, too lost in their own
private urgencies and hungers to run to him or anyone else.
And Salmagundi, standing alone a few minutes longer, waiting
in the gravel at the foot of the stairs to her apartment, waiting
for Jimmy DeSade.

"Sometimes he's late," Ariadne says and shuts the book she's
been reading for the last hour, her face close to the pages to see
the words in the flat gray January afternoon leaking into the
room. Something about Rosicrucians borrowed from Rat's pipe-
shop library, and she returns the smile, reflects the smile,
brushes tangled black hair from her eyes. Salmagundi is the
most beautiful woman, most beautiful thing, she's ever known;
one-third of her trinity, but more beautiful by ten than
either her lover or the smack; hair as gold as department-store
Christmas tinsel, slenderlong hands and marble skin, if marble
ever had the faint blush across Salmagundi's high cheekbones,
the candy red in her lips. Everything Ariadne trusts, all the light

she's ever seen, straight or stoned, and times like this she doesn't know why she ever needs the dope, why she ever needs anything but the certainty that she'll never be asked to leave the yard.

"He'll be here soon," and Ariadne hopes she sounds confident, reassuring, and Salmagundi sighs and turns back to her window, cold wind off the river fingering her hair. And she says, "When I close my eyes I can't find him," and she doesn't say anything else, and after a while, Ariadne goes back to her book.

Salmagundi's stingy fortune was exhausted long ago, and now there's only the yard and what it gives up to the patient salvages of the children; dollars and more often pennies for wreck and ruin, copper wire and pipe, bits and warped pieces of presses and drills and sheet-metal cutters, sold off for scrap. And the money and food that Jimmy DeSade brings them, the white powder he brings back from Mexico and turns into cash in Baltimore and Philadelphia and Newark. So, no one goes hungry and no one freezes in the winter and there are little comforts.

Rat and Jesus keep the keys and almost always find the best scrap. Rat who doesn't look anyone in the eye anymore, his face a wormpink scar and hair oiled back smooth with industrial lubricants. Jesus all stringy hard muscle and Cuban-Chinese good looks, and today they're breaking down a gap press that Rat found hidden away in the subbasement of one of the pre-outfitting shops. Two treacherous days of block and tackle to get it up into the sun, and their hands move sure as surgeons, or pathologists over a suspicious corpse, wrenches and acetylene fire for scalpels. Wren and Joey watch them, ready to help when they can, to bring water or roll cigarettes.

Wren hiding out here from the cops and juvie, sanctuary after she finally got too tired of her stepfather's dick between her legs, and she changed the rules with two shots from a .38 she found in a garbage can on West Forty-Second Street. Joey who just showed up at the gates one day, and maybe this'll be his last winter, endless diarrhea and losing so much weight, never mind the black market AZT that Jimmy brings.

Jesus shuts off his torch, squints and blinks behind tinted goggles like fish eyes. "How 'bout a smoke, Wren Bird?" and she reaches for the leather bag of tobacco around her neck as Ariadne steps through a rotted jumble of plywood pallets and pipe twisted like sections of robot intestine.

"Hi," Rat says, not looking at her, and she hands his book back, stands beside Wren and Joey and stares at the gap press, what's left of it and the scatter of its dissection spread across an oily drop cloth at their feet, motor still one piece, grungy bits she can't identify. Wren finishes rolling the cigarette, seals the paper expertly with one lick and passes it to Jesus. Zippo from his pocket, and he blows smoke the hopeless color of the sky. "He'll be here soon," Jesus says, and she nods, shrugs and sits on the crate with Wren and Joey.

"She's scared," and Ariadne realizes that she's scared, too; wishes Jenny Haniver were with her now instead of off digging mussels, hunting blue crabs along the mudflats at the old docks. "She's not eating," Ariadne says. "Won't do anything but sit at the window watching the road."

Same moment and same words from their mouths, "Nobody fucks with Jimmy," and, before Wren has a chance, Joey says "Jinx," and punches her in the arm. "Jinx yourself, Joseph," but Ariadne sees how scared she looks, too; all of them scared, like Salmagundi, all of them waiting, watching the road, each in his or her own way and in their own time. More scared because Salmagundi is scared.

"Damn straight," Jesus says. "Not more'n once they don't," and takes another drag off his cigarette before he flicks the roach away and turns the oxyacetylene torch on again and draws slicing fire down the gap press' steel skin.

Fading dusk, night already where the river winds away towards

Hudson Bay, the sea beyond, and across the water Manhattan burns like a grounded slab of Milky Way, as distant, as unfathomable as the stars. Jenny Haniver sits over her bubbling hot-plate stew, big dinged and dented pot full of the things she found along the shore, and the other children sit around her; all eyes on the pot or the cement floor of the mostly empty warehouse where they sleep and eat and keep themselves from the wind. No light but stubby candles, and she stirs the mussels and crabs, mud rinsed away and everything dropped in whole, lucky today so there's a small eel, too. Niggardly pinches of black pepper and salt, sage from her baby food jars of spices, almost empty now, and there'll be no more until Jimmy comes back.

"It smells good," Wren says, and her voice just seems to make the silence that lies like ice over the yard that much heavier, a hard blanket of unspoken fears, and Jesus says, "Yeah, it does," but Jenny only shrugs and the quiet rushes back to fill in even the tiniest unguarded space.

"Tell us a story," Joey says, looking at Ariadne Moreau where she sits on the floor next to Jenny. "Tell us about the city." Ariadne glances at Jenny Haniver and shakes her head. "You already know about the city, Joey. You know everything about the city you need to know."

"Then tell us about something else. Tell us about how the yard used to be when Salmagundi was a little kid."

And this is not so different from any other night, them asking her to talk to keep away the dark and all their ghosts, her complaining that they know all the stories, could recite them in their sleep: Silas Desvernine opening the yard a hundred years ago, longer than that, his ships built with rivets instead of welds, and the wars, then, and the fortunes handed down from Silas to his children, their children, grandchildren, Salmagundi's father. The bad times, finally, the yard closing, never a happy ending, and she doesn't know why they want to hear. Same tired story, the clanging Desvernine empire of steel and smoke lost because its last emperor was a drunk and the empress a gambler and she bet away four generations on a spinning wheel and a tiny black ball.

Same as ever, except for Salmagundi still sitting alone in her room, watching the road, and when Ariadne asked her if she was coming down for supper or wanted something brought up, she said no, I'm really not hungry, and her eyes never left the window. Same, except their minds are all somewhere else, waiting.

"Not tonight, Joey," Ariadne says softly, firmly and she shivers inside her raveling orange cardigan, holds Jenny's hand while dusk closes down and turns to barren darkness.

She fell asleep in the chair by the window, wrapped in quilts from her bed, her robes underneath, and now Salmagundi dreams that she's locked outside the gates of the yard. Chain-link and silver coils of razor wire, glinting blades in the moonlight and the lifeless or twitching bodies of rock doves and starlings trapped within the thorns. Her fingers so cold they're numb, but she tries to free one of the birds, slicing her thumb open, her blood and the starling's commingling painlessly, and it doesn't matter how loudly she calls out for Ariadne or the others. Shadows and dull shine off the cranes and tin roofs on the other side of the fence, span of jib cranes like the skeletons of dinosaurs sculpted in steel. Just blackness where the lights of New York City ought to be, and the bird dies in her bleeding hands.

"He's left you," her mother says, watching through the diamond weave of the fence. An old woman, which her mother never was; not the woman who died in a sanitarium upstate a long time before these wrinkles and crooked bones, this voice a dry place over naked gums. "There's always someone prettier," her mother says. "And very little you can do about it, in the end."

"No, Mother," and the old woman laughs, a laugh too full of the night behind that withered face: *I see myself in your face, she says. Myself locked up in you like light coming off a mirror...* but Salmagundi is calling for Ariadne, for Rat or Jesus, drowning her out, or simply drowning.

"They won't hear you," the old woman says. "They're all asleep, heads full of dust and sand in their eyes. They know he isn't coming back this time."

And Salmagundi turns away from the old woman that her mother never became, and there's the road instead, broken asphalt crumble, potholes filled with oilsheen water, new cracks at her feet as the razor wire grows around her like brambles, wriggles up from the dead soil and writhes across the tarmac. In the distance, just coming through the narrow cut in the bluff, she sees his headlights. Or the nighthungry eyes of something else altogether, but it doesn't matter which because the wire winds tighter around her, wraps her and slices her white skin, and the lights never get any closer.

"But what *is* it?" Ariadne asks as Rat and Jesus set the bulky piece of machinery down, odd something like a stubby fan, hub and maybe twenty rubber straps where blades would be, heavy black rubber and the ends of the straps flattened and four round and pimpled metal disks attached to each, exotic coins or worthless slugs.

"Centrifugal flagellater," Rat says, and Ariadne shakes her head. "Fanciest words you've come up with yet for a piece of junk," she tells him, and so he pulls a small book from the back pocket of his coveralls, grease-stained and yellow pages, and he flips to a diagram of the thing, almost an exact likeness, then shows it to Ariadne without looking at her. "See," he says. "What I said. For cleaning metal, getting rid of loose mill scale or rust. Those things on the rotary flaps are tungsten shot."

"Tungsten. That ought'a be worth a few bucks at least, eh, Ratboy?" Jesus smiling, sweating and filthy and tired, and it's almost enough to make her feel better, more like herself, less like the threatening sky overhead, the indigo cumulonimbus underside of the frostbite sky, dead cold pressing down towards earth, and there could be snow by afternoon.

Jesus sits on the ground, strong legs crossed, inspecting the device more closely, takes the book from Rat and makes a show of comparing the two. "Man, we need some sounds, Rat. Go get the box." And Rat comes back a few minutes later with the huge boom box Glitch left behind, and now they all share it when there are batteries. Pulls back strips of duct tape that hold the CD player's lid closed and slips in the Beastie Boys, *License to Ill*, and Jesus hums along.

None of them heard her coming up behind, but Ariadne knows it first, turns and Salmagundi dressed in velvet the color of smog and the long black leather overcoat Jimmy brought her last time. Sleepless bruisey red beneath those startling blue eyes, and when she talks Ariadne thinks it's more a ghost of Salmagundi and cringes inside where no one can see.

"Hello," a little slurred, and Ariadne wonders what she's on, Valium or Xanax or maybe she has needles of her own. "What have you found, Jesus?" Salmagundi says.

"I found it," Rat whispers, and Jesus nods his head, "Yeah, true fact, Ratboy found it." And then Rat explains the peening wheel for Salmagundi, explains again, more nervous but more detail than before, and the jittery hint of a stutter.

"It was in one of the painting sheds," Jesus adds. "Buried under a whole bunch'a crap," and Salmagundi stoops down for a better look, velvet dragging in the mud, and Ariadne sees she's barefoot. "Has anyone seen Wren and Joey today?" absent flat tone, and Salmagundi runs the tips of her white fingers over the blunt ends of the straps, her nails chewed ragged, raw cuticles.

"They were chasin' rats around the docks, went down there with Jenny," Jesus says, and Salmagundi pulls her hand back, then, jerks it away fast, and Ariadne sees the blood welling from the cut on her thumb, sees too the rustbrown sliver of steel like a stinger jutting from one of the rubber flaps. "Ah," and the thumb to her mouth, Ariadne bending to see. Salmagundi frowns and shakes her head, it's nothing, nothing serious, but when she takes her thumb out of her mouth Ariadne can see how deep the cut is, pad laid open, parted, and a little crimson left behind on Salmagundi's carnation lips.

"We should get some peroxide on it, at least, and a bandage," but no response from Salmagundi, and Rat's already run off for one of the first-aid boxes; there are no inconsequential cuts in the yard, no scratch so small that staph or lockjaw can't find its way in through the breach. Ariadne holds her hand, squeezes Salmagundi's thumb lightly so it will bleed away germs or filth, slow red drip to the gray earth and Salmagundi watches each drop of herself grow too heavy to resist gravity, each red spat.

"Something's wrong, Ariadne," she says. "Something's happened to him."

"Shit, it might just be his fucking car broke down again," Jesus says, and she turns on him. "Shut up," snarls Salmagundi, pulling free of Ariadne's grasp, and something in her eyes now that they've never seen there before, something wild and frightened and mean, someone she could have been all along, if things were different. Desperation and whatever comes between faith and loss of faith, the cold wind in her hair like it was taking sides.

"I'm sick of all of you pretending nothing's wrong, that it hasn't been days," and Salmagundi turns her back on them, and her feet make hardly any sound at all in the mud and gravel as she goes. Ariadne thinks that maybe Jesus will cry, and she doesn't want to see, so she looks at the ground and the small bloody place Salmagundi left behind.

⇒ 2 ⇐

Here's the scene: Jimmy DeSade and his junkyard Lincoln rolling mercuric smooth along the New Jersey Turnpike like asphalt was greased black glass, expert weave and tailgate, and the other cars get out of his way. Thrash from the tape deck, this pale man behind the wheel and the glow from the dash on his face, ghost glow of deep sea things, face past gaunt or hard and the sunglasses like his soul's windshield. Sleet for the past five miles, and here's his exit; he lights another cigarette, last one from the pack on the seat beside him, and glides off the freeway into the night crouched past the streetlights.

Almost a week since he slipped across the border near Matamoros, untouchable, just one more desert shadow and enough shit tucked away inside the car's secret places that his happy ass could stay put till spring. And then New Orleans and the Burgundy Street deal gone bad—no—nothing so simple or sane as bad, skullfucking incendiary to tell the truth, and a miracle he hadn't lost more than half the coke and a little skin besides. That the Haitians hadn't kept his teeth, hadn't kept his fucking balls for their gris-gris charms. The rest of the stuff dumped on his Philly connection, never mind that he almost had to give it away to unload that much that fast, a buyer's market, Jimmy, after all, and that Irish cocksucker grinning like a tetanus corpse as she split open a bag with her little pen knife, discreetest taste with the tongue-moistened tip of one finger.

"What's got you makin' sucker deals, Jimmy?" And she had another taste while he counted her money, counted it twice just to piss her off, his money now, and the fucking blow isn't his problem anymore. Just this Jersey night, broken yellow line and the lights from Weehawken off that way, so he tries to forget New Orleans and Ciara Gallagher and let the road pull him smooth across the ruined marshes and divided stones, down the poisoned land to the river.

And of course, the gates are locked. Jesus and Rat know it'd be both their asses if he came rolling up and found them any other way, and, of course, Jimmy DeSade has his keys. But the yard is still and cold as ash, everything turning silver oyster-white from the sleet changing to snow, and he shifts into park and gets out, steps around into the space between the Lincoln's headlights, and now he can see the new chains, new locks and sloppy loops of wire like barbed and bladed vines. "Hey," he shouts, and then "Jesus," but nothing and no one answers, just the wind that ignores his trench-coat black leather and everything underneath, insubstantial, numbing teeth at his skin. There are bolt cutters in the trunk and probably nothing on the gate he can't get through in half an hour or so, but no comfort there, nothing but affirmation, dread freezing hard as the ice and slag beneath his boots. So Jimmy DeSade stands in the gathering storm a minute longer, calling Jesus and Rat and Ariadne Moreau until his throat hurts, and calling for Salmagundi, last of all.

There's still a little candlelight in the room, and Jesus sits in one corner, an arm around Wren and an arm around Joey, holding them while they cry. Rat's been gone for hours, and Jenny Haniver sits at Salmagundi's dressing table, painting her face with white powder and cherry-ripe rogue. Ariadne has just started all over again, combing Salmagundi's golden hair, when the door to the apartment opens, opens hard and bangs loud against the wall, and there's Jimmy DeSade. Tall man of leather and studs and chains, and what she sees on his face now, she's always known that was there. Wren tries to pull free, to run to him, but Jesus holds her back.

"Ariadne?" he says, and "Jesus?" and his voice is rawer and colder than the wind flaying itself alive on the corners of the building. "We did everything we knew how to do, Jimmy," but three long strides and he's pushing her out of the way, her ass bump to the hard floor and the comb tangles, pulling away a handful of Salmagundi's hair. "Fuck this," he says. "Oh," and "Fuck this," and he shakes her, shakes the hollow shell that was her, and Salmagundi's head lolls rag-doll limp.

Most of the things they did to try and bring her back are hidden beneath the gown that Ariadne has dressed her in, silk the greenblack color of avocado skin and lace. And Jimmy just says the same thing, fuck me, oh, fuck me, over and over, and now Wren is crying again. Jimmy kisses Salmagundi hard, his living pale flesh against dead pale, looks like maybe he's trying mouth-to-mouth or just kissing her harder than Ariadne's ever seen anyone kiss anyone or anything before.

"She just cut her finger," she says, finally. "Cut her thumb on a piece of junk," and Jimmy DeSade comes up for air, glances at her, sunglass plastic where his eyes should be. "What?" and she knows better than to repeat herself, so stares down at the comb instead, the yellow strands of Salmagundi's hair caught in its teeth.

"You're saying she cut her fucking finger, and now she's fucking *dead*?" Ariadne nods, then, because she's afraid not to, but just once.

He holds up Salmagundi's right hand, nothing there but lifeless fingers, and then her left and the ragged bandages, mummy fist and ugly stains like oil and strawberry jam. Unwinds the gauze, and Salmagundi's thumb is still so swollen, mutilated where they tried to get the poison out of her blood, and the sound starts way down inside him, makes Ariadne think of a subway train on its way into the station, not so much a sound as something you feel in every cell, subsonic, seismic. This isn't sorrow and it isn't rage, the sound of a soul tearing, and he's picking Ariadne up off the floor before she knows it, the comb dropped from her fingers and skittering away.

"You goddamn fucking *junky*," last word like a Roman's nail, and maybe that's what he means to do: to nail her to this wall for their sin. "Haven't you ever fucking heard of a goddamn *hospital*?" No time for an answer, her feet dangling an inch above the floor, and he slams her into the wall so hard the world shimmers through her eyes.

"*Jimmy*," and Jesus is trying to pull him off her, Wren and Joey both wailing in their corner, and Ariadne catches a glimpse of Jenny Haniver, reversed in Salmagundi's mirror, mime face and smeared lips before she falls, a dazed lump at the silver-tipped toes of his boots. The sound of his fist hitting Jesus is very loud, or just the sound of Jesus' nose breaking, either one or maybe both.

"You let her die," he says. And Jesus is cradling his face in his hands, blood between his fingers, shaking his head like he's forgotten how to talk, no, Jimmy, no, we didn't, the words in his wide, dark eyes. "Yes, you *did*, Jesus. Yes, you fucking did. You *let* her die." Last thing he'll ever say to them, though Ariadne doesn't know that yet, all she can see is the gun that wasn't in his hands a minute ago, abracadabra and this huge fucking pistol black and perfect shiny even in the dim candlelight. He doesn't aim, just squeezes the trigger, and the world is too full of the sound of the gun for anything else, even breathing.

Then she's crawling towards Jesus, crawling past those boots, boots sharp and hard enough they could kill if they wanted to, crawling through the brittle, shellshock deafness after the shot. Jesus curled fetal, and she thinks that she can hear him whimpering, but that might just be the ringing in her ears. Nasty big gouge in the concrete floor, little crater and no sign of the slug. "Come on," she says. "Get up," hears her voice more inside herself than coming out her mouth, and she forces Jesus up, on his knees at least, *just get them out of here, just get us out, and maybe he won't kill us.*

Wren and Joey at her side without being called, neither of them crying now, scared past anything but wide-eyed, silent disbelief. And Jimmy sitting on Salmagundi's bed, leaning over her body, mother protective or threatful as a movie vampire, scarecrow fingers stroking her gray cheeks, black hair fallen forward and hiding his face. Ariadne goes to Jenny Haniver, tears streaking the sloppy Robert-Smith makeup now, kohl smudge around her eyes, holes and Jenny looking out at her through them.

"We were supposed to keep her safe," Jenny Haniver says, "That's all we had to do. Dig up junk and keep her safe," and Ariadne sees where the mirror's broken, Jimmy DeSade's bullet ricocheted off the floor and buried somewhere behind the spiderwebbed looking glass. She jerks Jenny up and off the stool, no cooperation but no resistance, either, just a lifeless zombie shuffle that pisses Ariadne off, makes her want to kick

Jenny, let her sorrow and fear lash out and bite someone the way Jimmy's has. Instead, she pushes them forward, only Jesus looking back over his shoulder, pushes them into the narrow hallway cold as ice, dark as the memory of night, and she closes the door behind her.

Two hours later, almost dawn, and Jimmy DeSade has found all the sheet metal he'll need in one of the cutting shops, that much and a hundred times more, and he's found Rat there, too, cringing alone in the rusting shadows. No words between them, nothing that can be said, but Rat helps him cut the steel plates down, carbon-alloy steel shaped for hulls designed and never realized, flame-sliced down into appropriate and manageable shapes, rough squares and rectangles from the blueprint in Jimmy's head, and his sunglasses traded for smoky welder's goggles. But heavy pieces, still, and they carry them one at a time through the fresh snow and ice slick, and Jimmy feels their eyes, watching, the eyes of the children of the yard hiding somewhere in the gloom. Trip after trip from the shop up the stairs to Salmagundi's apartment and back down to the shop and back to Salmagundi's apartment, her antiques, heirlooms for no one now, pushed aside, tipped over, as Jimmy and Rat lay the sections out on the floor.

"You're gonna need an outfit up here," Rat says finally, a flinching bold stroke against the gelatin silence. And Jimmy nods his head, yeah, yeah. "And glass," he says. "Good, sturdy glass, Rat. Can you find me that, too?"

"Yeah. No problem," and Rat sounds grateful and relieved and afraid. "In the warehouses there's lots of good glass, if you know where to look." They leave her alone again, her cold body on the bed, and an hour later, the sun rising behind the clouds, black to gray to grayer, and they have the big tank of oxygen and a smaller blue tank of acetylene, lengths of hose and a torch. But there's still the glass and Rat, huffing, out of breath, propped against a hand truck and watching his feet when he says "If Jesus helped, it'd be easier, go faster..." Jimmy wipes sweat off his face, shakes his head no, and so Rat doesn't bring it up again.

Rat leads him to the glass, neat rows a quarter inch thick and watery green under brown paper, shows him how to score it and tap hard enough to break along the groove without cracking or shattering the whole pane. And it's noon by the time they begin carrying the glass to Salmagundi's apartment, and the sky is almost the same color it was at dawn.

"Don't look directly at the flame," Rat says, then "You know that," apology, and he shows Jimmy how to stuff the legs of his black jeans down into his tall boots, some duct tape wrapped tightly around to keep them in and the melting filler metal out. And no more words after that, no need, lifting the sections into place one after another and in between, the metal-on-metal scrape of the spark lighter and supernova white from the torch, flux, and Rat keeping an eye on the four pressure gauges while Jimmy DeSade welds like he's done this all his life, or all his life has led to this moment of heat and light. And he turns steel to molten drops and fleeting puddles as the flame travels the jagged length of each seam, solidifying again, strong new alloy of filler rod and steel left cooling behind.

Once, he pauses, sweatgrime face and the frame almost done; it makes Rat think of a giant's unfinished fish tank, blind and empty, no water or guppies or plastic seaweed inside. Jimmy glances back at Rat, Rat and the canisters of compressed gas, the flare of his torch aimed careless and intentional at the oxygen; Rat understands, thinks he *might* understand, and waits while Jimmy DeSade decides their futures, considers this other solution, eyes secret behind his goggles; a few seconds longer than long minutes, and then he turns back to his work, and Rat feels no relief at all.

─ 3 ─

Colder and it's getting dark again, and not one of them moves, hardly breathes as the Lincoln spins its tires and pulls away, suddenly nothing left of Jimmy DeSade but a cloud of exhaust rising up and coming apart in the wind, nothing but the fading sound of his wheels rolling away over scabby earth. And even then they wait, shivering together in the fresh dark until Ariadne moves first, a first faltering step like she has to learn to walk all over again, and she doesn't think to let go of Jenny's hand, so she comes, too, and Jesus next, and Wren and Joey with him. Joey's been coughing hard the last couple of hours, and the sound makes Ariadne think of the river lapping, nibbling at the edges of the yard.

Their boots and tennis-shoe tatters quiet across the snow, maybe two inches deep now, to the wide snowbare place where Jimmy's car sat all day, and they each walk around that, to the stairs, that rickety iron path up to Salmagundi's apartment, and before she climbs it, Ariadne Moreau looks back at them. Four of the seven, small in the night, and the snow catching in their hair, on their clothes, and it would kindly bury them if they only stood still long enough to let it, by spring nothing remaining but clean bones and empty rags to disappoint the gulls. Another thing broken, she thinks, and remembering what Jenny Haniver said before Salmagundi's shattered mirror, *How'd we ever believe we could keep anything safe? How'd we ever believe...* and she starts up the stairs, trying in vain not to walk in Jimmy DeSade's footprints.

They follow her, not a word passing between them, slippery steps and the railing too cold to hold on to; the stairs creak and rustcry and sway a little from the wind and their weight.

At the top, Ariadne opens the door before anyone can stop her, before she can stop, and the room still has a little candle-light, enough she can see by and stare sick at all Salmagundi's threadbare fine furniture tossed about like it was only junk, like nobody ever loved it. Notices the splintered leg on an over-turned table before she even sees Rat and the thing that Jimmy DeSade has made, and there's Salmagundi, sealed inside. The straight black lines that come together in corners as sharp as the toes of Jimmy DeSade's boots, Rat with one cheek squashed against the glass, and the fat roll of bills in his hand; he's sobbing without making a sound, and his tears run down and streak like the glass has begun to melt from the heat of his face pressed too long against it.

They push in around her, Jenny Haniver and Jesus, Wren and Joey. And "Oh," Wren says. "Oh," said so very softly; Rat leaves a sticky print on the glass when he turns to see, snot and saltwater smudge, and he looks Ariadne in the eye.

"He ain't comin' back," Rat says. "*Never*," and now Ariadne looks away, at the gray face inside the cage of glass and solder, those closed and sunken lids safer than this boy's lost green eyes. "That's what he said, Jesus," and then Rat turns away from them again. And Ariadne Moreau walks past Salmagundi's glass coffin, waxlight shimmer, and she goes to the window. There's snow blown in under the plastic, a little drift on the floor, and she pushes back the drape. Outside, the yard is still and white, dulled beneath the snow like an old dog's teeth, and the road beyond is dark and nothing moves there, either.

Breakfast in the
House of the Rising Sun
(Murder Ballad No. 1)

Out here on the .tattered north rim of the Quarter, past sensible bricks to keep the living out and the dead inside, weathered-marble glimpses above the wall of St. Louis #1, and on past planned Iberville squalor and Our Lady of Guadalupe. Hours left till dawn, and the tall man in his long car turns another corner and glides down Burgundy. Almost dreaming, it's been too long since he slept or ate, so long since he left Matamoros and the long Texas day before of sun and gulf-blind blue. All that fucking coke sewn up in the seats, white blocks snug in plastic wrap beneath his numb ass, and he checks the Lincoln's rearview mirror, watching, watching in case some Big Easy pig doesn't like his looks. The fat veins in his eyes are almost the same shade of red as the little crimson pills that keep him awake, keep him moving. But there isn't much of anything back there—silhouette and streetlight shadow of a crazy old black man in the street, and he's pointing up at the sky and falls to his knees on the asphalt, but he's nothing for Jimmy DeSade to worry about. He lights another Camel, breathes gray smoke, and there's the House, just like every time before. Gaudy Victorian ruin, grotesquerie of sagging shutters and missing gingerbread shingles, the slow rot of time and Louisiana damp. Maybe it's leaning into itself a little more than last time, and maybe there are a couple of new dog or gator skulls dangling in the big magnolia standing shadowy guard out front. Hard to tell in the dark, no streetlights here, no sodium-arc revelation, and every downstairs window painted black as mourning whores. Jimmy DeSade drives on by, checks his mirror one more time, and circles around to the alley.

Rabbit opens his door a crack and watches the trick stagger away down the long hall, the fat man that stank like garlic and aftershave, fat man that tied Rabbit's hands behind his back and bent him over the bed, pulled down his lacy panties and whacked his butt with a wooden hairbrush until he pretended to cry. Until he screamed stop, Daddy, stop, I'll be a good little girl now. They still give him the creeps worst of all, the call-me-Daddy men. Rabbit eases the door shut again, whispering half a prayer there will be no more tonight, no more appetite and huffing desperation, and maybe he can have a little time alone before he fixes and falls asleep.

Let's not count on it, he thinks and kicks off the black patent pumps, walks the familiar five steps back to the low stool in front of his dressing table, sits down and stares at himself in the mirror. Every minute of twenty-two years showing in his face tonight—and then some—a handful of hard age shining out mean from beneath powder and mascara smears. Rabbit finds his lighter, finds the stingy, skinny joint Arlo slipped him earlier in the evening, and the smoke doesn't make it easier to face that reflection; the smoke makes it remotely possible. He pulls a scratchy tissue from the box, something cheap that comes apart in cold cream, and wipes away the magenta ghost of his lipstick, sucks another hit from the joint and holds the smoke until his ears begin to buzz, high electric sound like angry wasps or power lines, then breathes it out slow through his nostrils. And those gray-blue eyes squint sharply back at him through the haze—Dresden blue, his Momma used to say— pretty Dresden blue eyes a girl should have, and Rabbit licks thumb and forefinger, pinches out the fire and stashes the rest of the joint for later. Tucks it safely into the shadows beneath one corner of a jewelry box; later he'll need it more than he needs it now.

Rabbit restores the perfect bee-stung pout, Cupid's-bow artifice, a clockwise twist and the lipstick stub pulls back inside its metal foreskin. No point in bothering with the eyes again this late, but he straightens his dress, Puritan-simple black as if in apology for all the rest. He also straightens the simpler strand of pearls at his throat, iridescent plastic to fool no one lying against his milk-in-coffee skin, skin not black, not white, and there he is like a parody of someone's misconception of the mulatto whores of Old New Orleans. Bad romance, but *this* is real, this room that smells like the moldy plaster walls and the john's cum drying on the sheets, cheap perfume and the ghosts of tobacco and marijuana smoke.

This is as real as it gets, and you can sell the rest of that shit to the turd-for-brains tourists with their goose-necked hurricane glasses, Mardi Gras beads, crawdad T-shirts, and pennies for the dancing nigger boys with Pepsi caps on the soles of their shoes. Rabbit closes his eyes and makes room in his head for nothing but the sweet kiss of the needle, as if anticipation alone could be rush, and he doesn't move until someone knocks at the   bedroom door.

Arlo works downstairs behind the bar, and he sweeps the floors and mops the floors, scrubs away the blood or puke and whatever else needs scrubbing away. He sees that the boys upstairs have whatever keeps them going, a baggie of this or that, a word of kindness or a handful of pills. Sees that the big motherfuckers downstairs at the tables have their drinks, empties ashtrays, takes away empty bottles, and washes whiskey glasses. And Arlo isn't even his name. His real name is Etienne, Etienne Duchamp, but no one likes that Cajun shit up here, and one time some mouthy, drunk bitch said his hair made him look like some old folk singer, some hippie fuck from the sixties.

You know, man, Alice's Restaurant, and you can get anythang you waaaaaant...and it stuck. Good as anything else in here, and in here beats selling rock in the projects, watching for gang bangers and cops that haven't been paid or might not remember they've been paid.

Arlo pulls another beer from the tap and sets it on the bar, sweaty glass on the dark and punished wood, reaches behind him for the piss-yellow bottle of Cuervo, and pours a double shot for the tall man across the bar. The man just passing through on his way back to New York, the man with the delivery from Mexico City, the man whose eyes never come out from behind his shades. The man who looks sort of like a biker, but drives that rusty-guts land-yacht Lincoln. Jimmy DeSade (*Mr.* DeSade to Arlo and just about anyone else who wants to keep his teeth, who wants to keep his fucking balls), so pale he looks like something pulled out of the river after a good long float, his face so sharp, and lank blue-black hair growing out of his skull.

"Busy night, Arlo?" he asks, icicle voice and accent that might be English and might be fake, and Arlo shrugs and nods.

"Always busy 'round here, Mr. DeSade. Twenty-four, seven, three hundred and sixty-five." And Jimmy DeSade doesn't smile or laugh, but slowly nods his head and sips at the tequila.

Then a fat man comes shambling down the crimson-carpeted stairs opposite the bar, the man that's had Rabbit from midnight till now, and Arlo sees right off his fly's open, yellowed-cotton wrinkle peek-a-boo careless between zipper jaws. Stupid fat fuck, little eyes like stale venom almost lost in his shiny pink face. And Arlo thinks maybe he'll check in on Rabbit, just a quick *You okay? You gonna* be *okay?* before the two o'clock client. He knows the fat man wouldn't have dared do anything as stupid as put a mark on one of Jo Franklin's mollies, nothing so honest or suicidal, so not that kind of concern. But this man moves like a bad place locked up in skin and Vitalis, and when he hustles over to the bar, ham-hock knuckles, sausage fingers spread out against the wood, Arlo smells sweat and his sour

breath and the very faint hint of Rabbit's vanilla perfume—
Rabbit's perfume, like something trapped.

"Beer," grunts the fat man, and Arlo takes down a clean mug.
"No, not that watered-down shit, boy. Give me a real beer, in a
goddamned bottle."

Not a word from Jimmy DeSade, and maybe he's staring
straight at the fat man, staring holes, and maybe he's looking
somewhere past him, up the stairs; there's no way to know
which from this side of those black sunglasses, and he sips his
tequila.

"Jo knows that I'm waiting," Jimmy DeSade says, doesn't ask,
not really, the words rumbling out between his thin lips, voice
so deep and cold you can't hear the bottom. Arlo says yes sir, he
knows, he'll be out directly, but Arlo's mostly thinking about
the smell of Rabbit leaking off the fat man, and he knows better, knows there's nothing for him in this worry but the knot
winding tight in his guts, this worry past his duty to Jo, past his
job.

The fat man swallows half the dewy bottle in one gulp, wet
and fleshy sound as the faint lump where his Adam's apple
might be rises and falls, rises and falls. He swipes the back of a
porky hand across his mouth, and now there's a dingy grin,
crooked little teeth in there like antique cribbage pegs. And
"Jesus, sweet baby Jesus," he says. "That boy-child is as sweet a
piece of ass as I've ever had." And then he half turns, his big
head swiveling necklessly round on its shoulders, to look directly at Jimmy DeSade. "Mister, if you came lookin' for a sweet
piece of boy ass, well, you came to the right goddamn place.
Yessiree."

Jimmy DeSade doesn't say a word, mute black-leather gargoyle still staring at whatever the hell the eyes behind those
shades are seeing, and the fat man shakes his head, talking
again before Arlo can stop him. "That's the God's honest-fuck-
ing truth," he says. "Tight as the lid on a new jar of cucumber
pickles—"

"You done settled up with Rabbit? You square for the night?"

Arlo asks quickly, the query injected like a vaccination, and the fat man grows suddenly suspicious, half-offended.

"Have I ever tried to stiff Jo on a fuck? The little faggot's got the money. You think I look like the sort'a cheap son of a bitch that'd try to steal a piece of ass? *Shit*," and Arlo's hands out defensively, then, No, man, that's cool, just askin', that's all, just askin', and the fat man drains the beer bottle, and Arlo has already popped the cap off another. "On the house," he says.

Behind them, the felted tables, and one of the men lays down a double-six (no cards or dice, dominoes only in Jo Franklin's place, and that's not tradition, that's the rule), and he crows, answered with a soft ring of grumbled irritation round the spread of wooden rectangles the color of old ivory, lost money and the black dots end-to-end like something for a witch to read.

His hair not gray, cotton-boll white, and, even in the soft Tiffany light of his office, JoJo Franklin looks a lot older than he is, the years that the particulars of his life have stolen and will never give back. He closes a ledger and takes off his spectacles, rubs at the wrinkled flesh around his eyes. Rows of numbers, fountain-pen sums scrawled in his own unsteady left hand because he's never trusted anyone else with his books. He blinks, and the room stays somewhere just the other side of focused: dull impression of the wine-red, velvet-papered walls, old furnishings fine and worn more threadbare than him, the exquisitely framed forgery of Albert Matignon's *Morphine* that a Belgian homosexual had tried to pass off as genuine. He paid what the man asked, full in the knowledge of the deceit, small talk and pretended gratitude for such a generous price, then had the Belgian killed before he could cash the check; Jo forgot the man's name a long time ago, but he kept the phony Matignon, the three beautiful morphinomanes, decadent truth beneath Victorian delusions of chastity, and this fraud another level of delusion, so it's worth more to him than the real thing could ever be. The value of illusion has never been a thing lost on JoJo Franklin.

And now Jimmy DeSade's outside his door, waiting to do business, the simple exchange of pure white powder for green paper. JoJo puts his glasses back on his face, wire frames hooked around his ears, and the three ladies in the painting swim into focus, gently euphoric furies hiding one more deception, the counterfeit bills just up from Miami, stacked neatly in his safe, company for his ledgers and the darker secrets in manila and old shoe boxes; good as gold, better than.

The topmost drawer of his desk is open, and the little pistol is right there where it should be, tucked reassuringly amid the pencils and paper clips. Just in case, but he knows there'll be no ugly and inconvenient drama with Jimmy DeSade, creepy fucking zombie of a man, but a sensible zombie; no more trouble than with the Haitians the night before, the Haitians who are always suspicious of one thing or another, but these bills so goddamn real even they hadn't looked twice. Jimmy DeSade will take the money and carry it northwards like a virus, no questions asked, no trouble. In a minute or two, Jo Franklin will push the intercom button, will tell Arlo to send the smuggler back, but he's thirsty, and something about the pale and skinny man always makes him thirstier, so a brandy first and *then* the intercom, then the zombie and this day's transaction.

Jo Franklin rests his hand a moment on the butt of the pistol, cold comfort through fingertips, before he slides the drawer shut again.

Four knocks loud on the door to Rabbit's room, four knocks heavy and slow, reckless sound like blows more to hurt the wood than get attention, and he blots his lips on the cheap tissue, sparing a quick pout for the mirror before, "Yeah, it's open," and it is, the door, slow swing wide and hall light spilling in around them. Rabbit sees the men reflected without having to turn his head, and he sits very still, seeing them. Both dark, skin like black, black coffee and both so fucking big, and Rabbit can't really see their faces. Silhouettes with depth: one much thinner than the other and wearing sunglasses, the other bald and built like a wall. Concrete in a suit meant to look expensive. Pause, heartbeats, and "Come in," he says and wonders if he said it loudly enough because the men don't move, and his voice grown small and brittled in an instant. Christ, it's not like he hasn't done doubles before. Not like Arlo would ever let anyone come up those stairs that was gonna be a problem. Speaking to the mirror, scrounging calm, "Please," he says. "You can shut the door behind you."

A low whisper from one or the other, and the bald man laughs, a hollow, heartless laugh before Rabbit breathes in deep and stands to face them. The tall man first, his face so slack, his bony arms so limp at his sides, torn and dirty Mickey Mouse T-shirt and rattier pants, no shoes on his knobby feet. Movement underwater slow, sleepwalker careless, like those four knocks, and the bald man follows after. He shuts the door, and the lock clicks very loud.

"Three hundred and fifty for the both," Rabbit says, cowering rabbit voice that wants to be brave, that wishes for the needle and sweet heroin salvation; the bald man smiles, hungry-dog smile and one silver tooth up front catching the candlelight. "*Ou chich*," chuckled Creole and Rabbit shrugs, street-smart shrug even if he doesn't feel it. "Whatever. We're priced to sell round here," and the ice not breaking even though the trick laughs again, every laugh just that much more frost in aching veins, laugh and "You're a funny *masisi*, funny faggot," Caribbean-accented bemusement, Jamaican or Haitian or something; the tall man stands behind him, his back against the door, and doesn't smile or laugh or say a word.

Just part of their turn-on, trying to flip you out, and *Don't you let 'em fuck around with your head*, he thinks, trying to hear those words in Arlo's voice, or Chantel's, Chantel three doors down who never gets cold feet with weirdoes. But it's still just his own, small thing rabbit whispering from tall bayou grass.

And a fat-ass roll of bills comes out of the bald man's coat pocket, rubber band snap loud, and he's peeling off two, three, four, laying them down like gospel, like an exclamation point on the table by the door, the table with plastic lilies stolen late one night from a St. Louis vault. Sun-faded plastic lilies in a dry vase.

"Gonna fuck you till you can't sit down, funny *masisi*," and Rabbit looks to the money for strength, four one hundred dollar bills, crisp new paper, bright ink hardly touched, and there's an extra fifty in there, fifty free and clear of Franklin's cut. "Yeah," he says. "Whatever you want, Mr—" and the customary pause, blank space for an alias, your name here, but the bald man is busy getting out of his jacket, too busy to answer, or maybe he just doesn't want to answer. The tall, still man takes his jacket, drapes it gently across one thin arm, nightmare butler, and the bald man reaches for his zipper.

"What about him?" Rabbit asks, trying to sound hooker tough, but almost whispering instead, sounding scared instead and hating it, motioning at the man with his back pressed to the bedroom door. "He doesn't talk much, does he?"

"He don't talk at all, and he don't fuck. So you don't be worrying about him. You just gonna worry about *me*."

"You paid enough, for both—"

"*Fèmen bouch ou*," and a sudden flicker like lightning in the man's dark eyes, flickering glimmer down a mine shaft so deep it might run all the way to Hell. Rabbit doesn't understand the words, but enough meaning pulled from the voice, from those eyes and the hard lines of his face to know it's time to shut up, just shut the fuck up and play their game by their rules until it's over.

"Stop talking and take off that ugly dress," the man says, and Rabbit obliges, unzips quickly and lets the very plain black dress fall around his ankles, a pool of black cotton around his heels to step out of, reluctant step closer to the man. His pants down, gray silk trousers to match the jacket but no underwear, uncircumcised droop, bizarre and fleshy orchid, organ, but he's getting hard, and Rabbit knows he'll probably be using hemorrhoid pads tomorrow, shitting a little blood as well. The pants are hung on the tall man's arm now, too, and still no emotion in that face, every movement past slow or efficient, pared to jerky last stop before coma paralysis. Rabbit feels cold inside, more naked than can be explained by the discarded dress; the bald man makes a satisfied sound in his chest, mumbled approval, and Rabbit glances at himself in the dresser mirror. His thin body like a teenage girl's, almond skin, legs and underarms shaved smooth, and he's wearing nothing now but the black lace and satin, bra and panties trimmed with scarlet, naughty somber contrast, matching garter belt and thigh-high net stockings on his long legs: nothing to mar the cultured illusion of his femininity except the subtle bulge at his crotch and the flatness of his chest.

"Sure you a boy?" the man asks, and this is nothing new, this question and the answering so routine that Rabbit can almost relax a little, and he hooks a thumb into the front of his panties, pulls them down enough to reveal his own sex, the sex of his flesh, and the man nods, one hand rubbed across his hairless, glinting scalp. "Leave them on." he mutters.

"Sure, if that's what you want," and the man's big hands are on him then, sweat-warm palms and fingers over his cool skin. Hard kiss like something desperate, something forced that isn't, but needs to *feel* that way, faint cigar taste, tongue pushing past Rabbit's teeth and inside him, exploring teeth and palate and his own tongue. And then their lips parting, and a string of spittle between them to cling to Rabbit's chin.

"Bend over, bitch," the bald man says, and Rabbit bends over, hands on the bedspread, ass to Heaven, and he feels his panties coming down, draws a deep breath before two wet fingers shove their way inside him, probing, working his asshole, and he closes his eyes, braces knees against the sagging bed as those strong hands grip his thighs, purchase found, strong fingers to leave bruises behind, and there's the smallest whimper from Rabbit's lips as the bald man's cock pushes its way inside.

The very last door at the sunset end of a hall that is all doors, six choices with antique crystal knobs to ease decision, and that last door is Chantel Jackson's; been here longer than anyone, any of the boys, longer even than Arlo. Her end of the deal upheld after JoJo Franklin paid for her trip to Brussels, money she'd never have to resolve the quandary between her legs, and money he'd never miss. In return, she's the house specialty now, this one all the way, not just a pretty boy in frilly drawers, no shit, wanna know what it's like to fuck pussy that used to be dick? And she's got no complaints, so many ways things might have gone so much worse, and that resolution all she ever really wanted, anyway.

No complaints except that magnolia right outside her window, and there's a few minutes before her two-fifteen so she sits on her bed, smokes and watches that scary old tree, the sash down and locked, smudgy glass protection between her and those crooked limbs, big leaves like the iridescent green shells of a thousand gigantic beetles. Nothing good about that tree, and mostly she ignores it, keeps the blinds down and tries not to notice the shadows it makes on her walls day and night. But sometimes, like now, when the demons inside are worse than the demons outside, she tries to stare it down, make it blink first, make *it* flinch. She imagines that magnolia shriveling the way movie vampires do if the sun gets at them, all those leaves turning brown and dropping off, gone to dust before they even touch the ground, the gnarled trunk husk laid bare like a guilty heart, and wood cracks and splits, and the earth opens to take it back down to Hell. Or, maybe it bends itself over, pulls up its roots, tired of the masquerade if some tranny hooker bitch has its number, anyhow, and it shamefully drags itself back to the swamps, move over Mr. Catfish, move over Mr. Snapping Turtle, and it'll lie waiting in some black pool until everyone's forgotten it again.

"Silly fool," she whispers, knows it's goddamned silly to be scared of an ugly old tree when there's plenty enough else to be scared of in this city; silly bitch, but there's her church-neat line of charms and candles, anyway, painted saints and plastic Jesus and Mother Mary on the windowsill. Her careful shrine just in case it's not so silly to be afraid of ghosts after all, ghosts and worse things than ghosts.

They used to hang pirates from that tree, someone said, and thieves and runaway slaves, too. *Just about everyone got hung from that tree,* depending on who you happen to ask. And there's also the tale about the Storyville lovers: impossible and magic days a hundred years ago when hooking and gambling were legal, Storyville red-light before the whole district was razed for more legitimate corruption: a gentleman gambler from Memphis, or St. Louis, or Chicago, and he fell in hopeless love with a black girl, or a mulattress, under this very tree, except she was a *loup-garou,* and when she finally showed him her real face he went stark-raving bugfuck mad. *You can still find their initials carved in the trunk,* name-scars trapped inside a heart, *if you know where to look,* can still hear her crying if the moon and wind are right. Can still hear the green-stick snap of his bones between her teeth.

None of that shit even half as bad as the bleached animal skulls and little skeletons wired together wrong ways round, charms the voodoo women still leave in the limbs when no one's watching, the things JoJo won't ever cut down, won't even let Arlo get near them, never mind the awful racket they make whenever a storm blows up.

And tonight it just stares right back at her, that magnolia and all its guarded secrets, truths and lies and half-truths, steadfast, constant while the world moves around it. *Not tonight it ain't gonna blink for you or for nobody else, not a chance,* and Chantel Jackson crosses herself, then, reaches for the dangling cord to lower the blind, and down there in the always-shadow that grows beneath a tree like this tree she sees the men coming, the dark and confident men on the overgrown walk to the front door nailed shut. And one face glances up, and maybe it sees her, small and haunted in the frame of her window, and maybe it doesn't, but it smiles, either way, and she hears the

wind, and the bones in the tree, like champing teeth and judgment.

The door bursts open, cracking splinter-nail explosion, door
years sealed and boarded but off its rusted hinges in one small
part of an instant and split straight down the center. Arlo does-
n't wait to see, one hand beneath the bar and right back up
with the shotgun Jo keeps mounted there, twelve-gauge slide-
action always loaded, and he levels it at the bad shit pouring
through the shattered door. Men huge and black and hard
enough they barely seem real, skin like angry, living night, the
flat glint of submachine gun steel and machete blades; the
domino players cursing, scatter of bodies as Arlo levels the Winchester's barrel at the Haitians, white tiles flying like broken
teeth, tables and chairs up for shields before the thunder. God
of sounds so loud and sudden it wipes away anything else in
the buckshot spray, and he blasts the first big fucker through
the door, and he also hits a man named Scooter Washington,
slow and skinny shit into JoJo for almost ten thousand dollars,
and Scooter falls just as hard.

Jimmy DeSade is moving now, scrambled vault uninvited over
the bar and something coming out of his jacket, but no time for
Arlo to see just what as he pumps the shotgun again, empty
shell spit, and he makes thunder one more time before the
Haitians are talking back, staccato bursts chewing apart the
room, wood and plaster and flesh all the same. Hot buzz past
Arlo's left ear, and the long mirror behind the bar comes apart,
razor-shard rain as he drops to the floor, and it seems like every
bullet ever made is hitting the bar, punching straight through
the oak and finding the steel plating hidden underneath.

"Shit," he says, can hardly hear himself over the Uzis, but
"Shit, shit, *shit*" anyhow, and Jimmy DeSade doesn't say a word,
big-ass revolver in his steady white hands, the six-shot cylinder
flipped open, chambers full, snapped closed again, careful man
double-checking; the glass still falling on them, downpour of

glass and whiskey, rum and all the sweet and sticky liqueurs. And then silence as harsh and sudden as the gunfire, heady quiet weighted at the edges with the choking stink of gunpowder and spilled alcohol.

"Sonofa*bitch*," and Arlo knows how scared he sounds but doesn't care, and then the booming, pissed-off voice from the other side—"*Hey there, Mr. JoJo Franklin!*"—alligator-bellow voice pounding air still shocky from the guns. "*Where are you at, Mr. JoJo Franklin?*"

"You *know* these people?" and a full moment passes before Arlo realizes that the question is meant for him, Jimmy DeSade and his shiny black Smith and Wesson crouched back here with him, and he wonders if his chances are really that much better on this side of the bar. "Yeah," he says. "Yeah, I know them. They were around last night. Business with Jo, but I don't know what, honest. A bunch of Haitians from the other side of the river—"

"*I say, I done come to talk to you, Mr. JoJo Franklin!*"

Arlo swallows, fever-dry swallow, closes his eyes and digs down deep for calm, anything to make his hands stop shaking. "That one talking, he was with the Tonton Macoute, I think, before Duvalier went down."

"That's some reassuring shit, Arlo," words sizzling out between clenched teeth, and Jimmy DeSade stares up at the place where the mirror used to be.

"I don't know his name—"

"*Going to have to start shooting again if you ain't gonna talk,*" the Haitian shouts, and Arlo can hear the impatient, grinding sound of their boots on broken glass. "*Going to have to start killing some of these fine people out here, Mr. JoJo Franklin!*"

Jimmy DeSade bows his head, the tip of his sharp nose resting against the shark-fin sight at the end of the pistol's long barrel; he sighs, and that's another bad sound to make Arlo's stomach roll. "Stupid bastard's probably halfway to Baton Rouge by now," Jimmy DeSade whispers. "Wouldn't you say that's a fair enough guess, Arlo?"

"Yeah, probably," not like he's gonna disagree, and not like he has any fucking idea *where* Jo might be at the moment, just wishes he was there, too, and it was somewhere far away, wishes he'd taken Rabbit and hit the road a long time ago. "We're absolutely fucked," he says. And Jimmy DeSade looks at him, and the sunglasses have slipped down his nose a little ways, far enough that Arlo gets a glimpse of the gray-blue eyes back there, almost the same eyes as Rabbit's: *wolf* eyes, and now he thinks maybe he's going to throw up after all.

"Everybody's fucked, Arlo," Jimmy DeSade says calmly, resolutely, as he thumbs back the revolver's hammer and stands up.

After the bald man's cum, and Rabbit lies on his stomach on the bed, squeaky springs finally silent again and his asshole on fire, forget the witch hazel, he's gonna be wearing fucking maxi pads on his butt. Semen-wet, sweat-damp down there; blood, too, but he lies very still while the man puts his clothes on again, zips himself up, and Rabbit only clenches his fists a little because it hurts, and he wants to be alone. Wants to fix and go to sleep and forget these two ever happened.

"Good fuck, *masisi*," the man says, his satisfied grunt like Rabbit's stepfather pushing back from the dinner table after a big meal. "A shame that I have to kill a pretty piece of ass like you," and the words not quite registering, threat too many steps removed from here and now, as unreal and far away as the tall, death-quiet man standing at the door, but Rabbit's rolling over, turning so he can see the big bald man and his rumpled clothes and the machete in his right hand.

"It is nothing personal," he says, the sour hint of a smile at the thick corners of his mouth. "*Je suis un pauvre Tonton*, Miss Chantel, and I just do what my boss say to do, and he say it will teach JoJo Franklin a lesson if we kill his special whore."

Rabbit's mouth open and the words jammed in his throat, *I ain't Chantel*, words dead as corn in fear-dry fields, spit gone to paste. And the bald man's arm rises like proof of guilt and penalty being served.

"I ain't Chantel," ugly croak across Rabbit's lips, not his voice, but those were words, words this man should understand, even this man with an arm that ends in that long dark blade. "You got the wrong room—"

Abrupt apocalypse, then, downstairs cacophony and Hell coming up through the floorboards, everything there but the trumpets; Rabbit moving, belly scramble across the bed, and he can feel the shudder of shotgun blasts, one, two, before the machine-gun tattoo begins, and by then he's off the other side of the bed, falling like this was the edge of a flat world, no sound as he hits the floor because there's so much sound already. Blood in his mouth because he's bitten the tip of his tongue, and one hand's pushing in between the mattress and box springs, frantic grope, and it's there somewhere, it's always fucking there so why can't he find it. *I don't give a shit if it scares you*, Arlo said. *You're gonna take it and put it someplace you can get to it fast if you ever have to, okay?* But this isn't fast *enough*, not nearly fast enough.

Downstairs, the gunfire stops, and now there's just his heart and the bald man's footsteps coming round the end of the bed, the bald man cussing the stupid little faggot on the floor, and Rabbit's hand closes around the cold butt of the pistol.

"I can make it fast for you," the bald man says, "if you just be still for me," and then he's looking at the gun in Rabbit's trembling hand, Rabbit scooting backwards across the floor, hard bump into the nightstand, and something falls off, breaks loud and wet. The bald man is laughing now. "*Oh, you gonna shoot me, eh? You gonna shoot poor Charlot with that silly—*" And Arlo says so calm and patient, *Squeeze the trigger, just point it and squeeze the trigger,* so Rabbit squeezes, winces expectantly, but it's not such a big sound after all, bottle-rocket pop, firecracker pop, and then that hole opening up like magic in the bald man's neck. Neat little hole barely big enough to put a pinky finger in, just a little blood for him to look so surprised as the machete clatters to the floor and his big hands fumble for his throat.

Rabbit squeezes the trigger again, and the man stumbles, sinking slowly to his knees, and there's still nothing much on his face but surprise. Grin wide and white teeth bared, mouth open to speak but there's only more blood, a fat red trickle from the corner of his mouth and down his chin.

"Fucking *die*, goddammit," Rabbit growls, but it's like someone else said that, someone in a movie, and the next bullet hits the bald man square in the face; there's lots of blood this time, a warm and sticky mist that gets Rabbit before the man tumbles over on his side and lies dead on top of the machete. A quick glance at the tall man, almost-forgotten accomplice, Rabbit's adrenaline-stiff arms pointing the pistol that way, but he hasn't moved, slack face just as blank as before, the dead man's jacket still draped across one arm.

"Whatever this shit's about," says Jimmy DeSade, speaking so calmly to the big Haitian, "it doesn't have anything to do with me." And Arlo's still crouched on the floor with the shotgun, wondering if he can make the stairs without getting killed, maybe even make it all the way up to Rabbit's room, and then the both of them could duck down the rickety back steps to the alley and then get the fuck away from here, just as far and fast as they can run.

"Who the hell are *you*?" says the big Haitian, and Jimmy DeSade replies, "Nobody. Nobody that wants any trouble," and then he kicks Arlo hard in the hip with the sharp toe of one of his sharp black boot.

"All we *got* here tonight is trouble," says the Haitian and he laughs, laughter rumbling around the room like reckless desolation. "So you in the wrong damn place, Mr. Skinnybones White Man, if you don't want no trouble." And then Jimmy DeSade gives Arlo the boot again, and "*Fuck you*," he says, out before there's any stopping himself.

"I don't work for JoJo Franklin," says Jimmy DeSade. "Whatever he's done to you, it's got nothing to do with me. And I don't give a shit what you do to him. He probably has it coming."

Silence for a moment, like maybe the Haitian's thinking all this over, and Jimmy DeSade may as well be marble as flesh and bone, may as well be carved out of fucking ice, standing there with his finger on the trigger and the long barrel pointed straight ahead.

"But maybe I *don't* care 'bout that, Mr. Skinnybones," the Haitian rumbles. "Maybe I'm so pissed off tonight I just want to kill me all the ugly white motherfuckers I can find."

Copperhead words from Jimmy DeSade's pale lips, then, whisper-hiss dripping down on Arlo's ears—"Get the hell up here, Arlo, or I'm gonna shoot you myself." And because there's nothing left to do, because he doesn't have the guts to run, doesn't have the guts to stay put, Arlo stands up slowly. Slow as a man can move, slow as dawn at the end of the world's longest night. He clutches the shotgun to his chest, crucifix of steel, gunpowder rosary, and the two men are talking again, but there's no room in his head for anything now but the meat-hammer sound of his heart.

And the sudden, clumsy thump and thud of footsteps on the stairs.

It's not like the movies, not at all, slow-motion painful so everything makes sense even if there's nothing he can do to stop it; no time for regret and pointless dot-to-dot foresight. Time for nothing but scalding adrenaline and the Winchester coming down, pumped and both barrels emptied before Arlo knows it's Rabbit, Rabbit half naked on the stairs and the tall black man trailing behind, tall man in a Mickey-the-fucking-Mouse T-shirt and *Can you* believe *that shit*? Tall man there to catch the body, all that's left after the iron shot is done and only the crimson-black hole where Rabbit's belly was and the empty look on his pretty face that isn't surprise or accusation or pain or anything else Arlo's ever seen before.

A cold pearl sun almost up and the eastern sky turning oyster white off towards Biloxi and Mobile; Jimmy DeSade hunched behind the Lincoln's steering wheel, trying not to notice the muddy, dark waters of Lake Pontchartrain, the waves rough and sleek as reptile skin beneath the long bridge out of New Orleans. He lights a cigarette and keeps his eyes on the road, stares down the car's long hood, the tarnished ornament like his pistol's sight and his foot on the trigger.

Nothing he could have done back there, nothing else at all but what he did; twelve fat kilos of primo coke to the Haitians for his skin, and they let him walk away, luckiest fucking day of his shitty life, and there ought to be relief burning him up from the inside out, but there's just Arlo kneeling over the ruined body of the dark boy in women's underwear. Arlo screaming, tin and gravel man-scream, a sound to keep the dead awake nights, and everything so ridiculously goddamn still as the shotgun turned towards the Haitians. The cartoon sharp *bang* when Jimmy DeSade put a bullet in Arlo's head, *bang*, and the Winchester clattering to the floor. He knows it was the bullet that saved his life, not the fucking dope; that's a stone-cold fact, and there's nothing he can ever do to change it.

Jimmy DeSade stares out at the stark and brightening world from behind his tinted lenses, and his big car rolls east, and the sun makes no difference whatsoever.

RICHARD
KIRK

ESTATE

ROUGH AND HUNGRY BOY, BARELY NINETEEN, THAT first time Silas Desvernine saw the Storm King, laid bright young eyes to raw granite and green rash rising up and up above the river and then lost again in the Hudson morning mist. The craggy skull of the world, he thought, scalped by some Red Indian god and left to bleed, grain by mica grain, and he leaned out past the uncertain rails of the ferryboat's stern, frothy wake-slash on the dark water and no reflection there. He squinted, and there was the railroad's iron scar winding around its base, cross-tie stitches, and already the fog was swallowing the mountain, the *A. F. Beach*'s restless sidewheel carrying him away, upriver, deeper into the Highlands, towards Newburgh and work in Albany, and he opens his leathery old eyelids and it's deadest winter 1941, not that wet May morning in 1889. Old, old man, parchment and twigs, instead of that boy, and he's been nodding off again, drifting away, but her voice has brought him back. Her voice across the decades, and he wipes away a stringy bit of drool at the corner of his mouth.

"Were you dreaming again?" she asks, soft velvet tongue from her corner, and he blinks, stares up into the emptycold light spilling down through the high windows, stingy, narrow slits in the stone of the long mansard roof. And "No," he mumbles. *No,* but he understands damn well there's no point to the lie, no hiding himself from her, but at least he's made the effort.

"Yes. You were," she says, Jesus, that voice that's never a moment older than the first time and the words squeeze his tired heart. "You were dreaming about Storm King, the first time you saw the mountain, the first morning—"

"Please," no strength in him, begging and she stops, all he knows of mercy. He wishes the sun were warm on his face, warm where it falls in weak-tea pools across the clutter of his gallery. Most of his collection here, the better part, gathered around him like the years and the creases in his stubbled face. Dying man's pride, dead-man-to-be obsession, *possessions*, these things he spent a life gathering, stolen or secreted but made his own so they could be no one else's. The things sentenced to float out his little forever in murky formalin tombs, specimen jars and stoppered bottles, a thousand milky eyes staring nowhere. Glass eyes in taxidermied skulls, bodies stuffed with sawdust; wings and legs spread wide and pinned inside museum cases. Old bones yellowed and wired together in shabby mockeries of life, older bones gone to silica and varnished, shellacked, fossilized. Plaster and imagination where something might have been lost. Here, the teeth of leviathans, there, the claws of a behemoth; a piece of something fleshy that once fell from the sky over Missouri and kept inside a bell jar. Toads from stones found a mile underground. Sarcophagi and defiled Egyptian nobility raveling inside, crumbling like him, and a chunk of amber as big as an orange and the carbonized hummingbird trapped inside fifty million years.

A narwhal's ivory tooth bought for half a fortune, and he once believed with the unflinching faith of martyrs that it was a unicorn's horn. Precious bit of scaly hide from the Great Sea Serpent, harpooned off Malta in 1807, they said, and never mind that he knew it was never anything but the peeling belly of a crocodile.

"There's not much more," she says. "A day, perhaps," and even her urgency, her fear, is patient, wetnurse gentle, but Silas

Desvernine closes his eyes again, prays he can slip back, fifty-two trips wrong way round the sun, and when he opens them he'll be standing on the deck of the ferry, the damp and chill no match for his young wonder, his anticipation and a strong body and the river rolling slow and deep underneath his feet.

"No," she says. "I'm still here, Silas."

"I know that," he says, and the December wind makes a hard sound around the edges of this rich man's house.

After the War, his father had run, running from defeat and reprisal and grief, from a wasted Confederacy. World broken and there would be no resurrection, no reconstruction. Captain Eustace Desvernine, who'd marched home in '65 to the shallow graves of wife and child, graves scooped from the red Georgia clay with free black hands. And so he faded into the arms of the enemy, trailing behind him the shreds of a life gone to ash and smoke, gone to lead and worms, hiding himself in the gaslight squalor and cobbled industrial sprawl of Manhattan; the first skyscrapers rose around him, and the Union licked its wounds and forgot its dead.

Another marriage, strong Galway girl who gave him another son, Silas Josiah; the last dregs of his fortune into a ferry, the *Alexander Hamilton*, sturdy name that meant nothing to him, but he'd seen it painted on the side of a tall building. So, the Captain (as Silas would always remember him, the Captain in shoddy cap and shoddier coat on wide shoulders) carried men and freight from Weehawken to the foot of West Forty-Second Street. Later, another boat, whitewashed sidewheeler, double ender he'd named the *A. F. Beach*, and the year that Robert E. Lee died, the Captain began running the long route between New York and Albany.

And one night, when Silas was almost twenty years old, almost a man himself and strong, he stood beside his father in the wheelhouse of the *A. F. Beach*. The Captain's face older by the unsteady lamp as they slipped past the lights of West Point on their way downriver. The Captain taking out his old revolving pistol, Confederate-issue Colt, dullshine tarnish and his callused thumb cocking the hammer back while Silas watched, watched the big muzzle pressed against the Captain's left temple. Woman's name across his father's lips then, unfamiliar "Carrie" burned forever into Silas' brain like the flash, the echo of the gunshot trapped between the high cliffs, slipping away into the river night and pressed forever behind his eyes.

"Are you sure that's the way it happened?" she asked him once, when he told her. Years and years ago, not so long after he brought her to his castle on Pollepel Island, and she still wore the wings, then, and her eyes still shone new-dollar silver from between the narrow bars of her cage.

"I was young," he said. "Very young," and she sighed, short and matter-of-fact sigh that said something, but he wasn't certain what.

Whole minutes later, "Who was she?" and him already turned away, unpacking a crate just arrived from Kathmandu; "What?" he asked, but already remembering, the meaning of her question and the answer, absently picking a stray bit of excelsior from in his beard and watching those eyes watching him.

"Carrie," she said. "Who was Carrie?"

"Oh," and "I never found out," he lied. "I never tried," no reason, but already he felt the need to guard those odd details of his confessions, scraps of truth, trifling charms. Hoarding an empty purse, when all the coins have gone to beggars' hands.

"Ah," she said, and Silas looked too quickly back to the things in the crate, pilfered treasures come halfway around the world to him, and it was a long time before he felt her eyes leave him.

Pollepel Island: uneven jut of rock above water where the Hudson gets wide past the Northern Gate, Wey-Gat, the long stony throat of Martyr's Reach, greenscab at the foot of Newburgh

Bay; white oak and briar tangle, birch skin over bones of gneiss and granite. Bones of the world laid down a billion years ago and raised again in the splitting of continents, divorce of lands; birth of the Highlands in the time of terrible lizards, then scraped and sculpted raw, made this scape of bald rock and gorge during the chill and fever of ice ages. And Pollepel Island like a footnote to so much time, little scar in this big wound of a place.

Silas Desvernine already a rich man when he first came here. Already a man who had traded the Captain's ragtag ferries for a clattering empire of steel and sweat, Desvernine Consolidated Shipyard, turning out ironclad steamers, modern ships to carry modern men across the ocean, to carry men to modern war. And Pollepel chosen for his retreat from industry, the sprawling, ordered chaos of the yard, the noise and careless humanity of Manhattan. First glimpse, an engraving, frontispiece by Mr. N. P. Willis for *American Scenery*: tall sails and rowboat serenity, Storm King rising in the misty distance. The island recalled from his trips up and down the river, and the Captain had shown him where George Washington's soldiers sank their *chevaux-de-frises*, sixty-foot logs carved to spikes and tipped with iron, set into stone caissons and dropped into the river off Pollepel to pierce the hulls of British warships.

And this valley already a valley of castles, self-conscious stately, Millionaire's Row decades before Silas' architects began, before his masons laid the first stones, since the coming of the men of new money, the men who nailed shining locomotive track across the nation or milled steel or dug ore and with their fortunes built fashionable hiding places in the wilderness; cultivated, delusory romance of gentleman farmers in brick and marble, iron spires and garden pools. But Silas Desvernine was never a man of society or fashion, and his reasons for coming to Pollepel Island were his own.

Modest monstrosity, second-hand Gothic borrowed from his memory of something glimpsed on a business trip to Scotland, augmented with the architect's taste for English Tudor, and the pale woman he married, Angeline, his wife, never liked the great and empty halls, the cold and damp that never deserted the rooms. The always-sound of the river and the wind, restless in the too-close trees, the boats passing in the night.

If he'd permitted it, Angeline Desvernine would have named the awful house, given a name to tame it, to bind it, make it her home, maybe, instead of whatever else it was. But *No*, Silas said, stern and husbandly refusal, and so no poet ostentation, no Tioranda or Oulagisket or Glenclyffe on his island, just Silas' castle, Silas' Castle.

His dream, and the long night on the Storm King is never precisely the same twice and never precisely the way things happened. And never anything but the truth. The dream and the truth worn thin, as vellum soft, streampebble smooth, these moments pressed between the weight of now and then and everything before, and still as terrible.

Younger but not young, reaching back and she takes his hand, or Angeline takes his hand, neither of them, but an encouraging squeeze for this precarious slow climb up and up, above the river, while Prof. Henry Osborn talks, lecturing like the man never has to catch his breath. "Watch your step there. A lot of loose stone about," he says, and Silas feels sixty instead of forty-five.

Somewhere near the summit, he lingers, gasping, tearing-water eyes and looks down and back, towards his island; a storm coming, on its way up the valley and so twilight settling in early, the day driven like dirty sheep before the thunderheads, bruisebelly shepherds and the muddy stink of the river on the wind.

"A shame about this weather, though, really," Osborn sighs. "On a clear day, you can see the Catskills and the Shawangunks."

Of course, Osborn wasn't with him that day, this day, and he knows that dimly, dim dream recollection of another history;

another climb mixed in with this, the day that Osborn showed him a place where there was broken Iroquois pottery and arrowheads. Osborn, man whose father made a fortune on the Illinois Central and he's never known anything but privilege. The rain begins, then, wet and frying noise, and Henry Osborn squints at the sky, watches it fall as the drops melt his skin away, sugar from skeleton of wrought iron and seam welds; "On a clear day," he whispers from dissolving lips, before his jaw falls, clank and coppertooth scatter, and Silas goes on up the mountain alone.

No one ever asked him the *why* of the collecting, except her. Enough what's and where's and how's, from the very few who came to the island. The short years when Angeline was alive and she held her big, noisy parties, her balls for the rich from other castles down the valley, for gaudy bits of society and celebrity from New York City or Philadelphia or Boston. Minor royalty once or twice. The curious who came for a peek inside the silent fortress on Pollepel. Long nights when she pretended this house wasn't different, and he let her play the game, to dull the edge of an isolation already eating her alive.

Later, new visitors, after The Great War that left him more than wealthy, no counting anymore, and Angeline in her lonely grave on the western edge of the island, their son gone to Manhattan, the yard run by so many others   that Silas rarely left the island. Let whatever of the world he had need of come to him, and never more than one or two at a time, men and women who came to walk his still halls and wonder at this or that oddity. All of them filled with questions, each their own cyclopedia of esoteric interrogations, lean and shadowy catechists, a hundred investigators of the past and future, the hidden corners of this life and the next. Occultists, spiritualists, those whose askings and experiments left them on the bastard edges of science or religion. They came and he traded them glimpses of half-truths for the small and inconsequential things they'd learned elsewhere. All of them single-minded, and they knew, or mostly thought they knew, the why, so no point to ever asking.

That was for her, this one thing he'd brought back to Pollepel that he was afraid of and this one thing he loved beyond words or sanity. The conscious acquisition that could question the collection, the collector.

"I have too much money," he said once, after the purchase of a plaster replica of Carnegie's *Diplodocus* skeleton to be mounted for the foyer and she asked the sense of it "It's a way of getting rid of some of the goddamned money," he said.

She blinked her owlslow, owlwise blink at him, her gold and crimson eyes scoffing sadly.

"You know the emptiness inside you, Silas. These things are a poor substitute for the things you're missing." So he'd drawn the draperies on her cage and left them drawn for a week, as long as he could stand to be without the sight of her.

Nineteen eighteen, so almost three years after his son was pulled screaming from his wife's swollen body, pulled wet and blind into the waiting, dogjawed world; helpless thing the raw color of a burn. His heir, and Silas Desvernine could hardly bear the sight of it, the squalling sound of it. Angeline almost dying in the delivery nightmare of blood and sweat, immeasurable hours of breathless pain, and there would be no others, the doctor said. Named for father and grandfather's ghost, Eustace Silas, sickly infant that grew stronger slowly, even as its mother's health began to falter, the raising of her child left to indifferent servants; Silas seeing her less and less often, until, finally, she rarely left her room in the east wing.

And one night, late October and the first winter storm rolling down on Pollepel from the mountains, arctic Catskill breath and Silas away in the city. Intending to be back before dark, but the weather so bad and him exhausted after hours with thickheaded engineers, no patience for the train, so the night spent in the warmth and convenience of his apartment near Central Park.

Some dream or night terror, and Angeline left her rooms, wandered half-awake, confused, through the sleeping house, no slippers or stockings, bare feet sneakthief soft over Turkish carpets and cold stone, looking for something or someone real. Someone to touch or talk to, someone to bring her back to this world from her clinging nightmares. Something against the storm rubbing itself across the walls and windows, savage snow-pelt, wild and wanting in and her alone on the second story: the servants down below, her child and his nurse far away in another part of the house that, at that derelict hour, seemed to weave endlessly back upon itself. Halls as unfamiliar as if she'd never walked them, doors that opened on rooms she couldn't recall. Strange paintings to watch over her, stranger sights whenever she came to a window to stand staring into the swirling silver night, bare trees and unremembered statuary or hedges. Alien gardens, and all of it so much like the dream, as empty, as hungry; lost in her husband's house and inside herself, Angeline came at last to the mahogany doors to Silas' gallery, wood like old blood and his cabinet beyond, and how many years since she'd come that way? But *this* she recognized, hingecreak and woodsqueal as she stepped across the threshold, the crude design traced into the floor there, design within designs that made her dizzy to look directly at.

"Silas?" and no answer but the storm outside, smothering a dead world. Her so small, so alone at the mouth of this long and cluttered room of glass and dust and careful labels, his grotesquerie, cache of hideous treasures. Everything he loved instead of her; the gray years of hating herself flashing to anger like steam, then, flashing to scalding revelation. Something in her hands, an aboriginal weapon or talisman pulled from its bracket on the wall, and she swung it in long and ruthless arcs, smashing, breaking, shadow become destroyer. Glass like rain, shatter puddles that sliced at the soles of her feet, splinter and crash and the sicksweet stench of formaldehyde. Angeline imagining gratitude in the blank green eyes of a two-headed bobcat that tumbled off its pedestal and lay fiercely still, stuffed, mothgnawed, in her path.

And the wail rising up from the depths of her, soul's waters stagnant so long become a tempest to rival the fury and thundervoice of the blizzard. Become a war-cry, dragging her in its red undertow, and when she reached the far side, the high velvet drapes hiding some final rivalry: tearing at the cloth with her hands, pulling so hard the drapes ripped free of brass rings and slipped like shedding skin to the floor.

Iron bars and at first nothing else, gloom thick as the fog in her head, thick as jam, but nothing more. One step backwards, panting, feeling the damage to her feet, and the subtle shift of light or dark, then, all the nothing coalescing, made solid and beautiful and hateful, hurting eyes that she understood the way she understood her own captivity, her own loneliness.

And the woman with wings and shining bird eyes said her name, *Angeline*, said her name so it meant things she'd never suspected, some way the name held everything she was in three syllables. One long arm out to her, arm too long and thin to believe, skin like moonlight or afterbirth, fingers longer still and pointing to the door of the cage. Padlocked steel and the interlace design from the threshold again, engraved there like a warning. "Please," the woman in the cage said. "*Please*, Angeline."

Angeline Desvernine ran, then, ran from even the possibility of this pleading thing, door slammed shut behind her, closing it away and closing away the fading illusion of her victory. Almost an hour before she found her way back to her own room, trailing pools and crusting smears of blood from her ruined feet; crawling, hands and knees, at the end. She locked her door, and by then the sound of servants awake, distant commotion, her name called again and again, but there was no comfort left after those eyes, the ragged holes they'd put in her. No way not to see them or hear that silk and thorny voice.

Most of the storm's fury spent by dawn, by the time the maids and cooks and various manservants gave up and called for someone from the stables to take the door off its hinges. First leadflat morning light filling up the empty room, the balcony doors standing open wide and tiny drifts of snow reaching almost to the bed. They found her hanging from the balustrade, noose from curtain-cord tiebacks, snow in her tangled black hair, crimson icicles from the sliced flesh of her toes and heels. And her eyes open wide and staring sightlessly towards the Storm King.

"They're my dreams," he says, whispers loud, and she says "They're lies," and he keeps his eyes on the last colorless smudges of afternoon and says low, mumbled so she won't hear, "Then they're my lies."

This time, this dog-eared incarnation of the climb up Storm King, he's alone, except for the thunder and lightning and rain like wet needles against exposed skin, wind that would take him in its cold fist and fling him, broken, back down to the rocks below, to the impatient, waiting river. No sign anymore of the trail he's followed from the road, faintest path for deer or whatever else might come this way and now even that's gone. He can see in the white spaces after the thunder, flashpowder snapshots of the mountain, trees bending and the hulk of Breakneck across the river, Storm King's twin. Jealous Siamese thing severed by the acid Hudson, and he thinks *No, somewhere deep they're still connected*, still bound safe by their granite vinculum below the water's slash and silt.

Thunder that sounds like angels burning, and he slips, catches himself, numb hands into the roots of something small that writhes, woodsy revulsion at his touch, and he's shivering now, the mud and wet straight through his clothes. He lies so still, waiting to fall, to drown in the gurgling runoff, until the thunder says it's time to get moving again and so he opens his eyes. And soon he's standing at the summit, little clearing and the tall stone at its heart like a stake to hold the world in place. Gray megalith like things he's seen in England or Denmark or France, and in the crackling brief electric flash he can discern the marks made in the stone, marks smoothed almost away by time and frost and a hundred thousand storms before. Forgotten characters traced in clean rivulets like emphasis. He would turn and run, from the place and the moment, *If you had it to do over again, If you could take it back,* but the roots have twisted about his wrists, becoming greenstick pythons, and for all his clever, distracting variations, there's only this one way it can go.

She steps out of the place where the stone is, brilliant moment, thinnest sliver of an instant caught and held in forked lightning teeth; the rain that beads, rolls off her feathers, each exquisite, roughgem drop and the strange angles of her arms and legs, too many joints. The head that turns on its elegant neck and the eyes that find him, sharp face and molten eyes that will never let him go.

"Nothing from the Pterodactyle, I shouldn't think," says Professor Osborn, standing somewhere behind him. "Though the cranium is oddly reminiscent of *Dimorphodon*, isn't it?" and Silas Desvernine bows his head, staring down at the soggy darkness where his feet must be, and waits for the leather and satin rustle of her wings, gentle loversound through the storm. The rain catches his tears and washes them away with everything else.

The funeral over and the servants busy downstairs when Silas opened the doors of his gallery; viewed the damage she'd done for the first time, knew it was mostly broken glass and little that couldn't be put right again, but the sight hurt his chest, hurt his eyes. Heart already so broken and eyes already so raw, but new pain anyway. No bottom to this pain, and he bent over and picked up his dodo, retrieved it from a bed of diamond shards, and Silas brushed the glass from its dusty beak and rump feathers. Set it back on the high shelf between passenger pigeons and three Carolina parakeets. Another step closer to her cage, the drapes still pulled open, and his shoes crunched. Her, crouched in the shadows, wings wrapped tightly about her like a cocoon, living shield against him, and he said, "What did you do to her, Tisiphone?" And surprised at how calm his voice could be, how empty of everything locked inside him and clawing to get out.

The wings shivered, cringed and folded back; "That's not my name," she said.

"What did you do to her, Megaera?"

"Shut up," words spat at the wall where her face was still hidden, spat at him. "You know that I'm not one of the three, you've known that all along."

"She couldn't have hurt you, even if she'd wanted to," he said, hearing her words, but this is as close as he would ever come to being able to ignore them: her weak, and his grief too wide to cross even for her voice. "Did you think she could hurt you?" he asked.

"*No*," and shaking her head now, forehead bang and smack against brick, and he could see the sticky, black smear she left on the wall.

"Then you did it to get back at me. Is that it? You thought to hurt me by hurting her."

"No," she said, and that was the only time he ever saw her cry, if it was crying, the dim phosphorescence leaking from the corners of her eyes. "No, *no*—"

"But you know she's dead, don't you?" and "Yes," she said, small yes too quick and it made him want to wring her white throat, lock his strong hands around her neck and twist until he was rewarded with the pop and cartilage grind of ruined vertebrae. Squeeze until her tongue hung useless from her lipless mouth.

"She never hurt anyone, Alecto," he hissed, and she turned around, snake-sudden movement, and he took a step away from the bars despite himself.

"I asked her to *help* me," and she was screaming now, perfect crystal teeth bared. "I asked her to free me," and her hurt and fury swept over him, blast furnace heat rushing away from her, and the faint smell of nutmeg and decay left in the air around his head.

"I *asked* her to unlock the fucking cage, Silas!" and the wings slipped from off her back and lay bloody and very still on the unclean metal and   hay-strewn floor of the cage.

In the simplest sense, these things, at least, are true: that during the last week of June 1916, Silas Desvernine hired workmen from Haverstraw to excavate a large stone from a spot near the summit of Storm King, and that during this excavation several men died or fell seriously ill, each under circumstances that only seemed unusual if considered in connection with one another. When the foreman resigned (mink-eyed little Scotsman with a face like ripe cranberries), Silas hired a second crew, and in July the stone was carried down and away from the mountain, ingenious block-and-tackle of his own design, then horse and wagon, and finally, barge, the short distance upriver to Pollepel Island. Moneys were paid to a Mr. Harriman of the Palisades Interstate Park Commission, well enough known for his discretion in such matters, and no questions were asked.

And also, that archaeologists and anthropologists, linguists and cryptographers were allowed brief viewings of the artifact over the next year, though only the sketchiest, conflicting conclusions regarding the glyphs on the stone were drawn: that they might have been made by Vikings, or Phoenicians, or Minoans, or Atlanteans; that they might be something like Sanskrit, or perhaps the tracks of prehistoric sea worms, or have been etched by Silas Desvernine himself. The suggestion by a geologist of no particular note, that the stone, oily black shale with cream flecks of calcite, was not even native to the region, was summarily ignored by everyone but Silas, who ignored nothing.

One passing footnote mention of "the Butterhill Stone" in a monograph on Mahican pottery, and by 1918 it was forgotten by the busy, forgetful world of men and words beyond the safe-guarding walls of Silas' Castle.

"Wake up," she says. "You must wake up," and he does, gummy blink, unfocused, and the room's dark except for the light of brass lamps with stained-glass shades like willows and dragon-flies and drooping purple wisteria.

"You're dying, Silas," and he squints towards the great cage, cage that could hold lions or leopards, and she looks so terri-bly small in there. Deceptive contrast of iron and white, white skin, and she says, "Before the sun rises again..."

Big sigh rattle from his bony chest, and "No," looking about the desk for his spectacles. "No, not yet," but she says, "You're an old man, Silas, and old men die, eventually. All of them."

"Not yet," and there they are, his bifocals perched on a thick book about African beetles. "There's a new war, new ships that have to be built," and he slips them on, frame wire bent and straightened and bent again so they won't sit quite right on his face any longer. Walking cane within reach, but he doesn't stand, waiting for the murky room to become solid again.

"Let me go now," she says, as if she hasn't said it a thousand thousand times before, as if it were a new idea, never occurred to her before, and he laughs. Froggy little strangled sound more like a burp. "You're trying to trick me," he says, grinning his false-toothed grin at her and one crooked finger pointed so there can be no doubt. "You're not a sibyl," and it takes him five minutes to remember where he's put his pocket watch.

"I can hear your tired old heart, and it's winding down, like your watch," and there it is, in his vest pocket; 4:19, but the hour hand and minute hand and splinter second hand still as ice. He forgets to wind it a lot these days, and how much time has he lost, dozing at his desk? Stiffneck crane, and he can see stars through the high windows.

"You can't leave me here, Silas."

"Haven't I always *told* you that I won't?" still watching the stars, dim glimpse of Canes Venatici or part of the Little Bear, and the anger in his voice surprising him. "Haven't I said that? That I'll let you go before I die?"

"You're a liar, Silas Desvernine. You'll leave me here with all these other things that you've stolen," and he notices that her eyes have settled on the tall glass case near her cage, four tall panes and the supporting metal rods inside, the shriveled, leathery things wired there. The dead feathers that have come loose and lie scattered like October leaves at the bottom of the case.

"You would have destroyed them if I hadn't put them there," he mumbles. "Don't tell me that's not the truth," turning away, anything now to occupy his attention, and it was true, that part. That she'd tried to eat them after they'd fallen off, *Jesus Christ*, tried to *eat* them, before he took them away from her, still warm and oozing blood from their ragged stumps.

"*Please,*" she whispers, the softest snowflake excuse for sound, and "Please, Silas," as he opens a book, yellowbrown paper to crackle loud between his fingers, and adjusts his bent spectacles.

"I keep my promises," he grumbles, and turns a dry page.

THE LAST CHILD OF LIR

T HE ASS END OF ANOTHER MANHATTAN NOVEMBER, fuck Thanksgiving, fuck the goddamn holiday tinsel and Salvation Army Santa-Claus bullshit, and Glitch is sitting outside the free clinic, smoking on the steps, No Smoking inside, so here he is in the cold again, fog breath and tobacco cloud from his lips chapped so raw there's blood on the cigarette's filter; waiting for Jamie and Ladybird. Freezing, shivering bundle in his ratty, loose army jacket and jeans, watching the concrete gray and brick red of another Village morning. Everyone going somewhere, except him and the black dude across the street, bonethin dude asleep next to a parking meter, bed of plastic milk crates and cardboard, and one blanket the comfortless color of egg custard wrapped tight around him. Maybe he's dead, no way to tell, and Glitch thinks maybe he'll go see, someone should, so he flicks away the butt of his cigarette, but then the clinic door jingles open him, and this time it's Jamie, with Ladybird following a few steps behind. Brief scent of antiseptic and warmth from inside before the wind takes it away.

Ladybird, so thin the black guy under the custard blanket looks like the Ghost of Christmas Present, and he's clutching an amber prescription bottle in one hand. Jamie huddled in her fake-fur cocoon, how many fake leopards had to die for that? staring down at her boots, back turned to the gusts rolling mean down Charlton. "Can I have a smoke?" and so Glitch lights one and hands it to her, and finally he asks, "Well?" but nothing volunteered, so "What's the word?" And Ladybird looks up at the sky, bonecheeks and chin like the man in the moon where his pretty face used to be, bags beneath his eyes like bruises. But no answer.

"Yeah, never mind," Glitch says and gets up, starts walking for no other reason than he's sick of sitting outside the clinic watching the dying men and women going in and coming out. May as well be cold somewhere else. They turn up McDougal, heading for the park, the arch, and Jamie's walking as close to him as she can, half a foot shorter and so she has to walk twice as fast to keep up. Ladybird somewhere straggling behind. Past a long folding table and someone selling books, piled hardbacks with torn covers that flap in the wind. Ladybird stops to finger through a water-stained copy of *Valley of the Dolls*, ruined and swollen paper, until Glitch tugs at his sleeve. "*C'mon*, man," and they're moving again. Always moving, the time spent between squats and friends' apartments and the hallways outside friends' apartments.

Not so bad at first, late August and the eviction from their TriBeCa ratwarren. August since the band's last gasp, Crimson Stain Mystery buried in yellow pawn slips and the last rung down to the street. Jokes at first, before the cold and Ladybird getting so damn sick, jokes about suffering for their art and the stories they could tell MTV one day. Jamie screaming shit at the suits and ties, the trendy secure, "Punk rock nomads!" and "Kurt Cobain died for your sins!" at the top of her whiskeygravel voice. But whatever gritty romance faded now, like summer and bearable autumn and Ladybird's health. Nothing left but walking and squatting and time like cold, bitter coffee they can't afford.

Before the eviction, Glitch worked making pies and selling slices, him always stinking of tomato sauce and sausage and

Jamie always bitching about the smell. And she had a job in a fetish boutique near Broadway, latex and leather, stiletto pumps in men's sizes. Ladybird never working steady, but dancing drag here and there, wherever the pecking order of queens would let him steal a little stage time. So he brought in tips, and once a hundred dollars after he won amateur night at a place without a name, just a neon red tube of lipstick out front. Lip syncing Concrete Blonde's "Joey," the sort of stuff he always did and the reason why he rarely ever got to perform, no Mariah Carey or Madonna or fucking Whitney Houston. That night, that almost perfect night, Glitch and Jamie down front yelling for him so loud they were hoarse for two days.

Never any money from the band, though, just money into the band that should have been going for rent and gas and electricity. Groceries. Toilet paper. A little airtime on a couple of late-night goth shows, weehour radio for the dead children, one or two mentions in photocopied zines. Jamie's voice and Glitch's oilblack Gibson, Ladybird on bass and a procession of drummers, almost a different one every show until they gave up and paid for a very used drum machine. Worshipping Polly Jean Harvey and Nick Cave so much it showed, and they could have been playing covers, the way people stayed away. Might have been different, might have been okay, if they'd sounded too much like Bauhaus or Christian Death, instead.

And then Jamie accused of stealing twenty dollars and lucky they only fired her, lucky they didn't press charges, they said. Glitch never asked if she took the money or not, honestly didn't give a shit. Everyone stole, one way or another; just wishing she hadn't gotten caught if she had taken the twenty. Always hanging on by their fingernails and without her check bad to worse so fast and one month late on the rent before the old Polish fag super put them out on their butts, their shit out for garbage and the street people to scavenge. Selling what they could, instruments they swore to each other they'd have back before Halloween, Ladybird's dresses and shoes farmed out to other baby queens, the clothes they could carry and a ragged paperback, *The House At Pooh Corner*, stuffed into two backpacks and a gym bag. Jamie's boom box and a few tapes. The rest (which really wasn't all that much) just gone.

Glitch trying to keep the pizza job, but that gone too as soon as the owner found out he didn't have an address. "I don't hire bums. You don't even have a place to take a bath. I'll get closed down, kid." And that was that, nothing left but what they could do for each other, and then, finally, what they could do for Ladybird.

Mondays and Thursdays, the three of them hiking or panhandling subway fare to Central Park, the rough stone and castle turrets of the Museum of Natural History, because they know someone who sells tickets, a friend of Glitch's from another band years ago and he lets them in, sometimes, if they can manage to look halfway decent. Clean hands and faces, at least, but always *Not my ass if you guys get caught*, always, *I'll swear I never saw you before in my life*, like they've forgotten from the last time. But Glitch nods and thanks him, agreeable, grateful for a few hours' shelter and entry into this one place from the world before, one solid piece to hang onto and keep: church-sacred halls and dusty African savannas behind glass, tempera-tundra illusions and fiberglass-black seafloors. All frozen or suspended, held right there, still point in the chaos and monotony. And the Hall of Dinosaurs best of all, remodeled now and some of its old dignity shined away, solemn shadow traded cheap for sterile interactive flash and Disneyland tricks. But the bones still the same, mostly, holiest reliquary centerpiece, and Glitch has been teaching Jamie and Ladybird how to pronounce the names, catechism of Latin and phonetic patience: *Apatosaurus louisae, Oviraptor philoceratops, Tyrannosaurus rex.*

"*You* should'a been a scientist," Ladybird says almost every time, mother voice, no arguing with that tone. "You know *all* this shit," and Glitch shrugs his shoulders, maybe proud inside, and they move on to the next exhibit, mastodons or the mummified duckbill or stuffed Komodo dragons big as jungle cats, mounted fierce and sporting phony gore on their scaly snouts.

Jamie's favorite part a mural, imagined seascape sixty-five million years ago, sandwhite shore and tall cliffs and the sun setting golden warm as honey on the horizon, Maxfield Parrish sky for pterosaur wings, all held inside, within, the tall cream-marble arch; and she says, "I used to dream I could fly," and "That could be a window," as she closes her eyes, smiling softly like she can feel warmer air, clean and tropical twilight breeze, nostrils flared like she's smelling salt.

This isn't Monday or Thursday, just a Tuesday and the three of them sitting together on a bench in Washington Park, huddled close for body heat and company, Ladybird in the middle so he'll stay the warmest; a tape in the box because Ladybird pocketed some batteries yesterday, five-fingered drugstore discount and so Jamie humming along with Patti Smith. Glitch wonders how long before he gets caught, and if he'd be better off if he did, a hospital maybe instead of dying on the street. Even a fucking jail hospital better than dying of pneumonia or toxo or whatever it's going to be, sooner or later, dying out here like a rat or a pigeon or a lousy, goddamn wino.

He sees the Bonerman before the Bonerman sees him, standing over near the arch, smoking and talking with some college girls, three girls in identical, impeccable black, and they probably think they're slumming it, cool, talking to a junky. Glitch thinks about getting up, dragging the others after him. Really not in the mood today to listen to Boner's crackhead prattle. But Ladybird's meds have made him sick to his stomach again, ready to puke at the drop of a dime and paler even than usual. So he sits, still and helpless, hoping they won't be noticed, hoping Bonerman will wander away with the NYU chicks or have to hurry off to make his afternoon connection.

"Pretend like you don't see him," whisperhissed at Ladybird, who hasn't and "Who?" so Glitch has to point, one finger jabbed discreetly towards the arch, and that's enough movement to snag the Bonerman's jittery attention.

"Damn," Glitch mutters. "Never mind."

And Ladybird says, "Oh, *him*." and goes back to looking determinedly nauseous.

"Shit," says Jamie, and by then the Bonerman already past the fountain, cutting across parchment-yellow grass to reach them quicker, short, stiff-legged stride, stiff spring in each step, wound so tight that maybe they'll get lucky and he'll explode on the way.

"God, he makes me itch," says Jamie, little mouthcorner sneer, and Ladybird says, "Unh-huh," and nods. Glitch pulls his coat tighter, collar up high, turtlehead attempt at retreat. Pointless as spitting into an electric fan, and there's the Bonerman and the snotgreen cardigan he's been wearing for weeks, more holes now and raveling yarn, his hair like a malnourished fungus, one brown hand out to pump Glitch's like he can't stop.

Glitch tugs, frees himself, and then the Bonerman starts rubbing his palms together, skin like two frantic sticks, like flint for fire from flesh. "Fuckin' *cold* out here, man," he says, brrrrrrr. "*Too* motherfuckin' cold out here for *my* ass, I sure know that shit."

And, "I heard that," Glitch says.

Jamie's staring off towards Judson Memorial, distant eyes like maybe she's praying he'll go away soon, but Glitch knows she doesn't pray.

"Hey there, Lady," the Bonerman says to Ladybird, winks, and Ladybird sighs, says hey back, the most reluctant acknowledgment and anyone else would take it for contempt, but even that much an encouragement to the Bonerman, and "You lookin' a little rough today, Lady," he says.

"He's sick," Jamie says, her eyes still on the church. "His medicine's making him sick today."

"Oh, man, I'm real sorry to hear that shit," and "Yeah," Ladybird says. "Wanna see me puke?" and his left index finger held up, iceblue polish all but chipped away.

"No, man. But, hey. Look here. I was hopin' I'd run into you guys. I still owe you one, right?" and Glitch has no fucking clue what the Bonerman's talking about but easier to listen than start asking questions.

"You guys still needin' a good squat, right? Sure, and I heard of this place down on West Fourteenth, right down there—"

"We're fine," Ladybird says, interrupting, little gag, dry-swallow and then going on. "We ain't so hard up we need to start crashing in crackhouses in the fucking meatpacking district."

Big offended face from the Bonerman, then, half surprise and half practiced exaggeration. "You don't *look* so fine," pause, and "It ain't like that, it's just this empty warehouse down by the river, okay?" and he's started wringing his hands; that's worse than the rubbing, always drives Glitch bugfuck. And "I was just tryin' to help you guys out, I mean, I'd be down there *myself*, if it wasn't so far away from my peoples and all."

"It's okay, man," Glitch says, sees the storm coming gray and violent behind Ladybird's eyes and so he's talking fast. "Really, thanks, but maybe we should get together about it later. Maybe..." but Ladybird is standing, dizzy-stagger up from the bench, and the space left between Glitch and Jamie filled in at once with the greedy, eager cold.

"We don't need no favors from fucking *junkies*, okay! We *don't*," and the Bonerman takes a quick step back, two steps. "Hey, bitch! Watch it now," but Ladybird in pursuit, tripping over the boom box, falling, and he's vomiting before he hits the sidewalk. The little bit of breakfast they had, stalebland cherry Danish split three ways and his third coughed up now on the toes of the Bonerman's duct-taped sneakers.

"*Shit*! Holy Jesus *shit*!" and the Bonerman is staring down at his spattered shoes, the steaming, doughy pink mess all over them and his mouth hanging open stupid, revulsion and surprise fading fast to plain pissed off. "You plague-carryin', Sodomite mother*fucker*."

And Jamie up before Glitch is even sure what's happened, herself jammed in tight between the Bonerman and Ladybird still dry heaving on the ground. The Bonerman shoves her once, shoves hard and she tumbles over Lady, butt smack right back down on the bench, woodcrack and, "Hey, *hey*," Glitch holding both hands out. "He didn't mean it, Boner. I swear to God and Jesus, man. He didn't mean it. He's just sick, you know? He's just sick."

"Yeah, he's *sick* all right," and "You can catch that shit from puke, man, just like it was blood. Look at my shoes. What the hell am I supposed to do about my shoes?"

And then Glitch is leading the Bonerman away from their bench, apologizing like a broken record, mollifying, desperate silly words, and he glances back once to see Jamie kneeling beside Ladybird, arms around him, holding him close.

"Just *look* at my shoes, man," and Glitch does, but there's nothing he can do, so "I'm sorry as a motherfucker, honest, but it was just an accident." And when he's far enough away that Jamie can't hear and Ladybird can't hear, "Look, about that place, that warehouse—"

"Hey, don't you be askin' me to help your sorry asses out after that shit back there."

"I told you, man. He didn't mean it. The medicine makes him sick. We could really use a safe place. We need to get Lady in out of the cold for just a little while, that's all."

"Yeah, well, I hope the little faggot freezes to death."

"No you don't," Glitch says, looking back at them again, Jamie helping Ladybird up, lifting him, wiping his mouth with a scrap of something blue from her coat pocket.

"And you owe us, right?" he says, pushing his luck, no luck left so he might as well. The Bonerman is busy cursing and making disgusted noises, smearing his shoes back and forth in the dead grass, but he stops and stares at Glitch.

"The place is somewhere up by Tenth," finally, "But I'm just tellin' you so you'll get that fag sonofabitch outta here before I have to cut him or somethin'. I don't owe nobody nothin' after their AIDS-infected fag friend done puked on my fuckin' shoes. That shit makes us even."

One last I'm sorry and Glitch gives the Bonerman fifty cents, quarter and nickel and a bunch of pennies from his pants pockets, miserly compensation but all he has, and then he walks swiftly back to the bench, leaving the junky alone and still trying to scrape away the stains on his feet.

The warehouse is there, more or less where Glitch had expected from the Bonerman's grudging directions, far enough down Fourteenth he can see dingy steelbluegray glimpses of the Hudson between the buildings. Stinking maze of loading docks and wholesale butchers: diesel fumes, old fat, fresh blood; knives and meat hooks for everything down here. Past concrete and greasy plastic drums marked INEDIBLE—DO NOT EAT, and he knows this is the place, derelict, condemned bricks laid a hundred years ago or more, and Jamie tells the taxi driver to stop, they'll get out here, please. She pays the fare, precious, crumpled five bucks she's been holding back, gone, the bill and some change, and an ugly look from the driver when she apologizes for having nothing left for a tip.

All afternoon spent talking Ladybird into the move, and by then he's running a fever Glitch and Jamie can feel just standing close, cloudy eyes and the soft heat off his skin like he's begun to burn alive in there. Wet cough and Jamie telling him, finally, that it was going to be the squat or the ER and him giving in, giving up. And now they're all but carrying him, one on each side and his thin arms around their shoulders, not nearly as heavy as he ought to be.

Narrowlong alley squeezed between the warehouse and the building next door, and Glitch looking for a way in without leaving obvious tracks, big broken window or busted lock sign for the police or other homeless.

"I don't want to die down here in all this filth," Ladybird says, faint and runny echo of his voice, and Jamie frowns, "You're not gonna die, stupid. You just gotta get out of the wind and get some sleep."

"Oh, and chicken soup, too, please," Ladybird says. "I think I saw a nice, ripe one back there in the gutter." He tries to laugh and winds up coughing, instead.

Almost to the end of the alley, dead-end wall and so much colder way back here where the sun never comes.

"Jesus," she says. "Glitch, how are we supposed to get in?" and that makes him flinch, makes him cringe down inside, too tired, ashamed they've come to this, that *she's* come to this: frayed excuse for Jamie like rotten old shoelaces ready to snap, and he sees the hole, then, not big, but big enough. Some warped plywood and masonry nails where the bricks have fallen in, but nothing they can't pry open.

"Here," and it feels good to have the answer, any answer would feel good. Lowering Ladybird, careful, to sit against the wall, Glitch's jacket off and spread on the ground for a mat, protection from broken asphalt gravel and the damp. The pocketknife he carries out, and he tests the mortar, punkysoft from decades of the river's soggy breath, soft enough to gouge a little furrow without even trying. The knife folded closed again and all his fingers worked into the space between the board and wall. "Help me," he says to Jamie and both their hands in now, wedged slow, painful between scrub-raw brick and splinters, and pulling, more work than he'd anticipated before the nails start to squeal, reluctant, ugly sound, sliding free, and her corner pops loose first. *Pop*, and she stumbles, almost falling; one palm sliced, but she's still hanging on.

"You all right?" and she nods, white fog puffs and "Yeah," breathless, "I'm fine, c'mon," and the board comes completely off with the next big tug. From his spot on Glitch's jacket, Ladybird applauds weakly. "My heroes," he mumbles, smiling a wide, sloppy smile for them.

And Glitch looks inside, dark so deep and solid he thinks maybe he could scoop up a handful, dark and the musty smell of a place closed away for a very long time.

"Can you see anything?" she says, glancing back down the alley in case their noise has attracted attention and he shakes his head, no. "Well, I don't expect there's much worth seeing," she says.

"Help Lady up," and Glitch ducks inside before he can change his mind, swallowed whole by that black dust-reek. Cigarette lighter left in the pocket of his jacket, and so he stands up slow, blind and hands out for obstacles. Nothing but the dark, though; his eyes adjusting, gradual, almost imperceptible fade-in from nothing to the dim impression of a large and vacant space, big empty, and neat rows of a lesser darkness on the other side, rectangle smudges one after the other. Windows painted over, and he almost screams when something bumps his legs from behind, rough and sudden nudge, and he reaches back, fingers tangling in hair and it's only Jamie, just Jamie.

"*Hey*, will you please watch the fuck out?" she says and slaps his hand away.

"There's nothing in here," Glitch says, as they help Lady to his unsteady feet, and he's so hot, human furnace and skin slippery; Glitch tries to remember if that's supposed to be a good sign, the sweating, if it means the fever's breaking. Ladybird begins to shiver, teeth chattering like an involuntary reply.

"It isn't the Ritz-Carlton, is it?" Lady wheezes, and Jamie says *shhhhhhhh*, but he's already coughing again, the awful rattle from his chest that frightens Glitch.

They move slowly away from the hole, bright, hopeless way back, supporting Ladybird between them, three moving as one, bizarre six-legged thing. Something that might belong here, that might thrive off this freezing box of night.

"I can't die yet," he said, out of his head fevergrin, and "She hasn't given me permission...the bitch," that grin and the fear in his eyes glowing hot as his face. But he did, disobedient and dead hardly an hour later, maybe an hour left until dawn. The nest they made for him in one corner of the warehouse, most of their clothes spread out on the icy cement, their coats wrapped around him and so Glitch and Jamie shivering through the long night. The batteries running low on the boom box, so the Tom Waits Lady asked to hear playing slower and slower, "Blind Love" and "Walking Spanish" stretched and slurred; Ladybird mummyswaddled and Jamie holding his hand at the end, begging him to let Glitch find a phone, call an ambulance.

"*No*," Ladybird said and squeezed her hand twice as hard. "We made a deal," and they had, a week after the death of Ladybird's last lover, and he'd made them both swear it would-n't be like that for him, no lingering hospitalwhite death scene on antiseptic sheets, plugged into machines to breathe for him and shit for him, while his body wasted down to bone and yellowjaundice skin and things he couldn't even pronounce ate away his brain.

Lady squeezing so hard it hurt, his nails biting her and Jamie pleading. And then he sighed and closed his eyes and wasn't squeezing her hand anymore. And it was over, no debate, no decisions left to make. That simple, that easy.

Neither of them crying, not yet, sitting with his body, without words, their coats retrieved and Jamie brushing Ladybird's hair, patient fingers working through the day's snarls.

Until, finally, "What do we do with him?" Glitch whispers, and he's glad he can't see her face very well.

No place else to go, and so they stayed there in the old ware-house on Fourteenth Street. Ladybird's body lugged three blocks south the next night and left slumped in a doorway, dead boy alone and no colder than the night around him; Jamie called the police from a pay phone, Glitch telling her it was too dangerous, stupid, and her telling him to fuck off, she didn't give a shit anymore.

Two days later, Jamie sitting in the one small pool of after-noon sun that gets through a high place where the paint has flaked away or the brush missed, sitting alone with *The House At Pooh Corner* and all Ladybird's things stuffed, bulging, into his nylon backpack beside her. Glitch went out for food earlier, came back with a couple of hard bagels and a plastic three-liter Coke bottle full of water. Bread and water, and she just looked at him when he said that, blank eyes, blank face, bread and water, hah fucking hah.

So he goes up to the second floor by himself, wooden stairs past rickety, set way back near an old freight elevator that might still work, if there was electricity. Suicidal-dumb climb through the darkness, right hand never leaving the railing and every step like being in the hull of a movie pirate ship, sway and creak, counting the steps for a charm to keep them anchored to the wall: fifteen, eighteen, twenty-one and he's at the top. Heart in his throat, in his fucking mouth, but both feet on the landing, second tier of concrete flooring and it's so dark he only knows that there's a door in front of him because his hand fumbles, blind-man lucky, across the knob.

Of course, it'll be locked, he thinks, it absolutely has to be locked, right? but the knob turns oilsmooth, faint hasp click as the door swings inward, swinging open, and never so much light in the world. Never in this world, never this brilliant and drowning, hands up over his eyes, squinting out between his fingers while his pupils shrink down to make sense of it all; and it's only that they didn't bother to paint out the windows up here. Glitch steps blinking into the looking-glass twin of the room below, sun-choked yang to an ebony yin. Not just the light, though: this room as full as the one downstairs is empty, wall-to-wall stuffed with wooden crates and drop cloths, some of the crates big enough to hold trucks or zoo elephants. The walls resolving to bleached swimming-pool blue, rising up to the windows and then a rusty network of steel girders, bare ribs for the pitched roof overhead.

Neat rows, building-block neat stacks, and the shoulderwide paths left winding between, shipping-crate canyon stretching away from him. Glitch almost turns and calls back down the stairs for Jamie, but stops, goes instead to the nearest line of boxes and touches the one at the bottom, this box almost big enough it could hold their last couple of apartments, and he touches it. *Just checking to see if it's real, really here,* he thinks and aloud, "Bullshit, it's a fucking warehouse, ain't it?" His fingers brush cautiously across the wood, strong lumber bearing the weight of all the crates piled above for God knows how long. Callused fingertips across the words stenciled there, whatever original red sunfaded now to dullest redorange: desvernine consol-lot 5 and the arrow pointing towards the ceiling or the stars and this end up.

"You have to come see," he says again, as Jamie scoots her butt over a little more, following the drowsy track of the sun, keeping herself in its favor. She looks up at him from the safety of the Hundred-Acre Wood and says, cold as the floor, "I don't *have* to do anything, Glitch."

"It's a whole lot warmer up there. And we'll be safer, okay?" New strategy if she doesn't care about the crates, practical tactic, but she only shrugs and goes back to her book.

"I'm trying to read, Glitch. Just leave me alone."

"Jesus," and he sits down in front of her, arms hugging his own knees, the scuffed toes of his boots almost touching the scuffed toes of hers. He says nothing else for a long time, watches her reading, ignoring him, until the sun's almost down and he knows she can't see the pages anymore.

"You think it was my fault, don't you? Because I brought us down here," and her eyes up again, impenetrable anger for everything they see.

"*I'm* the one who talked him into coming," she says. "Not you. This isn't even about you."

"It was his choice," Glitch says, reaching for her as she pulls away. "Fuck off," and that's all, the book closed, laid aside, and she turns away from him.

He works alone while she sleeps below. Baby-aspirin orange

light leaking in from the streets, city light strained through the flyblown windows. A crowbar he found among the crates and the muffled rumble of thunder somewhere far away, storms coming, and he's prying the crates open one after another, carelessly careful not to upset the stacks so it all comes crashing down on top of him. Crying at first, loud and racking sobs that he thinks will never end, will tear him apart, pain enough to eat him alive; but his grief and fury poured into the work, release through tear ducts and straining muscles. And inside each crate a different miracle, Glitch pushing or digging his way through dustdry seas of excelsior and cotton padding to the treasures hidden inside, impossible pearls to find here among the rat nests and spiders.

This shit doesn't even make sense, these things he lifts gently from their prisons with unsteady hands: life's work of a dozen lunatic taxidermists in the first three or four boxes, beautiful horrors, song birds with bat wings, motheaten ape with a crocodile's tail, two-headed bobcat or lynx and the stitches, forgery's fingerprint, plain enough to see through the fur that falls away at his touch. And then a crate filled with a hundred glass jars and each wrapped in moldering straw and brittle newspaper, filled with alcohol or formaldehyde for the scales and spiny fins and skin as pale as cheese floating within. A zoologist's nightmares, too pitiful or perverse for exhibition, and Glitch sets down a quart jar of pickled flesh and gristle and smoothes a page of newspaper packing out flat on the lid he's pried away. *The Times* and the date across the top barely legible, February 17, 1943. Thirty years before he was born, ten years before his *mother* was born; half a century or more since these jars were wrapped and secreted away.

Glitch's hand against crumbling newsprint, casual, critical contact of typescript disintegration and his living skin, his twenty-five years and the weighted certainty of time he's never felt anywhere else but the Museum: Hall of Saurischian Dinosaurs, Hall of Ornithischian Dinosaurs, and the visible heft of petrified bones. The empty socket gaze of an *Allosaurus* skull and the confined smell from these crates washing over him.

Glitch turns to the next box and picks up the crowbar, crudest tool become a key, and another lid comes away, another after that: Roman statues and Egyptian tablets, a skull that he would swear was a unicorn's if he ever believed in unicorns, and all the time he's moving deeper and deeper into the ordered labyrinth of wood and nailsteel, messy trail of uncounted unlikelihoods left behind. Too much left to see, to divulge, for him to pause, give in to lazy curiosity, and finally these two crates set apart from all the others. Like they've been waiting here for him all along, at the still heart of this room, heart of this building left for dead.

One tall and narrow, not much larger than a phone booth and the other so long, wide enough to conceal a city bus. *She must be right beneath me now*, he thinks, standing at the center of this room and Jamie asleep in the middle of the one downstairs, Ladybird's things held close to her; fragile stenciled redorange across the wood, same as all the ones before, handle with care. His arms hurt, and he tries to remember where he left his coat, barely remembers taking it off, hot and sweatsoaked from exertion despite the cold, despite the wind at the windows.

Go ahead. Open them, and "Oh," he says, "I am so sorry, Lady. I'm so goddamned sorry."

And when he's done, and the crates are boards and bent nails, there's no strength left in him to be amazed, the fact of his awe left but not the passion, and so he can only stand and stare and wonder that he still has tears left to cry.

The simple cabinet of glass and fine, varnished wood that holds the wings, tattered things of ivory and dappled gray, wired stiff to an iron armature, but drooping anyway, as many feathers lying scattered at the bottom of the case as are left on the wings. Wings that must have once belonged to something huge, a condor he thinks, or an albatross.

And the circus cage, straight off a cardboard carton of Barnum's animal crackers, absurd and ornate frame of wrought iron and bronze filigree, inviolable bars hidden politely behind rotting velvet the gangrenous color of old avocados, and when he pushes them aside, ties them back, Glitch can see nothing in there but more straw, more dust. He breaks the padlock with the crowbar and climbs inside, sits staring back out at the room, the gutted crates, their menagerie of atrocities and treasures scattered about. Outside, it has started to snow, might have been snowing for hours, for all he knows. White gusts hard against the panes, and it makes him cold again, seeing the storm, and he wishes he had his coat, though not enough to climb out again and hunt for it. He lies down in the straw and closes his eyes, and in a moment he's asleep.

"I used to dream I could fly," someone says, and Glitch turns around to see who, knows her name without her having to tell him, Maeve, tall and her skin like eggshell and chalk on a blazing summer sidewalk. Naked, perfect, and he looks away, back out to the smooth green sea, the high cliffs where the land drops away, the procession of white-apron men in between, plump and pigsnouted men, marching along with their cleavers and bloodstained feet.

The wind is warm and smells like salt and rain, flows around and through him, lifts him up, above the world and its taut, indifferent soul. His wings are stronger than arms could ever be. His swan voice more beautiful than Jamie's (*Fuck off*, she said. *Fuck off*, and she walked away with the rabbit and the bear and the donkey's tail in her hand), envy from wheeling gulls and kestrels and jealous pterosaurs. This shimmering freedom beyond the simple absence of restraint and the wild, wild wind draws tears from his black eyes, and they roll off his beak and fall into the sea.

Aware, then, that she's somewhere above him, her shadow and his playing tag over the waves. "*See?*" she asks him, "Isn't it beautiful?" but he's already sipping from the cup his mother has handed him, water or cherry Kool-Aid, and the kitchen is filled with their screams, his terrified brother and sisters. Child-screams from birdmouths as bones stretch and snap and bend into new shapes, as feathers burst through their bleeding skin. And Aoife says, "This one gift I can give you," sarcasm smirk, and she lights a cigarette, blows cartoon smoke rings that settle over them, and "They'll hunt you for it, though."

And then Glitch is pulling Jamie back, a handful of sweater, and she's leaning so far over the rails, through the arch of milk-pale marble into the sunset. Standing on her toes and leaning out, reaching for that last Cretaceous sunset, or Ladybird alone on the beach. His back is turned to them, and Maeve says "The others went back to their skins, when they could," but Glitch doesn't care; if there's some lesson in this screw it, he only wants to fly. And, "I couldn't give this up," she cries in notes as sharp as crystal shards and sweet as cream soda.

They ride low now, skimming inches above the whitecaps, dart and shimmer of fishsilver beneath the surface and her banking, leading him back towards shore and the tall, rough cliffs glowing orange as the western ocean swallows the sun and the clouds overhead catch fire.

"He wanted everything terrible for himself," she says, and there's Ladybird, his bare feet in the surf, wickerbrown basket of ammonite shells in his hands. The dead boy smiles and waves as they pass overhead, up past the leathery things that cling to the cliffs, and Jamie's leaning so far out that she'll fall for sure, will tumble head over fucking ass, and "He held me for a long, long time. Even after he died, he held me," and Glitch is pulling Jamie back, both of them falling to the polished museum floor, hitting hard. Glitch bites his tongue, mouthful of coins and needles, but nothing compared with the pain in his shoulder blades as she takes back his beautiful alabaster wings, tears them free, and so he holds tight to Jamie, all that's left him; holds her fiercely and will *not* let her go, pressing his face into the sticky warmth of her cheek.

And opens his eyes.

"Glitch?" she says, Jamie, standing in the mess of disemboweled crates, holding onto a stuffed and mangy dodo by one stubby leg. "Glitch?" she asks. Confused, red eyes, and "What is all this?" He blinks, freezing and stiff all over from the floor of the cage, itching from the straw. Opens his mouth to answer her, and through the bars he sees what's left of the tall display cabinet.

"I had a really bad dream," she says, but Glitch can't take his eyes off the glitter of powdered glass around the cabinet's base, the twisted stump of the armature that held shriveled gray wings. And nowhere a single fallen feather.

"God, Glitch, I miss Lady so much," and she's crying, crossing the room to him, picking through and over all the shit piled in her way. A big jar kicked over, smashed, and Glitch is crying too, realizes he's been crying since he awoke. He feels the draft before he looks up and into the bone and charcoal sky hanging low above the warehouse, and the single broken window, and the snow getting in and falling softly to the floor.

A Story for Edward Gorey

THE ALLEY SO HOT, AND ERICA'S BEEN WATCHING THE dark third-floor window for almost an hour. Dark hole left in the brickwork, dark space so cool and every now and then the lace curtain the color of purple jelly beans moves a little, stirring from the useless summer breeze or maybe someone inside. Maybe a cat stretched out fat and panting on the windowsill, all-black cat so Erica can't see it up there, can't even see its slit-green eyes looking down at her. Erica's neck is starting to hurt, watching the window so long from the alleyshadow. Another half hour and the sun will come up over the rim of the building and she'll have to find another place to stand, or sit, some place out of the noon burn. She lights her last cigarette and sits down so she can lean her head back against something, dumpster steel not yet hot, but not cool either, not like the window.

A month now since she came to Atlanta, too old to be a runaway, but the one time she blew a quarter calling home that was what her mother called her anyhow. "Mom, you can't be nineteen *and* a runaway," she said. "I'm legal," and that just made her mother cry. A month and still living on the streets, still begging spare change at Little Five Points, still sleeping wherever; sometimes lucky and someone lets her have a little bit of floor for a night or two, but mostly it's doorways and parks.

And it's still better than home and better than the shitty little white-trash planet and her shitty fast-food jobs, even now that it's turned summer proper and the nights aren't much cooler than the days. This is *still* better. Even a little sex, a couple of other baby dykes, both younger than her, jailbait girls with their redfresh piercings and sweet girlsweat smells, so much of what she left home for there between their thighs, beneath their T-shirts.

The curtain moves again and Erica doesn't take her eyes off it, pulls another mouthful from the Camel, smoke out slow through her nostrils, but the curtain doesn't move again. Not even really a curtain, just a piece of purple cloth stuck up for a curtain, filter for the sun and the black inside. Probably just nailed up there, or maybe a staple gun instead of nails, but you can't really call that a curtain.

"Shit," she whispers around the cigarette's filter, and the lace is already still again.

Three hours later and the sun up and over, heading back down, fireball pissed off at the whole goddamn world, wanting to set it on fire and coming so close, but no cigar. Three hours dodging a couple of cops and hanging around outside the stores, catching the tourists and the hipster kids spending Daddy's money on their way out or in. Better when they're on the way out, holding plastic or paper bags of clothes or shoes or CDs, red-handed, easy marks. Guilt to grease the gears— she's getting good at this, tips from Vincent and a couple of others who've been here a lot longer than she has. More than five dollars this afternoon, most of it in quarters, and the pockets of her baggy gray trousers feel ready to burst, duct tape on the seams, but they jingle a little when she walks and bump hard against her legs. She rests a few minutes in the tiny plaza across from the shop that sells crystals and wind chimes and tarot cards, brown grass and crape myrtle trees, watches the board weasels kicking around their hacky-sack ball and the Rasta woman trying to sell her beads and incense sticks.

"Hey bitch," and when she turns around it's just Bennie, little Bennie in her too-big overalls and the same L7 T-shirt worn a week now, starting to look like someone washed a car with it or something. Head shaved closer than Erica's, down to skin and just a little yellow fuzz. "Hey, Bennie," Erica says, and Bennie sits down beside her. "Got a cig?" and Bennie shakes her head no, and "Fuck. That figures."

"There's a party tonight," Bennie says and scootches closer, close enough that Erica can smell her, body odor and the vanilla oil she wears. "I don't know the people but it's supposed to be free and we could go, if you want. There'll be beer, at least, and a dj. We could dance—"

"Sure," doesn't know if she means it, the way Bennie almost always winds up getting on her nerves, but "Sure," anyway, and so a big smile from Bennie.

"Cool. Hey, look, I gotta go find someone, but let's meet back here later, okay?" Erica nods, and Bennie hugs her, quick cheek kiss, and then she's gone and the hot air still smells like her. Erica stares up at the sun through the crooked little branches and thinks about the alley and the lace curtain. Late enough there's probably shade again by now, if she can stand the stink from the dumpster. Worth the sour curry rot from the Indian restaurant's garbage, worth a little funk to watch that cool black hole.

The smell is even worse than she expected, all the fresh and not-so-fresh crap in the dumpster baked by the July sun, and she bets if she peeked inside there'd be maggots. She sits down a few feet from the dumpster and wishes she'd remembered to stop at the Jiffy Mart for smokes on her way, sucks on a pinkie finger, instead. Watches the red and chocolate bricks, dull redorange like lipstick and chocolate brown like semi-sweet Hershey bars, old bricks worn as wrinklesmooth as the skin of old women. And the black window and the purple lace. No air conditioning or the window wouldn't be open, probably, but she can imagine, knows how cool the air past that curtain must be. No heat to that quality of dark, blessed sanctuary chill of supermarkets, frozen-food aisles, heavy air, and *maybe* if she stood directly under the window some might come pouring out and down the wall, spill right over her.

And the face at the window, then, so white and sudden she jumps, startled, caught, tries to look like she wasn't sitting there staring in, peeping tom, nosy pervert. But those eyes squinting down at her, nowhere to go unless she fucking runs, and the woman says "Who are you?" Voice as cool as ice-cream sandwiches, Georgia drawl that doesn't seem to match such perfect porcelain skin.

Erica doesn't answer, tongue gone to lead, dead meat in her mouth; she just stares back, deaf-mute idiot stare until the woman shakes her head, hair so black it's hard to see, frame for that face, white hands braced on the windowsill, nails long and polished, but Erica can't tell what color.

"What? Do you think people never look out their windows?"

And Erica's talking, tongue unlocked and moving before she can hold it back. "I really like your curtains," she says, stupid, goddamn stupid thing to say, but the woman smiles at her, surprised eyebrows, and "My curtains? *This?*" and tugs at the purple lace. "You like *this?*"

"Um, yeah. I do," and before she can say anything else the woman asks, "What's your name?" so at least she can say something that makes sense. "Erica," she says. "My name's Erica," and the beautiful, pale woman in the cool black window says, "You wanna come up for a while, Erica?"

"Uhm," and Erica glances back towards the street, the asphalt melt and concrete glare, and the pale woman says, "I could fix you a glass of iced tea. If you wanna come up, I'll buzz you in. You like iced tea with mint?" and all Erica can think about is how the woman's skin would feel, white and so smooth, marble-statue chill; to be held in arms like that, arms to take away the fever for a little while. "Erica?" the woman says, and Erica nods, "Yeah. Yeah, sure."

Big freight elevator with silver walls to shine back dull; scratched and dull Erica looking back at herself in smeary reflections and above her head the constant hiss and electric fluorescent buzz. The elevator smells like old piss and makes an ugly pinging noise as it counts off the floors, two, three and the blurry Erica watching her splits down the middle, pulled apart as the doors slide reluctantly open. She steps out, anxious to be free of that clanking mirror box, steps out into the long hall and the only light up here coming in through a window way down at the other end, but bright enough that she can see the plaster walls painted dark red or maroon, worn carpeting to match. And the air stifling, soupy thick, no better than the street, maybe worse for the odors getting out past the unnumbered doors she passes, each one a different color like big dingy Easter eggs.

The blue door, the woman in the window said, but here's a door the bleached blue of empty swimming pools and the next one down gaudy bright like peacock feathers. Erica knocks on the swimming-pool door, hesitant knock, uncertain knuckles on wood, and Jesus, she's sweating, nerves and the heat and maybe this was a bad idea, maybe she shouldn't be bothering people she doesn't know. But the unlocking sounds begin before she can change her mind, safety-chain rattle and hard deadbolt click; "Hi, Erica," the woman says when the door swings open. "Come inside."

Immediate disappointment, the apartment dark, but almost as hot as the hall, stuffy and nothing but a noisy little electric fan, antique-store relic on the floor recycling the sticky air. She tries not to *look* disappointed, smiles and shakes the woman's hand, which isn't cool either. Sweatslick palm and Erica says, "It was awful nice of you to ask me up."

An hour later and Erica lying naked and exhausted on the woman's bed, black sheets, ebony wrought iron and the filmy white canopy like spider silk. A slight breeze slips in through the open window, late afternoon smells, light breeze to finger the lace curtain, and *I'm on this side*, she thinks. And it's such a strange and simple thought: *I'm on this side.*

The woman has gone to the kitchen again, gone for more of the sweet, minty tea, the woman named Isabel, and so Erica lies very still, listens to the music coming from the expensive stereo (when asked, *I mostly like rap*, she said, and the woman smiled and put on classical) and stares at the apartment around her. Mostly just this one big room filled up with furniture, as far as she can tell; stuff like she remembers from the old ladies' houses her mother used to clean back home. Burgundy-velvet sofa and high-backed chairs of dark, carved wood, something that isn't a chair or a sofa, something in between, but Erica doesn't know what it's called. Bronze lamps with softly glowing stained glass shades like wisteria and dragonflies, satin shades with beaded fringe; a huge oriental rug covering most of the floor, hardwood crust around the tattered edges, crimson and gold weave worn thin by feet and dust and time. Walls lined with tall, lighted display cabinets and a patchwork of pictures in expensive-looking frames, pictures hung almost all the way up to the tall ceiling and hardly an inch of bare wall anywhere.

The pictures are pretty, landscapes and women too beautiful to ever be real, but the cabinets are crowded with old books and bones, rocks and stoppered jars. Jars filled with murky liquid and dead things floating inside, and she doesn't like to look at them. Doesn't like to think about the staring milky eyes, or what might be in those books, so she just looks at the pictures, instead.

And then the black doll, unnoticed all this time, dangling from the ceiling near the open window. What might be a coat hanger bent open and one end run straight through its cloth body, the other end twisted closed around a small hook set into the plaster. Featureless thing, raglimp legs hanging down and no arms at all; only smooth, blank nothing where a face might be.

"Do you like Maxfield Parrish?" the woman asks, and Erica makes herself look away from the awful doll. Isabel carrying a silver serving tray and two tall glasses, tea and ice cubes and a green sprig of fresh mint on each. She sets the tray on a table beside the bed, then offers one glass to Erica. It's slippery with condensation, so cold it almost hurts to hold.

"Is that who painted all these pictures?" and the woman sits down beside her and sips from her own glass.

"Not all of them, but most," she says.

The sudden screech of tires outside, car horns, and Isabel rubs her glass across her forehead.

"That one, up there," and Erica follows her finger, grateful she's not pointing in the direction of the black doll. "That's *Salammbô*. It was painted by Gabriel Ferrier in 1881."

The painting high on the wall, a woman with skin as pale as snow, paler than Isabel's, lying on a bed and an enormous snake, a python or boa constrictor, twined tight around her body. In the background, another figure, indistinct man or woman playing what looks like a harp. The snake poised to strike or kiss and the woman, lips parted slightly, eyes half-mast, impossible to tell if that's pleasure or pain, if she's fainted, and Isabel's already pointing to another, even farther up the wall, almost lost in shadow. Erica has to strain to see.

"That one's by Antoine Magaud. I don't remember the year," and it's another woman, standing before an elaborately-framed mirror, dress down and maybe a hint of her breasts, lips pressed gently to the looking glass, to the reflection of her lips.

"It's called *A Kiss in the Glass*."

"Are they real?" and Isabel laughs, but not a mean laugh. "No, dear. They're only prints."

"Oh," and she feels so sleepy, so long since she's been this comfortable, anything like this content, and Isabel is taking the glass from her hand. "Have a nap," she says. "I hate to think where you've been sleeping," and Erica's already closing her eyes, uneasy glance back to the black doll to see it still there, and she thinks maybe she can see a place where a stitch has raveled and a bit of stuffing is poking out, cotton as black as the cloth. But she can't see it with her eyes shut, and Isabel's fingers, her long nails the color of evergreens, feel so good against Erica's scalp. Softest kiss at her ear, warmth and a whispered confidence, something Erica knows she won't remember, before she's asleep.

This old house down near the creek, through the woods behind her mother's house. Old house where a black man used to live, but doesn't, anymore. Nothing left of him now, bare floor, bare walls, ghosts of pictures marked by less-faded wallpaper patches. Wallpaper peeling like skin in calico strips and molding house bones underneath. Erica's sitting in a corner, hard wooden chair that hurts her butt, straight back and the sun so bright outside. Bright as the butterfly sparrows lighting on the eaves of busted windows, staring in, waiting.

"Hide them," the girl says, the girl that was the woman named Isabel only a moment ago, but now she's a girl, Tonya making wads from magazines at the fireplace. Pages torn and crumpled, tossed in with twigs and pine-straw tinder. "Jesus, Erica, you said nobody would know. You said nobody would ever find out."

And Tonya's striking a match, big kitchen match, wood and little redwhite sulfur head to blaze. *Scritch*, and all the magazines are burning. All the pretty women eaten by the flames, swallowed by the crackle and rising up the chimney, bare breasts and hips and lips and eyes to rising flakes of shitbrown ash. The room smells like the sun and burning paper.

"I'm sorry," she says, and "There's no point in being *sorry*, Erica," Tonya says. "Sorry's not gonna make it better. My daddy's gonna beat the shit outta me."

And the clopping sound as the little horses march across the floor, the pretty plastic horses, palominos and stallions black as midnight, ponies the color of pecans, marching to the fire. Tonya doesn't do anything to stop them; crying now and they gallop past her, more fuel for the hungry flames.

"You don't care what people think of you," Tonya sobs and smears snot and mascara with the back of her hand. "You're just a fucking dyke, anyway."

Something Erica wants to say, comfort or self-defense, but the clopping grown so loud now, so many little horses, and when she says "No, Tonya," she can't even hear herself.

"I just don't know what to do, I just don't," and why can she *still* hear Tonya? Why can't she get up and step over the fucking horses and shake Tonya and make her stop? "I just don't know," Tonya's words like the straight razor in her hand and the greenblue veins in her wrists. And Erica sees it on the mantle, then, the black doll, slumped over so the empty place where its face should be is hidden.

clop clop

"He'll send me off somewhere..." and the black doll is falling forward, tumbling (*clop clop*) into the brilliant space between the beat of tiny horseshoes, between Erica and Tonya, the sunwhite light flashing off the razor's blade, and it's a long way down to the floor.

"I *asked* you who the hell she *is*?" the man's voice says again, growls like a dog on a chain, and Erica's lying motionless beneath the sheets, head too full of the dream to think. Big man voice somewhere in the darkened room, and she can still hear the horses, their hooves against the floorboards of the old shack, so maybe she's *still* dreaming.

"She's none of your goddamn business, Eddie," and Erica knows the clopping noise is coming from the same place as the woman's voice, off towards the kitchenette, and she opens her eyes halfway. Flickering light like candles, and so it must be very late, already after dark, and she'll have missed Bennie, missed the party. The clopping stops and starts again.

No, not clopping. Chopping. She's cutting something up in there, and Erica's too afraid to move.

"If you're fuckin' the little bitch in *my* bed, it is too my goddamn business," the man says and something breaks, a muffled shower of glass across the rug, and Erica flinches but doesn't close her eyes again. Moves her head so slow until she can see the kitchen counter, Isabel's face in the glow of a white pillar candle.

"It's not *your* bed, Eddie. You don't own the bed or me, okay? You don't own shit."

And she brings the knife down again, steel into cutting-board wood, the broad butcher's blade glinting, and Erica risks another inch, her face inching slowly across the pillow.

"You're a fucking whore, Isabel," the man says, and Erica imagines the mad-dog foam on his lips, spit flying from clenched teeth, sharp mad-dog teeth. "A goddamn fucking whore. How old is *this* one, anyway? How old is she?"

The blade down and into something soft she can hardly see from the bed, meaty lumps and shreds, deepest, stringy red, wet smears on the blade as it rises again, and now there's a bit of something stuck to the metal.

"How much are we gonna have to pay this one to keep you out of jail, Isabel?"

Isabel moves, turning quickly to face the place the dog man's voice is coming from, and Erica can see her, her hair wild around her white face, wild tangle and eyes like the sky before a summer storm. And her lips sticky red, bloodsticky smear across her chin and throat.

"Get the fuck *away* from me, Eddie! *Now!*" and she's pointing the knife, arm outstretched and that blade at the end, rigid muscles trembling and more smears on her hand and arm all the way up to the elbow. "I'll cut your fucking throat if you don't leave me the hell alone!"

"Yeah, well, fuck you," he says. "Okay? *Fuck you*, Isabel. I'm not going to be here this time, all right? So fuck you. I don't care if you screw every little dyke in the whole city."

When the door slams, it sounds like a shotgun and all the pictures rattle on the walls, nervous, brittle rattle from inside the display cases, too, and Erica closes her eyes again. Doesn't want to see any more, those eyes and the raw red stains on those lips. In the dark behind her eyelids, there's only Isabel crying, loud sobs and maybe words stuck in between. And finally, bare feet across the floor, another door opening and closing before the desolate, choking sound of vomiting.

And later, an hour or longer, when there's nothing to hear but the street noise getting in through the open window and the muted voices from other apartments, Erica gets up, gathering her raggedy clothes, and she dresses quickly, moving cat-slow and as quietly as she's able, but every sound magnified times ten, anyway—bed springs and her feet, the jingle of all those quarters and nickels and dimes in the pockets of her pants.

Past the bed, and she's careful not to look into the kitchen, extra careful not to see whatever's left on the cutting board and countertop. But she does turn, not wanting to turn, and the black doll is still there, strung on its wire. The tear in its side seems wider than before, a little more of its dark stuffing showing, but that's probably only a trick of the candlelight; she turns her back on the black doll, and "I'm sorry, Isabel," whispered to the closed bathroom. When there's no answer, Erica opens the front door and pulls it silently shut behind her.

Outside, the hall is dark and very, very hot.

SALAMMBÔ

POLLEPEL ISLAND, LIKE A ROCKY BIT OF SOMETHING undigested, indigestible, in the long cold gut of the Hudson, there where the river widens past Martyr's Reach and the mistyraw hump of the Storm King. The island with its high and empty castle, abandoned almost twenty years now, and so the two sisters, great-granddaughters of the man who built the castle, lived with their mother and a meager few servants in a cottage that had been built for servants only. Not twins, and no one had ever mistaken them for twins: the youngest by four years, Salmagundi, with hair like sun spun into fine gold thread, and Salammbô, elder shadow, ripe blackberry hair, hair like a raven's eye. Both milkpale and their mother's Wedgwood eyes, their father's pretty nose and cheekbones. The haunted father who'd fled the island when the sisters were still babies, provisions made for the wife and children he'd left behind, and Coen Desvernine had drunk himself to death in Chicago, or perhaps Detroit. No one was ever certain where he'd died, but his body, the rum- and whisky-pickled fatherhusk, neatly boxed, returned and shut away in the marble row of crypts near the center of the island. The girls old enough to remember his funeral and the thing their mother had said when the minister had finished; "No one really gets away, lambs, not for long," and her eyes already beginning to show the flat and vacant, somewhere-else look.

Flowers for his grave, birthdays and Father's Day, and when the sisters were finally old enough to visit the crypts alone, they sat together, sometimes, and watched the river flowing swift around the island, as deep and icy and perfectly indifferent as the time passing them by.

"At least *I* wasn't named for a box of chocolates," an old, familiar taunt from her sister, and Salmagundi sighed, wished Salammbô would at least try to think of something original. It was true, though, that their mother had named her after a painting on an old Whitman's Sampler tin. Brennen Desvernine still had the tin, age-dulled and a little rust marring the once-bright Mucha portrait of a beautiful, blonde woman. Kept it on her nightstand with the antique copy of Flaubert's *Salammbô*, red leather spine and brittle-yellowed pages to crumble at the touch, namesake totems beside silver-framed photographs of her daughters.

The April afternoon getting in through the parlor windows, thick and bright as orange marmalade, and "At least I wasn't named for a *whore*," Salmagundi replied, not quite a whisper, and anyway, it wasn't a very good comeback, because she knew Salammbô was proud of the literary inspiration for her name.

"Not a whore," Salammbô smiling now but not bothering to look up from the *Life* magazine laid open across her lap, black-and-white photos of soldiers in Vietnam and one finger twisting in her dark hair. "A powerful priestess—"

"A very wicked, idolatrous priestess," Salmagundi interrupted, trying hard now to sound righteous, fumbling for the vicious tone her mother reserved for Democrats and hippies. "A godless, pagan *witch*."

"You talk an awful lot, baby girl," Salammbô said and turned a glossy page, President Johnson and Ladybird in Texas, then spared a quick and slicing glance at her sister, "for someone named after a box of chocolates."

Another relic, the greenhouse, hunched and hollow Victorian ruin of steel and glass erected by the sisters' great-grandfather, and, when their father was a boy, it had still been filled with lush and growing things: exotic flora from far away and always-warm places like Brazil and Madagascar, ginkgoes and tree ferns, banana plants and the drooping, fleshy blooms of the rarest varieties of wild orchid. But there had been a storm, years ago, before the girls were born, and the damage to the greenhouse had never been repaired, and its treasures had withered in the fierce New England winters. Nothing left now but dirt and broken windows, cracked terra-cotta and rusted gardening tools.

Salammbô called it "the arboretum," *her* arboretum, always, but to Salmagundi it was just the greenhouse, and she rarely went there. She disliked the crosshatch shadows and the rank, earthy smell of the disused flower beds, and, besides, it was where Salammbô kept her snakes.

She'd captured the first one three or four days after Salmagundi's eighth birthday, two years ago; a tiny garter snake she'd cornered near the house and imprisoned in an old pickle jar, holes punched through the lid for air. Salammbô had kept the snake in their bedroom at first, hiding it from the maid and their mother. There'd been the usual threats from Salammbô, and so not a word from Salmagundi, even though she felt sorry for the little thing, coiled like living ribbon at the bottom of the old Vlassic jar, waiting in their closet for the crickets and slugs her sister caught for it in the vegetable garden and smuggled upstairs in the pockets of her skirts.

Soon there'd been other jars, other garters, a big green snake she'd found in the rose bushes behind the cottage, and when her menagerie had finally, inevitably, been discovered, when she'd been ordered to release them, Salammbô had pouted, a few convincing tears, and "Yes, Mother," she'd said, and "Of course, whatever you say," before she'd simply moved them all out to the old greenhouse.

Lying in the darkness before sleep, Salmagundi had asked,

"You didn't turn them loose, did you?" and from across the room her sister, whisperhiss from the direction of Salammbô's bed, "Yes I did. I put them in your chifforobe with your panties and socks. So watch your fingers, baby girl. They'll get hungry in there." Salmagundi had known she was lying, had crouched rabbit-silent and watched her sister through the branches of a hedgerow as Salammbô had carried the jars into the greenhouse. "Liar," defiant as she'd dared, but Salammbô had laughed, and Salmagundi had worn the same underwear the next three days.

The two sisters rarely left their island, rarely crossed the dark, restless water that surrounded and defined them. Brennen Desvernine would have no talk of schools, either private or public, parochial or secular, for her daughters, not in a country sinking deeper and deeper into sexual and political anarchy. So a tutor made the trip down from Newburgh three times a week for their lessons; dour and plain and safe Miss Wesley to teach them the things their mother felt they should learn from the books she approved. Sometimes, the sisters watched from the uncertain little pier below the castle as Miss Wesley was ferried across from the river's eastern shore, the old man with his flat-bottomed boat and beard like dead moss, their only link with the world. A pair of opera glasses Salammbô had found in the top of her mother's closet and, taking turns but Salammbô's always longer, they could see Miss Wesley's shiny red Ford parked near the rocky beach, candyapple new and chrome reminder of everything forbidden.

"Scientists who study snakes?" and Miss Wesley squinted curiously at Salammbô, her scrutinizing regard that always made Salmagundi feel like something single celled and squirming beneath a microscope. "They're called herpetologists. But they don't just study snakes. They study all reptiles and amphibians: snakes, lizards, turtles, frogs, salamanders."

And Salammbô slowly repeating the word, hard-candy consideration between her tongue and palate, savoring its length and flavor, syllables like sugar.

"From the Greek *herpeton*," and Miss Wesley was always delighted when the sisters seemed to have stumbled on some line of inquiry all their own, questions unprescribed by their mother, and her next visit she brought books, subversive encouragement hidden at the bottom of her satchel. Gifts for Salammbô from a used bookshop in Newburgh: *Reptiles of the World* and *A Field Guide to Reptiles and Amphibians of Eastern and Central North America.*

So, two new sacred texts added to Salammbô's scriptures, the herpetology books to follow Flaubert, and Salmagundi watching from outside, always outside her sister's thoughts and desires, and beginning to feel cold somewhere deep in her stomach. The way she felt every year when the skies turned leadflat gray and the first snows swept down on the Hudson Highlands. The way the river sometimes made her feel, if there was too much of a particular shade of blue in the sky. Or the smell of dead roses. But dread she kept for herself, always for herself, and especially if her sister was involved.

Late into the nights, May going to June, and Salammbô reading the secret books by moonlight or flashlight or a stub of candle on their windowsill. Salmagundi lying still in her bed, listening as her sister carefully pronounced the names aloud, whispering as if she might break them, or their mother might hear; benediction of scales and teeth and claws like a chant, and sometimes Salmagundi wrapped her pillow tight about her head so she couldn't hear, scared for no reason she could understand and ashamed of her fear, but just as scared; angry at herself for not simply confessing her sister's obsession, and their teacher's thoughtless complicity, to her mother, and then maybe it would stop.

"*Thamnophis sirtalis sirtalis,*" or "*Diadophis punctatus,*" or "*Nerodia sipedon,*" a hundred others, names or phrases that meant nothing to Salmagundi, but slipped awe swollen from Salammbô's lips. As if their repetition, their correct and demanding pronunciation, had power, to hold back something terrible, or call forth something worse.

And sometimes Salmagundi imagined other sounds in the darkness, softer than her sister's voice, dry and slithering sounds across the floor, sibilant rustlings, and she would turn to face the wall, blanket over her head, and then the long wait until sleep, or morning, found her.

Pollepel an island more of stones than trees or anything else growing, and Salammbô found the flat slab of granite behind the greenhouse, one side weatherbleached and white as old bone shot through with diamond shards of mica, the other dark and muddy from soil and the messy lives of insects and worms.

Salmagundi watched from her hiding place in the hedge, half an afternoon for her sister to drag the heavy slab to the spot she wanted it, leaned like a headstone against an outside wall of the greenhouse, and another hour spent crouched over it, chipping away, brick hammer and cold chisel from a tool shed. And then Salammbô moved aside so that Salmagundi could see the shallow marks she'd cut into the sunfaded side of the stone. But there was only one she understood, one that mattered: one sinuous, arrowheaded form, and the rest just gibberish, glyphs meant for no one but Salammbô.

No one human but Salammbô, Salmagundi thought, and she knew that now there were dozens of jars in the dilapidated greenhouse, jars and impromptu terrariums her sister had made from loose panes of glass and rubber cement and screen wire. Salmagundi had watched Salammbô prowling the wild edges of the island, stolen pillowcase in one hand, an old golf club in the other. Her eyes always on the ground, and occasionally she'd stop to roll aside a big rock or break apart a rotten log. And sometimes the pillowcase was empty, and sometimes it twitched and writhed, bulged with the things she'd dragged into daylight. Cottonwhite cocoon stained with dirt and mud, and now the stone, a warning or a welcome, depending how high your belly rode above the earth.

One night, when she was absolutely certain that Salammbô was asleep, almost an hour past sure, before Salmagundi slipped out of her bed and downstairs. Floors she'd never heard a peep from before complaining loud beneath her bare feet, kitchen-door hingecreak loud enough to wake the entire house, and then she was outside. No moon, high clouds, and so maybe a storm before dawn; Salmagundi moving swiftly as she dared across the lawn, glancing back only once and there was their bedroom window, windowblack hole where her sister might be watching, invisible, where anything might be watching her sneaking progress towards the greenhouse.

The narrow swath of old trees, then, closing limbs and hun-gry leaves about her, hiding her and smothering, and in this deeper shade of night Salmagundi stumbled, stubbed a big toe against a rock, and she bit her tongue to keep from crying out. Limping the last ten or twenty yards uphill to what had once been her great-grandfather Silas' garden, grandfather Eustace's garden, and her own father had played between the rows of carefully tended shrubbery. All gone wild now, wild as the river, wild as the withdrawn and zealous distance in her sister's gray-blue eyes.

Salammbô retreating farther and farther into herself, or some other place Salmagundi couldn't follow, wouldn't even if she'd known how, until it seemed her sister had been taken away and something furtive, detached and unfathomable, left behind to fill up the dry socket. Salmagundi had never felt this alone before—the knowledge of their shared isolation on the island, but isolation is not loneliness, not necessarily. And then she'd seen the blood on Salammbô's sheets, dry smear the wounded color of pressed rose petals and almost as big as Salmagundi's hand. So much blood, but everyone acting as if nothing was wrong.

Salmagundi pushed through the last clinging tangle of briars and creeper vines, and finally the trees were behind her, the stingy bit of old growth that might recall the time before her great-grandfather came to tame the island and so might hold a grudge, might be whispering to her sister even now, *Salmagundi's gone to the greenhouse, the arboretum* and *Hurry, Salammbô, hurry or she'll see*; it wasn't hard to hear them if she listened, branchsnap words in sapgreen voices and Salmagundi shivered, summer night but still a chill. Goose-across-her-grave, and she hugged herself, ignoring her traitorous imagination. No one knew she was there, because she'd been very careful, and *Trees can't talk*, she reminded herself, *not even very old and bitter trees.*

And there was the greenhouse, then, waiting for her in the shadow that always seemed to lie pooled in the lee of the empty castle. Waiting with broken glass like shedding scales, dragon scales, dragon cold worse than fire, jagged teeth to slice and grind before burying her in its loamy gut. Weedy grass wet and slick beneath her feet, now, and she moved quick past the dry and crumbling fountain, disintegrating mermaid of concrete and wire and its court of crumbling gray fish, to the cobbled walk leading up to Salammbô's granite marker and into the greenhouse beyond.

A last glance over her shoulder, but no one and nothing there, wishing she'd brought a flashlight even though it might have given her away. The greenhouse looming above her, and Salmagundi paused at the door, squinting for a better look at what her sister had chiseled into the stone. The crude snake scraped across its center and the other marks above and below that meant no more to her up close than far away. She thought of smashing the stone, promised herself she would come back with a hammer another night and break it into a thousand pieces, scatter the pieces across the island. And then Salmagundi stepped quickly across the threshold, fast before she could change her mind, and the greenhouse accepted her.

Salammbô's jars and homemade tanks gathered together on one long table, warped pine that might once have held bright and fragrant flats of peonies or African violets, hidden way back in the best-preserved part of the greenhouse, so relatively safe from the rain and wind; Salmagundi hadn't expected there would be half this many, two or three dozen, maybe more, and each one a little box of midnight, dozens of unblinking eyes to watch her, flicking tongues, and she saw that there were candles, too, set about the table and floor, and a box of scarlet-tipped kitchen matches.

Much colder here, unaccountable cold concentrated and alive, getting in easy through her flannel robe and nightgown, settling in her bones and teeth, the space behind her eyes. Ice for her heart now, and Salmagundi knew this was the place that was taking her sister away from her, this devouring, jealous chill. Hands trembling as she was striking a match across the rough strip on one side of the box, then, no memory of even picking up the box, but the sandpaper scritch and sulfur-stinking flare anyway, light so sudden she was blind for a moment. Unsteady flame transferred to blackened wicks, one after another, while Salmagundi blinked at hovering purple blotches, and when her hand passed too near one of the larger tanks, something inside hissed loudly and the greenhouse filled with the dry and warning sound of rattling.

"Do you *like* him?" Salammbô whispered from the shadows behind Salmagundi, the night made more solid by the wavering patch of candlelight; Salmagundi did not take her eyes off the timber rattlesnake behind the glass, taut coil of muscle and bronzeflake scales, dark spots like her sister's dried menstrual blood spaced out along its back and sides. Alert and catslit eyes that followed her hand and the match burning itself down towards her fingers.

"I think he likes *you.*"

The fire reached her skin and Salmagundi cried out, dropping the match, a small sound of pain and surprise from her throat as the big snake struck, hard thump against the glass, and now Salmagundi was screaming, helpless backward topple, but her sister there to catch her. Strong arms to haul her roughly back to her feet, and she saw that the snake had already coiled again, two pus-colored streaks of venom running down the inside of the glass and the tip of its tail loud as machine gunfire in the musty closeness of the greenhouse.

"I could take him out, so you could play with him, Salmagundi. Would you like that?" and Salammbô's hands squeezing very hard around her upper arms now, hands like steel police cuffs to hold her, to force her forward. Her face held very close to the tank, and she could see the tiniest, hairline crack where the snake had hit the transparent wall of its prison; Salmagundi shut her eyes tightly, tears hot on her cheeks, and she was begging, pleading, "I'm sorry," and "I'm so sorry."

"I could *make* you sorry, you snooping little bitch."

The rattler struck the glass, and Salmagundi screamed again, opened her eyes to see that the crack had grown, concentric spider's web fracture now.

"You won't tell Mother *anything*," her sister's breath wet and warm in her right ear, "You won't say one fucking word about any of this to her or anyone else, do you understand?"

"Yes, *please, god, please*," but Salammbô still talking, spitting voice hot as the poison dripping honeyslow down the fractured glass. "I'll slip him into bed with you, Salmagundi. You'll wake one morning with him coiled up on your flat little chest, and you won't even have time to scream."

Salmagundi swearing every promise she could imagine, every oath, meaning every word, and suddenly she was free, shoved aside and landing hard on hands and knees, frantic scramble in the dirt and shattered bits of tile.

"Don't ever come back here, baby girl," Salammbô growled, and Salmagundi ran from her sister and the threats that followed her out into the night and trailed her across the ruined garden and into the trees.

Air that smelled like dead fish and muddy little snails, the river lapping hungry at the breakwater, and the sisters sat together with the pilfered opera glasses, the old ritual observed for the first time in weeks, watching Miss Wesley and the ferryman, the red car sparkling on the far shore. Usually, the car made Salmagundi think of running away, escaping and how it would feel not to spend each long night alone with Salammbô, and she remembered that there had been a time when the car made her think of other things, but she wasn't sure anymore what those other things might have been.

Dreaming, Salmagundi is standing on her father's crypt, high and craggy roof of the island and such an awful place to put the dead, ground too stony for digging graves so these marble crates instead; neat rows, names and dates and all the family's departed around her. Faintest silent hint of their old comfort; the sun almost down, midsummer dusk, and she's watching fireflies dance like fairies behind the castle, the castle where night always comes early. The fireflies are huge, chartreuse-blinking carnival bulbs, and she can hear the barker's voice drifting urgently on the warm, river-scented breeze, can hear other voices, too, and so Salmagundi climbs down, marble steps the ripening color of cheese or rotting under water that lead her between the trees, past their cottage, and there's her mother and a maid and Miss Wesley watching her go. Her mother at the window, and Salmagundi smiles and waves before her mother turns away.

"From the Greek," Miss Wesley calls after her, and she can see that the fireflies really are incandescent bulbs, hundreds strung in the overgrown garden and the big tent set up where the greenhouse used to be, before she told Miss Wesley and her mother called the workmen from Cornwall to tear it down. Tent like an empty skin of something giant and the garish tattoos across its canvas hide: SEE! WONDERS OF THE ANCIENTS! and SEE! MYSTERIES OF SCIENCE—FREAKS OF NATURE! A man like a living skeleton and an impossibly fat woman holding hands; SHOCKING ELECTRA and another painting, a girl not much older than Salmagundi, both arms raised to a stormblack sky and lightning forking down, HUMAN LIGHTNING ROD, acrylic-bright fire twined sizzling about her wrists and arms.

The crowd dissolves, melts, and Salmagundi is alone again, alone with the tent where the greenhouse isn't anymore; behind her, the castle whispers, mortar and musty derelict-hallway caution she doesn't understand, the secret language of abandoned houses, before the tent opens itself wide for her, canvas flayed back, batwing flap, and she's already inside; dark and narrow aisle, the parching reek of alcohol. There are things around her, still and taxidermied things, and she keeps her eyes on the sawdust floor.

"He swallows every time," a man mumbles, "every time," and Salmagundi risks a glimpse at the pit, quick impression of naked skin and blood, drifting rain of feathers and coins thrown from cigarette-smoke clouds; she keeps moving. "From the geek," Miss Wesley says, and they're standing together before a great tank, elaborate cast iron and carved wood to frame thick plate glass. Grass-sweet smell of straw, filthy straw to cover the floor of the tank, and the thing inside looks up and out at them with lidless eyes, vertical pupils and grayblue irises. Not even stumps, greasepaint scales to hide scarred shoulders and chest, a leathery stocking cinched about its waist so the legs don't matter, and the thing in the tank trails away into the shadows. Might go on that way forever, its tail lost somewhere in the molten core of the world.

"I want to go," she says, and Miss Wesley squeezes her hand tight. "I want to go *now*."

"In a just moment, dear. We've already paid for our tickets," and Salmagundi has to look away, then, because the thing in the tank is trying to speak, even though its new tongue is much too long, too many teeth. And there's Salammbô, and she's smiling a cruel and gentle smile for Salmagundi, and she holds the knife in her hands.

Salmagundi awoke and lay listening to the heavy, calming sound her heart made in the darkness of the bedroom, almost a quarter past three by the softly glowing Mickey Mouse and Pluto alarm clock; the curtains had been left drawn so that she couldn't see the stars above Pollepel Island, the velvetwide Appalachian sky and she was glad for that. She could see that Salammbô's bed was empty, pillow lumps arranged carefully beneath the covers, just in case anyone looked in on them. Too easy to imagine the candle glow from the greenhouse, too hard not to think of Salammbô, alone and busy in the night. So she stared at the clock, its ticking grown louder or her heart grown quieter, played number games with its face, circumference and diameter, until the dream faded and she slept again.

Salmagundi stood alone beneath the dead copperhead in the little row of cherry trees at the end of the yard. Tiptoe stretch, and if she dared, she could almost touch the end of its tail. Lifeless chain of autumn orange and brown and the darker slash across its spine from the blade of Mr. Tom's hoe. The handyman had killed it that morning and put it there, a certain charm against the high and emptyblue sky, the two weeks now without rain, air dry enough to burn and the vegetables beginning to wither in the sweaty last-week scorch of July.

"We're not a superstitious family, Mr. Tom," her mother had told him. "I don't like to encourage that sort of thing." Salmagundi listening from the window seat where she'd been trying to read Nancy Drew, but too heatdazzled to concentrate, and so she'd kept reading the same paragraph over and over again.

"Honestly, I'd rather you just got rid of it."

"Oh, that's not a superstition, Ma'am," and Salmagundi had caught the faintest hint of Mr. Tom through the open window, pleasant reek of snuff and chewing gum, aftershave and hair oil; she'd often wondered if that's the way her father had smelled. "Hang a dead snake in a tree when you need rain. I've seen it work," and he'd started across the lawn towards the gate, the hoe over one shoulder like a soldier's rifle and the copperhead draped across the end, limp head and tail swinging back and forth as he walked away.

"Then at least put it somewhere the children won't find it," and Mr. Tom had called back, "Yes, Ma'am."

One hand flat against the trunk of the cherry tree to steady herself, and if she had another half-inch her index finger would brush against it. Her mouth cottondry at the thought, those rough, cold scales against her skin, but *It's only meat now,* she told herself again, dead meat for the flies and ants, but scared anyway, and the half inch might as well have been another foot, another ten feet.

"Did *you* do that?" and Salmagundi jumped, almost losing her balance, almost falling as she turned around too fast to find Salammbô standing there. Hands clenched and something frantic in her eyes that Salmagundi had never seen before

"No," and Salmagundi was shaking her head, insistent, stepping away from the tree, away from Salammbô. "It was Mr. Tom, I swear. I can't even reach that high, and—"

"*Liar,*" vicious sound from her sister's throat, sound meant to hurt, to scar, threatful growl like a cat makes hanging onto a dying mouse. "I *saw* you put it there. I watched you, Salmagundi."

And Salammbô's hand too quick to see, snake-strike punch and the saltywarm taste of blood in Salmagundi's mouth before she was even sure what had happened.

"Go *on!* Run, you murderous little bitch! Run away and tell Mother!" Salammbô was screaming, shrieking, and she bent down, furiously gathering rocks with both hands.

"I swear to God, it wasn't me. I didn't do it," and Salammbô rising, hands full and nothing in her eyes like belief or mercy. So Salmagundi ran, but not back towards the house, a mindless, terrified dash instead towards the castle and the first rock that Salammbô hurled buzzed past her left ear like an angry red wasp. It struck the ground somewhere in front of her, and a second later, another; hot and stinging slash across her right shoulder just before she reached a low stone wall and scrambled behind it. Still in range and the missiles raining down around her, bouncing loud off the wall, digging ragged furrows in the dirt, wounds meant for flesh, and she made herself very small, arms around her knees, head down tight.

"I didn't do it, Salammbô, I didn't do it," desperate pleading litany through snot and tears and blood, but no one to hear her now, and nothing to do but wait until the rocks stopped falling from the sky.

Salammbô buried the copperhead in the greenhouse, shallow grave scraped out with her hands and then the earth pushed back into place, an old piece of corrugated tin and some broken slate roofing tiles piled on top so nothing could dig it up again.

Salmagundi watched from her old hiding place in the hedge, dull throb starting in her shoulder, muscles bruised and stiffening, something broken, perhaps. She could tell that Salammbô knew she was there, had seen her following all the way up from the cherry trees or had maybe felt her sister's eyes; occasionally Salammbô would pause and glance towards Salmagundi, black hair sweatplastered to cheeks flushed the color of beet-stained linen, eyes swollen and red from crying for the dead snake. Baleful, acid glances that said more than words ever could, the promise that this crime was past forgiving, and Salmagundi knew there would be no convincing Salammbô that she was innocent. No way she could go to Mr. Tom or her mother without revealing her sister's secrets, so she was damned either way.

After Salammbô had stacked the last weathered bit of tile, she sat beside the grave and read aloud from a book, nothing Salmagundi recognized and too far away to make out the cover or even follow the words, just the hoarse and hitching rhythm of her sister's voice. Before Salammbô finished, there was thunder, a sudden rumble from off towards Newburgh Bay, and a light rain began to fall.

A week later, Salmagundi had sat alone and watched the ferryman bringing Miss Wesley across the deep and narrow eastern channel separating Pollepel Island from the mainland. A strong, warm wind in her hair and no sign of Salammbô. Her sister hadn't shown up for their lessons, either, and by sunset their mother had been near panic. An exhausting search of the cottage and the grounds had turned up nothing. Salmagundi had gone with her mother to the greenhouse and all the tanks were there, all the jars, but every one of them empty now, and her mother had not stopped to ask what they meant, if she'd even noticed them.

Next morning, and the sheriff arriving before dawn, the sheriff and sheriff's deputy of Duchess County and twelve men with them, and they'd combed the island, had finally searched the castle itself. Nothing found, though, and for days the river around and below the island had been dragged. After a week, the sheriff had shaken his head and taken his men away; there had been no funeral, no death certificate, no evidence that she was dead, and Brennen Desvernine refused to admit even the possibility. But Adrian Cotswold, the ferryman, quit soon afterwards, and when questioned by the police, he admitted to having given the girl a ride across for thirty-five dollars and some change. Said that Salammbô had told him she was only planning to hitchhike into Newburgh for a movie, specifically *Bandolero!* with Jimmy Stewart and Raquel Welch, she'd said, and so they let him go. There were private detectives retained in Albany and Manhattan, but, while their services had cost the family a considerable portion of its dwindling finances, they'd never found any sign of the missing sister.

And the river took no notice, rolled on through its gneiss and granite trough carved twenty thousand years before by the grinding weight of ice two miles thick. And on the island,

Salmagundi grew towards womanhood, time-lapse metamorphosis, fifteen already when a tattered postcard came to Pollepel from Los Angeles. Cheerful cartoon sun, cartoon-broad grin and black sunglasses, shining down on palm trees and bare-chested boys on surfboards. The card left on her bed, anonymously, and for a long time she only sat and stared at it, ink as unintelligible as Sanskrit, at first, too much to believe, the airmail stamp and smudged postmark—May 17, 1973—and finally, she read it aloud, once and then again and again: "It isn't true, Sal, what Mother said at Father's funeral. We *can* get away. Love, always, your sister, Salammbô D.," and nothing else. No return address.

Just before dark, Salmagundi took the postcard with her to the greenhouse where she often spent evenings, reading by candlelight, and she read the postcard again, aloud, to the empty jars and tanks, still where her sister had left them, to the grave of the long-dead copperhead. And then she sat and listened to the night, the frog- and cricketwhisper sounds of another spring coming to the island. Sometime before dawn she dozed, and dreamed of sandy, far-away beaches, and snakes sunning themselves on desert rocks.

> *Wearied at last with her thoughts she would rise...*
> —Gustave Flaubert, *Salammbô* (1862)

PAEDOMORPHOSIS

Nasty cold for late May, rain like March; Annie sat on one of the scrungy old sofas at the front of the coffeehouse, sipping at her cappuccino, milkpale and bittersweet, savoring the warmth bleeding into her hands from the tall mug. The warmth really better than the coffee, which always made her shaky, queasy stomach if she wasn't careful to eat something first. Beyond the plate glass, Athens gray enough for London or Dublin, wet Georgia spring hanging on, Washington Street asphalt shimmering wet and rough and iridescent stains from the cars passing by or parked out front. The rest of the band late as usual, but no point getting pissed over it, baby dykes living in their own private time zone. Annie lit another cigarette and reminded herself that she really was cutting back, too expensive and no good for her voice, besides.

The door opened, then, and the cold rushing in, sudden rainsmell clean to mix with the caffeinated atmosphere of Bean Soup, air forever thick with the brown aroma of roasting beans and fresh brewing. Jingled cowbell shut again, Ginger and Mary and Cooper in one soggy clump, stupid happy grin on Mary's face and Cooper sulking, wet-hen disgust, and she set her guitar case down beside Annie.

"What's with this fucking weather, man, that's what I want to know? I think my socks have fucking mildewed."

"Maybe if you changed them every now and then," Ginger sniggered, and Mary giggled; Cooper groaned, shook her head and "These two have been sucking at the weed all afternoon, Annie," she said. "It's a wonder I finally pried them away from the bong." Mary and Ginger were both giggling now.

"Well, you know I got all day," Annie said over the steaming rim of her mug, and that was true, three days now since she'd quit her job at the diner, quit before they fired her for refusing to remove the ring in her right eyebrow.

"Yeah, well, I'm about ready to kick both their stoner asses, myself," and another hot glance back at the drummer and bass player, Ginger and Mary still blocking the doorway, sopping wet and laughing. "I'm gonna get some coffee. *You* see if you can do something with them."

"Okay, ladies, you know it's not nice to pester the butch," and of course that only got them laughing that much harder, and Annie couldn't help but smile. Feeling a little better already, something to take her mind off the low and steelblue clouds as cold and insubstantial as her mood.

"She's such a clodosaurus," Mary said, tears from giggling and she stuck her tongue out at Cooper, in line at the bar and her back to them, anyway. "Hey, can you spare one of those?" and Mary was already fishing a Camel from Annie's half-empty pack.

"No, actually, but help yourself," and Cooper on her way back now, weaving through the murmuring afternoon crowd of students and slackers, Cooper with her banana-yellow buzzcut and Joan Jett T-shirt two sizes too small to show off her scrawny muscles. Annie still amazed that their friendship had survived the breakup, and sometimes, like now, still missing Cooper so bad it hurt.

"Thank you. I will," and then Mary bummed a light from Ginger.

Cooper sat down in a chair across from them, perched on the edge of cranberry naugahyde and sipped at her mug of black, unsweetened Colombian, plain as it got, no decaf pussy drinks for Cooper.

"They still going at it down there?" and Cooper stomped at the floor like a horse counting, and Annie nodded, "Yeah, but I think they're winding up."

And "*See,*" Ginger said, mock-haughty sneer for Cooper, "it's a *good* thing we were late. The sad widdle goffs ain't even done yet," and Cooper shrugged, "Unh huh," and she blew on her coffee. "We gotta find another fucking place to practice."

Honeycomb of identical rooms, gray cubicles beneath Bean Soup rented out for practice space, but down here the cozy scent of fresh-ground espresso replaced by the musty smell of the chalk-white mushrooms they sometimes found growing in the corners, the mildew and dust laid down like seafloor sediment.

Concrete poured seventy or eighty years ago, that long since the sun into this space, never mind the single hundred-watt bulb dangling from the ceiling. Something painful bright but not light, stark illumination for the sickly little room so that they could see to tighten wing nuts and tune instruments, so Annie could read lyrics not yet memorized from her scribbly notes. Ten feet by ten, or that's what they paid for every month, but Annie had her doubts, maybe a different geometry than her idea of ten square. But at least the steel fire door locked and the pipes that laced the low ceiling like the coffeehouse's varicose intestines had never broken. Enough electrical outlets(when they'd added a couple of extension cords) for their monitors and Mary's dinky mixing board.

Thick layers of foam rubber glued to the walls, Salvation Army blankets stapled over that, and they still couldn't start practice until Seven Deadlies had finished. No way of shutting out the goth band's frantic nextdoor drone and "Those assholes have the bitchmother off all subwoofers crammed in there," Cooper had said more than once, an observation she must have thought bore repeating. Sound you could feel in your bowels, bass to rattle bones and teeth, that passed straight through concrete and the useless soundproofing.

Complaints from some of the other bands, but Annie thought it was a shitty, pointless thing to do, bitching about another band playing "too loud," and besides, the complaints all summarily ignored. So TranSister always waited until Seven Deadlies were done for the afternoon before they started. Simpler solution and no toes stepped on, no fear of petty reprisals.

One long and narrow hall connecting all the cubicles, cheapest latex maroon coming off the walls in big scaly flakes, and TranSister's space way down at the end. Passing most of Seven Deadlies on their way out (eight of them, despite the name), painful skinny boys and girls, uncertain androgynes with alabaster faces and kohlsmudged eyes. Pretty in their broken porcelain ways and usually only the most obligatory conversation, clash of subcultures, and Cooper sometimes made faces behind their backs. But one of the girls waiting for them this time, tall, thin girl in fishnets and a ratty black T-shirt, Bauhaus and a print Annie knew came from *The Cabinet of Dr. Caligari*, tall girl with her cello zipped snug inside its body-bag cover.

"Hi," she said, shy but confident smile, and Annie said hi back, struggling with the key, and she could feel Cooper already getting impatient behind her.

"I'm Elise," she said, was shaking Mary's hand. "Would you guys mind if I hang around and listen for a while?"

Immediate and discouraging grunt from Cooper, and Mary said, quick, "I don't know. It's really pretty close in there already and all..." and Elise countering, satin voice and a smile to melt butter, "I don't take up much room, honest. And I can leave this in our space," pointing to her instrument. Before another word, "Sure," from Annie, and to the others, "She can sit in the big chair, okay?"

"Yeah," half a snarl from Cooper. "She can sit in the big chair. Right," and pushing her way past Annie, unlocking the door and inside, Mary and Ginger pulled along sheepish in her wake.

Five times through the set, a couple of the newer songs more than that, only three nights until they opened for Lydia Lunch and Michele Malone at the 40-Watt Club, and everyone was getting nervy. Finally too tired for any more and Annie too hoarse, Ginger's Sailor Moon T-shirt soaked straight through so you could see she wasn't wearing a bra. Cooper and Mary dripping sweat, dark stains on the concrete at their feet. Annie had left the door open, against the rules, but hoping that some of the stormdamp air from above might leak down their way.

Cooper sat on the floor and lit a cigarette, smoke ring aimed at the light bulb, and she pointed a finger at Elise.

"Damn, girl, don't you fucking sweat?" and getting nothing but that mockshy smile back, Elise who'd sat quietly through the entire practice, legs folded in a half-hearted lotus on the broken-down recliner, slightest shrug of her black shoulders.

"Well, I do," said Mary, propping her Barbie-pink Gibson bass against the wall, static whine before she switched off her kit. "I sweat like a goddamn pig," and she made loud, oinking noises for emphasis.

"Well, whatever, but you can fuck this heat," Cooper calling it a night, so time for a beer at the Engine Room; hazy, cramped bar next door to Bean Soup, pool tables and Mortal Combat, PBR by the pitcher half-price because Cooper once had a thing with one of the bartenders.

Annie sat on the arm of the recliner next to Elise, top twisted off her water bottle, and she took a long swallow. Bottle that had once upon a time held water from "wild Canadian springs," but recycled from the tap in her apartment time after time, and now it tasted mostly like warm plastic and chlorine. Something to take the edge off the dryness in her throat, at least; she glanced down at Elise, had glanced at her a lot while TranSister had punched and yowled their way through carefully re-hearsed riot grrrl anger. And every time, Elise had been watching her, too, enough to make Annie blush, and maybe she was starting to feel horny for the first time since she and Cooper had called it quits.

"What about it?" she asked Elise. "Wanna go get a beer with us?"

"I don't drink alcohol," and Ginger rolling her eyes, squeezed herself out from behind her drums and past the big chair. "Well, they got Cokes and stuff, too," she said.

"Hey, we'll catch up with you guys in a little bit, okay?" Annie said, braver than she'd felt in months, the rest of the band exchanging knowing looks, but at least they waited until they were all three in the hall to start snickering.

"Sorry about that," when they were gone and feeling like maybe they'd taken her new boldness with them, so another drink from the bottle because she didn't know what else to do or say.

"That's okay. I understand," and Elise's voice cool and smooth and sly as milk on broken glass.

"Thank god," and Annie sighed, relief and now maybe her heart could slow the fuck down. "I was afraid maybe I was making an ass of myself."

"Nope," Elise said, up onto her knees now and her lips brushing Annie's. "Not at all. Want to see something neat?"

The space where Seven Deadlies practiced like a weird xerox, the same four walls, the same pipes snaking overhead, same mushroomy funk. But these walls painted shiny black and draped in midnight velvet (or at least velveteen), a wrought iron candelabra in one corner and plaster saints in the other three. Dusty, threadbare Turkish rug to cover the entire floor, a hundred faded shades of red and orange and tan, the overall design obscured by speakers and keyboard stands; a wooden table made from two saw horses and an old door, crowded with computers and digital effects equipment.

"Shit, did one of you guys win the Lotto?" and Elise laughed, shut the door behind them. "Jacob, our vocalist, comes from money," she said. "The old Southern type. It comes in handy."

Annie nodded, "With all this gear, no wonder you guys can make such a racket."

"Mostly we're working with MIDI programs right now," Elise said, standing just behind Annie, and for the first time she noticed the heady, sweet reek of vanilla off the girl, and something else, something wild that made her think of weekends at her parents' river cabin when she was a kid.

"You know, Sound Forge and some other stuff. Lots of sampling," Elise was saying, "on Jacob's Mac."

"I don't know shit about computers," Annie said, which was true, not just a line to get away from shop talk, and Elise smiled, another kiss on Annie's cheek. And that smell stronger than before, or maybe she was just noticing it now.

"Anyway, I wanted to show you something," and Elise stepped past her, past the computers, and she was folding back a section of the velvet (or velveteen) curtain. "Down here."

Annie followed, six steps to the other side of the room and then she could see the crack in the concrete wall, a foot wide, perhaps a little more where it met the floor, stooping for a better view, and *This is where it's coming from*, she thought. The waterlogged, mudflat smell of boathouses and turtles, and she wrinkled her nose at the dark inside the hole, the fetid air drifting from the crack.

"Man, what a mondo stinkorama," trying too hard to sound funny, and Annie realized that she was sweating, cold sweat and goosebumps and no idea why. Something triggered by the stench from behind the wall, a memory she wasn't quite remembering or something deeper, maybe, primal response to this association of darkness and the rotting, wet smell.

"Oh, it's not that bad," Elise said, taking Annie's hand, and she slipped through the hole, gone, like the concrete wall had swallowed her alive and there was nothing left in the world but one arm, detached, silver bracelet and ragged black nails, one hand still holding Annie's tight.

"Aren't you coming?" she asked. "Don't you want to see?" Elise's voice muffled and that speaking-in-an-empty-room quality to it now, sounding much farther away than she should've. "No," Annie said. "Not really, now that you mention it." But a tug from Elise, and she almost pitched forward, one hand out so she didn't smack her forehead on the wall. Sweatcool palm against cold cement and a sudden gust or draft from the crack, stale pocket dislodged by Elise, and Annie was beginning to feel a little nauseous.

"I'm *serious*," she said, tugging back, and Elise's white face appeared in the crack, irked frown for Annie like something from an old nightmare, like the sleepwalker on her T-shirt.

"I thought dykes were supposed to be all tough and fearless and shit," she said.

Annie shook her head, swallowed before she spoke. "Big ol' misconception. Right up there with the ones about us all wanting dicks and pickup trucks."

Elise was crawling out of the crack, dragging more of that smell out behind her, dustgray smears on her black shirt, dust on her Doc Marten's and a strand of cobweb stuck in her hair.

"Sorry," she said, but smiling now like maybe she really wasn't sorry at all. "I guess I just don't think about people being bothered by stuff like that. My dad's a paleontologist, and I spent a lot of time as a kid crawling around in old caves and sinkholes."

"Oh," Annie said and sat down on the rug, grateful for something between her and the concrete. "Where are you from, anyway?"

The loose flap of cloth falling back in place, once again concealing the crack. "Massachusetts," Elise replied, "but no place you've probably ever heard of."

"Yeah, like Athens is the white-hot center of the solar system," and a dry laugh from Annie, then, laughing just to make herself feel better, and she fluttered her eyelashes, affected an air-headed falsetto, "'*Athens*? Athens, *Georgia*? Isn't that where R.E.M.'s from?'"

"And the B-52s," Elise added, sitting next to Annie. "Don't forget the B-52s," and "Yes," Annie agreed. "*And* the stinkin' B-52s." Both of them laughing and Annie's abrupt uneasiness fading almost as fast as it had come, only the slimmest silver jangle left in her head, and Elise bent close, kissed her and this time their tongues brushed, fleeting, teasing brush between mouths before she pulled away.

"Play some of your stuff for me," Annie said, and when Elise looked doubtfully towards her cello, "No, no, no. A tape or something," and Annie motioned towards the black cabinets and consoles, row upon numbered row of dials and gauges. "With all these cool toys, surely you guys have put something down on tape by now," and Elise nodding, still doubtful but *yes*, anyway; she stood, began digging about on the door *cum* table, loud and brittle clatter of empty cassette cases, and a moment later she slipped a DAT cartridge into one of the machines.

"Jacob would probably have a seizure if he knew I was fucking around with this stuff," she said.

And nothing at first, at least nothing Annie could hear, and then the whisperchirp of crickets and more faintly, a measured dripping, water into water. Elise returned to her spot on the floor next to Annie, an amber prescription bottle in her hand. "You *do* get stoned, don't you?"

The crickets getting louder by degrees, droning insect chorus, and Annie thought she could hear strings buried somewhere in the mix, subliminal suggestion of strings, but the dripping still clear, distinct *plop* and more distinct space between each drop's fall.

"Mostly pot," Annie said, and Elise had popped the cap off the bottle, shook two powder-blue pills into her open palm. "This is better," she said. And Annie already feeling like a pussy for not following her into the hole in the wall, so accepting the pills, dry swallowing both before she had a chance to think better of it.

"What are they?"

Elise shrugged, "Mostly codeine, I think. One of our keyboardists gets them from her mother." Then three of the tablets for herself before she screwed the cap back on the bottle and tossed it back onto the table.

"Okay, now listen to this part," and Annie's attention returning to the tape: the crickets fading away, but there were new sounds to take their place: a slow, shrill trilling, and then another, similar but maybe half an octave higher; a synth drum track almost as subtle as the strings.

"Are those *frogs*?" Annie asked, confused, wishing she had her water bottle because one of the mystery pills had stuck halfway down, and Elise shook her head. "No," she said. "Toads."

Later, but no sense left for her to know how much later, wrapped up tight in the twin silken embrace of Elise and the pills, time become as indefinite as the strange music that had swelled until it was so much bigger than the room. Understanding, now, how this music could not be held within shabby concrete walls. Feral symphony and Annie listening, helpless not to listen, while it took her down and apart and Elise made love to her on the shimmering carpet like all the colors of autumn lying beneath still and murky waters. Held weightless between surface tension and siltdappled leaves; the certain knowledge of dangerous, hungry things watching them from above and below, but sanctuary found in this girl's arms.

And the second time Elise offered to show her what was on the other side of the wall, Annie didn't say yes, but she didn't say no, either; dim sense that she'd acted silly earlier, afraid of the dark and getting her hands dirty. Elise still in her shirt, but nothing else, Annie in nothing at all, and she followed, neither eager nor reluctant, scraped her shoulder squeezing through, but the pain at least a hundred harmless miles away.

"Watch your head," Elise whispered, library whisper like someone might overhear. "The ceiling's low through here."

So hands and knees at first, slow crawl forward, inch by inch and the muddy smell so strong it seemed to cling to Annie's bare skin, scent as solid as the cobwebs tangling in her hair. A vague sense that they were no longer just moving ahead, but down as well, gentle, sloping descent and then the shaft turned sharply, and Annie paused, "Wait," straining to see over her shoulder. Pinhead glimmer back the way they'd come, flyspeck of light like the sun getting around an eclipse and a sudden, hollow feeling in her gut that made her wish they had stayed in the warm pool of the Turkish carpet, tadpole shallows, drifting between the violins and keys, the twilight-pond sounds.

"It's so far back," she said, the compressing weight of distance making her voice small. "No," Elise replied. "It's not much farther at all."

Finally, the shaft opening wide and they could sit up, the impression of a vast and open space before them and the unsteady flame of the single pillar candle Elise had brought from the room revealing high, uneven walls to either side, old bricks wet and hairy with the colorless growth of some fungus or algae that had no need of sunlight or fresh air. "Be careful," Elise said and her arm out and across Annie's chest like a roller coaster safety bar, and she saw that they were sitting on a concrete ledge where the crawl space ended abruptly. Short drop down to rubble and the glint of water beyond that.

"Where are we?" and Annie heard the awe in her voice, little girl at the museum staring up at a jumble of old bones and daggerteeth awe; Elise pointed up, "Right beneath the old Morton Theater," she said. "But this goes on a long way, beneath most of downtown, and *that* way," and now she pointed straight ahead of them, "that way goes straight to the Oconee River. Old basements and subbasements, mostly. Some sewer lines. I think some of it must be pre-Civil War, at least," and Annie wished halfheartedly she wasn't so fucked up, so she could remember how long ago that was.

And then Elise was helping her down off the ledge, three or four feet to an unsteady marble slab, and then showing her the safer places to put her feet among the heap of broken masonry.

"I never had any idea all this was down here," Annie said and realized that she had started crying, and Elise kissed her tears, softest flick of her tongue as if salt might be too precious to waste. "No one ever has any idea what's below their feet," she said. "Well, *hardly* ever, anyway."

Misstep, ankletwist, and Annie almost fell, but Elise there to catch her. "Are you okay?" but Annie only nodding her head, guessing she must be since nothing hurt. A few more careful, teetering steps and they were already to the black water, mirrorsmooth lake like glass or a sky without stars or moon. And Annie sat down again, winded and dizzy, a little queasy, and that was probably the pills, the pills and the smell. "How deep?" and Elise smiled, Elise holding the candle out above the surface, and the water stretched away as far as they could see. "That depends. Only a few feet right here, but a lot deeper in other places. Places where the roofs of subbasements have fallen in and the structures below have been submerged."

"Shit," Annie muttered, her ass cold against the stones, and she hugged herself for warmth.

"There are a lot of cool things down here, Annie," and Elise was crouched right at the water's edge now, one hand dipped beneath the surface, spreading ripples that raced quickly away from the candlelight.

"Things that have gotten in from streams and rivers and been down here so long they've lost their eyes. Beautiful albino salamanders and crayfish," she said, "and other things." She was tugging her shirt off over her head, the candle set carefully aside, and it occurred to Annie how completely dark it would be if the flame went out.

"Want to swim with me, Annie?" Elise asked, seductive coy but Annie shivered, not the damp air or her nakedness but remembering now, swimming with a cousin when she was nine years old, a flooded quarry near her house where kids skinny-dipped and thieves dumped the stripped hulks of cars and trucks. Being in that water, beneath glaring July sun, but not being able to see her feet, dog paddling and something slimy had brushed fast across her legs.

"I'll wait here," she said and reached for the candle, held it close and the flame shielded with one hand, protective barrier between the tiny flame and any draft or errant breeze, between herself and the native blindness of this place.

"Suit yourself," and there was a loud splash before Elise vanished beneath the black surface of the pool. More ripples and then the surface healing itself, ebony skin as smooth as before and Annie left alone on the shore. Every now and then a spatter or splash that seemed to come from very far away, Annie feeling sleepy and the pills playing with her sense of distance, she knew. Trying not to think of how filthy the water must be, everything washed down sinks and toilets and storm drains to settle here. But Elise would be back soon, and then they could leave, and so Annie closed her eyes.

Sometime later, a minute or an hour, and she opened them again, headachy and neckstiff, the nausea worse; Elise was there, dripping, and her hands cupped together, something held inside them for Annie to see. Something fetal the pinkwhite of an old scar, floating indifferent in the pool of Elise's hands, and she said, "Isn't she wonderful? She looks a little like *Gyrinophilus palleucus*, but more likely she's a whole new species. I'll have to send one back to my father."

And then the salamander released, poured from her hands back into the lake, and she bent to kiss Annie. Slick arms around Annie's waist and lips so cold, so wet they might be a drowned girl's, drowned Ophelia risen, *And will 'a not come again, and will 'a not come again*; faint and fishy taste passed from Elise's mouth, and she pulled away, was reaching for her T-shirt, lying where she'd left it on the rocks.

"You should have come. I really hope you didn't get bored," she said. Annie shook her head.

Elise lifting her arms, and Annie saw the crimson slits where her armpits should be, the feathered edges bright with oxygen-rich blood, gasping slits like twin and puckered mouths, and then the Bauhaus shirt down, and Annie almost made it to the edge of the water before she vomited.

The last week of June and TranSister moved their gear into a new space across town, a big loft above a pizza place, the rent too high but they were sharing the cost with two other groups. And the wet weather passed into the blistering swelter of early summer, and Annie stayed away from Bean Soup. There were other coffeehouses, and when she saw Elise on the street she smiled, polite recognition, but never spoke. A few prying questions from Mary and Ginger, but she only had to tell them once to shut the fuck up.

And sometimes, late at night and especially when the summer storms came riding high and swift across the land and the sky rumbled like it was angry at the world, she would lie awake in her apartment on Pulaski, trying not to remember the throbbing, amphibian voices threaded into the fabric of Seven Deadlies' music, *Elise's* music, trying not to think about the vast and empty spaces that might sprawl somewhere beneath her. And unable to think about anything else.

There are strange things living in the pools and lakes in the hearts of mountains...

—J. R. R. Tolkien (1937)

POSTCARDS FROM THE KING OF TIDES

HERE'S THE SCENE: THE THREE DARK CHILDREN, THREE souls past twenty but still adrift in the jaggedsmooth limbo of childhoods extended by chance and choice and circumstance, their clothes impeccable rags of night sewn with thread the color of ravens and anthracite; two of them fair, a boy and a girl and the stain of protracted innocence strongest on them; the third a mean scrap of girlflesh with a blacklipped smile and a heart to make holes in the resolve of the most jaded nihilist, but still as much a child as her companions. And she sits behind the wheel of the old car, her sagegray eyes staring straight ahead of her, matching their laughter with seething determination and annoyance, and there's brightdark music, and the forest flowing around them, older times ten hundred than anything else alive.

The winding, long drive back from Seattle, almost two days now, and Highway 101 has become this narrow asphalt snake curving and recurving through the redwood wilderness, and they're still not even as far as San Francisco. Probably won't see the city before dark, Tam thinks, headachy behind the wheel and her black sunglasses because she doesn't trust either of the twins to drive. Neither Lark nor Crispin have their licenses, and it's not even her car; Magwitch's piece-of-shit Chevrolet Impala, antique '70s junk heap that might have been the murky

green of cold pea soup a long, long time ago. Now it's mostly rust and bondo and one off-white door on the driver's side. A thousand bumper stickers to hold it all together.

"Oooh," Lark whispers, awevoiced, as she cranes her neck to see through the trees rushing past, the craggy coast visible in brief glimpses between their trunks and branches. Her head stuck out the window, the wind whipping at her fine, silkwhite hair, and Tam thinks how she looks like a dog, a stupid, slobbering dog, just before Crispin says, "You look like a *dog*." He tries hard to sound disgusted with that last word, but Tam suspects he's just as giddy, just as enchanted by the Pacific rain forest, as his sister (if they truly are brother and sister; Tam doesn't know, not for sure, doesn't know that anyone else does either, for that matter).

"You'll get bugs in your teeth," he says. "Bugs are gonna fly right straight down your throat and lay their eggs in your stomach."

Lark's response is nothing more or less than another chorus of *ooohs* and *ahhhs* as they round a tight bend, rush through a break in the treeline and the world ends there, dropping suddenly away to the mercy of a silveryellowgray sea that seems to go on forever, blending at some far-off and indefinite point with the almost colorless sky. There's a sunbright smudge up there, but sinking slowly westward, and Tam looks at the clock on the dash again. It's always twenty minutes fast, but still, it'll be dark a long time before they reach San Francisco.

She punches the cigarette lighter with one carefully-manicured index finger, nail the color of an oil slick, and turns up the music already blaring from the Impala's tape deck. Lark takes that as her cue to start singing, howling along to "Black Planet," and the mostly bald tires squeal just a little as Tam takes the curve ten miles an hour above the speed limit. A moment in the cloudfiltered sun, blinding after the gloom, before the tree shadows swallow the car whole again. The cigarette lighter pops out, and Tam steals a glance at herself in the rearview mirror as she lights a Marlboro: yesterday's eyeliner and she's chewed off most of her lipstick, a black smear on her right cheek. Her eyes a little bleary, a little red with swollen capillaries, but the ephedrine tablets she took two hours ago, two crimson tablets from a bottle she bought at a truck stop back in Oregon, are still doing their job and she's wider than awake.

"Will you sit the fuck down, Lark, before you make me have a goddamn wreck and kill us all? Please?" she says, smoky words from her faded lips, and Lark stops singing, pulls her head back inside and Crispin sticks his tongue out at her, fleshpink flick of I-told-you-so reproach. Lark puts her pointy black boots on the dash, presses herself into the duct-taped upholstery, and doesn't say a word.

They spent the night before in Eugene and then headed west, following the meandering river valleys all the way down to the sea before turning south towards home. Almost a week now since the three of them left Los Angeles, just Tam and the twins because Maggie couldn't get off work, but he told them to go, anyway; she didn't really want to go without him, knew that Lark and Crispin would drive her nuts without Magwitch around, but the tour wasn't coming through LA or even San Francisco. So she went without too much persuading, *they* went, and it worked out better than she'd expected, really, at least until today.

At least until Gold Beach, only thirty or forty miles north of the California state line, where Crispin spotted the swan neck of a *Brachiosaurus* towering above shaggy hemlock branches, and he immediately started begging her to stop, even promised that he wouldn't ask her to play the PJ Harvey tape anymore if she'd Please Just Stop and let him see. So they lost an hour at the Prehistoric Gardens, actually paid money to get in and then spent a whole fucking hour wandering around seventy acres of dripping, wet trees, listening to Crispin prattle on about the life-sized sculptures of dinosaurs and things like dinosaurs, tourist-trap monstrosities built sometime in the 1950s, skeletons of steel and wood hidden somewhere beneath sleek skins of wire mesh and cement.

"They don't even look real," Tam said, as Crispin vamped in front of a scowling stegosaur while Lark rummaged around in her purse for her tiny Instamatic camera.

"Well, they look real enough to *me*," he replied, and Lark just shrugged, a suspiciously complicit and not-at-all-helpful sort of shrug. Tam frowned a little harder, no bottom to a frown like hers. "You are really such a fucking geek, Crispy," she said under her breath, but plenty loud enough the twins could hear.

"Don't call him that," Lark snapped, defensive sister voice, and then she found her camera somewhere in the vast, black-beaded bag and aimed it at the pretty boy and the unhappy-looking stegosaur. "A geeky name for a geeky boy," Tam sneered, as Lark took his picture; Crispin winked at her, then, and he was off again, running fast to see the *Pteranodon* or the *Ankylosaurus*. Tam looked down at her wristwatch and up at the sky and, finding no solace in either, she followed zombie Hansel and zombie Gretel away through the trees.

After the Prehistoric Gardens, it was Lark's turn, of course, her infallible logic that it wasn't fair to stop for Crispin and then not stop for her and, anyway, all she wanted was to have her picture taken beside one of the giant redwoods. Hardly even inside the national park and she already had that shitty little camera out again, sneaky rectangle of woodgrain plastic and Hello Kitty stickers.

And because it was easier to just pull the fuck over than listen to her snivel and pout all the way to San Francisco, the car bounced off the highway into a small turn-around, rolled over a shallow ditch and across snapping twigs; Lark's door was open before Tam even shifted the Impala into park, and Crispin piled out of the backseat after her. And then, insult to inconvenience, they made Tam take the photograph: the pair of them, arm in arm and wickedsmug grins on their matching faces, a mat of dry cinnamon needles beneath their boots and the boles of the great sequoias rising up behind them, primeval frame of ferns and underbrush snarl all around.

Tam sighed loud and breathed in a mouthful of air so clean it hurt her Angeleno lungs, and she wished she had a cigarette. *Just get it the fuck over with,* she thought, sternpatient thought for herself. But she made sure to aim the camera just low enough to cut the tops off both their heads in the photo.

Halfway back to the car, a small squeal of surprise and delight from Lark, and "*What?*" Crispin asked, "What is it?" Lark stooped and picked up something from the rough bed of redwood needles.

"Just get in the goddamned car, okay?" Tam begged, but Lark wasn't listening, held her discovery out for Crispin to see, presented for his approval. He made a face that was equal parts disgust and alarm and took a step away from Lark and the pale yellow thing in her hands.

"*Yuck,*" he said. "Put it back down, Lark, before it bites you or stings you or something."

"Oh, it's only a banana slug, you big sissy," she said and frowned like she was trying to impersonate Tam. "See? It can't hurt you," and she stuck it right under Crispin's nose.

"*Gagh,*" he moaned. "It's *huge,*" and he headed for the car, climbed into the backseat and hid in the shadows.

"It's only a banana slug," Lark said again. "I'm gonna keep him for a pet and name him Chiquita."

"You're going to put down the worm and get back in the fucking car," Tam said, standing at the rear fender and rattling Magwitch's key ring in one hand like a particularly noisy pair of dice. "Either that, Lark, or I'm going to leave your skinny ass standing out here with the bears."

"And the sasquatches!" Crispin shouted from inside the car, and Tam silenced him with a glare through the rear windshield.

"Jesus, Tam, it's not gonna *hurt* anything. Really. I'll put it in my purse, okay? It's not gonna hurt anything if it's inside my purse, right?" But Tam narrowed her eyes and jabbed a finger at the ground, at the needle-littered space between herself and Lark.

"You're going to put the motherfucking worm *down*, on the ground," she growled, "and then you're going to get back in the motherfucking car."

Lark didn't move, stared stubbornly down at the fat slug as it crawled cautiously over her right palm, leaving a wide trail of sparkling slime on her skin. "No," she said.

"*Now*, Lark."

"No," she repeated, glancing up at Tam through the cascade of her white bangs. "It won't hurt anything."

Just two short, quick steps and Tam was on top of her, almost a head taller, anyway, and her teeth bared like all the grizzly bears and sasquatches in the world. "Stop!" Lark screeched. "Crispin, make her stop!" She tried too late to turn and run away, but Tam already had what she wanted, had already snatched it squirming from Lark's sticky hands, and Chiquita the banana slug went sailing off into the trees. It landed somewhere among the ferns and mossy, rotting logs with a very small but audible *thump*.

"Now," Tam said, smiling and wiping slug slime off her hand onto the front of Lark's black Switchblade Symphony T-shirt. "Get in the car. *Pretty* please."

And for a moment, the time it took Tam to get behind the wheel and give the engine a couple of loud, warning revs, Lark stood, staring silently towards the spot in the woods where the slug had come down. She might have cried, if she hadn't known that Tam really would leave her stranded there. The third rev brought a big puff of sooty exhaust from the Impala's noisy muffler, and Lark was already opening the passenger-side door, already slipping in beside Tam.

She was quiet for a while, staring out at the forest and the stingy glimpses of rocky coastline, still close enough to tears that Tam could see the wet shimmer in the window-trapped reflection of her blue eyes.

~~≈~~

So the highway carries them south, between the ocean and the weathered western slopes of the Klamath Mountains, over rocks from the time of Crispin's dinosaurs, rocks laid down in warm and serpent-haunted seas; out of the protected cathedral stands of virgin redwood into hills and gorges where the sequoias are forced to rub branches with less privileged trees, mere Douglas fir and hemlock and oak. And gradually their view of the narrow, dark beaches becomes more frequent, the sharp and towering headlands setting them one from another like sedimentary parentheses.

Tam driving fast, fast as she dares, not so much worried about cops and speeding tickets as losing control in one of the hairpin curves and plunging ass-over-tits into the fucking scenery, taking a dive off one of the narrow bridges and it's two hundred feet straight down. She chain smokes and has started playing harder music, digging through the shoe box full of pirated cassettes for Nine Inch Nails and Front 242, Type-O Negative and Nitzer Ebb, all the stuff that Lark and Crispin would probably be whining like drowning kittens about if they didn't know how pissed off she was already. And then the car starts making a sound like someone's tossed a bucket of nails beneath the hood and the temp light flashes on, screw you Tam, here's some more shit to fuck up your wonderful fucking afternoon by the fucking sea.

"It's not supposed to do that, is it?" Crispin asks, backseat coy, and she really wants to turn around, stick a finger through one of his eyes until she hits brain.

"*No*, Einstein," she says instead. "It's not supposed to do that. Now shut up," settling for such a weak little jab instead of fresh frontal lobe beneath her nails. The motor spits up a final, grinding cough and dies, leaves her coasting, drifting into the breakdown lane. Pavement traded for rough and pinging gravel, and Tam lets the right fender scrape along the guardrail almost twenty feet before she stomps the brakes, the smallest possible fraction of her rage expressed in the squeal of metal against metal; when the Impala has finally stopped moving, she puts on the emergency brake and shifts into park, then turns on the hazard lights.

"We can't just stop *here*," Lark says, and she sounds scared, almost, staring out at the sun beginning to set above the endless Pacific horizon. "I mean, there isn't even a here *to* stop at. And before long it'll be getting dark—"

"Yeah, well, you tell that to Magwitch's fine hunk of Detroit dogshit here, babycakes," and Tam opens her door, slamming it closed behind her, and leaves the twins staring at each other in silent, astonished panic.

Lark tries to open her door, then, but it's pressed smack up against the guardrail and there's not enough room to squeeze out, just three or four scant inches, and that's not even space for her waif's boneangle shoulders. So she slides her butt across the faded green naugahyde, accidentally knocks the box of tapes over and they spill in a loud clatter across the seat and into the floorboard. She sits behind the wheel while Crispin climbs over from the backseat. Tam's standing in front of the car now, staring furiously down at the hood, and Crispin whispers, "If you let off the brake, maybe we could run over her," and Lark reaches beneath the dash like maybe it's not such a bad idea, but she only pulls the hood release.

"She'd live, probably," Lark says. "Yeah," Crispin replies, and begins to gather up the scattered cassettes and return them to the dingy shoe box.

The twins sit together on the guardrail while Tam curses the traitorous, hissing car, curses her ignorance of wires and rubber belts and radiators, and curses absent Magwitch for owning the crappy old Impala in the first place.

"He said it runs hot sometimes, and to just let it cool off," Crispin says hopefully, but she shuts him up with a razorshard glance. So he holds Lark's hand and stares at a bright patch of

California poppies growing on the other side of the rail, a tangerine puddle of blossoms waving heavy, calyx heads in the salt and evergreen breeze. A few minutes more and Lark and Crispin both grow bored with Tam's too-familiar indignation, tiresome rerun of a hundred other tantrums, and they slip away together into the flowers.

"It's probably not as bad as she's making it out to be," Crispin says, picking a poppy and slipping the stem behind Lark's right ear. "It just needs to cool off."

"Yeah," she says. "Probably," but not sounding reassured at all, and Lark stares down the precarious steep slope towards the beach, sand the cinder color of cold apocalypse below the gray shale and sandstone bluff. She also picks a poppy and puts it in Crispin's hair, tucking it behind his left ear, so they match again. "I want to look for sea shells," she says "and driftwood," and she points at a narrow trail just past the poppies. Crispin looks back at Tam once, her black hair wild in the wind, her face in her hands like maybe she's even crying, and then he follows Lark.

Mostly just mussels, long shells darker than the beach, curved and flaking like diseased toenails, but Lark puts a few in her purse, anyway. Crispin finds a single crab claw, almost as orange as the poppies in their hair with an airbrush hint of blue, and she keeps that, too. The driftwood is more plentiful, but all the really good pieces are gigantic, the warped and polished bones of great trees washed down from the mountains and scattered about here, shattered skeletons beyond repair. They walk on warm sand and a thick mat of sequoia bark and spindle twigs, fleshy scraps of kelp, follow the flotsam to a stream running down to meet the gently crashing sea, wide and shallow interface of saltwater and fresh. Overhead, seagulls wheel and protest the intrusion; the craggy rocks just offshore are covered with their watchful numbers, powdergray feathers, white feathers, beaks for snatching fish. *And pecking out eyes*, Lark thinks. They squawk and stare, and she gives them the finger, one nail chewed down to the quick and most of the black polish flaked away.

Crispin bends and lets the stream gurgle about his pale hands. It's filled with polished stones, muted olive and bottle-green pebbles rounded by their centuries in the cold water. He puts one finger to his lips and licks it cautiously. "Sweet," he says. "It's very sweet."

"What's that?" Lark asks, and he looks up, across the stream at a wind-stunted stand of firs on the other side and there's a sign there, almost as big as a roadside billboard sign and just as gaudy, but no way anyone could see this from the highway. A great sign of planks painted white and lettered crimson, artful, scrolling letters that spell out, alive and untamed! monsters and mysteries of Neptune's bosom! and below, in slightly smaller script, mermaids and miracles! the great sea serpent! Men-eaters and devilfish!

"Someone likes exclamation points," Lark says, but Crispin's already halfway across the stream, walking on the knobby stones protruding from the water; she follows him, both arms out for balance like a trapeze acrobat. "Wait," she calls to him, and, reluctantly, he pauses until she catches up.

The old house trailer sits a little distance up the slope from the beach, just far enough that it's safe from the high tides. Lark and Crispin stand side by side, holding hands tight, and stare at it, lips parted and eyes wide enough to divulge a hint of their mutual surprise. Lark's left boot is wet where she missed a stone and her foot went into the stream, and the water's beginning to seep past leather straps and buckles, through her hose, but she doesn't notice, or it doesn't matter, because this is that unexpected. This old husk of sunbleached aluminum walls, corrugated metal skin draped in mopgray folds of fishing net, so much netting it's hard to see that the trailer underneath might once have been blue. Like something a giant fisherman dragged up from the sea, and finally, realizing what he had, this inedible hunk of rubbish, he left it here for the gulls and the weather to take care of.

"Wow," Lark whispers, and Crispin turns, looking over his shoulder to see if maybe Tam has given up on the car and come looking for them. But there's only the beach, and the waves, and the birds. The air that smells like dead fish and salt wind, and Crispin asks, "You wanna go see?"

"There might be a phone," Larks says, still whispering. "If there's a phone, we could call someone to fix the car."

"Yeah," Crispin replies, as though they really need an excuse beyond their curiosity. And there are more signs leading up to the trailer, splintery bread crumbs teasing them to take the next step, and the next, and the next after that: THE MOUTH THAT SWALLOWED JONAH! and ETERNAL LEVIATHAN AND CHARYBDIS REVEALED! As they get close they can see other things in the sandy rind of yard surrounding the trailer, the rusting hulks of outboard motors and a ship's wheel nailed to a post, broken lobster cages and the ivorywhite jaws of sharks strung up to dry like toothy laundry. There are huge plywood and canvas façades leaned or hammered against the trailer, one on either side of the narrow door and both taller than the roof: garish seascapes with whitefanged sea monsters breaking the surface, acrylic foam and spray, flailing fins like Japanese fans of flesh and wire, eyes like angry, boiling hemorrhages.

A sudden gust off the beach, then, and they both have to stop and cover their eyes against the blowing sand. The wind clatters and whistles around all the things in the yard, tugging at the sideshow canvases. "Maybe we should go back now," Lark says when the wind has passed, and she brushes sand from her clothes and hair. "She'll wonder where we've gone."

"Yeah," Crispin says, his voice grown thin and distant, distracted. "Maybe," he says, but they're both still climbing, past the hand-lettered signs and into the ring of junk. Crispin pauses before the shark jaws, yawning cartilage jaws on nylon fishing line, and he runs the tip of one finger lightly across rows of gleaming, serrate triangles, only a little more pressure and he could draw blood.

And then the door of the trailer creaks open and a man is standing in the dark space leading inside, not what either expected if only because they hadn't known what to expect. A tall man, gangly knees and elbows through threadbare clothes, pants and shirt the same faded khaki; bony wrists from buttoned sleeves too short for his long arms, arthritis-swollen knuckles on his wide hands. Lark makes a uneasy sound when she sees him and Crispin jerks his hand away from the shark's jaw, sneakchild caught in the cookie jar startled, and snags a pinkie, the soft skin torn, and he leaves a gleaming crimson drop of himself behind.

"You be careful there, boy," the man says with a voice like water sloshing in a rocky place. "That's *Carcharodon carcharias* herself hanging there, and her ghost is just as hungry as her belly ever was. You've given her a taste of blood and she'll remember now—"

"Our car broke down," Lark says to the man, looking up at his face for the first time since the door opened. "And we saw the signs." She points back down the hill without looking away from the man, his cloudy eyes that seem too big for his skull, odd, forward sloping skull with more of an underbite than she ever thought possible and a wormpink wrinkle where his lower lip should be, nothing at all for the upper. Eyes set too far apart, wide nostrils too far apart and a scraggly bit of gray beard perched on the end of his sharp chin. Lank hair to his shoulders and almost as gray as the scrap of beard.

"Do you want to see what's inside, then?" he asks, that watery voice, and Lark and Crispin both look back towards the signs, the little stream cutting the beach in half. There's no evidence of Tam anywhere.

"Does it cost money?" Crispin asks, glances tentatively out at the man from underneath the white shock of hair hiding half his face.

"Not if you ain't got any," the man replies and blinks once, vellum lids fast across those bulging eyes.

"It's getting late, and our car's broken down," Lark says, and the man makes a noise that might be a sigh or might be a cough. "It don't take long," he tells her and smiles, showing crooked teeth the color of nicotine stains.

"And you've got all the things that those signs say, in there?" Crispin asks, one eyebrow cocked, eager, excited doubt, and the man shrugs.

"If it's free, I don't expect you'll be asking for your money back," as if that's an answer, but enough for Crispin and he nods his head and steps towards the door, away from the shark jaws. But Lark grabs his hand, anxious grab that says "Wait," without using any words, and when he looks at her, eyes that say, *This isn't like the dinosaurs, whatever it is, this isn't plaster and plywood,* and so he smiles for her, flashing comfort and confidence.

"It'll be something cool," he says. "Better than listening to Tam bitch at us about the car, at least."

So she smiles back at him, small and nervous smile, and she squeezes his hand a little harder.

"Come on, if you're coming," the man says. "I'm letting in the flies, standing here with the door wide open."

"Yeah," Crispin says. "We're coming," and the man holds the door for them, steps to one side, and the trailer swallows them like a hungry metal whale.

Inside, and the air is chilly and smells like fish and stagnant saltwater, mildew, and there's the faintest rotten odor some-where underneath, dead thing washed up and swelling on the sand. Crispin and Lark pause while the man pulls the door shut behind them, shutting them in, shutting the world out.

"Do you live in here?" Lark asks, still squeezing Crispin's hand, and the old man turns around, the tall old man with his billy-goat beard, and gazing down on the twins now as he scratches at the scaly, dry skin on his neck.

"I have myself a cot in the back, and a hot plate," he replies, and Lark nods; her eyes are adjusting to the dim light leaking in through the dirty windowpanes, and she can see flakes of dead skin, dislodged by his fingers and floating slowly down to settle on the dirty linoleum floor of the trailer.

The length of the trailer has been lined with wooden shelves and huge glass tanks, and there are sounds to match the smells, wet sounds, the constant bubble of aquarium pumps, water filters, occasional, furtive splashes.

"Wonders from the blackest depths," the old man sighs, wheezes, tired and sickly imitation of a carnie barker's spiel. "Jewels and nightmares plucked from Davy Jones' Locker, washed up on the shores of the Seven Seas—"

The old man is interrupted by a violent fit of coughing, then, and Crispin steps up to the nearest shelf, a collection of jars, dozens and dozens of jars filled with murky ethanol or formalin, formaldehyde weak-tea brown and the things that float lifelessly inside: scales and spines, oystergray flesh and lidless, unseeing eyes like pickled grapes. Labels on the jars, identities in a spidery handwriting, and the paper so old and yellow he knows that it would crumble at his most careful touch.

The old man clears his throat, loud, phlegmy rattle, and spits into a corner.

"Secrets from the world's museums, from Mr. Charles Darwin's own cabinets, scooped from the sea off Montevideo in eighteen hundred and thirty-two—"

"Is that an octopus?" Lark asks, and the twins both stare into one of the larger jars, three or four gallons and a warty lump inside, a bloom of tentacles squashed against the glass like something wanting out. Crispin presses the tip of one finger to the glass, tracing the outline of a single, dimewide suction cup.

The old man coughs again, throaty raw hack, produces a wadded and wrinkled, snot-stained handkerchief from his shirt pocket and wipes at his wide mouth with it.

"*That*, boy, is the larva of the Kraken, the greatest of the cephalopods, Viking-bane, ten strangling arms to hale dragon ships beneath the waves." And then the old man clears his throat, and, in a different voice, barker turned poet, recites, *"Below the thunders of the upper deep, far, far beneath in the abysmal sea, his ancient, dreamless, uninvaded sleep the Kraken sleepeth."*

"Tennyson," Lark says; and the old man nods, pleased.

Crispin leans closer, squinting through the gloom and dusty glass, the clouded preserving fluids, and now he can see something dark and sharp like a parrot's beak nested at the center of the rubbery mass of molluskflesh. But then they're being hurried along, past all the unexamined specimens, and here's the next stop on the old man's tour.

Beneath a bell jar, the taxidermied head and arms and torso of a monkey sewn onto the dried tail of a fish, the stitches plain to see, but he tells them it's a baby mermaid, netted near the coast of Java, a hundred years ago.

"It's just half an old, dead monkey with a fish tail stuck on," Crispin says, impertinent, already tiring of these moldy, fabricated wonders. "See?" and he points at the stitches in case Lark hasn't noticed them for herself.

The old man makes an annoyed sound, not quite anger, but impatience, certainly, and he moves them quickly along, this time to a huge fish tank, plate-glass sides so entirely overgrown with algae there's no seeing what's inside, just mossygreen like siren hair that sways in whatever dull currents the aquarium's pump is making.

"I can't see anything at all in there," Crispin says, as Lark looks nervously back past the mermaid towards the trailer door. But Crispin stands on his toes, peers over the edge of the tank, and "You need to put some snails in there," he says. "To eat some of that shit so people can see."

"*This* one has no name, no *proper* name," the old man croaks through his snotclogged throat. "No legend. This one was scraped off the hull of a Russian whaler with the shipworms and barnacles, and on Midsummer's Eve, put an ear to the glass and you'll hear it *singing* in the language of riptides and typhoons."

And something seems to move, then, maybe, beyond the emerald scum, feathery red gillflutter or a thousand jointed legs the color of a burn, and Crispin jumps, steps away from the glass and lets go of Lark's hand. Smug grin on the old man's long face to show his yellowed teeth, and he makes a barking noise like seals or laughing.

"You go back, if you're getting scared," the old man says, and Lark looks like that's all she wants in the world right now, to be out of the trailer, back on the beach and headed up the cliff to the Impala. But Crispin takes her hand again, this very same boy that's afraid of banana slugs, but something here he has to see, and something he has to prove to himself or to the self-satisfied old man. "What's next, sea monkeys?" he asks, defiantly, mock brave.

"Right here," the old man says, pointing to something more like a cage than a tank. "The illegitimate spawn of the Great Sea Serpent and a Chinese water dragon." A sloppy construction of planks and chicken wire on the floor, almost as tall as the twins, and Crispin drags Lark along towards it. "Tam will be looking for us, won't she?" Lark asks, but he ignores her, stares instead into the enclosure. There's muddy straw on the bottom and motionless coils of gold and chocolate-brown muscle.

"Jesus, it's just a stupid python, Lark. See? It's not even as big as the one that Miss Alexandra used to have. What a rip-off—" and then he stops, because the snake moves, shifting its chain-link bulk, and now he can see its head, the tiny horns above its pearlbead eyes, and farther back, a single, stubby flap of meat along one side of its body that beats nervously at the air a moment and then lies still against the filthy straw.

"There's something wrong with it, Crispin, that's all," Lark says, argument to convince herself, and the old man says, "She can crush a full-grown pig in those coils, or a man," and he pauses for the drama, then adds, resuming his confident barker cadence, sly voice to draw midway crowds—"Kept inside a secret Buddhist monastery on the Yangtze and worshipped for a century, and all the sacrificial children she could eat," he says.

The flipper thing on its side moves again, vestigial limb rustle against the straw, and the snake flicks a tongue the color of gangrene and draws its head slowly back into its coils, retreating, hiding from their sight or the dim trailer light or both; "Wonders from the blackest depths," the old man whispers. "Mysteries of the deep, spoils of the abyss."

And Lark is all but begging, now. "*Please*, Crispin. We should go," but her voice almost lost in the burbling murmur of aquarium filters.

Crispin's hand about her wrist like a steel police cuff, and she thinks, *How much more can there be, how much can this awful little trailer hold?* When she looks back the way they've come, past the snake thing's cage and the green tank and the phony mermaid, past all the jars, it seems a long, long way; the dizzying impression that the trailer's somehow bigger inside than out, and she shivers, realizes that she's sweating, clammy coldsweat in tiny salt beads on her upper lip, across her forehead and leaking into her eyes. *How much more?* but there's at least *one* more, and they step past a plastic shower curtain, slick blue plastic printed with cartoon sea horses and starfish and turtles, to stand before the final exhibit in the old man's shabby menagerie.

"Dredged from the bottom of Eel Canyon off Humboldt Bay, hauled up five hundred fathoms through water so inky black and cold it might be the very moment before Creation itself," and Crispin is staring at something Lark can't see, squinting into the last tank; cold pools about Lark's ankles, one dry and one still wet from the stream, a sudden, tangible chill that gathers itself like the old man's words, or like heavy air spilling from an open freezer door.

"And this was just a *scrap*, boy, a *shred* ripped from the haunches or seaweed-crusted skull of a behemoth."

"I can't see anything," Crispin says, but then, "*Oh*. Oh shit. Oh, Jesus."

Lark realizes where the cold is coming from, that it's pouring out from under the shower curtain, and finally she slips her hand free of Crispin's grasp. He doesn't even seem to notice, can't seem to stop staring into the murky, ill-lit tank that towers over them, filling the rear of the trailer from wall to wall.

"And *maybe*," the old man says, bending very close, and he's almost whispering to Crispin now, secrets and suspicions for the boy twin and no one else. "Maybe it's growing itself a whole new body in there, a whole new organism from that stolen bit of flesh, like the arm of a starfish that gets torn off."

Lark touches the folds of the curtain, and the cold presses back from the other side. Cold that would burn her hand if she left it there, lingered long enough. She glances back at the old man and Crispin to be sure they're not watching, because she knows this must be forbidden, something she's not meant to see. And then she pulls one corner of the shower curtain aside, and that terrible cold flows out, washing over her like a living wave of Arctic breath and a neglected cat box smell and another, sharper odor like cabbage left too long at the bottom of a refrigerator.

"Fuck," Crispin says behind her. "No fucking way," and the old man is reciting Tennyson again.

"There hath he lain for ages, and will lie, battening upon huge sea worms in his sleep, until the latter fire shall heat the deep—"

There is dark behind the shower curtain, dark like a wall, solid as the cold, and again, that vertigo sense of a vast space held somehow inside the little trailer, that this blackness might go on for miles. That she could step behind the curtain and spend her life wandering lost in the perpetual night collected here.

"... *Then once by man and angels to be seen*," the old man says, somewhere back there in the world, where there is simple light and warmth, "*In roaring he shall rise and on the surface die.*"

Far off, in the dark, there are wet sounds, something breaking the surface of water that has lain so still so long, and she can feel its eyes on her then, eyes made to see where light is a fairy tale and the sun a murmured heresy. The sound of something vast and sinuous coming slowly through the water towards her, and Crispin says, "It *moved*, didn't it? Jesus, it fucking moved in there."

It's so close now, Lark thinks. *It's so close and this is the worst place in the world and I should be scared, I should be scared shitless.*

"Sometimes it moves," the old man says. "In its sleep, sometimes it moves."

Lark steps over the threshold, the thin, tightrope line between the trailer and this place, ducks her head beneath the shower curtain, and the smell is stronger than ever now. It gags her, and she covers her mouth with one hand, another step and the curtain will close behind her and there will be nothing but this perfect, absolute cold and darkness and her and the thing swimming through the black. Not really water in there, she knows, just *black* to hide it from the prying, jealous light— and then Crispin has her hand again, is pulling her back into the blinding glare of the trailer and the shower curtain falls closed with an unforgiving, disappointed *shoosh*. The old man and his fishlong face is staring at her, his rheumy, accusing eyes, and "That was not for you, girl," he says. "I did not show you that."

She wrenches her hand free of Crispin's and almost manages to slip back behind the curtain before anyone can stop her, the only possible release from the sudden, empty feeling eating her up inside, like waking from a dream of Heaven or someone dead alive again, the glimpse of anything so pure and then it's yanked away. But Crispin is stronger and the old man is blocking her, anyhow, grizzled Cerberus standing guard before the aquamarine plastic, a faint string of drool at one corner of his mouth.

"Come on, Lark," Crispin says to her. "We shouldn't be here. We shouldn't ever have come in here."

The look in the old man's eyes says he's right, and already the dream is fading, whatever she might have seen or heard already bleeding away in the last, watercolor dregs of daylight getting into the trailer.

"I'm sorry," Crispin says as they pass the shriveled mermaid, and he pushes the door open, not so far back after all. "I didn't want you to think I was afraid."

"No," she says. "No," but doesn't know what to say next, and it doesn't really matter, because now they're stumbling together down the trailer's concrete-block steps, their feet in the sand again, and the air is filled with gentle twilight and the screaming of gulls.

Tam has been standing by the stream for half an hour, at least that long since she wandered down to the beach looking for the twins, after the black man in the pick-up truck stopped and fixed the broken fan belt with an old pair of pantyhose from the backseat of the Impala and then refilled the radiator. "You take it easy, now, and that oughta hold far as San Francisco," he said, but then she couldn't find Lark or Crispin. Her throat hurts from calling them. It's nearly dark now, and she's been standing here where their footprints end at the edge of the water, the past thirty minutes spent shouting their names. Getting angrier, getting fucking scared, the relief that the car's running again melting away, deserting her for visions of the twins drowned or the twins lost or the twins raped and murdered.

Twice she started across the stream, one foot out and plenty enough stones between her and the other side to cross without getting her feet wet, and twice she stopped, thinking that maybe she glimpsed dark shapes moving just below the surface, undulating forms like the wings of stingrays or the tentacles of an octopus or squid, black and eel-long things darting between the rocks. And never mind that the water is crystal clear and couldn't possibly be more than a few inches deep. Never mind she *knows* it's really nothing more than shadow tricks and the last glimmers of the setting sun caught in the rippling water. These apprehensions too instinctual, the thought of what might be waiting for her if she slipped, sharp teeth eager for stray ankles, anxiety all but too deep to question, and so she's stood here, feeling stupid, calling them like she was their god-damn mother.

She looks up again and there they are, almost stumbling down the hill, the steep dirt path leading down from the creepy old trailer, Crispin in the lead and dragging Lark along, a cloud of dust trailing out behind them. When they reach the stream they don't even bother with the stepping stones, just splash their way straight across, splashing her in the bargain.

"Mother*fucker*," Tam says and steps backwards onto drier sand. "Will you please watch what the fuck you're doing? Shit..." But neither twin says a word, stand breathless at the edge of the stream, the low bank carved into the sand by the water; Crispin stares down at his soggy Docs, and Lark glances nervously back towards the trailer on the hill.

"Where the hell have you two bozos been? Didn't you hear me calling you? I'm fucking hoarse from calling you."

"An old man," Lark gasps. "A terrible old man." wheezing the words out, and before she can say anything else Crispin adds, "A sideshow, Tam, that's all," speaking quickly like he's afraid of what Lark will say if he doesn't, what she might have been about to say. "Just some crazy old guy with a sort of a sideshow."

"Jesus," Tam sighs, tired and pissy sigh that she hopes sounds the way she feels, and she reaches out and snatches a wilted poppy from Crispin's hair, tossing it to the sand at their feet. "That figures, you know? That just fucking figures. Next time, Magwitch comes or your asses stay home," and she turns her back on them, then, heading up the beach towards the car. She only stops once, turning around to be sure they're following and they are, close behind and their arms tight around one an-other's shoulders as if they couldn't make it alone. The twins' faces are hidden in shadow, night-shrouded, and behind them, the sea has turned a cold, silvery indigo and stretches away to meet the rising stars.

Rats Live on No Evil Star

"I think that we're fished for," Olan says, menthol cigarette smoked almost down to the filter, and he's sitting at the unsteady little card table by the window, staring out at the high January sky, that disheartening sky like a flawed blue gemstone, and Jessie stops smearing peanut butter on slices of soft white bread and looks at him.

"What?" she asks, and he only nods at the sky so that she has to ask again. "What did you say, Olan?"

"I think we are *fished* for," the words repeated loudly and more slowly, as if she's only deaf and stupid, after all, and he's making perfect sense.

"I don't know what you're talking about," not meaning to sound annoyed, and she puts two pieces of thickly peanut-buttered bread together, another sandwich for this lean and crazy man who lives down the hall, this man to whom she is neither related nor can call her friend. But if no one looks in on him, he doesn't eat. Jessie cuts the sandwich into neat triangles, trims away the crust because he only pulls it off anyhow. She places it on one of the pink saucers that she's rescued from the kitchen's clutter of filthy dishes, wasteland of cracked plates and coffee cups for the cockroaches to roam. She had to bring the soap from her own apartment down the hall, of course, and a clean dishrag.

"I don't mind listening," she says, setting his sandwich down in front of him. "If you want to try to explain."

Olan exhales, stubbing out his cigarette in a ceramic ashtray shaped like Florida, dozens of butts and cindergray ash spilling onto the top of the table; he looks at the sandwich instead of the sky, but his expression doesn't change, the one as much a mystery to him as the other. He takes a hesitant, small sip from the beer that Jessie has brought him. She doesn't often do that, but sometimes, just a bottle of the cheap stuff she drinks while she writes, Old Milwaukee or Sterling or PBR sacrificed to his reliable indifference.

"Never mind," he says and glances at her through his spectacles, wire and some Scotch tape wrapped around one corner, thick glass to frame his distant eyes. He takes a bite of the sandwich and looks at the sky while   he chews.

"What are you working on today, Jessie?" he asks around the mouthful of peanut butter as she sits down across the table from him. "Anne Sexton," she says. Same answer as always, but that doesn't matter, because she knows he only asks to be polite, to seem to care. And now her eyes are drawn to the window, too, past the dead plant in its clay pot on the radiator, leaves gone to dry and wiltbrown tendrils, and out there the railroad glints dull silver beneath the white, white sun, parallel lines of steel and creosote-stained cross ties, granite and slag ballast, the abandoned factories and empty warehouses on the other side, a few stunted trees to emphasize the desolation.

And then she looks away, back down at her own lunch, bread with the crust still on, something mundane to break the spell. "I'm beginning a new chapter this afternoon," she says, not feeling hungry anymore.

"The Death Baby?" he asks and she shakes her head no, "I'm done with the Death Baby for now."

"*There,*" Olan says and presses the tip of one finger against the flyblown glass, pointing at something he sees in the sky. "Right there. See it?" And Jessie looks. She always looks, and she's never seen anything yet. But she doesn't lie to him, either.

"I don't see it," she says. "But my eyes are going to shit. I spend too much time staring at fucking computer screens."

"Well, it's gone now," he says very quietly, as if to let her off the hook, because his eyes don't leave the window. Olan takes another bite of the sandwich, another sip of beer to wash it down, and his eyes don't leave the window.

The tiny apartment on the west side of a city that once knew thriving industry and has seen long decades of decay, foundries and mills closed and the black smoking skies gone and the jobs gone with them. Not the Birmingham of his childhood, only the shell of the memory of that city, and further east the hungry seeds of gentrification have been planted. In the newspapers he has read about the "Historic Loft District," a phrase they use like Hope or Expectancy. But *this* apartment existing on its own terms, or his terms, this space selected twenty years ago for its unobstructed view of the sky, and that hasn't changed.

Three very small rooms and each of them filled with his books and newspapers, his files and clippings and folders. The things he has written directly on the walls with Magic Marker because there wasn't time to find a sheet of paper before he forgot. Mountains of magazines slumped like glossy landslides to bury silverfish and roaches, *Fate* and *Fortean Times*, journals for modern alchemists and cryptozoological societies and ufology cults. Exactly 1,348 index cards thumbtacked or stapled to plaster the fragile, drained color of dirty eggshells and coffee-ground stains. Testaments uncorrelated, data uncollated, and someday the concordance and cross-reference alone will be a hundred thousand pages long.

After the girl has left (The Academic, as he thinks of her), Olan finds the fresh and stickybrown smear of peanut butter on the kitchen window, his shitcolored fingerprint still there to mark the exact spot, and he draws a black circle onto the glass around it. There are other circles there, twenty-three

black *and* red circles on this window, and someday he will draw
interconnecting lines to reveal another part of the whole, his
map of the roof of the sky.

"I don't see it," he whispers, remembering what she said and
something a doctor told him to say years ago, when he was still
a boy and might have only been a man who could say "I don't
see it" when he does.

Olan sits at the window, new ink drying as the sun sinks towards twilight. Black ink to indicate a Probable Inorganic, ten-
tative classification of the shimmering orb he saw hanging in
the empty sky above the city. A pencil sketch already in one of
his notebooks, and best-guessed estimates of height and di-
mension underneath it, something like a bowling ball as perfectly motionless as the train tracks down below.

"Visible for approx. 14 minutes, 1:56 until 2:10 p.m. CST," he
wrote, not sure of exactly how long because the girl kept talking and talking, and then he saw her to the door, and when he
got back it wasn't there anymore, had fallen or vanished or simply drifted away.

"I don't see it," he says again, her borrowed words and in-
flection, and then he takes off his glasses and rubs at his tired
and certain eyes.

This is Page One. Which is to say—this is where the story begins when he is asked to tell it as a story, when he *used* to tell it
for the doctors who gave him pills and advice and diagnoses.
The linear narrative that has as little and as much truth as any
necessary fiction ever has, any attempt to relate, to make the
subjective objective.

"I was seven, and we lived on my granddaddy's farm in Bibb
County, after my father went away and my mother and I lived
there with my grandmother because my granddaddy was already dead by then. It wasn't a *real* farm anymore, but we did
have chickens and grew okra and tomatoes and collards. I had
a dog named Biscuit.

"One day—it was July—one July day in 1955, when I was seven, Biscuit chased a rabbit into the woods. And I was standing in the field beside the house calling him, and there were no clouds in the sky. No clouds at all. I'm sure there were no clouds. I was calling Biscuit, and it began to rain, even though there weren't any clouds. But it wasn't raining water, it was raining blood and little bits of meat like you put into a stew, shreds of red, raw meat with white veins of fat. I stopped calling Biscuit and watched the blood and meat hitting the ground, turning it red and black. There was a crunchy sound, like digging in a box of Rice Krispies for the toy at the bottom, a very faint cereal-crunching sound that came from the sky, I think.

"And then my mother was yelling and dragging me back towards the house. She dragged me onto the front porch, and we there watching the blood and meat fall from the clear sky, making puddles and streams on the ground.

"No, Biscuit never came home. I couldn't blame him. It smelled very bad, afterwards."

He has a big jar on the table beside the mattress where he sleeps, quart mayonnaise jar, and inside is the mummified corpse of something like a mouse. It fell out of the sky three years ago, dropped at his feet while he was walking the tracks near the apartment building, this mouse-thing husk from a clear sky, and he has labeled it in violet, for Definitive Organic.

The girl from #407 doesn't usually bring him supper, but she did one night a month ago now, and she also brought some typed pages from her dissertation. She cooked him canned ravioli with Parmesan cheese and made a fresh salad of lettuce with radish and cucumber slices, and they ate it together, sitting on the paper-cluttered floor while she talked about the work of a poet who had committed suicide in 1974. He had never read the poet, but it would have been impolite not to listen, not to offer a few words when he thought he wouldn't sound too foolish.

"It's a palindrome from a barn somewhere in Ireland," the girl said, answering a question about the title to one of the poems. "Someone had painted it on a barn," and then she produced a tattered paperback that he hadn't noticed in among her pages, and she read him the poem that began with the title from the barn. He didn't understand it, exactly, Adam and Eve and the Fall, words that sounded good put together that way, he supposed. But, those words, STAR. RATS STAR, those words like a hand placed flat against a mirror, like bookends with nothing in between.

"Sometimes she called herself Ms. Dog," the girl said, and he saw the trick at once—Dog, God.

"I would very much like a copy of that poem," he said to her, chewing the last bite of his salad. And three days later she brought him a photocopy of those pages from the paperback, and he keeps them thumbtacked to a wall near the window. He has written RATS and STAR and RAT'S STAR on the wall in several places.

The sun is down, down for hours now, and Olan sits at the card table by the window, studying by the dim fluorescent light from the kitchenette. He has The Book of the Damned by Charles Fort opened to page 260, and he copies a line into one of his notebooks: "Vast thing, black and poised, like a crow, over the moon." This is one of the books that makes him nervous—no, one of the books that frightens him; The Golden Bough makes him nervous, Gilgamesh makes him nervous, and this book, this book frightens him. Goosebumps on his arms for a sentence like that: "Vast thing, black and poised..." Things that were seen casting shadows on the moon in 1788, things between earth and moon, perhaps, casting shadows.

He flips back two pages and copies another line: "Was it the thing or the shadow of a thing?" Fort's taunting question put down in Olan's obsessive-neat cursive, restated in precisely the same ten words. He pauses and lights a Newport and sits smoking, staring out the window, trying to find the sense in the question, the terrible logic past his fear.

There is only a third-quarter sliver of moon tonight, and that's good, he thinks, too poor a screen for anything's shadow.

And down on the railroad tracks there is movement, then, and a flash, twin flashes of emerald, a glinting reflection like cats' eyes caught in a flashlight or headlights. Olan sits very, very still, cigarette hanging limp from his lips, cough-drop smoke coiling about his face, and he does not even blink. Waits for it to come again, and if there were a moon tonight he might see a little better, he thinks, a moment ago happy there was no more light in the sky but now, the not knowing worse than the knowing, and so he strains his eyes into the night. But nothing else, so in a moment he goes to the buzzing fluorescent bulbs above the sink and switches them off, then sits back down in the dark. There's still a little glow from the next room, but now he can see the tracks better.

"I don't see it," he says aloud, but he does, that thin shape walking between the rails, the jointed, stiltlong legs, and if there are feet he cannot see them. "It *could* be a dog," he whispers, certain of nothing but that it   isn't a dog. He thinks it has fur, and it turns its head towards him, then, and smiles, yes, yes, Olan, it's smiling, so don't pretend it isn't, don't fucking pretend. He squeezes his eyes shut, and when he opens them again it's still there. He sits very still, cold sweat and smoke in the dark, as it lingers a moment more on the tracks, and then gallops away towards the row of abandoned factories.

"Did you ever talk about this with your mother or grandmother afterwards?" the doctor (not doctor, not real doctor—therapist) asked him, and he shook his head.

"No," he said. "We didn't talk about that day."

"I see," the therapist said and slowly nodded her head. She

did that a lot, that slow up and down agreement or reassurance nod, and chewed the eraser end of her pencil.

"What else can you remember about that day, Olan?" she asked him.

He thought a moment, what to say, what to hold back, what could never be explained, thoughtsifting, filtering, and finally said, "We went inside, and she locked all the doors and windows. My grandmother came out of the kitchen and watched with us, and she prayed. She held her rosary and prayed. I remember that the house smelled like butter beans."

"You must have had it all over you, then? The blood."

"Yeah," he said. "When it stopped falling my mother took me to the bathroom and scrubbed my skin with Ivory Soap. She nearly scrubbed me raw."

"Did your mother often give you baths, Olan?" the therapist asked, and he looked at her a while without answering, realizing how angry he had become, the sudden fury nested in him for this woman who nodded and feigned comprehension and compassion. "What are you getting at?" he asked her, and she took the pencil eraser from her mouth.

"Was it out of the ordinary, that degree of intimacy between you and your mother?"

"I was covered in blood," he said, hearing the brittle edge in his voice. "Both of us, and she was scared. We thought maybe it was the end of the world."

"So it was unusual? Is that what you're saying?"

And he remembered his mother dragging him down the hall, a redblack handprint smear he left on the wall, and her crying and stripping off his ruined clothes, the suspicion that it was somehow *his* fault, this horrible thing, and Where's Biscuit? he'd kept asking her, where's Biscuit?

"I have to go now," he said, and the therapist put down her pencil and apologized for nothing in particular, apologized twice if she'd upset him. He paid her, twenty-five dollars because she was seeing him on a sliding scale, she'd explained at the start. A twenty and three ones and some change, and she gave him a receipt. "Will you be back next week? I have you down for three o'clock on Thursday, but if that's too late—"

"I don't know," he said, dishonest, and she nodded again, and Olan never went back to her office.

"Well?" he asks the girl, the Academic, "Are you going to open it or not?" and she looks up slowly from the brown paper bag in her hands, confused eyes, surprise and a scrap of a smile on her lips.

"Is this a present?" she asks. "Are you giving me a present, Olan?" And he can hear the caution, the do-I-want-to-encourage-this-sort-of-thing wariness in her voice. But he knows that she will accept what's in the bag, because she's brought him food and beer and talked to him, and rejecting such a small reciprocation would seem unkind. He has noticed that the Academic has a great unwillingness to seem unkind.

"It's not much," as the hallway silence is interrupted by the rustle of the paper bag when she opens it. She reaches inside and takes out the padlock and hasp set, the shrinkwrapped Yale he bought at a hardware store seven blocks away. "It's not much," Olan says again, because it isn't, and because he thinks that's the sort of thing you say when you give someone a gift.

She stares at it a moment without saying anything, and he says, "It's a rough neighborhood. It didn't used to be, but it is now."

"Yeah," she replies, and he can see that she's still rummaging for words. "Thanks, Olan. That's very thoughtful of you. I'll put it on the door this afternoon."

"You're welcome," and to change the subject, because it's not hard to see how uncomfortable she is, he asks "How's the new chapter coming along?"

"Ah, um, well, you know. It's coming," she says and smiles more certainly now, shrugs, and "God, I'm being so rude, letting you just stand out there in the hall. Do you want to come in, Olan? I needed to take a break anyway—"

"No," he says, maybe a little too quickly, but he has notes he must get back to, and the walk to the hardware store has cost him the better part of the afternoon already.

"Are you sure? I could make us some coffee."

He nods to show that yes, he is sure, and "It's in the Southern Hemisphere," he says; she looks confused again, and he recognizes the familiar patience in her confusion, the patience that shines coolly from her whenever she doesn't immediately understand something he's said.

"Sextens," he says. "The Sextant constellation. The Rat's Star," and now, the vaguest glint of comprehension in her, surfacing slow like something coming up from deep water for a breath of air. And, "I didn't know if you knew that. If you knew much about astronomy," he says.

"No, I didn't know that, Olan. That could be interesting. I mean, I don't think anyone's ever drawn a connection before," and now she's staring back down at the padlock like maybe she's just noticed it for the first time.

"There are three actually," he says. "Three stars in an isosceles triangle, like this," and Olan tries to show her with his hands, geometry of thumb against thumb, the intersection of index fingers. "Like a ship's sextant," he adds.

"That could be very helpful to know."

"I have books, if you ever need them," and he's already turning away from her, can sense that he's made her uneasy, has spent plenty enough years making people uneasy to see the signs. "I have a lot of books on stars, if you ever need any of them. I know you take good care of books."

And she says "Thanks," as he walks away towards his own apartment door at the other end of the hall. "And thanks for the lock, Olan," she says, like an afterthought.

On one wall he has taken down twenty-seven index cards, accounts of living things found encased in solid stone, toads and worms mostly, and he has written live evil where the cards were. Two elements of the palindrome taken out of context and reconnected, like rat's star. Sometimes the truth is easier to see when things are disassembled and put back together another way. That what the Academic does, he thinks, takes apart the words of dead women and puts them together differently, trying to find the truth hidden inside lines of poetry. That's what he does with his books and newspapers.

Now Olan lies in the dark on his springshot mattress that smells like sweat and tobacco smoke and maybe piss, too, and the only light is coming in through the window above his head, falling in a crooked rectangle on the opposite wall, so he can read LIVE EVIL where he took down the cards.

He lies still, listening to the building and the city outside, and he thinks: there is never any getting closer to the truth, no matter what you write on paper cards or plaster walls, no matter how you rearrange the words. Because the truth is like the horizon, relative to where you're standing, and it moves if you move. And he thinks that he should get up and turn on a lamp and write that in one of his notebooks, that he might forget it before morning, and then he hears the sound: broomsticks thumping on the stairs, that staccato wooden quality to the sound, broomsticks or stilts maybe, and he remembers the long-legged thing from the train tracks the night before. He wonders if its long legs might not make that sound coming up the stairs. And his heart is beating faster, listening, as the sound gets closer, not on the stairs any longer, thump, thump, thumping in the hallway, instead. But way down at the other end, near the Academic's door, not his, and he lies very, very still hoping that she has done what she said, that she has put the extra lock on her door.

And then he realizes that there is another kind of noise, fainter, but worse to hear, a wet and snuffling sort of noise, like something sniffing along the floor, or the narrow crack beneath a closed door. A purposeful, searching noise, and he stares across the shadow-filled room towards the door, getting cold from his own sour sweat despite the radiator. In a few minutes, the snuffling noise stops and the thumping begins again, as whatever's in the hall moves on to the next door down.

"I don't hear it," Olan whispers, and he hides his face in his pillow and waits for daylight.

Morning like clotted milk hanging in the sky, and Jessie, her arms loaded with overdue library books stacked up to her chin, dreading the cold outside and the bus ride to school. Jangle of her key ring in the quiet hallway: key for the doorknob and the dead bolt and the door out to the street, key to the laundry room and mailbox, one more for her shabby little office at the university; all hung together on a shiny loop of brass and a tarnished brass tab with her initials engraved there, Christmas gift five years old from a now dead father. It's a sideshow contortionist trick, locking the door, shifting the books, and the one on top slides off, *The World Into Words* falling to the dusty floor. Jessie leaves the key ring dangling in the lock and stoops to retrieve the fallen book, cursing loudly when the rest of the stack almost tumbles over as well, but she catches them by leaning quickly forward against the door.

"*Fuck*," she says, hard and angry whisper, and her breath foggy in the cold air; it's too fucking early for this shit. She rests her forehead against the wood, swallows, pushing down the camera flash of rage, knows that she's overreacting, knows that's what her shrink would say.

And then, looking down, she sees the marks in the wood, the deep gouges near the floor, and for a second she thinks it's just something that has always been there and she never noticed, that's all. But there are splinters on the floor, too, old wood freshly broken, and a fresh scatter of scaly paint flakes the color of bile. And, last thing to notice, a faint, unpleasant smell, lingering in the heavy cold, smell like a wet dog and something gone bad at the back of a refrigerator, smell like animal and mildew and mushrooms.

"Jesus," not bothering to whisper anymore. "Jesus H. Christ," and she carefully sets the books on the floor and explores one of the gouges with the tip of a finger, the rough and violated wood sharp against her soft skin. Jessie turns and looks down the hall, and there are similar marks on other doors, and a wide, diagonal slash across Olan's so big that she can see it all the way from her end. She shivers, not a cold shiver, but a prickling at the back of her neck, shorthair tingle down her arms at the sight of each of the doors with their own, individual scars. But all of them are closed, no sign that whoever made the gouges actually managed to break into a single one of the apartments.

Jessie locks her door, thinking of the gift from Olan, unopened and lying useless on her coffee table; *It's a rough neighborhood* he said, and she picks up her books again, more attention to balance this time. She tries not to think about junkies with crowbars, crackheads with tire irons wandering the building while she slept, shit like that. When she gets home she'll dig out a screwdriver and hammer and put Olan's shiny new padlock on the door.

A seeker of Truth. He will never find it. But the dimmest of possibilities—he may himself become Truth.
      —Charles Fort, *The Book of the Damned* (1919)

SALMAGUNDI
(NEW YORK CITY, 1981)

ELGIN IS SIPPING HIS SECOND BEER AND WATCHING the empty space past the footlights that haven't been turned on yet, matte-black plywood hole hardly big enough to call a stage, small by even the frugal standards he's gotten used to the last two years; these two years frantically divvied between New York and LA, Seattle and San Francisco, watching, interviewing, writing up everything from guerrilla street theater to post-feminist performance art for *The Village Voice* and anyone else who will pay him enough to pretend this is journalism. Fuck that, just anyone willing to publish what he says, what *they* say to him, and now this piece for *RE/Search*, for a volume on industrial culture, and he looks at the flyer again, torn off a telephone pole on Bleecker Street. Paper the color of a blood stain, maybe, or a ketchup stain, at least, and the sort of cut-up art he would have expected; violent, disconnected images from anonymous sources, and handprinted across the top, "Salmagundi" and a date and an hour and the address of this place where a rat would think twice about taking a dump. SubAllegory, the sign above the door says, though that wasn't on the flyer.

Elgin folds the ragged piece of red paper and stuffs it back into his shirt pocket. His beer is warm and tastes like something made from fermented cornflakes.

And then the lights come up, dazzling sudden white in the smoke and gloom, and so now it is a stage, or at least a place where something is about to happen, so it'll have to do. The murmuring crowd jammed into SubAllegory stops murmuring and their heads turn that way, their eyes turn, as the eyes of one multibodied organism turning to see, hungry and maybe there will be something edible in a moment. But there's only a mountain of bone, jackstraw pyramid of carefully balanced and interlocked femora and skulls, ribs and dry shoulder blades; mostly cow and pig, Elgin guesses, maybe some sheep, bonetrash gathered from meat packers and butchers. He has his stenographer's pad and his pencil, and he's long since learned to make notes in the dark, graphite scrawl he can decipher later in brighter places.

There are other things, suspended by metal wire or nylon fishing line and hooks, crimsongray chunks of meat and organs, a heart, a liver, a length of oysterviolet intestine at varying heights, hung to form a rough and floating mandala about the bones. And now that he thinks about it, Elgin realizes that he can smell the meat, old blood and a faint hint of rot in the cold basement air of the place—"a faint odor like fetid subtext," he writes quickly without taking his eyes off the stage.

There must be speakers he can't see because there's sound now, a painful eruption of sound as sudden as the light, feedback whine and an arrhythmic clatter like chains against shattered glass. Sound to make him wince, to make them all wince, the audience creature rediscovering forgotten and instinctual reactions, but not smart enough to run, not smart enough to cower or hide. And the sound climbs an octave, gouging its way deeper into Elgin's head. He thinks there may be a voice somewhere inside the cacophony, more than one voice, perhaps, mumbling words he can almost hear, subliminal current of words that could be threats, that *feel* like whispered threats overheard, or could be casual perversities, or could be nothing at all. His mouth feels dry, and the beer sits forgotten on the bar.

On the stage, the mound of bones seems to shift, rearranging itself subtly, an almost imperceptible sort of movement, and Elgin squints through the glare and cigarette smoke and noise to be sure. And yes, they are indeed moving, each bit of skeleton independent of the other, flexing or contracting somehow without sending the whole precarious thing clattering over. It makes him think of the hide of some great armored reptile, impossible, warped alligator or crocodile, in pain or dying or waking up, and he writes that down, as well.

Violin-string squeal that melts by grating slow degrees into a scream or piercing howl, something calling out in pain so terrible it can only be expressed in this endless, agonized lament. And past that, *within* that, an audible cracking, then, fracturing, shell-brittle pop, loud enough that it manages to pull free, achieving singularity, and Elgin feels it hit him, a fist driven against his chest, an invisible cudgel that almost knocks the breath from him. The audience creature seems to lean slightly forward, expectant, impatient for its extinction, an end to their boredom, their jaded enlightenment. Elgin knows that whatever's happening, it can only end in disappointment for them, that no revelation is even half equal to their need.

And then the bones do break apart, a silent tear or slit in the side facing him, jagged mouth or vagina; thick liquid squirting out, dark and syrupy gouts like a punctured carotid, and two or three sitting right up front move back a little, wipe at their clothes or faces or hair with fingers reluctant to touch the substance, curious to know, disgusted and excited by disgust. And the howl is fading now, growing distant or imploding, and it leaves behind a dullheart thump-thump-thump that's more metal than flesh, steamhammer pound in air raped into stillness, into vacuum, by sound.

The slit grows a little wider, and Elgin can see something membranous inside, pressing itself outward, a glinting surface slimy with whatever a mound of bones can bleed. And the thumping is getting louder, steel slammed against steel, and he wants to close his eyes, wants to look away, but he doesn't. It's not his job to look away; his job to watch, no matter what, to watch what they have to show and put it into words.

The crowd gasps collectively as the membrane bursts, rips wide, and spills its huge fetus onto the stage. Hesitant motion inside a caul the raw color of living viscera, and he can see the winding umbilicus leading back inside the slit, back inside this writhing thing's dead and fleshless mother. The smell of rotting is stronger, suddenly, and he can see the maggots squirming in the lights, hundreds or thousands of them, and now the audience creature is breaking up, losing cohesion as more and more of its constituent parts back away from the stage.

The mechanic heart crashes, pumps train collisions and the inevitable collapse of skyscrapers, steel and concrete, as she tears herself free, hands and arms as pale as skin that has never seen the sun, that cannot imagine warmth or light, thrust towards them all. The caul heaves once, slides heavily to one side, heaves again, and she's free and ripping at the cord leading back into that appalling, dead womb, tearing at it with vicious teeth, furious, grinding jaws; her long hair flails and slaps wetly from side to side, slinging drops of liquid and maggot afterbirth into the crowd.

And Elgin doesn't remember standing, defeated, but he's pushing people aside, roughly shoving his way through the press of bodies to the door, out into the south Manhattan night air that has never smelled so clean, never half so pure. He climbs the cement stairs leading up to the street, then leans gasping against a brick wall, trying to force the cloying sweet decay smell from his nostrils, and when Elgin Murray glances down at his stenographer's pad, there's hardly anything written there at all.

"You're Murray," the girl says, doesn't ask but says it like an order, like he might have ever thought he had some choice in the matter. "The guy that wants the interview," and he nods, yeah, dropping the butt of his cigarette to the sidewalk and crushing it out with the toe of his boot. The girl's hair is the color of pomegranates, and she's wearing blue jeans and a sweatshirt stained with streaks of something that might be oil or stage blood. "C'mon then," she says, a hint of irritation or displeasure in her voice, and he follows her around the corner, away from SubAllegory.

"She don't talk to a lot of people," the girl says. "Not just anybody, you know. You gotta understand that. You're lucky, man, gettin' to interview her."

"Yeah," Elgin says, and the girl leads him down a flight of stairs, dark burrow below a porn shop, no light at the bottom and the February air like soup down here, the cold that condensed, that gelid. "Watch your step," she says. "There might still be some ice," and the girl hammers on a door with her fist, blam, blam, blam, and in a moment there are voices from the other side.

"Who's there?" one of the voices asks, and the girl hits the door again, punching the wood for a reply. "Fuckin' ConEd, motherfucker," she growls. "Who do you think? Open the door. I'm freezin' my ass off out here, goddamnit. It's just me and the guy," and the metal sound of locks being turned, then, entrance being reluctantly granted, and Elgin hastily combs at his hair with his fingers.

"Sorry," the girl says to him as the door opens. "We gotta be careful, you know. Since that show in Jersey. Man, that was a total freakin' shitstorm."

And a big black man lets them in, finally, and there's someone smaller standing behind him, but this man is all that matters, muscles like a threat beneath ragged clothes; he glares at Elgin, suspicious eyes paid to be that way, and then the girl is towing him forward, out of the night into a narrow hallway painted glossy tangerine. Not much warmer in here, and that doesn't surprise him, but at least they're out of the wind. She takes him past doors with numbers that seem to have been assigned at random, no perceptible order, metal numerals nailed to orange doors, 8 and 21 and 3, and the air smells like dust and mildew and someone cooking meat with curry.

"I didn't see her come out," Elgin says, watching the doors, part of him still looking for the pattern, and the girl says, "There's a back way in, straight from the studio. There's all sorts of shit down here, man. It's like a goddamn rat maze under these buildings."

"Oh," he says as they stop at the door numbered 12, fifth in line but it gets to be 12 anyway, and there's a pencil-thin junky sitting on the floor outside, flipping through a tattered *Hustler* magazine. "Is she ready for us?" the girl asks him, and the junky sniffles loudly and wipes his nose on the back of one hand. "He's the guy?" the junky asks, rheumy eyes on Elgin, and the girl says, "Yeah, he's the guy. Is she ready or not?"

"Ready as she'll ever be," the junky says and smiles, uneven, yellowrot smile and goes back to his magazine, the gaudy nudes spreading themselves on shiny paper, and the girl says, "You know you're just wastin' your time, Willy. How many months now since you had any kinda hard-on? You know you're just torturin' yourself with that shit."

"Hey, baby, I do *remember*, okay? I haven't forgotten what it *feels* like, so it doesn't hurt me to look," and the junky gives the girl the finger as she knocks three times and turns the knob to door number 12.

"I don't know why she keeps that piece of shit around here," the girl confides to Elgin, as if the junky can't hear, and Willy mumbles something obscene but doesn't bother to look away from the magazine.

The room is small, almost warm and not the cultured squalor he expected at all. Unanticipated mix of scruffy Victorian and Art Deco, a clutter of antiques ruined by time and neglect and the places that they've been. Pleasantly muted incandescence after the hallway from fringed table lamps and stained glass torchères; a framed Erté print on one wall and a Beardsley on another, something he remembers from a book of Poe or Wilde; a chaise lounge upholstered in burgundy velvet beneath a makeshift canopy of scarves and lace, a dressing table nearby and Elgin and the girl looking back at themselves from its wide, revealing mirror.

"Does she carry all this stuff around with her?" he asks and the girl's reflection nods. She points him to a chair, dark scrolled wood scuffed, mother-of-pearl inlay, and more patched velvet the color of spilled wine, so he sits down and opens his stenographer's pad again. The girl closes the door behind her, leaving him alone, and Elgin stares at the almost-blank page that he should have filled with notes during the performance. Hopes that what he remembers about the show is anything like what really happened, and from the next room someone says "Just shut up about it, Jimmy, okay? Jesus, just shut up about it," and Elgin sits up straight, didn't even realize there was another room but now he can see the door past the chaise, a dog skull hung there, its snout pointing down towards the floor and the filthy Turkish carpet he notices for the first time.

The door swings open then, and she steps into the room, final heir to a great grandfather's lost fortune, lost great grand-daughter of the Gilded Age, and his first sight of her outside photocopied art zines and then that fetal thing that she became on stage. And "Breathtaking," he will write in the inter-view, though after an argument with an editor he'll cut that word and substitute "disarming," knowing that it doesn't really matter either way because neither is any closer to the truth. Salmagundi Desvernine: blonde, blonde hair still wet and waterdark from a shower, bare feet, and her maroon bathrobe something cheap to pass for silk, her face like porcelain that might break at the gentlest touch, like ice or porcelain, and she stops and squints across the room towards him.

"Hello," she says, lips the palest pink not smiling, and the voice to match the face exactly, voice like crystal chimes tinkling in underground winds, and "Hello," he says back.

"Did I keep you waiting?" and he shakes his head, no, "I just got here."

"Good," she says. "Would you like a drink?" and then Elgin

sees the man behind her, still standing in the doorway, closer to a boy than a man, really, but tall, taller than her, *paler* than her, and his eyes hidden behind black wraparound shades. He chews nervously at one black fingernail and stares past Salmagundi, black-plastic stare towards Elgin that makes him feel nine or ten years old again and facing the rat bastard of all school-yard bullies. He glances back down at his notepad. "That would be nice," he says. "A drink would be nice."

"Jimmy? Pour Mr...?" and "Murray," Elgin volunteers at once, "Elgin Murray." She smiles for him, painful soft smile and perfect sapphire eyes. "Pour Mr. Murray a drink. Is brandy okay? We have brandy and cognac."

"Brandy's fine," Elgin says, smiling back and watching her, not looking at her ashen-skinned companion in black leather and ripped up T-shirt, black jeans and lizardskin cowboy boots.

"*Brandy's fine,*" the tall man sneers, mocking him; there are a couple of decanters on a small table nearby, cut glass half filled with liquid amber, and the tall man pours Elgin a drink from one.

"They told me that you don't like tape recorders," Elgin says to Salmagundi, and she nods, sitting down at the dressing table only a few feet away from him now and stares at herself. "I don't like hearing my voice that way," she says. "Knowing that someone can push a button and make you say things you might not mean anymore. Things you might never have meant in the first place."

"But it's okay if I take notes?" Elgin asks, holding up the pad so she can see it in the mirror, and yes, she nods, smiling again, but not such a welcoming smile this time, as if the mirror's distracting her.

The tall man walks across the room and hands Elgin a big snifter of brandy, the glass badly chipped around the rim and the initials "S.D." engraved on one side like etched frost. "Thank you," Elgin says, accepting the drink, and the man's face is blank, blank disregard for this polite intruder, and Elgin can see himself in the black sunglasses. He doesn't like what he sees there, as if he's seeing someone else's disapproving impression of him times two, and it's better to focus on the questions that he's spent a week putting together.

Salmagundi picks up a tarnished silver brush from the dressing table, pulls it carefully through her long wet hair, and "That was an amazing performance tonight," he says to her, and the interview begins.

An old tin box from one of the drawers as she talks, dents and the gold paint flecked off in places, rust like a skin disease; Elgin recognizes the portrait on the lid, the perfect profile at the center of an intricate mosaic of color like Muslim tiles of paint for ceramic. If the design isn't actually one of Alphonse Mucha's, then a clever enough forgery, and the beautiful Nouveau face close enough to the woman sitting at the dressing table to give Elgin a serious case of the heebie-jeebies. salmagundi printed in blocky red letters underneath, stylized "Whitman's" in the lower left-hand corner and "chocolates" in the lower right.

"Then it is true?" he asks, trying not to sound surprised and failing. "About your name, I mean."

Salmagundi Desvernine pauses, the lid of the box already half open, and she glances sidewise at him, not using the dressing mirror as a middle man this time, but looking directly at him, instead, and then back at the box as if she hasn't really looked at it in a very long time, and maybe it's not only a tin box, but something more that she *pretends* is only a tin box.

"It was my mother's," she says. "It was my grandmother's, and she gave it to my mother."

"And that's where she got your name, off that tin?"

"It used to really make my sister laugh, that I was named after a box of candy."

And then she opens the box the rest of the way, and there's a small plastic baggie of white powder inside, a razor blade and a mirror that might have been popped out of a compact. Other things too, crammed in there, but she closes the box before Elgin can see what they are. She untwists the rubber band holding the baggie closed and carefully pours cocaine onto the little mirror, minces it with the razor blade, and Elgin looks down at his notepad, trying hard to remember what he was going to say next.

"You were asking me about the film project," she says, and "Yeah," he replies, "...*Between the Gargoyle Trees*, why didn't you finish it?," embarrassed but relieved to be reminded, relieved to get on with it. The tall, pale boy in leather and sunglasses is watching him now, and he imagines the kind of eyes those glasses might hide, intent and predatory eyes, jealous eyes the color of jade idols or a stormy autumn sky.

"I saw a clip last year in Montreal, a very brief clip, but it was definitely—"

"It was bullshit, Elgin," Salmagundi says quickly, finishing his sentence for him, and she's made three neat lines of the coke, uses a shortened bit of straw to snort the first two. She closes her eyes then, fists clenched, jaw clenched and a hint of her white teeth. Thirty seconds, forty, and "It was a mistake," she says and wipes her nose with a Kleenex from a box on the dressing table. "A lumbering, pretentious mistake. I'm just glad I figured that out before I wasted any more time on the damned thing.

"Jesus, it was worse than the poems. I thought maybe I could explain these ideas with film, explain them visually, since they've killed poetry."

"Who's killed poetry?"

And she looks at him a long moment, wry hint of a smile pulling at the corners of her mouth like fishhooks; Salmagundi shakes her head, and her sapphire eyes sparkle.

"*They*, Elgin. They. Everyone since fucking Yeats and T. S. Eliot. Jesus, whatever all these fuckers call themselves today. *They*. The 'poet-citizens.' You can't really touch people with poetry anymore because it's been taken apart, eviscerated, and no one even *half* remembers how to put it back together." And then she snorts the third line and closes her eyes again.

Elgin nods uncertainly; he wants a cigarette so bad it almost hurts, thinks about lighting one but there are no ashtrays anywhere in the room. "The stuff that you're doing now is so reminiscent of Mark Pauline," he says, instead, and tries not to think about the boy named Jimmy.

"Yeah, I saw *Male/Female Relations* last August, and then I talked with Mark afterwards. He showed me how to build a lot of the things I'm using, got me thinking in the right direction, anyway. Organic machines, reanimation."

"But you're still dealing with the same fundamental issues you were speaking to in... *Between the Gargoyle Trees*, right? The post-industrial landscape."

And she puts one hand to her forehead, one finger pressed between her eyes, "Jesus, Jimmy, put on some music, okay?" and "What?" he asks her without moving from his chair in the shadows. "Anything. Anything at all. I can hear the cars. Anything so I can't hear the goddamn cars and the people talking upstairs." So Jimmy gets up and goes to an old reel-to-reel on a shelf near the door leading back out to the tangerine hall, hits a switch, and The Velvet Underground's "All Tomorrow's Parties" blares from the speakers.

"I hate that phrase," she says, "I loathe it," and before Elgin can ask what she means, "Post-industrial," she adds. "As if there's nothing left now but the aftermath, like post-modern, as if there's no way that we can possibly define ourselves except in relation to... Christ, Jimmy, is that the only tape we *own*?"

"You just said it didn't matter," Jimmy sighs, sullen-voiced, returning to his chair. "And your hour's up, Mr. Murray," He says. "It was up five minutes ago."

"Yeah," Elgin replies, and he checks his wristwatch. "Just a couple more questions, okay, and then I'll get out of your hair."

"I said, your hour is *up*," and Jimmy is speaking deliberate and threatful now, and he leans forward, leans towards Elgin and his eyebrows rise slowly into dark arches above his black shades.

"Mr. Murray, I won't repeat myself again."

Elgin looks to Salmagundi for support, but she's laid her head on the dressing table, eyes closed, one hand resting on the antique candy box as if for comfort. Her damp hair hides most of her pretty face.

"You really should go now, Elgin," she says, not unkindly. "You only asked for an hour."

And so he closes his pad, has learned not to push these things, and surely he has enough for the article. Jimmy stands and opens the door for him, and "Thanks," Elgin says. "I really do appreciate your time." He looks back once, just before the door closes and locks behind him, and he sees her face framed in the mirror, that porcelain face still stained by the Hudson Valley money it came from, watching him leave, and her gemstone eyes are bright and weary and something tiny and white like a single living grain of rice falls from her forehead and lies wriggling on the dressing table by the Whitman's tin.

> *Their eyes mid many wrinkles, their eyes,*
> *Their ancient, glittering eyes, are gay.*
> W. B. Yeats, "The Gyres" (1938)

In the Water Works
(Birmingham, Alabama 1888)

R ED MOUNTAIN, WEATHERED TIP END OF APPALACHIA'S
long and scabby spine, this last ambitious foothill before
the land slumps finally down to black-belt prairies so flat
they've never imagined even these humble altitudes. And as if
Nature hasn't done her best already, as if wind and rain and
frost haven't whittled aeons away to expose the limestone and
iron-ore bones, Modern Industry has joined in the effort,
scraping away the stingy soil, and so whenever it rains, the
falling sky turns the ground to sea slime again, primordial mire
the color of a butchery to give this place its name, rustdark
mud that sticks stubbornly to Henry Matthews' hobnailed
boots as he wanders over and between the spoil piles heaped
outside the opening to the Water Works tunnel.

Scarecrow tall and thin, young Mr. Henry S. Matthews,
lately of some place far enough north to do nothing to better
the reputation of a man who is neither married nor church-
going, who teaches geography and math at the new Powell
School on Sixth Avenue North and spends the remainder of his
time with an assortment of books and rocks and pickled bugs.
The sudden rumble of thunder somewhere down in the valley,
then, and he moves too fast, careless as he turns to see, almost
losing his footing as the wet stones slip and tilt beneath his
feet.

"You best watch yourself up there, Professor," one of the workmen shouts, and there's laughter from the black hole in the mountain's side. Henry offers a perfunctory nod in the general direction of the tunnel, squinting through the haze of light October rain and dust and coal smoke at the rough grid of the little city laid out north of the mountain; barely seventeen years since John Morris and the Elyton Land Company put pen to ink, ink to paper, and incorporated Birmingham, drawing a city from a hasty scatter of ironworks and mining camps. Seventeen years, and he wonders for a moment what this place was like before white men and their machines, before axes and the dividing paths of railroad tracks.

The thunder rolls and echoes no answer he can understand, and Henry looks back to the jumbled ground, the split and broken slabs of shale at his feet. The rain has washed away the thick dust of the excavations, making it easier for him to spot the shells and tracks of sea creatures preserved in the stone. Only a few weeks since he sent a large crate of fossils south to the State Geological Survey in Tuscaloosa, and already a small museum's worth of new specimens line the walls of his cramped room, sit beneath his bed and compete with his clothing for closet space, with his books for the shelves. An antediluvian seashore in hardened bits and pieces, and just last week he found the perfectly preserved carapace of a trilobite almost the length of his hand.

A whistle blows, shrill steam blat, and a few more men file out of the tunnel to eat their lunches in the listless rain. Henry reaches into a pocket of his waistcoat for the silver watch his mother gave him the year he left for college, wondering how a Saturday morning could slip by so fast; the clockblack hands at one and twelve, and he's suddenly aware of the tugging weight of his knapsack, the emptiness in his belly, hours now since breakfast but there's a boiled egg wrapped in waxed paper and a tin of sardines in his overcoat. The autumn sky growls again, and he snaps his watch closed and begins to pick his way cautiously down the spoil towards the other men.

Henry Matthews taps the brown shell of his hard-boiled egg against a piece of limestone, crack, crack, crack, soft white insides exposed, and he glances up at the steel-gray sky overhead; the rain has stopped, stopped again, stopped for now, and crystal drops cling to the browngoldred leaves of the few hickory and hackberry trees still standing near the entrance of the tunnel. He sits with the miners, the foreman, the hard men who spend dawn to dusk in the shaft, shadowy days breaking stone and hauling it back into the sunlight. Henry suspects that the men tolerate his presence as a sort of diversion, a curiosity to interrupt the monotony of their days. This thin Yankee dude, this odd bird who picks about the spoil like there might be gold or silver when everyone knows there isn't anything worth beans going to come out of the mountain except the purple-red ore, and that's more like something you have to be careful not to trip over than try to find.

Sometimes they joke, and sometimes they ask questions, their interest or suspicion piqued by his diligence, perhaps. "What you lookin' for anyways, Mister?" and he'll open his knapsack and show them a particularly clear imprint of a snail's whorled shell or the mineralized honeycomb of a coral head. Raised eyebrows and heads nodding, and maybe then someone will ask, "So, them's things what got buried in Noah's flood?" and Henry doubts any of these men have even heard of Lyell or Darwin or Cuvier, have any grasp of the marvelous advancement that science has made the last hundred years concerning the meaning of fossils and the progression of geological epochs. So he's always politic, aware that the wrong answer might get him exiled from the diggings. And, genuinely wishing that he had time to explain the wonders of his artefacts to these men, Henry only shrugs and smiles for them. "Well, actually, some of them are even a bit older than that," or a simple and noncommittal "Mmmmm," and usually that's enough to satisfy.

But today is different and the men are quiet, each one eating his cold potatoes or dried meat, staring silent at muddy boots and lunch pails, the mining-car track leading back inside the tunnel, and no one asks him anything. Henry looks up once from his sardines and catches one of the men watching him. He smiles, and the man frowns and looks quickly away. When the whistle blows again, the men rise slowly, moving with a reluctance that's plain enough to see, back towards the waiting tunnel. Henry wipes his fingers on his handkerchief, fish-oil stains on white linen, is shouldering his knapsack, retrieving his geologist's hammer, when someone says his name, "Mr. Matthews?" voice low, almost whispered, and he looks up into the foreman's hazel eyes.

"Yes, Mr. Wallace? Is there something I can do for you today?" But Warren Wallace looks away, nervous glance to his men for a moment that seems a lot longer to Henry who's anxious to get back to his collecting.

"You know all this geology business pretty good, don't you, Mr. Matthews? All about these rocks and such?" and Henry shrugs, nodding his head. "Yes sir, I suppose that I do. I had a course or two—"

"Then maybe you could take a look at somethin' for me sometime," the foreman says, interrupting, looking back at Henry, and there are deep lines around his eyes, worry or lack of sleep, both maybe. The foreman spits a shitbrown streak of tobacco at the ground and shakes his head. "It probably ain't nothing, but I might want you to take a look at it sometime."

"Yes. Certainly," Henry says. "Anytime you'd like," but Warren Wallace is already walking away from him, following his men towards the entrance of the tunnel, shouting orders. "Be careful up there, Mr. Matthews," he says, spoken without turning around, and Henry replies that he always is, but thanks for the concern anyway, and he goes back to the spoil piles.

Fifteen minutes later, it's raining again, harder now, a cold and stinging rain from the north and wind that gusts and swirls dead leaves like drifting ash.

~≈~

May 1887 when the Birmingham Water Works Company entered into a contract with Judge A. O. Lane, Mayor and Alderman, and plans were drawn to bring water from the distant Cahaba River north across Shades Valley to the thirsty citizens of the city. But Red Mountain standing there in the way, standing guard or simply unable to move, and its slopes too steep for gravity to carry the water over the top, so the long tunnel dreamed up by engineers, the particular brainchild of one Mr. W. A. Merkel, first chief engineer of the Cahaba Station. A two thousand, two hundred foot bore straight through the sedimentary heart of the obstacle, tons of stone blasted free with gelignite and nitro, pickaxes and sledge hammers and the sweat of men and mules. The promise of not less than five million gallons of fresh water a day, and in this bright age of invention and innovation, it's a small job for determined men, moving mountains, coring them like ripe and crimson apples.

A week later, and Henry Matthews is again picking over the spoil heaps, a cool and sunny October day crisp as cider, an autumnsoft breeze that smells of dry and burning leaves, and his spirits are high, three or four exceptional trilobites from the hard limestone already and a single, disc-shaped test of some species of echinodermia he's never encountered before, almost as big as a silver dollar. He stoops to get a better look at a promising slab when someone calls his name, and he looks up, mildly annoyed at the intrusion. Foreman Wallace is standing nearby, scratching at his thick black beard, and he points at Henry with one finger.

"How's the fishin', Professor?" he asks, and it takes Henry a moment to get the joke; he doesn't laugh, but a belated smile, finally, and then the foreman is crossing the uneven stones towards him.

"No complaints," Henry says and produces the largest of the trilobites for the foreman's inspection. Warren Wallace holds the gray chunk of limestone close and squints at the small dark *Cryptolithus* outstretched on the rock.

"Well," the foreman says and rubs at his beard again, wrinkling his thick eyebrows, and he stares back at Henry Matthews. "Ain't that some pumpkins. And this little bug used to be alive? Crawlin' around in the ocean?"

"Yes," Henry replies, and he points to the trilobite's bulbous glabellum and the pair of large compound eyes to either side. "This end was its head," he says. "And this was the tail," as his fingertip moves to the fan-shaped lobe at the other end of the creature. Warren Wallace glances back at the fossil once more before he returns it to Henry.

"Now, Professor, you tell me if you ever seen anything like this here," and the foreman produces a small bottle from his shirt pocket, apothecary bottle Henry thinks at first, and then no, not medicine, nitroglycerine. Warren Wallace passes the stoppered bottle to the schoolteacher, and, for a moment, Henry Matthews stares silently at the black thing trapped inside.

"Where did this come from?" he asks, trying not to show his surprise, but his wide eyes still on the bottle, unable to look away from the thing coiling and uncoiling in its eight-ounce glass prison.

"From the tunnel," the foreman replies, then spits tobacco juice and glances over his shoulder at the gaping hole in the mountain. "About five hundred feet in, just a little ways past where the limerock goes to sandstone. That's where we hit the fissure."

Henry Matthews turns the bottle in his hand, and the thing inside uncoils, stretches chitinous segments, an inch, two inches, almost three, before it snaps back into a legless ball that glimmers iridescent in the afternoon sun.

"Ugly little bastard, ain't it?" the foreman says and spits again. "But you *ain't* never seen nothin' like it before, have you?"

And Henry shakes his head, no, never, and now he wants to look away, doesn't like the way the thing in the bottle is making him feel. But it's stretched itself out again, and he can see tiny fibers like hairs or minute spines protruding between the segments.

"Can you show me?" he asks, realizing that he's almost whispering now, library or classroom whisper like maybe he's afraid someone will overhear, like this should be secret. "Where it came from, will you take me there?"

"Yeah. I was hopin' you'd ask," the foreman says and rubs his beard. "But let me tell you, Professor, you ain't seen nothin' yet." And after Warren Wallace has taken the bottle back, returned it to his shirt pocket so that Henry doesn't have to look at the black thing anymore, the two men begin the climb down the spoil piles to the entrance of the tunnel.

A few feet past the entrance, fifteen, twenty, and the foreman stops, stands talking to a fat man with a pry bar while Henry looks back at the bright day framed in raw limestone and bracing timbers, blinking as his eyes slowly adjust to the gloom. "Yeah," the fat man says. "Yeah," and Warren Wallace asks him another question. It's cooler in the tunnel, in the dark, and the air smells like rock dust and burning carbide and another smell tucked somewhere underneath, unhealthy smell like a wet cellar or rotting vegetables that makes Henry wrinkle his nose. "Yeah, I seen him before," the fat man with the pry bar says, wary reply to the foreman's question and a distrustful glance towards Henry Matthews.

"I want him to have a look at your arm, Jake, that's all," and Henry turns his back on the light, turning to face the foreman and the fat man. "*He* ain't no doctor," the fat man says. "And I already seen Doc Joe, anyways."

"He's right," Henry says, confused now, no idea what this man's arm and the thing in the jar might have to do with one another, blinking at Wallace through the dancing whiteyellow afterimages of the sunlight outside. "I haven't had any medical training to speak of, certainly nothing formal."

"Yeah?" the foreman says, and he sighs loudly, exasperation or disappointment, then spits on the tunnel floor, tobacco juice on rusted steel rails. "C'mon then, Professor," and he hands a miner's helmet to Henry and lifts a lantern off an iron hook set into the rock wall. "Follow me, and don't touch anything. Some of these beams ain't as sturdy as they look."

The fat man watches them, massages his left forearm protectively when the schoolteacher steps past him, and now Henry can hear the sounds of digging somewhere in the darkness far ahead of them. Relentless clank and clatter of steel against stone, and the lantern throws long shadows across the rough limestone walls; fresh wound, these walls, this abscess hollowed into the world's thin skin. And such morbid thoughts as alien to Henry Matthews as the perpetual night of this place, and so he tells himself it's just the sight of the odd and squirming thing in the bottle, that and the natural uneasiness of someone who's never been underground before.

"You're wonderin' what Jake Isabell's arm has to do with that damned worm, ain't you?" the foreman asks, his voice too loud in the narrow tunnel even though he's almost whispering. And "Yes," Henry replies. "Yes, I was, as a matter of fact."

"It bit him a couple of days ago. Made him sick as a dyin' dog, too. But that's all. It bit him."

And "Oh," Henry says, unsure what else he should say and beginning to wish he was back out in the sun looking for his trilobites and mollusks with the high Octoberblue sky hung far, far overhead. "How deep are we now?" he asks, and the foreman stops and looks up at the low ceiling of the tunnel, rubs his beard. "Not very, not yet... hundred and twenty, maybe hundred and thirty feet." And then he reaches up and touches the ceiling a couple of inches above his head.

"You know how old these rocks are, Professor?" and Henry nods, trying too hard to sound calm when he answers the foreman.

"These layers of limestone here...well, they're probably part of the Lower Silurian system, some of the oldest with traces of living creatures found in them," and he pauses and realizes that he's sweating despite the cool and damp of the tunnel, wishing again he'd declined the foreman's invitation into the mountain. "But surely hundreds of thousands, perhaps *millions* of years old," he says.

"Damn," the foreman says and spits again. "Now that's somethin' to think about, ain't it, Professor? I mean, these rocks sittin' here all that time, not seein' the light of day all that time, and then *we* come along with our picks and dynamite—"

"Yes sir," Henry Matthews says and wipes the sweat from his face with his handkerchief. "It is, indeed," but Warren Wallace is moving again, dragging the little pool of lantern light along with him, and Henry has to hurry to catch up, almost smacks his forehead on the low, uneven ceiling. Another three hundred feet or so and they've reached the point where the gray limestone is overlain by beds of punky reddish sandstone, the bottom of the Red Mountain formation; lifeblood of the city locked away in these strata, clotthick veins of hematite for the coke ovens and blast furnaces dotting the valley below. "Not much farther," the foreman says. "We're almost there."

The wet, rotten smell stronger now, and glistening rivulets meander down the walls, runoff seeping down through the rocks above them, rain filtered through dead leaves and soil, through a hundred or a thousand cracks in the stone. Henry imagines patches of pale and rubbery mushrooms, perhaps more exotic fungi, growing in the dark. He wipes his face again, and this time keeps the handkerchief to his nose, but the thick and rotten smell seeps up his nostrils, anyway. *If an odor alone could drown a man*, he thinks, is about to say something about the stench to Warren Wallace when the foreman stops and holds his lantern close to the wall, and Henry can see the big sheets of corrugated tin propped against the west side of the tunnel.

"At first I thought we'd hit an old mine shaft," he says,

motioning towards the tin with the lantern, causing their shadows to sway and contort along the damp tunnel. "Folks been diggin' holes in this mountain since the forties to get at the ore. So that's what I thought, at first."

"But you've changed your mind?" Henry asks, words muffled by the useless handkerchief pressed to his face.

"Right now, Professor, I'm a whole lot more interested in what *you* think," and then Wallace pulls back a big section of the tin, lets it fall loud to the floor, tin clamor against the steel rails at his feet. Henry gags, bilehot rush from his gut and the distant taste of breakfast in the back of his mouth. "Jesus," he hisses, not wanting to be sick in front of the foreman, and the schoolteacher leans against the tunnel wall for support, pressing his left palm against moss-slick stone, stone gone soft as the hide of some vast amphibian.

"Sorry. Guess I should'a warned you about the stink," and Warren Wallace frowns, grim face like Greek tragedy, and takes a step back from the hole in the wall of the tunnel, hole within a hole, and now Henry's eyes are watering so badly he can hardly see. "Merkel had us plowin' through here full chisel until we hit that thing. Now it's all I can do to keep my men workin'."

"Can't exactly blame them," Henry wheezes and gags again, then spits at the tunnel floor, but the taste of the smell clings to his tongue, coats it like a mouthful of cold bacon grease. The foreman gestures for him to come closer, close enough he can peer down into the gap in the rock, and Henry knows that's the last thing he wants to do. But he loathes that irrational fear, fear of the unknown that keeps men ignorant, keeps men down, and all his life gone to the purging of that instinctual dread, first from himself and then his students. And so Henry Matthews holds his breath against the stench and steps over the mining car tracks, glancing once at Warren Wallace, and to see a strong man so afraid and hardly any effort into hiding it is enough to get him to the crumbling edge of the hole.

And that's the best word—*hole*—a wide crevice in the wall of the tunnel maybe four feet across and dropping suddenly away into darkness past the reach of the lantern, running west into yet more blackness but pinching closed near the tunnel's ceiling. A natural fault, he thinks at first, evidence of the great and ancient forces that must have raised these mountains up, and the smell could be almost anything. Perhaps this shaft opens somewhere on the surface, a treacherous, unnoticed pit in the woods overhead, and from time to time an unfortunate animal might fall, might lie broken and rotting in the murk below, food for devouring mold and insects. And the thing in the jar is probably nothing more or less than the larvae of some large beetle new to entomology or perhaps only the hitherto unknown pupa of a familiar species.

"Take the lantern," Warren Wallace says, then, handing the kerosene lamp to the schoolteacher. "Hold it right inside there, but don't lean too far in, mind you," and Henry feels the foreman's hand on his shoulder, weight and strength meant to be reassuring.

"Hold it out over the hole," he says, "and look down."

Henry Matthews does as he's told, already half-convinced of his clever induction and preparing himself for the unpleasant (but perfectly ordinary) sight of a badly decomposed raccoon or opossum, maybe even a deer carcass at the bottom, and the maggots, maybe more of the big black things that supposedly bit Mr. Isabell's arm. He exhales, a little dizzy from holding his breath, then gasps in another lung full of the rancid air rising up from the pit. One hand braced against the tunnel wall, and he leans as far out as he dares, a foot, maybe two, the flickering yellow light washing down and down, and he almost cries out at the unexpected sight of his own reflection staring back up at him from the surface of a narrow subterranean pool.

"It's flooded," he says, half to himself, half to the foreman, and Warren Wallace murmurs a reply, yeah, it's flooded, and something else that Henry doesn't quite catch. He's watching the water, ten feet down to the surface at the most, water as smooth and black as polished obsidian.

"Now look at the *walls*, Professor, where they meet the water," and he does, positions the lantern for a better view, and maybe just a little braver now, a little more curious, so he's leaning farther out, the foreman's hand still holding him back.

At first he doesn't see anything, the angle a little less than ninety degrees where black rock meets blacker water, and then he does see something and thinks it must be the roots of a tree growing in the pool, or, more likely, running down from the forest above to find this hidden moisture. Gnarled roots as big around as his arm, twisted wood knotted back upon itself.

But one of them moves, then, abrupt twitch as it rolls away from the others, and Henry Matthews realizes that they're *all* moving now, each tendril creeping slowly across the slick face of the crevice like blind and roaming fingers, searching. "My God," he whispers. "My God in Heaven," starts to pull away from the hole, but the foreman's hand holds him fast. "No. Not yet," Warren Wallace says calmly. "You watch them for just another second, Professor."

And one of the tendrils has pulled free of the rest, rises silently from the water like a charmed cobra. Henry can see that it's turning towards him, already six or seven feet of it suspended above the dark water, but it's still coming. The water dripping off it very, very loud, impossible drip, drip, drip like a drumbeat in his ears, like his own racing heart, and then he notices the constant movement on the underside of the thing and knows at once what he's seeing. The worm thing in Wallace's bottle, coiling and uncoiling, and here are a thousand of them, restless polyps sprouting from this greater appendage, row upon writhing row, and now it's risen high enough that the thing is right in front of him, shimmering in the lantern light, a living question mark scant feet from Henry Matthews face.

And later, lying awake in his room or walking at night along Twentieth Street, or broad daylight and staring up towards the mountain from the windows of his classroom, this is the part that he'll struggle to recall: Warren Wallace pulling him suddenly backwards, away from the hole as the tendril struck, the lantern falling from his hand, tumbling into the hole, and maybe he heard it hit the water, heard it splash at the same moment he tumbled backwards into the dark, tripped on the rails and landed hard. And the foreman cursing, the sounds of him hastily working to cover the hole in the tunnel wall again, and lastly, the dull-wet *thunk*, meatmallet thud again and again from the other side of the tin barrier.

Minutes later that seem like days, and the schoolteacher and the foreman sit alone together in the small and crooked shed near the tunnel, sloppy excuse for an office, a table and two stools, blueprints and a rusty stovepipe winding up towards the ceiling. Coal soot and the sicklysweet smell of Wallace's chewing tobacco. Henry Matthews sits on one of the stools, a hot cup of coffee in his hand, black coffee with a dash of whiskey from a bottle the foreman keeps in a box of tools under the table. And Warren Wallace sits across from him, staring down at his own cup, watching the steam rising from the coffee.

"I won't even try," Henry starts, stops, stares at the dirt floor, and then begins again. "I *can't* tell you what that was, what it is. I don't think anyone could, Mr. Wallace."

"Yeah," the foreman says, shaking his head slowly as he sips at his coffee. Then, "I just wanted you to see it, Professor, before we bring in a fellow to brick up that hole next week. I wanted someone with some education to see it, so somebody besides me and my men would know what was down there."

And for a while neither of them says anything else, and there's only the rattle and clatter of a locomotive passing by a little farther up the mountain, hauling its load of ore along the loop of the L. & N. Mineral Railroad. In the quiet left when the train has gone, the foreman clears his throat and, "You know what 'hematite' means?"

"From the Greek," Henry answers. "It means 'blood stone,'" and he takes a bitter, bourbon-tainted sip of his own coffee.

"Yeah," the foreman says. "I looked that up in a dictionary. Blood stone."

"What are you getting at?" Henry asks, watching the foreman, and Wallace looks a lot older than he ever realized before, deep lines and wrinkles, patches of gray in his dark beard. The foreman reaches beneath the table, lifts something wrapped in burlap, and sets it in front of Henry Matthews.

"Just that maybe we ain't the only thing in the world that's got a use for that iron ore," he says and pulls the burlap back, revealing a large chunk of hematite. Granular rock the exact color of dried blood, and the foreman doesn't have to point out the deep pockmarks in the surface of the rock, row after row, each no bigger around than a man's finger, no bigger around than the writhing black thing in Warren Wallace's nitroglycerine bottle.

The chill and tinderdry end of November: Mr. W. A. Merkel's tunnel finished on schedule, and the Water Works began laying the two big pipes, forty-two and thirty inches round, that would eventually bring clean drinking water all the way from the new Cahaba Pumping Station. Henry Matthews never went back to the spoil heaps outside the tunnel, never saw Warren Wallace again; the last crate of his Silurian specimens shipped away to Tuscaloosa, and his attentions, his curiosity, shifted instead to the great Warrior coal field north of Birmingham, the smoke-gray shales and cinnamon sandstones laid down in steamy Carboniferous swamps uncounted ages after the silt and mud, the ancient reefs and tropical lagoons that finally became the strata of Red Mountain, were buried deep and pressed into stone.

But the foreman's pitted chunk of hematite kept in a locked strongbox in one undusted corner of Henry's room, and wrapped in cheesecloth and excelsior, nestled next to the stone and floating in cloudy preserving alcohol, the thing in the bottle. Kept like an unlucky souvenir or memento of a nightmare, and late nights when he awoke coldsweating and mouth too dry to speak, these were things to take out, to hold, something undeniable to look at by candle or kerosene light. A proof against madness, or a distraction from other memories, the blurred, uncertain recollection of what he saw in that last moment before he fell, as the lantern tumbled towards the oil-black water and the darker shape moving just beneath its mirrored surface.

All would be well.
All would be heavenly—
If the damned would only stay damned.

—Charles Fort (1919)

The Long Hall on the Top Floor

THREE MONTHS SINCE DEACON SILVEY PULLED UP
stakes and left Atlanta, what passed for pulling up stakes
when all he had to begin with was a job in a laundromat in the
afternoons and a job at a liquor store half the night, three hundred and twelve dollars and seventy-five cents hidden in the toe
of one of his boots; and man, some motherfucker's gonna walk
in off the street one night, some dusthead with a .35, and blow
your brains out for a few bills from the register, and then it's
the goddamn *laundromat* that gets held up, instead. Three Hispanic kids with baseball bats and a crowbar, and he sat still and
kept his mouth shut while they opened the coin boxes on every
washer, every drier, watched them fill a pillow case almost to
bursting with the bright and dull quarters that spilled like noisy
silver candy. And then they were gone, door cowbell ringing
shut behind them, and Deke too goddamned astonished to do
anything but sit and stare at the violated Maytags and Ken-
mores, at Herman and Lily Munster on the little black and
white television behind the counter and turned the sound all
the way down.

So a week later he was on the bus to Birmingham, everything
he owned in one old blue suitcase and a cardboard box, Tan-
queray box from behind the liquor store to hold his paperbacks
and notebooks and all his ratty clothes stuffed into the suit-

case. And some guy sitting next to him all the way, smoking Kools, black guy named Owen smoking Kools and watching the interstate night slip by outside, Georgia going to Alabama while he told Deacon Silvey about New Orleans, his brother's barber shop on Magazine Street where he was gonna work sweeping up hair and crap like that.

"Hell, man, it's worth a shit job to be down there," and Deacon thinking the man talked like he fell backwards off a Randy Newman song and landed on his head.

"How old you be, anyways?" and the man lit another Kool, menthol-smooth cloud from his lips and leaning across the aisle of the bus towards Deke. And "Thirty-two," Deacon answered. "Shit. Thirty-two? I'd give my left big toe to see thirty-two again. Thirty-two, the womens still give a damn, you know?" And the bus rolled on, and the man talked and smoked, until 3:45 a.m. when the Greyhound pulled up under the bug-specked   yellow glare of the station and Deacon got off in downtown Birmingham.

So now Deacon works at the Highland Wash'N'Fold every other night and a warehouse in the mornings, sleeps afternoons, not much different from Atlanta except mostly it's old drag queens and young slackers in the Wash'N'Fold and no laundromat pirates so far. His new apartment a little bigger, two rooms and a bathroom, one corner for a kitchen, in a place that's built to look like a shoddy theme park excuse for a castle, Quinlan Castle in big letters out front and four turrets to prove it. But the rent's something he can afford, and the cockroaches stay off his bed if he sleeps with the light on, so it could be worse, has been worse lots of times.

And tonight's Friday, so no laundromat until tomorrow, and Deacon's sitting on a bench in a park down the hill from the castle, sipping a bottle of cheap gin, tightrope balancing act, staying drunk and making the quart last the night. August and here he is, sitting under the sodium-arc glare on the edge of a basketball court, not even midnight yet, just sipping at his gin and reading *The Martian Chronicles* by Ray Bradbury, "Mars is Heaven" and "Dark They Were and Golden-Eyed," and hoping he doesn't run out of gin before he runs out of night.

"Hey, man," and Deke looks up, green eyes tracking drunk-slow from the pages to Soda's face, hawk-nosed Soda and his twentysomething acne, battered skateboard tucked under one arm, and he never smiles because he's lost too many teeth up front. "What's kickin'," and he's already parking his skinny ass on the bench next to Deacon like he's been invited; Deke slips the McCall's into the crook of one arm, knows that Soda's already seen the bottle, but better late than never. "What do you want?" but Soda doesn't answer, stares down at the raggedy cuffs of his jeans, at the place where the grass turns to concrete, and Deacon's about to go back to his book when Soda says, "I heard you used to work for the cops, man. That true? You used to work for the cops, back in Atlanta?"

"Fuck off," Deke says, and he's wondering what it feels like to be hit in the head with a skateboard when Soda shrugs and says, "Look, I ain't tryin' to get in your shit, okay. It's just somethin' I heard."

"Then maybe you need to clean out your damn ears every now and then," Deke says and steals a sip from the bottle while Soda's still trying to figure out what he should say next.

"Yeah, well, that's what I heard, okay?"

"Soda, do I look like a goddamned cop to you?"

And Soda nervously rubs at a fat pimple on the end of his chin, rubs until it pops and the pus glistens wet under the street lights. "I didn't say you *were* a cop, asshole. I said, I heard you *worked* for them, that's all," and then the rest, quick, like he's afraid he's about to lose his courage, so it's now or never. "I heard you could do that psychic shit, Deke. That they used to get you to find dead people by touching their clothes and find stolen cars and that sort of thing. I wasn't sayin' you were a cop."

Deke wants to hit him, wants to knock the bony little weasel down and kick his last few front teeth straight down his throat. Because this isn't Atlanta, and it's been four years since the last time he even talked to a cop. "Where the hell did you hear something like that, Soda? Who told you that?"

"Look, if I tell you... Jesus, man, that just don't matter, okay? I'm tellin' you I heard this 'cause I gotta *ask* you somethin'. I'm about to ask you a favor, and I don't need you freakin' out on me when I definitely did *not* say you were a cop, okay?" And now Deke's nodding his head, careful nod like a clock ticking, tocking, closing Ray Bradbury and his eyes fixed on Soda's chest, on his Beastie Boys T-shirt and a stain over one nipple that looks like strawberry jelly, but probably isn't.

"What, Soda? What do you want?"

"It ain't even *for* me, Deke. It's this chick I know, and she's kinda weird," and Soda draws little circles in the air, three quick orbits around his right ear. "But she's all right. And it ain't even really a favor, man, not exactly. Mostly we just need you to look at somethin' for us. *If* it's true, you workin' with the cops and all. You bein' psychic."

"How many *other* people have you told I was a 'psychic'?" and Deacon makes quotation marks with his fingers for emphasis.

"Nobody. Jesus, it ain't like I'm askin' you for money or dope or nothin'," and Deke snarls right back at him, "You don't have any idea *what* you're asking me, Soda. That's the problem." And Soda's mouth open, but Deke still talking or already talking again, not about to give him a chance.

"Whatever I did for the fucking cops, they *paid* me, Soda. Whatever I did, it wasn't for goddamn charity or out of the goodness of my heart."

And Soda makes an exasperated, whistling sound through the spaces where his missing front teeth should be, then shakes his head and risks half a disgusted glance at Deacon. "What happens to make someone such a bitter motherfucker at your age, Deke? Fuckin' wino. I oughta have my head examined for believin' you ever done anything but suck down juice and watch people doin' their laundry." For a minute neither of them says anything, then, and there's only the cars and the crickets and what sounds like someone banging on the lid of a garbage can a long way off. Until Deacon sighs, takes a long pull from the bottle of gin and wipes his mouth on the back of his hand.

"Rule number one, Soda. If I do this, it's once and once only, and you're never going to ask me for anything like this ever again."

Soda shrugs, shrug that'll have to pass for understanding, for agreement. "Yeah. So what's rule number two?" and Deke looks up at the sodium streetlight glare where the stars should be. "Rule number two, you tell anyone—no—if I find out you've *already* told anyone else about this, I'm going to find you, Soda, and stick the broken end of a Coke bottle so far up your ass your gums will bleed."

A little bit more than an understatement to say that Sadie Jasper is weird; three counties south of weird and straight on to creepy more like it. She's standing on the corner by Martin Flowers, staring in at the darkened florist shop, real flowers and fake flowers and plaster angels behind the plate glass, and when she turns and looks at Deacon Silvey and Soda her expression makes Deke think of a George Romero zombie on a really bad batch of crank, that blank, that tight, and her eyes so pale blue under all the tear- and sleep-smeared eyeliner and mascara that they almost look white, boiled-fish eyes squinting from that dead face.

"This is Deke," Soda says, and Sadie holds her hand out like she's a duchess and expects Deacon to bow and kiss it. "He's the guy I was tellin' you about, okay?" Deacon shakes the girl's hand, and she almost manages to look disappointed.

"So you're the skull monkey," she says and smiles like it's something she's been practicing for days and still can't get quite right. "The psychic criminologist," she says, drawing the syllables out slow like refrigerated syrup, and tries to smile again. "Not exactly," Deacon says, wanting to be back on his bench in the park, reading about Martians, enjoying the way the gin makes his ears buzz, or all the way back in his apartment; anything but standing on a street corner with Soda and this cadaver in her black polyester pants suit and too-red lips and Scooby Doo lunch-box purse.

"Yeah, well, Soda told me you used to be a cop, but they fired you for being an alcoholic," she says, and Deacon turns around and kicks Soda as hard as he can, scuffed toe of his size-twelve Doc Marten connecting with Soda's shin like a leather sledge hammer, and Soda screams like a girl and drops his skateboard. It rolls out into the street while Soda hops about on one foot, holding his kicked leg and cursing Deacon, fuck you, you asshole, fuck both of you, you broke my goddamn leg, and then a Budweiser delivery truck rumbles past and runs over his skateboard.

Deacon walks a hesitant few steps behind Sadie Jasper, all the way to the old Harris Transfer and Warehouse building over on Twenty-Second. Just the two of them now, because when Soda finally stopped hopping around and cursing and saw what the Budweiser truck had done to his skateboard—flat, cracked fiberglass, three translucent yellow rubber wheels squashed out around the edges like the legs of a dead cartoon bug that's just been smacked with a cartoon fly-swatter, the fourth wheel rolling away down the street, spinning, frantic blur escaping any further demolition—when he saw it, took it all in, Soda made a strangled sound and sat down on the curb. Wouldn't talk to either of them or even go after what was left of his board, so they left him there, a pitiful lump of patched denim and scabs, and Deacon almost wished he hadn't kicked the son of a bitch, might actually have managed to feel sorry for him if not for Sadie, the fact that somehow his unfortunate promise to look at whatever it was they were going to look at had not been broken along with Soda's skateboard.

"I *wasn't* a cop," Deke says again, and Sadie stops walking and looks back at him, waits for him to catch up, and she's still squinting as if even the pissyellow street lights are too much for her smudgy, listless eyes. "But the psychic part, he wasn't lying about that, was he?" she asks, and Deacon shrugs. Instead of answering her, he says, "I don't think Soda meant to lie about anything. I think he's just stupid." And she smiles then, smiles for real this time instead of that forced and ugly expression from before, and it makes her look a little less like a zombie.

"You really don't like to talk about this, do you?" she asks, and Deke stops and stares up at the building, turn-of-the-century brick, rusted bars over broken windows and those jagged holes either swallowing the light or spitting it back out because it's blacker than midnight in a coffin in there, black like the second before the universe was switched on, and Deke knows he needs another mouthful of gin before whatever's coming next.

"No," he says, unscrewing the cap on the bottle, "I don't." And Sadie nods while he tips the gin to his lips, while he closes his eyes and the alcohol burns its way into his belly and bloodstream and brain. "It hurts, doesn't it?" she whispers, and Maybe I'm going to need two mouthfuls for this, Deke thinks and takes another drink.

"I knew a girl, when I lived down in Mobile," Sadie says, confession murmur like Deke's some kind of priest and she's about to give up some terrible sin. "She was a clairvoyant, and it drove her crazy. She was always in and out of psych wards, you know, and finally, she overdosed on Valium."

"I'm not clairvoyant," Deacon says. "I get impressions, that's all. What I did for the cops, I helped them find lost things."

"Lost things," Sadie says, still talking like she's afraid someone will overhear. "Yeah, that's a good word for it." Deke looks at her, looks past her at the night-filled building; "A good word for what?" he asks.

"You'll see," she says, and this time when Sadie Jasper smiles it makes him think of a hungry animal or the Grinch that stole Christmas.

They don't go in the door, of course, the locked and boarded door inside the marble arch, *Harris* chiseled deep into the pediment overhead. She leads him down the alley instead, to a place where someone's pried away the iron burglar bars and there are three or four wooden produce crates stacked under the window. Sadie scrambles up the makeshift steps and slips inside, slips smooth over the shattered glass like a raw oyster over sharp teeth, like she's done this a hundred times before, and for all he knows she has, for all he knows she's living in the damn warehouse. Deacon looks both ways twice, up and down the alley, before he follows her.

And however dark it looks on the outside, it's twice that dark inside, and the broken glass under Deke's boots makes a sound like he's walking on breakfast cereal. "Hold on a sec," Sadie says, and then there's light, weak and narrow beam from a silver flashlight in her hand, and he has no idea where she got it, maybe from her purse, maybe stashed somewhere in the gloom. White light across the concrete floor, chips and shards of window to diamond twinkle, a few scraps of cardboard and what looks like a filthy, raveling sweater in one corner; nothing else, just this wide and dust-drowned room and Sadie motions towards a doorway with the beam of light.

"The stairs are over there," she says, and leads the way. Deacon stays close, spooked, feeling foolish, but not wanting to get too far away from the flashlight. The air in the warehouse smells like mildew and dust and cockroaches, rank, closed away from the world odor that makes his nose itch, makes his eyes water a little.

"Oh, watch out for that spot there," Sadie says and the beam swings suddenly to her left and down and Deke sees the gaping hole in the floor, big enough to drop a truck through, that hole, big enough and black enough that Deke thinks maybe that's where all the dark inside the building's coming from, spilling up from the basement or subbasement, maybe, and then the flash-light sweeps right again and he doesn't have to see the hole anymore. A flight of stairs instead, ascending into the nothing past the flashlight's reach, more concrete and a crooked steel handrail Deacon wouldn't trust for a minute.

"It's all the way at the top," Sadie says, and he notices that she isn't whispering anymore, something excited now in her voice, and Deke can't tell if it's fear or anticipation.

"What's all the way at the top, Sadie? What's waiting for us up there?"

"It's easier if I just show you, if you see it for yourself without me trying to explain," and she starts up the stairs, two at a time and taking the light away with her, leaving Deke alone next to the hole. So he hurries to catch up, chasing the bobbing flashlight beam and silently cursing Soda, wishing he'd taken the bottle straight back to his apartment instead of sitting down on that park bench to read. Up and up and up the stair-well, like Alice falling backwards, and nothing to mark their progress past each floor but a closed door or a place where a door should be, nothing to mark the time but the dull echo of their feet against the cement. She's always three or four steps ahead of him, and Deacon's out of breath, gasping the musty air, and he yells at her to slow the fuck down, what's the god-damn hurry. "We're almost there," she calls back and keeps going.

And finally there are no more stairs left to climb, a landing and a narrow window, and at least it's not so dark up here. Deke leans against the wall, wheezing, trying to get his breath, his sides hurting, legs aching; he stares out through flyblown glass at the streets and rooftops below, a couple of cars, and it all seems a thousand miles away, or a film of the world, and if he broke this window there might be nothing on the other side at all.

"It's over here," Sadie says, and the closeness of her voice does nothing about the hard, lonely feeling settling into Dea-con Silvey. "This hallway here," she says, jabbing the flashlight at the darkness like a knife as he turns away from the window. "First time I saw it, I was tripping and didn't think it was real. But I started dreaming about it and had to come back to see. For sure."

Deacon steps slowly away from the window, three slow steps and he's standing beside Sadie. She smells like sweat and tea-rose perfume. Safe, familiar smells that make him feel no less alone, no less dread for whatever the fuck she's talking about. "There," she says and switches off the flashlight. "All the way at the other end of the hall."

For a moment Deacon can't see anything at all, a darting afterimage from the flashlight and nothing much else while his pupils swell, making room for light that isn't there.

"Do you feel it yet, Deacon?" she asks, whispering again, excited, and he's getting tired of this, starts to say so, starts to say he doesn't feel a goddamn thing, but will she please turn the flashlight back on. But then he *does* feel something, cold air flowing thick and heavy around them now, open-icebox air to fog their breath and send a painful rash of goosebumps across his arms. And it isn't *just* cold, it's indifference, the freezing temperature of an apathy so absolute, so perfect; Deacon takes a step backwards, one hand to his mouth, but it's too late, and the gin and his supper come up and splatter loudly on the floor at his feet.

"You okay?" she asks, and he opens his eyes, wants to slap her just for asking, but he nods his head, head filling with the cold and beginning to throb at the temples. "Do you want me to help you up?" she asks, and he hadn't even realized he was on the floor, on his knees, and she's bending over him. "Jesus," he croaks, throat raw, sore from bile and the frigid air. He blinks, tears in his eyes, and it's a miracle they haven't frozen, he thinks, pictures himself crying ice cubes like Chilly Willy. His stomach rolls again, and Deacon stares past the girl, down the hall, that long stretch of nothing at all but closed doors and a tiny window at the other end.

No, not nothing. Close, but not exactly nothing, and he's trying to make his eyes focus, trying to ignore the pain in his head getting bigger and bigger, threatening to shut him down. Sadie's pulling him to his feet, and Deke doesn't take his eyes off the window, the distant rectangle less inky by stingy degrees than the hall. "There," she says. "It's there."

And he knows this is only a dim shadow of the thing itself, this fluid stain rushing wild across the walls, washing water-color thin across the window; shadow that could be the wings of a great bird or long, jointed legs moving fast through some deep and secret ocean. Neither of those things, no convenient, comprehensible nightmare, and he closes his eyes again. Sadie's holding his right hand, is squeezing so hard it hurts. "Don't look at it," he says, the floor beneath him getting soft now and he's slipping, afraid the floor's about to tilt and send them both sliding helplessly past the closed doors, towards the window, towards it.

"It doesn't want to be seen," he says, tasting blood and so he knows that he's bitten his tongue or his lip. "It wasn't *meant* to be seen."

"But it's beautiful," Sadie says, and there's awe in her voice and a sadness that hurts to hear.

There's a new smell, then, burning leaves and something sweet and rotten, something dead left by the side of the high-way, left beneath the summer sun, and the last thing, before Deacon loses consciousness, slips mercifully from himself into a place where even the cold can't follow, the last thing, a sound like crying that isn't crying and wind that isn't blowing through the long hall.

Twenty minutes later and they're sitting together, each alone, but one beside the other, on the curb outside the Harris Trans-fer and Warehouse building; Deacon still too sick to finish the gin, too sober, and Sadie quiet, waiting to see how this ends. A police car passes by, slows down and the cop gives them the hairy eyeball, and for a second Deacon thinks maybe someone saw them climbing in or out of the window. But the cop keeps going, better trouble somewhere else tonight. "I thought he was going to stop," Sadie says, trying to sound relieved.

"Why the fuck did you guys want me to see that?" Deke asks, making no attempt to hide the anger swirling around inside his throbbing head, yellow hornets stinging the backs of his eyes. "Did you even have a reason, Sadie?" She kicks at the gravel and bits of trash in the gutter, but doesn't look at him, drawing a circle with the toe of one black tennis shoe.

"I guess I wanted to know it was real," she says, faint defiant edge in her voice, defiance or defense but nothing like repentance, nothing like sorry. "That's all. I figured you'd know, if it was. Real."

"And Soda, he never went up there with you, did he?"

Sadie shakes her head and barks out a dry little excuse for a laugh. "Are you kidding? Soda gets scared walking past funeral parlors."

"Yeah," Deacon says, wishing he had a cigarette, wishing he'd kicked Soda a little harder. Sadie Jasper sighs loudly, and the rubber toe of her left shoe sends a spray of gravel onto the blacktop, little shower of limestone nuggets and sand and an old spark plug that clatters all the way to the broken yellow center line.

"I know that you're sitting there thinking I'm a bitch," she says and kicks more grit after the spark plug. "Just some spooky bitch that's come along to fuck with your head, right?" Deacon doesn't deny it, and, anyway, she keeps talking.

"But Christ, Deacon. Don't you get sick of it? Day after motherfucking day, sunrise, sunset, getting drunk on that stuff so you don't have to think about how getting drunk is the only thing that makes your shabby excuse for a life bearable? Meanwhile, the whole shitty world's getting a little shittier, a little more hollow every goddamn day. And then, something like *that* comes along," and she turns and points towards the top floor of the warehouse. "Something that means *something*, you know? And maybe it's something horrible, so horrible you won't be able to sleep for a week, but at least when you're afraid you know you're fucking alive."

Deacon's looking at her now, and her whiteblue eyes glimmer wetly, close to tears, crimson lips trembling and pressed together tight like a red-ink slash to underline everything that she's just said. No way he can tell her she's full of shit, because he knows better, has lived too long in the empty husk of his routine not to know better, but no way he can ever admit it, either. So he just stares at her until she blinks first, one tear past the eyeliner smear and down her cheek, and then she looks away.

"Jesus, you're an asshole," she says.

"Yeah? Well, maybe you wouldn't say that if you got to know me better," and he stands up, keeping the building and its ragged phantoms at his back. "Just promise me you'll stay away from this place, okay? Will you promise me that, Sadie?"

She nods, and he guesses that's all he's gonna get for a promise, more than he expected. And then he leaves her sitting there by herself, walks away through the warm night, through the air that stinks of car exhaust and cooling asphalt, and Deacon Silvey tries not to notice his long shadow, trailing along behind.

SAN ANDREAS
(1998)

B ARELY TEN IN THE MORNING AND CRISPIN ALREADY
drunk, starting on his third Cape Cod of the day and a couple of Xanax, besides, and still the sky is too blue and the sun
too bright and the smog-shrouded Los Angeles skyline seems at
least a million miles away. Cast-iron patio furniture that used to
be white, rustcancer eating the paint that peels away like diseased skin, so it's mostly the color of dried blood, now, canvas-
ragged patio umbrella faded the dullest green, like sage, green
just before gray. And Crispin leans back in his rusty chair and
stares down from the Hollywood hills at the red tile roofs and
winding, narrow streets sloping away south, to hell and the sea
beyond.

Somewhere down the canyon someone's honking a car horn,
and the sound makes Crispin wince, squeeze his eyes shut and
rub hard at the place between them that always seems to hurt
these days, no matter how much he drinks or how many pills he
takes. The honking stops, and he opens his eyes again, another
sip of his drink, bittertart cranberry juice and sour lime, but
the vodka and ice there to smooth the sharp edges off the taste
and the jagged morning light. Day like a broken bottle, cut
yourself on a day like this and bleed to death looking for the
night, and Crispin sets his glass back on the table and tries to
remember where he left his sunglasses this time.

"You're getting too much sun, Crispin," Randall said last night, has said more than once, but last night sounding angry about it. "It's beginning to ruin your poor, beautiful skin," and Crispin wishing now the sun would burn him the color of the cracked and weathered verandah tiles, scorch him terra-cotta brown, and then maybe they would both be free, him and Lark, ruin the set so maybe Randall and Lucy would send them both packing. Spoil their bedroom games with a tan, so simple, and Crispin picks up his glass, stands on unsteady legs, and the air smells like the red bougainvillea blossoms crawling along the patio railing, that heavy, that sweet. Bougainvillea and carbon monoxide and the chaparral starting to heat up beneath the California summer sun. Crispin leans against the chair, used to the dizziness, but the smell of the flowers is making him feel a little sick, and he stares sickly back at himself from the plate-glass doors, his reflection against the heavy black velvet drapes to keep the sun always on this side of things.

The thin and drunken boy watching him from the glass still pretty enough, yes, and skin still fair enough that porcelain isn't as much a lie as exaggeration, but there's something new in the face, wary something hard and trapped that frightens Crispin, face too old for his twenty-three years, and he pulls his robe closed, wrapping himself tightly in silken skin to hide the old scars on his chest and throat.

He reaches for the doorknob, cool brass and it turns so easily in his hand, easier than walking away, with or without Lark, and the air-conditioner chill spills out thick and soothing from behind the velvet curtains, and he lets it lead him back into the house.

Crispin and Lark were still living in their one-room NoHo apartment when they met Randall and Lucy Farraday, still working together at the dark little shop on Melrose that sold antique medical and mortician's instruments, obscure and out-of-print books on human anatomy and diseases of the skin and Venus, Victorian mourning jewelry, cemetery trinkets, and it was usually enough to pay the rent and a few dollars extra left over. The twins who kept shop for Miss Alexandra (who rarely spent time in the store herself); and, come in off the baking streets on a Saturday or a Thursday, step into the dustcool shadows of Cerement and talk awhile with Lark and Crispin about trocars or rubber eyecaps, a 1705 first edition of Thomas Greenhill's *NEKPOKH◻EIA, Or The Art of Embalming*, examine stoppered, amberglass bottles that once upon a time held formaldehyde. And for all they cared, the twins, it might have gone on that way forever, Lark and Crispin with their paleperfect skin and whiter hair, kohl-smeared eyes and the cyanotic lips of drowned androgynes.

But a year ago, almost, early summer, a late June afternoon and less than half an hour to go before closing time; London After Midnight playing the Palace that evening so the twins just wanting to be done with work, maybe grab some Thai or Vietnamese take-out on their way home, but the man and woman walking in, then, both of them laughing, and the door jingled shut behind them. The tall man and taller woman, impeccable black leather, blacker silk, the two almost as dark as the twins were pale; mismatched, grown-up shadows, perhaps.

"Can we help you find anything?" Lark asked, and Crispin caught the glint of hasty fascination in her eyes, the sudden, impetuous attraction in her voice, and he was instantly annoyed with himself, annoyed at his automatic jealousy.

"Is that what you're here for, dear, to *help* people?" the woman asked, heavy accent that might have been German or Dutch, smiling, secret wink for the man, and "Is there an extra charge if I say yes?" she asked. Lark blushing then, carnation-soft wash across her round cheeks, and she looked quickly away as the woman laughed again.

"We heard you might have a print we've been after," the man said, trying to look serious, now, serious business face for Crispin and one hand held out; Crispin accepting it, the man's wide, smooth palm wrapping itself tightly around his own for a moment, and something unexpectedly intimate in the simple act of a handshake. "Farraday," the man said. "Randall Farraday."

"Well, Mr. Farraday, we have a lot of prints," Crispin said, almost stuttering, fumbling for words as the man gave his hand back to him and Crispin tried to remember what he was supposed to say next. "*La Morgue*," the man said. "1840, from *Tableaux de Paris*, if it's an original. If it's not an original, we're really not interested." And "Of course," Crispin said, leading Randall Farraday towards the back of the shop, the walnut cabinet where Alexandra kept all the old woodcuts and lithographs. This would seem very important, later, only a few seconds in the shop and already the Farradays putting distance between the twins, drawing one away from the other, divide and conquer; so obvious, but not until later, when hindsight would be as good as blind.

The print was there, which surprised Crispin because he hadn't really expected it to be, and the man stood, silent, thoughtful, inspecting the time-brittle mortuary scene in the dim light the way a jeweler might examine a peculiarly cut diamond or ruby. And Crispin inspecting him, stealing nervous glimpses when he thought the man probably wouldn't notice; something fragile in Randall Farraday's face, or something already broken, maybe, sharp face that might have been handsome ten years ago, dark stubble on his cheeks, darker circles beneath eyes the rough and uncertain color of the ocean before a storm.

The kind of face the movies or television would give a man who was a werewolf, Crispin thought, and Lark began laughing then, and he glanced over his shoulder towards her. She'd taken something out of one of the cases, and Lucy Farraday was holding it in the palm of her hand. Lark laughed again.

"Well, that's very good, then," the man said, and so Crispin turned back to the walnut cabinet, back to Mr. Farraday. "You don't know how long we've been looking for that print," he said and coughed.

Three hundred dollars scribbled on the orange price tag stuck to the protective polypropylene bag holding the print, but Alexandra made a habit of knocking off ten or fifteen percent if the customer looked like they might come back, if they looked like serious collectors, and it didn't take a genius to tell the genuinely morbid from the merely curious. "Does two hundred and seventy sound okay?" Crispin asked, and Randall Faraday smiled a gentle smile and nodded.

"That's extremely generous," he said, handing the print to Crispin, turning and calling to the woman. "They have it, Lucy. The print. Isn't that marvelous?"

Three knocks on the bathroom door, hesitant knocks that Crispin knows by heart, as familiar as her voice, and Lark whispers, "Can I come in?" Sure, Crispin replies, thinks he must have replied because she opens the door, too drunk now to be sure, but there's a draft of cooler air from the hallway mixing with the steamy bathroom atmosphere, and he slips a little farther down to get away from it, only his head held an inch or two above the soapy water now. The warm water, the alcohol and Xanax in his bloodstream, and he's been sitting in the Faraday's cast-iron, lion-footed tub for half an hour, thinking dimly about Jim Morrison and how easy it might be to drown.

"Hey," she says, sounding far away, because he's so fucked up, because time passes and things drift apart, and Crispin opens his eyes and blinks until they focus. Lark is sitting on the edge of the tub, wearing nothing but her panties, holding a rubber octopus in one hand, the other rubbing at her eyes, and for a second she almost looks like herself again, and so maybe he's just waking up from a bad dream, that's all, a nightmare or a bad batch of something they shouldn't have dropped or snorted the night before.

"They're both still asleep," she says, still whispering, and Crispin sees the track marks on her arms and stops pretending.

"What time is it?" he asks, tongue that feels too heavy for his mouth, dead meat behind his teeth, and he can hear the clumsy way the words slur and spill together.

"Almost two," she says. "I thought Lucy had a meeting this afternoon, but she's still asleep."

Lark stops rubbing at her eyes, eyeliner smears on her fingers, now but still caked around her blue eyes, too, and she looks down at the rubber octopus, eight warty arms the color of a boiled lobster. "It means they're angry, I think," she says. "When they're this color," and she drops the toy octopus into the water with Crispin, splashing him, and it sinks slowly below the surface. Crispin smiles for her, reaches for his drink and it's still right where he left it in the hanging wire basket on the side of the tub with all the bottles of shampoo and bath oil and a big gray sponge.

"You're drinking too much," she says, an expression that wants to be a scowl, and Crispin takes a sip and swallows before he answers her. "Close the door," he says. "You're letting in cold air." Steam off his wet hand, crystal beads of condensation on the glass. "Don't tell me Randall's worried about his tab at the liquor store."

"Jesus, Crispin, you didn't used to be such a hateful bastard, you know?" and she turns away and stares down at the aquamarine floor tiles instead of him. "Yeah," he says, another sip of the Cape Cod and Crispin carefully returns his glass to the wire basket, then fishes around in the water until he finds the rubber octopus where it came to rest against his right thigh.

"I'm trying to talk to you, Crispin, and lately, every time I try to talk to you, you start a fight," she says. "Do you have any idea how long it's been since we talked?" And part of him, some small and hidden part that never gets drunk, brain cranny too remote for vodka or anger, knows how badly he misses her, and maybe she's scared, too, and maybe the whole goddamn world doesn't revolve around him, after all. But something like a rush when he makes her sound this way, contact high off her pain or confusion, the novelty of cruelty. So, quickly, before there's any chance he might think better of it, "Aren't you afraid they'll hear you, Lark?" he asks. "Aren't you afraid they'll be jealous?"

"What's happening to us, Crispin?" like she didn't hear him or it simply doesn't matter anymore, questions needing to be asked even if she knows he won't or can't answer her. "It was never supposed to be like this," and then she hugs herself tightly, white arms around bare, steam-slicked shoulders and she risks a glance at Crispin, but now he's trying to stare down the octopus.

"I'm never warm anymore. I'm always so fucking cold," she says.

"Then you should put some clothes on. That is, if you still remember how."

The soft, staccato sound of the faucet dripping, small splashes of water dripping off the octopus and his arm as Crispin lifts the toy cephalopod higher above the surface and stares into its bulging black eyes, depthless acrylic eyes that neither condemn nor condone, and Lark doesn't say anything else. She sits on the edge of the tub for a few more seconds, a minute, and then she leaves and gently pulls the bathroom door shut behind her.

So, the fetish ball and London After Midnight, latex poseurs and vampire songs, and then the twins went home with the Farradays. More to it than that, of course, but nothing more that mattered, coincidence that wasn't, seductions that would seem unremarkable, later, that would seem inevitable, flies and spiders, flattery and money will get you anything in the store. Crispin still distrustful of werewolfy Mr. Farraday, but it was good to feel wanted, good to see the glow on Lark's face even though it made him jealous, and they rode in the cramped backseat of the shiny black Jaguar, racing along snake-narrow, rockslide roads, climbing up and up from city chintz and squalor into lofty canyon privilege.

A full moon that night, only one night past full, anyway, so the Hollywood sign shining white and huge like a foghorn beacon, something bright and fixed against the dark, and Lark whispering in his ear how it was all like that first scene in *The Hunger*. Lark high on White Russians and the little blue pills that Lucy Farraday had given her at the ball, "Maybe they'll cut our throats," she whispered and giggled softly. "Maybe they'll kill us and do unspeakable things to our dead bodies." One last hairpin turn, then, gravity pressing the twins together, and Crispin glanced up before he saw the Farradays' house for the first time, glanced up and the Hollywood sign was almost directly overhead, towering so close, so white, and there was something terrible in that whiteness, something hollow and absolute.

Let's go back, he almost said. *Take us back*, but knowing it was just the dope making him paranoid, the dope and Lark trying to give him the creeps somewhere in the bargain. So fuck you, Mr. Tourist Postcard Sign, and then the Jaguar slowed and nosed suddenly, sharply, downhill.

"Hang on, kids," Lucy Farraday said. "It's a bit steep, at first," meaning the driveway, concrete-steep plunge and the garage door already opening wide, say Ahhhh, but Crispin's head and stomach feeling a lot more like this was the first, precipitous drop on a roller-coaster ride. And it wasn't like no one had ever asked the twins to let them watch, let them play, too, not like this was the first time they'd let someone take them home, so no good reason he should have felt afraid, should have felt trapped, as the garage shadows replaced the moon-drenched night and the electric door clanked and rattled and slid slowly shut on greased steel tracks behind them.

And that first night, all they did was watch.

After the bath, Crispin's skin still pink and wrinkled from the water, and he goes back to the verandah, pushes aside the velvet drapes and Lark is sitting alone at the rusty umbrella table. A black T-shirt, slouchy black skirt, and she's smoking, staring southeast towards the white and distant dome of Griffith Observatory perched alone on its crumbly eyrie high above the city. Telescope eyes that never look down, glass eyes for Heaven only no matter how sweetly Babylon whispers from its desert cradle; Crispin almost backs away, not up to this shit, and there are at least a dozen other places to wait out the afternoon, not up to facing Lark again, but the door's already swinging wide, opening though he doesn't remember turning the knob, and so he steps reluctantly out onto the verandah.

The sun slipping from the sky, slow fall towards the western horizon, and in another half hour it'll be a muddy orange puddle of fire half-hidden by the Santa Monica mountains and Pacific haze. The air already getting cool, chilly breezes scented with night-blooming jasmine. Lark doesn't say anything or turn around, no sign she even knows he's there, and she just smokes her cigarette and stares at the far away white speck of the observatory. Crispin pulls one of the heavy chairs from beneath the edge of the table, but Lark's still pretending she hasn't heard him.

"Would it make any difference if I said I'm sorry?" he asks her, and she shrugs, exhales loudly and a gray cloud of smoke hangs for a moment around her head until the breeze takes it apart. "Would it really make any difference if I said yes?" she replies, and Crispin doesn't know the answer, sits silent, wishing he weren't so drunk, so he could think, or just a little drunker, so he wouldn't care.

I miss you, and for a second he's afraid he might have said it aloud, but she turns around slowly, then, and he can tell from the blank expression on her face that he didn't. The slack and drowsy look she gets after she's fixed, eyelids at half-mast, but glancing back towards the house, wary glance like maybe the house itself is watching them, listening, waiting for the wrong word, the wrong move. Stucco white spy walls, and "I want you to tell me something, Crispin," she says, so quietly that he can barely hear, but he leans forward, nods yes. "Why don't we run away?" she whispers. "Why don't we just fucking *leave*?"

"Where would we go?" and the sudden glint of something small and scared in her eyes when he says that, but she nods once, nods and looks down at the ugly needle marks on her arms, and he wishes he hadn't said anything at all. Lark turns around again and goes back to smoking and staring at the observatory.

"There's that party tonight," he says; Lark nods again, and below the verandah there's a rustling noise, dry and weed-rattle noise from the underbrush before something small cries out, sudden agony silenced halfway through, and Crispin thinks about the ribsy coyotes he's seen walking the streets at sunset, coyotes and rabbits, and Lark chuckles softly to herself.

And the second night, the Pantomime began.

Lark's prosy shorthand for the long and enervating nights that followed, for the Farradays' inclinations, the things they asked the twins to do, and finally, eventually, Lark's expression for what their lives had become. The Pantomime, and seeming innocent enough in the beginning, the twins as amused with these two strange people and their passions and perversions as the Farradays were fascinated by the twins, but fascination flashing to need, need that maybe no one had ever filled before Lark and Crispin came to their high white house in the hills. Some terrible void in the man and woman, something lost or never there to begin with, something they'd carried together for years, experimenting when they couldn't ignore it any longer, and then, such a simple and cooperative resolution found in a musty shop on Melrose Avenue. *Can we help you find anything?* and no way that Lark could have known that the question she was asking and the one that Randall and Lucy Farraday had *heard* were worlds and ages apart.

Nothing at first that the twins hadn't done before, or thought about, or at least heard of, timid necrophiliacs with nervous suggestions, nervous requests, and enough money and baubles offered up front that they couldn't really say no, could they? A week of ice water baths, a week of lying very still, shallow breathing while the Farradays kissed and caressed their pretend *rigor mortis*, and then they'd be right back at Cerement with wild, ridiculous stories for Miss Alexandra and money to buy more than shelter and cheap take-out food. That was how it started, a week of their time, seven of their nights, and Crispin not even caring if he looked like some street urchin who'd never had two pennies to rub together in his whole life when Randall Farraday gave him the thousand, two five hundred dollar bills, one for Lark, one for him.

Seven days and seven nights, and the hardest part was managing to keep a straight face.

But when the week was over there was another offer, and if the requests this time out were a little more outlandish, so was the remuneration, five thousand dollars, in advance, and Lark said yes before Crispin had a chance to say no or anything else. Miss Alexandra was not nearly so understanding when the twins asked for a second consecutive week off, but she'd already found someone to fill in and the someone was perfectly willing to stay on another week.

"Very good," Randall said, and smiled his wolfnarrow smile, and "Yes," Lucy said. "Very, very good, indeed."

"Just hang up," Lucy Farraday says again from the kitchen, louder now like maybe Randall didn't hear her the first time. "Just hang up the goddamn phone."

And Crispin's sitting alone in the purple-walled room, the Mummy Room whenever Lark mentions it, but she never actually comes in here; straight and narrow shaft of track-lit space lined with fish tanks that have never held water; black widow spiders and huge pus-yellow scorpions, the most poisonous snakes shipped all the way from Australia or India and a couple of listless, glaring Gila monsters the harvest colors of Halloween. Nothing in here that can't kill, except the mummy, tiny clay sarcophagus on its pedestal at one lonely end of the room, clay-red coffin for a cat dead three thousand years. And for the last twenty minutes Crispin's been sitting on the floor watching all the legless bodies and pinching claws, pretending he has the nerve to start smashing glass, that maybe he's finally that drunk, and then he realized he could hear the Farradays arguing.

"Hang up!" and this time Randall does what she says, dull clack when he slams the receiver back into its cradle, plastic hard on plastic, and "That motherfucker," Randall says. "That lowlife motherfucker," and he almost sounds scared. *Wouldn't that be a first?* Crispin thinks and smiles, grim and secret smile, stingy gratification.

"I told you not to get mixed up with that crazy son of a bitch, Lucy. I begged you, goddamn it—" and Crispin then hears her slap him, meat-on-meat sharp and hard like a delayed echo of the phone hanging up.

"Jesus, Randall. Shut the fuck up, okay? You think he doesn't know you're terrified of him? You think he'd say half the things he says to you if he didn't know you were ready to shit yourself every time you hear his voice?"

Little whimper, a whipped-dog sound from the wolfy man, and Crispin leans closer to the wall, straining to hear, his face so close to glass now and the scales and muscle coiled an inch away.

"I never said no to anything..." Randall says and pauses, panting and something whispered quick that Crispin doesn't catch, scared and angry murmur, and then he raises his voice again. "Not *once*, Lucy. Not *once*, until *you* wanted to get mixed up with a lowlife *ghoul* like Jimmy DeSade."

"Christ. You make it sound like a dirty word, Randall," and there's more, the Farradays going at each other, money at the heart of it, money and fear, but now they sound far away, inconsequential voices suspended in the quiet, sweat-damp place between violet walls and the sound of Crispin's heart beating too hard, too fast.

Jimmy DeSade, and for a long, long moment the binding cords of dope and cash and manipulation that have tied the twins to Randall and Lucy Farraday are almost forgotten, trivialized by a name. Five years and a whole life before this, never mind the details, the year, the exact and sordid pains faded like the sour-sweet scent of dried roses or the phantom itch of missing fingers. Jimmy DeSade, the name all that matters, the man to teach you how bad bad can be, tall man to hold your life in his cold white palm and give you back the shriveled husk when he's done. Done with you, little boy, and Crispin says that name once, aloud, sick and solemn whisper to remind himself how much worse it could be, and then, nailed into the narrow purple space between Purgatory and Damnation, he closes his eyes and sits very still.

And if he were asked, no one thing that Crispin could ever name, no single turning point where the descent began, where they knew that there was no way back. More money, for a month, two months, Miss Alexandra firing them and then the unspoken understanding, each of them knowing what they had become for the Farradays, but keeping it to themselves; Lucy tying Lark to them with the heroin that Crispin wouldn't touch, Crispin drinking to dull thoughts of unthinkable things that had become everyday, every-night amusements. No single answer to how? or when? but moments like buoys in a whirlpool, moments standing out to mark the steady fall, around and around and down, and once he almost made a list of them.

The night they locked Lark inside a shiny black casket, and she screamed until dawn, clawed at the lining and her hands in white bandages for a week.

The make-up artists they hired to transform the twins into rotting zombies or charred corpses or bodies dragged from mangled automobiles.

The first night the Farradays brought a *real* corpse home. The first night that the corpse was human.

The smell of road kill and formaldehyde and calla lilies.

The restless, rainfall sound of live maggots on satin sheets.

All these things and a hundred more, and if he were asked, Crispin might list subtler things, a glance from Lucy, the weight of Randall's hand against his forehead, the sound of the front door opening, a car in the driveway. But no one moment, except the first, perhaps, the night at Cerement when they might have said no, when they might have ignored the Farradays' fishhook flattery and gone to the Palace alone.

An hour left until the party and Lark so fucked up that Crispin has to dress her, dress her like some living rag doll; junklimp, hypo-scarred arms through spiderweb sleeves, corsetry cinched tight around her waist. And all the time she's talking, talking or crying, slurred apologies for being such a pain in the ass, or else she's cursing him for not leaving her the hell alone. Her pulse so slow, eyes wandering when they're even open, and every few minutes he presses his thumb to her wrist, needing a drink so bad it hurts but trying to stay halfway sober because she's scaring him tonight. No idea how many times she's shot up today, and Jesus, it's just another one of the Farradays' cotillions for perverts and morticians, their dark circle of compatriots, another occasion to trot out the twins like prized and hoarded poodles, nothing they haven't already lived through a dozen times.

"Please," she mutters. "Please just go away, Crispin," and he's trying to finish lining her eyes but Lark's head keeps lolling forward. "C'mon," he says, coaxing, pleading, wanting to slap her and wanting to hold her, keep her safe from the hours between now and sunrise. "It'll be over before you know it," and now he's whispering. "It always is, and then you can sleep, Lark. Then you can sleep."

"It's never, ever over," she says, eyes almost focusing, dope-swollen pupils that could swallow him alive. "It won't ever *be* over."

And Crispin does slap her then, ugly sound even over the

music booming from their stereo, uglier mark on her cheek, red echo of Crispin's hand on her milky skin. A crimson trickle from her nose, and *I didn't do that*, he thinks. *I didn't fucking hit her*, but he did, the blood there for proof, and now his fingers are digging deep into her bare shoulders, bird-frail bones anyone could crush with just a little effort.

"Snap out of it, Lark! What the fuck do you think they'll do if they see you like this?" and her eyes are still fixed on him, hard, silent tears streaking her makeup, black rivulets from the corners of her eyes, but no surprise in her expression, as if she always knew it could come to this, always knew he could be pushed this far.

"Not as bad as what they'll do to you, Crispin," she says, "Nothing *half* as bad, if you leave a mark on me."

He releases her, because he knows she's telling the truth and he hasn't sunk so far that he can't still be afraid of what the Farradays can do. Releases her because there's no way to reach her, anyway, no way left for him to save her or himself, and he turns his back, dresses himself, matching outfits for the twins, the belles of the wake, and in just a little while, it's time to go upstairs.

The party in the Green Room, perfect, verdant Edwardian and velvet wallpaper like dark moss growing on the walls, room crowded with cigarette smoke and the press of bodies, the anise smell of absinthe. "Hold my hand," someone whispers in Crispin's ear, and when he turns around, expecting anyone else, it's Lark and he can see that she's been crying again. He holds her hand and they sit together on the peacock-green récamier beneath a gold-framed coffin photograph of Sarah Bernhardt. "Don't let go," she says, her voice desperate, and he doesn't intend to, nods his head, okay, but "No, *say* it, Crispin, please say you won't let go of my hand." So he says it, and she's staring at Lucy Farraday, Lucy and the old Mexican man who makes movies of autopsies and embalmings.

"I'm going to kill them," she says, but he's heard her say it too many times before, nothing shocking in that hollow, wishful declaration. "I'm going to kill them both, tonight."

"No you're not," he tells her, "So stop talking shit, Lark," because he's not up to the game tonight, too much effort just staying sober to waste energy humoring her. But then she reaches deep into a fold of her skirt, white fingers rustling beneath silk and chiffon, and when she pulls her hand out again the big pistol glints smooth and black as polished midnight in her palm. Randall's gun, the huge .44 he's shown them more than once, never threatening, not really, but one more thing for the twins to fear.

"Jesus, Lark, get rid of that fucking thing," and he grabs for the gun but it's already gone, vanished back into some secret furrow of her skirt, and Crispin glances at Lucy Farraday but she hasn't seen a thing, is laughing at something the Mexican said. No evidence that anyone else in the room has seen anything, either; Randall at the stereo, his back to them, and in a moment the air is filled with organ music, antique funeral music.

"You're out of your mind," Crispin whispers, scared and sweating, heart racing, heart creeping up his goddamned throat to choke him to death.

"I think so," Lark says, sounding lost and so far away that he's never going to find her again. "I think I am crazy, Crispin," and her eyes never waver from Lucy Farraday.

And then it's time for the show again, the scene, Lucy and Randall's entertainment for their sallow, eager guests, something simple tonight, something elegant. Randall leads the twins to one shadowy corner of the room, most of the props already in place, waiting there for them: the casket and the chair and a marble-topped table with a vase of fleshy lilies. Lark doesn't resist when Randall lifts her off the floor, and Crispin's waiting for the Magnum to come tumbling out of her skirt, then, waiting for the clatter of the pistol against the floorboards, but Lark smiles for him, smiles for everyone as she's helped into the casket, as she lies down in red roses and snow-white silk. Randall Farraday shuts the lower half of the casket's lid, and Lark closes her eyes, peaceful dead-girl smile still plastered on her face. Crispin takes his seat beside the casket, his familiar mourning position; he reaches inside and Lark squeezes his hand, squeezes hard, her nails digging into him so she won't stop smiling.

Randall Farraday steps to one side, silently presenting this modest *tableau de la mort* for the carrion-hungry men and women who have come to see, to stare, to envy such a precious possession as the twins. Crispin knows his cue, practiced so often now that even his fear doesn't get in the way, and a single, hot tear leaks from his left eye and rolls slowly down his cheek. Approving murmurs from the crowd, and then the softest applause, and Lark squeezes Crispin's hand even harder.

Five minutes later and no one's moved an inch, no one's said a word, and Crispin's face is slick with tears and snot, crying for real now, head bowed, sobbing and his hand gone numb, painful pins-and-needles tingle all the way up to his shoulder. Lark's expression hasn't changed at all, no sign she's even breathing. And then someone's clapping their hands, loud and listless clap to shatter the stillness, to break the spell, and Crispin looks up, but his eyes are too full of tears to see, stinging salt blur instead of sight, and "Bravo!" someone shouts from the other side of the room. "Bravo, Mr. Farraday, sir."

And he knows that voice, something terrible and long ago that he's tried to forget, but he may as well have tried to forget his own name or the sound of thunder, and Crispin wipes his eyes on the back of his hand, squints and he can see Randall and Lucy now, and it's hard to tell which of them looks more afraid.

"I never knew what I was missing," the voice says, the tall man with a voice like gravel and ice water, rail-thin man in leather and chains, and Crispin knows the cold, autumn-sky color of the eyes he keeps hidden behind his cheap plastic sunglasses. "Honestly, I would have come up for one of your soirées sooner, Randy, if you'd told me."

And people are getting out of his way, seeping out of the Green Room while there's still time, and pretty soon there won't be anyone or anything standing between Jimmy DeSade and the Farradays. "What do you want?" Lucy asks, and the tall man looks hurt, looks offended, takes one step closer and Crispin sees the shotgun in his right hand a second before he raises it and points it like an accusing finger at the Farradays.

"Now who said I wanted anything, Lucy? Did I say I wanted anything?"

Adrenaline surge like acid in his veins, acid and fire to burn Crispin to a living cinder from the inside out if he doesn't move soon, if he doesn't fucking run, but Lark hasn't budged, hasn't even stopped smiling. And then Jimmy DeSade motions towards the twins with the barrel of his shotgun, and Crispin pisses himself, warm and helpless rush of urine to soak straight through his underwear and camisole and spatter the floor.

"Where did you dig these two up, anyway," Jimmy DeSade says and takes another step towards the Farradays. "I know I sure as hell didn't bring them to you. Don't tell me you're buying from someone else, Mr. Farraday. After everything I've done for you?"

"Just tell me what you want," Lucy says again, her voice still so big and bold, but Crispin can hear the strain, the way she's trying so hard to hide the trembling just beneath the surface, Lucy Farraday always in control of everything, always. "Tell me what you want, and I'll give it to you, and then you can get the hell out of my house," she says.

Jimmy DeSade walks over and puts the barrel of the shotgun against her forehead, his finger tight around the trigger, and Randall's sinking to his knees now, like he would worship this terrible, pale man, would offer up frantic pagan prayers to save them all, to save himself.

"I *want* the twenty-five grand you owe me, Mrs. Farraday. For the drowned girl. I don't give that shit away, you know."

"Please," Randall says. "Please, for god's sake, don't do this—" and Jimmy DeSade kicks him, the silver-sharp toe of one cowboy boot cracking ribs, and Randall Farraday doubles over and lies gasping for air at the tall man's feet.

"Shut up, motherfucker. I bring you sick fucks your goddamn toys, and I expect to be paid, do you fucking *understand* me, Mrs. Farraday?" No sound from Lucy, but she nods her head, once, and Jimmy DeSade cocks the shotgun, uses it to push her back against the wall. "So I expect to be fucking paid for my trouble, on *time*, and instead I have to drag my ass all the way up to your little party and find out that, not only have you not paid me, you've gone and bought a dead girl from somebody else."

"I'm not dead, asshole," and Crispin looks away from Lucy Farraday and the tall man, and Lark's standing up in the casket, the .44 in both hands and aimed straight at Jimmy DeSade's head. She isn't smiling anymore, and Crispin stares stupidly down at his arm, at the hand he never felt her release, hanging numb at his side.

And Jimmy DeSade laughs, a dry, desert sound, rattlesnake and heatstroke laugh, and he presses Lucy's head hard against the velvet wall. "Well, I guess I owe you an apology, Mrs. Farraday," he says, then laughs again and turns his head slowly towards the twins. "So what's it gonna be, dead girl? You think you're gonna save this bitch? You think you're gonna be a hero, and maybe these two bags of shit will pay you a little extra for your performance?"

Lark glances at Lucy and then back to Jimmy DeSade. "Pull the trigger," she says, and the tall man smiles.

Still an hour or two left until dawn and the black Jaguar rushes along between the bluffs of shale and sandstone, Interstate 5 winding northwest between steep cliffs carved from the mountains before the twins were born, through Tejon Pass and the city lights are already far behind them, the scrub and sand-scorch wastes stretching out ahead, towards San Francisco, Portland, Seattle, anywhere but here. Motion the only thing that really matters now, distance, not destination, and Crispin behind the wheel, Lark in the seat next to him, staring silently out at the night, the star-crowded sky hung so low, gaudy indigo and pin-prick fire drooping down towards the world.

Crispin watches the headlights on the road, trying not to think about the roar and flash of the shotgun, the blooddark smears down green velvet, the frenzied promises Randall made before he died; but trying harder not to remember the first time they met Jimmy DeSade, the long summer after the riots, and that time he took almost everything but their lives. And this time, this time giving them that much back, some terrible, unspoken pact between him and Lark, or old scores settled, calling it even, and the tall man took his money and left them alone with the corpses of Lucy and Randall Farraday.

Trying to think of nothing but the road, nothing but escape.

"Are you sure you're okay?" he asks.

"Yeah," Lark replies, even though he knows she'll be hurting in a few hours. But there's a fat baggie of dope from Lucy's stash with all the other shit they took from the house, and Lark's kit, too, her needles and spoon, the length of clear plastic tubing she uses for a tourniquet. "Just drive," she says. "I'll be fine now." And so Crispin drives while Lark watches the sky, and she doesn't fall asleep until the sun has set the eastern horizon on fire and the only thing left of the night is trapped deep inside their souls.

MERCURY
(ATLANTA, 1986)

THE GIRL WATCHED DEACON SILVEY AS HE SMILED A sloppy, oblivious sort of smile for her and poured himself another glass of the cheap tequila. She was starting to get on his nerves, watching him from her place on the floor, the *way* she had of watching a person, or only the way she had of watching him, whichever. He wanted a cigarette, but knew better; she never let him smoke in her room. A little of the Montezuma trickled down the side of the bottle, and he caught it with an index finger before it could drip to the ugly yellow-orange carpet. The liquor more precious by far than his sorry, withering soul, of that much he was certain—waste not, want not—and he screwed the cap tightly back on the bottle and set it down on the crooked, cluttered table beside her bed.

"Look at it that way," she said, "and it's only a matter of finding an effective catalyst, something to trigger a postembryonic morphogenesis," sounding very serious, because she never sounded any other way.

"Hell, that ought to be a fucking breeze," and he tipped his glass towards her in a mock toast, then emptied half the drink in one long swallow and wiped his mouth on the back of his hand.

"You're making fun of me again," she said, neither sullen nor angry, but maybe a tad or two disappointed in him, and Jesus

H. Crap, Deacon thought, how the hell much can a crazy girl expect from a goddamn drunk?

"I am not," he replied unconvincingly. "Cross my heart and hope to die. Scout's honor." And then he drained the glass and belched

"You were never a Boy Scout."

"Sure I was. Weren't you? Baby, I've been *lots* of things."

"You don't believe a word I've said."

Deacon nodded his head and squinted at her through the dim, summer evening light filling up the hotel room. "Don't you take it personally," he said. "I hardly ever believe anything I say, either," and he laughed, expecting her to laugh, too, though she rarely ever laughed at anything. But the girl just sat there and stared at him with those bright and secretive eyes that were either green or brown, depending on the light and her mood. She was sitting on the floor across the room from him, her back pressed firm against the door and her long skirt spread out around her like the petals of an   enormous black flower. She'd been sitting there for almost an hour, watching him drink. As far as he could tell, she never touched the stuff, and if she had any other vices or bad habits, she kept them well hidden.

"Never mind," Deacon said, beginning to wish that he'd stayed in his own room tonight, and he reached for the bottle again. He'd known the girl for almost two months, ever since she'd shown up one afternoon with a couple of battered Samsonite suitcases and a cardboard box of books and moved into the room next door to his. Her name was Audrey, she said, and she also said she was from Los Angeles, though he thought maybe there was a hint of something Mid-Atlantic in her accent. She wore her long brown hair pulled back in a ponytail, tied up with a bit of what looked like package string. Her face was too thin, too pale, her cheekbones too high, but she was as close as anyone was ever likely to come to pretty in a dump like the Clermont Motor Hotel, and Deacon Silvey figured that she'd at least be more interesting to talk to than the squalid menagerie of winos and hookers and junkies that nested like cockroaches in the old hotel. And besides, he'd never actually met a real, live transsexual before.

"Most of the time, I might as well be talking to myself as talking to you," she said. "I might as well be talking to the walls."

"Now, kiddo, *that's* a goddamn fact. You can write that shit in ink. And you can bet twenty dollars that the walls won't ever go and piss you off by talking back."

"It's one thing to have all this stuff in your head," Audrey said, almost whispering now. "It's another thing not to have anyone who'll listen. Sometimes, it's like my head is full of bees."

"I listen," Deacon replied. "I listen to everything you say. Every single syllable."

"No, Deke, you *hear* me, and that's all you do."

"Well, listen to *this*, lady. I'm not your goddamn shrink, you know. I'm just the drunk next door."

"I think you could be a lot more than that, if you had the nerve. If you'd stop drinking. You're so smart. You're—"

"Getting ready to leave, sunshine," Deacon grumbled, picking up the half-empty bottle of Montezuma. "I get plenty enough of this shit from my own conscience."

And "No," she said, "please don't go," desperation and regret like dull shreds of tinfoil in her voice, not standing up, but holding one hand out towards him as if she knew some magic trick that could keep him from leaving. "I don't want to be alone tonight. I'm sorry about what I said. I talk too damn much, that's all. I've got to learn when to keep my mouth shut."

"You don't talk too much," Deacon said and sighed, wishing he'd bought two bottles, knowing there was no way one was going to get him through the night. "But, you know, people come to a place like this," and he motioned at the peeling wallpaper and the shabby furnishings and the water-stained ceiling, "they're here for a reason. Maybe they don't want to be told there's anything else out there. They don't like to hear that shit. They want to keep the blinders on, all snug and tight."

"Is that what the booze is for you, your 'blinders'?"

"Something like that."

He'd helped her carry her stuff in, had browsed through her box of books while she unpacked her clothes and bathroom stuff. Nothing much he'd read, or even heard of, which was saying something: *The Historical Background of Chemistry, Occult Chemistry* from a theosophical publishing house, *Reason, Experiment and Mysticism in the Scientific Revolution*, as well as *The Hermetic and Alchemical Writings of Paracelsus the Great*, Charles Fort's *Wild Talents*, books on transhumanism and genetics and AI, books on anatomy and evolution, a battered paperback of *Frankenstein*. He'd read the Fort, and he'd read *Frankenstein* way back in junior high.

"What do you read for fun?" he had asked, and she'd stopped transferring her bras and panties from one of the Samsonite suitcases to one of the dresser drawers long enough to stare at him, a baffled, slightly offended stare like he'd just asked her how often she got it on with farm animals, like he was speaking a foreign, heathen tongue.

"I read a lot of sci-fi," Deacon had told her, and she'd shrugged and gone back to her unpacking.

"There's so little time," she'd said.

And two weeks later, sitting with her back to the door, "There's no time for blinders," she said and stared intently at the ugly carpet, as though deciphering the secret language of cigarette burns and mystery stains. "Sometimes I know I'm very, very close."

"Close to what? That catalyst you're always going on about?"

"Maybe. If I'm very lucky. That or something else. Sometimes we find exactly what we're looking for only by looking for the wrong thing. Sometimes we find what we need, and it's not what we were looking for at all."

"Is that some sort of Buddhist riddle? You're starting to sound like Yoda."

"It's not a riddle," she said and stopped staring at the floor so she could stare at the ceiling, instead. "Who's Yoda? I don't know all that much about Buddhism."

"Never mind," Deacon said again, because he was too drunk to try to explain to this strange girl who and what Yoda was, this girl who never seemed to have seen a movie in her life, this girl who read medieval   alchemical texts and politely turned up her nose when he tried to loan her *The Martian Chronicles* or *Dune*.

"Sometimes, the thing we need the most, we can't even begin to imagine."

"And what'll happen when you find it?" Deacon asked and poured himself another drink, deciding he was definitely going to have to walk all the way back down Ponce de Leon to Green's for another bottle before they closed. "What then?"

"What then," she said like a parrot, like an echo slumming around in flesh and rags, and Audrey closed her eyes.

"Yeah. That's what I'm *asking* you."

"'We shall not cease from our exploration, And the end of all our exploring, will be to arrive where we started, and know the place for the first time.' That's from—"

"I *have* read Eliot," he said before she could finish, but the way she quoted "Little Gidding," it still sounded like she was asking him a riddle. He sipped at his tequila, making it last, thinking what he really needed was a bottle of gin, a big bottle of Gilbey's maybe.

"I know you've read Eliot."

"So, what are you trying to say?" and he looked at her even though she still had her eyes shut and couldn't see that he was looking at her. "Are you starting to think you made a mistake, letting them cut off your dick and all?"

"Jesus Christ, Deke," she groaned and opened her eyes just so he could see her roll them, or at least that's the way it seemed to him. "I know you're not that ignorant. And I've already told you, nobody cut anything *off.*"

"You know what I mean."

"No. If you don't *say* what you mean, I don't *know* what you mean."

Outside, a police siren wailed along Ponce, banshee wail to rise above and drown the traffic noise; Deacon waited until it was past to say anything else. He took a deep breath and drained his glass again.

"Are you saying you're sorry you did it?" he asked her, trying to pick his words more carefully, fumbling for them through the clinging haze of alcohol and indifference. "That you changed your sex?"

"What I'm *saying*, Deacon Silvey, is that I see circles everywhere I look, that's all. I don't see beginnings, and I don't see ends. Just old Ouroboros, round and round and round."

"Oh. I didn't know we were talking about the Ouroboros," he said, realizing he must be a lot more confused than he'd thought and wondering if he has time to get to Green's before they closed.

"We're *always* talking about the Ouroboros," she said, "all of us, whether we know it or not."

"I'm gonna take your word for that, kiddo. You need anything from the store?"

"The liquor store?" she asked, and Deacon bobbed his head and poured more of the Montezuma into his glass. "How about a root beer?"

"You better watch that shit. It's hardcore. It'll stunt your growth."

"I could walk with you, if you want," Audrey said hopefully, and Deacon took a swallow of tequila and ran his fingers through his dirty brown hair.

"Yeah, well, you could," he said. "But I think I better go alone this time. I need some air. A&W, right?"

"Whatever they have is okay," she replied, trying not to sound disappointed that he didn't want her tagging along, but he could see that she was; just the latest blow to the crush on him that she wore as subtly as a flashing neon sign, and that was probably another problem that he wasn't dealing with. One more black mark beside his name, if anyone out there or up there or down there was keeping score.

"I won't be gone long," he said, finishing his drink and setting the glass down beside the bottle.

"You could read me another story tonight," she said, too eager, standing up quickly and brushing dust off her black skirt. "I liked that last one."

"Did you? You fell asleep."

"*Before* I fell asleep."

Deacon checked a back pocket for his wallet, checked his wallet for cash, and "Sure," he said. "A story and a root beer. It's a date."

"No, it's not," she said and almost smiled. "But I know what you meant."

"That makes one of us," he replied and left her alone in the little room that stank of dust and mildew and the gas heat, age and neglect and hopelessness and all the long decades of lost souls that had washed up at the Clermont.

We're always talking about the Ouroboros, she said in her voice that wasn't quite female, but certainly not male, *all of us, whether we know it or not*. And yeah, that was Deacon Silvey, sure as shit enough, inside out and sideways—tail-swallower to the crowned heads of nowhere, circularity extraordinaire; eternal, rolling continuation, just like Audrey said, coachwhip serpent leading itself round and round and round, because that's all he'd ever known how to do. No reckoning the times he'd wished for the simple courage to open his jaws wide and let his teeth release their hold on his own scaly ass, opening the circle at last, making it a line that might lead him *somewhere*.

Deacon had been a loyal denizen of the Clermont ever since he finally left Emory, midway through the spring semester and a guaranteed-useless undergraduate degree in philosophy, a rainy April afternoon when he finally just couldn't see the point of it anymore. Sitting on a gray stone bench outside Bowden Hall, watching as a nervous flock of starlings pecked about on the green, waiting for his Thursday afternoon class—"Introduction to Epistemology"—to begin. And suddenly the decision had been no decision at all. The only next step possible, because he couldn't imagine sitting though another two-hours-that-felt-like-six of Dr. Parkinson's droning lectures on reflection-correspondence theory or the Kantian synthesis. Couldn't stomach even the *thought* of it. The prospect alone brought on a sudden and dizzying wave of nausea so acute that he'd actually thought he might vomit, right there on the pavement at his feet. And maybe that was exactly the sensation Sartre had meant by "nausea," and maybe it wasn't. Either way, he found a dime, called his mother and told her he was dropping out. No room for discussion, no second thoughts, because the whole thing was too absurd to keep going and, anyway, it wasn't her life.

"It's not the money," she'd said. "Don't worry about the money. We want to see you *make* something of yourself, Deke. You have so much potential."

He told her that he'd see her and Dad at Thanksgiving or maybe at Christmas, and then hung up while she was still going on about potential and The Future and lost opportunities. Deacon took the bus back to his apartment near Candler Park, walking the last two or three blocks and feeling as shiftless as ever. But at least the weight of expectation had lifted. He hadn't told his mother about his drinking, or his migraines, or the reasons why he got the fucking migraines in the first place. It hadn't seemed like any of her business and, besides, it was nothing she'd ever believe, no matter how many different ways he explained it.

There'd been a little money left in his savings account, and a couple of credit cards that he'd never used, and he'd figured it was probably enough to keep him going at least until the holidays, if he ditched the apartment on Oakdale and found someplace cheaper to live. As far as he could tell, the Clermont Motor Hotel was as cheap as anyone could live, without resorting to cardboard boxes and stolen shopping carts and panhandling. A hot plate in the room, so he could make do on Ramen and Campbell's soup, splurging for eggs and toast and bacon at the Majestic every once in awhile, when he was actually, sincerely hungry and needed a good hangover meal to get him moving again.

That was his sob story. At least that was all the parts he figured anyone would ever need to hear, his sob story given a cheap suit and a haircut and a close shave. As for Audrey's, he had only a few grudging hints and slips of the tongue and contradictions that didn't really add up to anything coherent. She'd been in LA for a while, after she'd been in San Diego, after she'd been in Tijuana. She'd started taking hormones in high school, but he wasn't sure when she'd had the surgery. Sometime after college, or sometime before college, or sometime during college, and she'd had it done in Belgium or Trinidad, Colorado, depending on which day of the week you asked her.

She had a doctorate in something from somewhere, but Deacon could never quite figure out what it was or where she'd gotten it. She'd worked as an extra in the movies for a few months, but she'd never seen a single one of the films she'd walked through. She ate sunflower seeds and dry cereal straight from the box, and rarely seemed to eat much of anything else. She drank A&W root beer whenever he brought it to her. If she had a last name, she'd never volunteered it, and Deacon hadn't asked.

"Once, I saw humpback whales off Vancouver," she'd said, almost smiling, right in the middle of a story he was reading her from William Gibson's *Burning Chrome*. Deacon had waited for her so say more, perhaps to explain what relevance whale-watching had to "Hinterlands," but she hadn't, and in a little while he'd gone back to reading.

Sometimes, Audrey asked him what he'd do when the money finally ran out, asking each time as though she'd never asked before, and he'd tell her he was going to get a job when the money ran out, or he'd mention the pristine credit cards in his wallet, or he'd say he was going to hit his parents up for some cash. He wasn't sure which of those choices was more ridiculous, but any one of them always seemed to satisfy her. Deacon was never sure where Audrey's own money came from. She had enough to get by, enough to cover her room and the little that she ate, enough to buy a used book every now and then (but they were never anything he wanted to read). Once, she'd shown up with a secondhand Monopoly game, and had pestered him until he'd agreed to play. A bunch of the pieces were missing, but they'd played anyway.

But mostly she talked, and mostly he listened. Audrey talked like someone who'd been alone her entire life, her head so full of thoughts that she probably had migraines of her own, and there had never been anyone she could confide in. Or she just wanted him to think that there hadn't. Or she didn't care what the hell he thought. She talked about alchemy and the metamorphosis of butterflies and leopard frogs, about nanotechnology and advances in genetics, about secret European societies dedicated to turning this to that to the other. And sometimes, when she was tired of talking, he read her stories about spaceships and aliens and the lonely places inside men that would still be lonely a thousand, thousand years from now.

"Hey, college boy, I done heard all about how you was tight with a sex change these days," the bum chuckled. Deacon set the quart bottle of Gilbey's back down on the shelf and glared at the ugly little man in an oil- and food- and sweat-stained Adidas t-shirt, a Braves baseball cap, and pink flip-flops. "And I heard he's a looker, too," the bum added. "Almost good as fish—"

"Who the hell even let you in here, Harley?" Deacon asked, because he knew that the bum was caught shoplifting from Green's only a month or so back, and he also knew it'd be better if he ignored the anger winding itself up hot like a knot of elastic in his empty belly.

"Man, I go wherever I *want* to go, and I don't have to answer to no   goddamn homo college-boy perverts, neither."

"If you've got any teeth left in that mouth you want to keep, you're gonna shut your yap," Deacon told the bum. "I thought you were still in jail."

"Does it *feel* like real pussy? See, I heard it don't even feel like real pussy."

Deacon looked back at the bottle of gin, at *all* the bottles of gin lined up neat and orderly on the shelf, crystal-clear quarts of solace, and what the hell was it to him what some rummy jailbird motherfucker thought he was doing with Audrey. But he also knew one thing that would feel even better than the booze, one thing that would absolutely take care of that knot in the pit of his stomach. And he could always say Harley started it, which was true. Of course, he might end up banned from the store, if he punched the bum, and then he'd have to walk all the way to Little Five Points for liquor.

"He got fake titties?" the bum chuckled and then spit on the concrete floor. "I bet he does. I bet he's got himself some of those fine fake *silicon* titties."

"Sili*cone*, you dumb sonofabitch," Deacon growled very quietly, though he didn't know whether Audrey had implants or not, and his voice, reverberating inside his skull, sounded like a sleepy grizzly bear that someone had been poking with the pointy end of a sharp stick; he felt his right hand close into a fist. He kept his eyes on the gin. The gin was one of the gods in his trusty, distilled pantheon, and his gods rarely ever let him down. Eighty-proof consolation waiting behind that red and silver label, and all he had to do was fucking ignore Harley, pick up the bottle up again, and walk down the aisle to the checkout counter.

"You some kinda goddamn fancy-pants faggot, college boy? That it? Or maybe you just can't get yourself no *real* pussy. Yeah, maybe *that's* it—"

Deacon turned and shoved the man hard, and he tripped and fell into a display of foam-rubber Budweiser can holders, which tumbled and bounced and rolled merrily away in every direction, and the bum just lay on his back, sputtering and f lailing like something that's never learned to walk or talk. One of his pink flip flops had come off and his toenails were the unhealthy yellow-brown of old mustard or the cast-off shells of deep-sea mollusks. Deacon glanced towards the front of the store and saw that the nervous Pakistani clerk was looking his way, and the rent-a-cop was already headed towards him, one beefy hand resting on the butt of his revolver.

"Harley, you're a fucking idiot," Deacon muttered, as he bent over and offered the bum a hand, the same hand that had been curled into a fist just a moment before. The bum named Harley continued sputtering and flailing and kicking foam-rubber can holders across the floor.

"What the sam hell's going on back here?" the cop asked, and Deacon shrugged convincingly and stood up again.

"I think he's having some sort of fit," Deacon said and pointed at the bum. "He asked me for spare change, and then, you know, he just keeled over like that."

The cop eyed Deacon a moment and then squatted down next to Harley.

"He might be epileptic," Deacon suggested. "Looks kind of like a seizure to me."

"You some sort of doctor or what?" the cop asked, and Deacon could tell from the tone in the his voice that it was time to take the quart of Gilbey's and move along to the register, horse make tracks, get out of Dodge while the getting was good. But he spared a quick, cold glare at Harley, making absolutely shit-sure that the bum caught the unspoken threat in his eyes: *Next time, motherfucker, it'll hurt. Next time, you won't fucking walk away. Next time, there won't be a cop waiting to save your ugly ass.*

"You sick, Mister?" the cop asked, and Harley made a noise like a dying turtle and glared back at Deacon with his cloudy eyes. "We need to call an ambulance for you?"

Deacon paid the Pakistani clerk and left with his bottle wrapped up safe in a brown paper bag. He looked back once, just in time to see the rent-a-cop helping Harley to his feet. And then he walked quickly back up Ponce to the Clermont, past a tattoo parlor and a sports bar, past other bums and telephone poles and the intersection with Bonaventure Avenue. He was almost to the front door of the hotel when he remembered the root beer.

Another night, weeks later, summer turning finally towards fall, September to October, and she was in his room for a change. She'd shown up with a half-dozen Krispy Kreme glazed dough-nuts and made him eat three of them because she said that he never ate enough. Sticky, sugared fingers, and he licked them clean and poured a glass of gin and watched as Audrey made herself comfortable on his floor.

"Why do you always sit with your back to the door?" he asked, wondering why he'd never asked her before and trying to recall if he'd ever seen her sitting any other way.

"I don't know. I've never thought about it."

"Well, it kinda looks like you're trying to make sure that noth-ing gets in, or nothing gets out."

"I've never thought about it," she said again.

The night before, he'd tried to lure her downstairs for a drink in the dingy lounge in the hotel's basement. Except, of course, she didn't drink, and she didn't like being around all that cig-arette smoke because it made her head hurt, she said. Deacon couldn't really blame her for not wanting to hang out in the Clermont Lounge. On beyond sleazy, matte-black walls and cheap draft beer and a couple of pathetic strippers who'd never make the cut in the classier meat markets out along Piedmont. So, instead, she'd talked about pollywogs, lecturing him on the regression of the tadpole's horny teeth and internal gills, resorption of the tail and limb development, the replacement of a cartilaginous skull by a bony skull, development of tongue muscles, the herbivorous tadpole's large intestine shrinking as it prepared for the adult frog's carnivorous eating habits, and so on and on and on, until Deacon had known that she was right. Most of the time, he *wasn't* listening, just sort of half *hear-ing* what she said. When she got tired of talking, he'd read her

"Dune Roller" by Julian May from a paperback collection of science-fiction short stories.

"What was I saying?" she asked him, furrowing her brow and putting a half-eaten doughnut back into the box.

"That you've never thought about—"

"No, *before* that."

"California," Deacon told her, and then he took another drink and leaned back against the headboard of the bed, which he thought made them seem sort of like bookends. Her with her back to the west, his to the east, one to watch the sunrise and the other sunset. "You were telling me about your boyfriend, the one who did special effects."

"Yeah. He was an ass," Audrey said and frowned, poking at the doughnut like she might have changed her mind and wanted the rest of it after all. "But we did some neat shit. I almost miss him sometimes."

Deacon fixed his eyes on the old brass doorknob to the right of Audrey's head. He was drunk enough now that it helped to find an anchor somewhere in the room and keep it in sight, just in case he began to drift a little too far this way or that. Audrey had been talking about her boyfriend in LA, who'd worked with Rick Baker on *The Howling* and Rob Bottin on *The Thing*. She had never seen either of the movies, but talked animatronics and latex prosthetics like a pro. At least, she sounded like a pro to Deacon, but what the hell did he know? The boyfriend had died in a car wreck somewhere in the Hollywood Hills.

"I might have married the creep, if he'd ever bothered to ask me."

"Can you do that, get married?" and the question earned Deacon another of her exasperated stares. "Oh, come on, Audrey. How am I supposed to know something like whether or not transsexuals can get married in California? You're the first one I've ever met."

Audrey pushed the doughnuts away and sucked at her right thumb for a moment.

"He never asked me," she mumbled around her thumb, "so it's not like it really matters, anyway. I don't even think we were in love. We just had the same fetish, that's all. We were both process whores."

"I'm not even going to pretend to know what the hell you're talking about now," Deacon said sleepily and reached for the bottle on the floor beside his bed.

"I mean, a finished thing is never any good. It's the act of *creating* it, that's what matters. The process—"

"Oh, I see," Deacon replied, even though he didn't.

"What's a chicken? What's a butterfly? Finished, that's all they are. Finished. It's the egg that matters, Deacon, the egg, and the chrysalis, and the tadpole."

And then she talked about all the things she'd done with the dead man she hadn't loved, the long year and a half that she'd spent as his willing canvas; the time he made her into a silver-blue shark-finned mermaid with razor teeth, a gnarled tree, a charred corpse, a werewolf. All of it wonderful, until they were done and there was only the perfect, finished illusion, only the emptiness that follows close behind inevitable orgasm, the climax that could never match the foreplay, and then she finished eating the glazed doughnut.

"Lady, I don't know when you're telling me the truth and when you're just sitting there making shit up," Deacon said, because he was too drunk to think better of it.

"I have a photo album," she said, not sounding offended, as though she had never expected him to believe her. "It's full of pictures of all the things we did. I'll show it to you some-time."

"Well, there you go," and Deacon settled back against the headboard with a fresh drink.

"But I can't stay here too much longer," she said.

Deacon glanced at the alarm clock on the nightstand beside his bed. It wasn't even midnight yet. "It's still early," he protested and pointed at the clock. "What did you come after? A ball of fire?"

"No, I mean I can't stay *here* much longer. I can't stay in Atlanta. I'm going to need to move along soon."

"Oh," Deacon muttered into the turpentine fumes rising from his glass. "Is that a fact?"

"You should think about moving along, too, Deacon Silvey. It's not good to stay in one place too long. It's not good to stagnate."

"Baby, I'm afraid whatever the hell I am, it's definitely not a process whore," and he was surprised that there was anger wedged in between the words, dividing them one from another. It was anger he hadn't intended, but didn't exactly feel like apologizing for, either. "Maybe I like stagnation. Maybe stagnation's what I do best."

"Maybe," Audrey said. "But maybe you're just like all the others. Maybe you're just afraid of change."

"If you say so."

And then she stood up, carefully straightened her skirt, which wasn't quite the color of storm clouds, and walked across the hotel room to stand at the side of his bed. Deacon stopped peering into his gin glass and stared up at her, instead.

"You're not finished," she said. "I know you think so. I know you think it's all a dead end, but maybe that's only because you think there's someplace or someone you're supposed to be." And before he could ask what she'd meant by that, Audrey leaned down and kissed him. Her sugary tongue slipped past his lips and teeth, into the cavity of his alcoholic's mouth. In a moment more, he put his hard, thin arms around her.

"Stuck in a groove," Audrey whispers, in the dream, and Deacon looks up from the book he found behind the toilet in her hotel room, the book with a Latin name that he won't remember when he wakes. The fluorescent light above the bathroom sink buzzes and flickers, because it's about to blow, because there are yellow jackets and red wasps crawling out from behind it. But none of them have wings, and they tumble helplessly, one by one, or in pairs, into the rust-stained porcelain sink. He turns his head, and Audrey's somewhere in the shadows behind him, talking to his mother and father.

"Penile inversion," Audrey says with perfect clinical detachment, and then she laughs, but it isn't exactly her laugh. It's the laugh that would have been her laugh, if she hadn't been born male, and then his parents laugh, too. "*Nobody* knows," Audrey tells them. "Nobody knows, because it's something that no one wants to think about."

There's a splash from the toilet bowl, and when he looks, the water's filled with tadpoles that aren't tadpoles. Squirming, blind things the color of semen or raw oysters, wriggling frantically past one another as their pale bodies struggle to sprout new appendages. Deacon puts the book back on the floor behind the toilet, exactly where he found it, so Audrey won't think he was snooping.

"We have a morbid, instinctual fear of mutability," Audrey says. "It's something hardwired into us. And that's what really frightened the Victorians about Darwin, the proposition that immutable forms were constantly changing. And now, now the world will have to face the mutability not only of species over geological time, but of the *individual*, from one day to the next, from hour to hour."

Deacon wipes the gray-white dust from the cover of the book off his hands onto his jeans, then flushes the toilet. The water swirls clockwise, sucking all the tadpole things away to the sewer. Where they belong, he thinks, then tries not to imagine what they might grow into, down there in the tunnels and pipes below the city, down there in the shit-stinking dark.

"No, I was never a *man*," Audrey says, that last word spoken like the most distasteful syllable in the universe, like some bit of offal clinging to the tip of her tongue. And Deacon realizes that she isn't talking to his parents anymore, that they aren't even inside the Clermont now. She sits naked on a blanket of moss, cross-legged, with the sun falling warm across her upturned face, brilliant honey-sun shafts slipping down between the shadows cast by the fronds of gigantic tree ferns and the boles of horsetails grown as tall as redwoods. Her eyes are shut, and he doesn't know if she remembers that he's there, waiting for her to see him.

"I'm so tired, Deacon," she says, so at least he knows that she's aware of his presence. "This skin, it's a prison, and I'm trapped inside." There are small peacock-blue and sage-green scales around the edges of her face and the backs of her hands, scattered across her thighs and belly and encircling her nipples. Variegated snakeskin patches that catch the sun and wink iridescent, so pretty that he wants to reach out and touch her again.

"Sometimes, I think that it will strangle me," she says, and when she opens her eyes tears spill out across her cheeks and drip to the mossy ground. "Sometimes, I think that it will crush me to a pulp." Here, in this place, this time, her eyes are a serpent's, and now her vertical pupils have contracted to narrow, painful slits.

"We are going," she says. "We are all of us going."

He doesn't think to ask her where, or why, or when, because there are sounds coming from the strange forest, sounds like great beasts moving through the undergrowth. A discordant symphony of hisses and shrieks and growls, and he flushes the toilet again, because one of the tadpole things is still in the bowl. It clings to the porcelain with misshapen forelimbs and suction-cupped toes, and it cries like a baby before the tiny maelstrom tears it free and drags it down to the same dark, putrescent hell that's taken all the others.

The water is turning red.

"'My body is that part of the world which my thoughts can change,'" she says, and in the dream Deacon knows that Audrey is quoting Lichtenberg to his parents, and if that's not enough to make him laugh, nothing ever will be. He closes the toilet's lid, laughing, so that he won't have to look at the red water anymore.

"Deacon has so many gifts," his mother says.

"But I think it's best if we don't talk about those," his father replies.

Deacon holds Audrey so tightly, the warmth of her, the faintly spicy, sweaty smells of her, and her hands move across his body like great five-legged spiders, things possessed of their own unknowable wills. Streetlight through the dirty windows of the hotel room, through the grimy curtains, and her body writhing, changing, never one thing long enough for him to be sure what he's seeing. Eyes that come and go, mouths that open and vanish without a trace, arms and legs and skin that stretches so thin and unyielding over jackstraw bones. Scales and feathers, fur and then something rough and soft and sticky like touching a garden slug. And he's in her, and she's in him, and they bleed together until there's no telling the one apart from the other.

And then, one morning in early October, she was gone. He was up earlier than usual and going down for a paper. The door to her room was standing wide open, the Hispanic maid inside making a jet-engine racket with her antique vacuum cleaner, and Deacon could see that all of Audrey's things were gone. Her books and the Samsonite luggage and the little knick-knacks that she'd kept on the dresser. He stood in the hall for a moment, not particularly surprised, staring in through the open door, until the maid turned and gave him a dirty, suspicious look. He would have asked her if she knew where Audrey had gone, but he knew the woman didn't speak English, and he didn't speak Spanish.

There was a message waiting for him at the front desk. The bald old man whom almost everyone in the Clermont called Mr. Jim Beam handed him the envelope, and Deacon opened it and read what she'd written on a single sheet of unlined paper. Not much, just a few unsentimental lines, and he realized that he'd never seen her handwriting before. This could be anyone's handwriting, anyone's at all. But he knew that it wasn't, and he read the message through two or three times, standing there in the lobby, the Friday *Atlanta Journal-Constitution* rolled up tight and tucked into his left armpit.

"Now maybe you can find you a *real* girlfriend," Mr. Jim Beam mumbled around his loose dentures.

"She didn't say where she was going?" Deacon asked. "She didn't leave a forwarding address?" and the old man shook his head.

"She's *gone*, buddy. So I guess you better find yourself a new playmate. Shouldn't be hard. This town's stinko with she-males and pretty boys, if that's what it takes to get you off." The old man smiled, and his dentures were crooked and tobacco stained. "Why don't you just mind your own goddamn business," Deacon said, and then he folded the sheet of paper and slipped it back inside the envelope with his name written on it and went upstairs again.

LAFAYETTE
(MURDER BALLAD NO. 2)

"I DIDN'T STEAL THE MONEY," RABBIT SAYS AGAIN, speaking through clenched teeth. "I didn't steal shit," repeating himself for what seems like the tenth or fifteenth time since the ghouls pulled up outside JoJo Franklin's molly house on Burgundy Street; their old station wagon the color of a rotting pumpkin parked in the narrow alleyway, and Rabbit sat on the back stoop for half an hour waiting for them to show, sitting alone in the dark and the November drizzle, watching the night from underneath his umbrella and praying that maybe they wouldn't come and JoJo would have to think up some lesser punishment. But it's been years since anyone's bothered to answer one of Rabbit's prayers, and now he's sitting in the backseat, smoking and trying not to notice the way the car smells, as the Ford grumbles and coughs its way across Canal; leaving the Quarter behind, slipping west and south past the brick and corrugated tin walls of the warehouse district, the razor-wire loops and chain link and guard-dog signs.

"Yeah, well, whatever," the ghoul in the passenger seat says, the one named Sticky, and then she rubs at the inside of the windshield with a gray rag in an unsuccessful attempt to wipe away the stubborn condensation, but really just smearing the water back and forth across the glass.

"Stop. You're only making it worse," the ghoul driving the car says, reedy-tall boy and his hollow-cheeked face so pale and scarred by acne that it makes Rabbit think about the moon and green cheese. His name is Harper, and he leans forward and squints over the steering wheel at the narrow, rain-slick street, frowns and squints through the watery smear left by Sticky's rag, past the lazy sweep of the insufficient windshield wipers.

"Yeah, well if you weren't so goddamn cheap you could get the heater fixed," Sticky says. "Then maybe we could see where the hell we're going when it rains." No reply from Harper, just that frown on his cratered face, and then Sticky turns around in her seat and stares at Rabbit.

"It ain't so bad," she says and smiles, and Rabbit notices for the first time that she's pretty, wispy goth-girl pretty, and her eyeliner running from the rain. "I know JoJo Franklin probably told you all sorts of crazy shit, 'cause he wants to scare the crap outta you for stealing from him."

"I said I didn't steal anything," Rabbit mumbles, and then he turns away from her to stare out the window at the rain and the streetlights.

"Yeah, I know, I know," and Sticky nods her head. "But as long as Mr. JoJo *thinks* you did, we gotta go through the motions. You're lucky, kiddo. I've heard about him doing lots worse to people he *thinks* are rippin' him off. This'll be over before you even know it."

"It isn't right," and Rabbit is almost whispering now. "Breaking into dead people's graves and stealing their stuff, stealing their bones. It's sacrilegious."

Sticky rolls her eyes and laughs at him. "Well, now. Don't *that* beat all?" she says. "Little Miss crossdressing whore-boy here givin' *us* a lecture on what's right and what's wrong. D'you even *believe* this shit, Harper?"

"Robbing graves is lots worse than being a hooker," Rabbit says, knows he's pissing Sticky off now, and that'll probably only make this whole thing that much harder on him, but saying these words makes him feel the tiniest bit better way down deep inside. Quick glance at Sticky, her green eyes gone cold, angry, and Rabbit smiles and turns back to the window.

"Christ, you're a self-righteous little bitch," Sticky sighs, and "How about you stop fuckin' with the kid and put in a tape," Harper tells her, and so she turns back around, leaving Rabbit alone with his thoughts again. Plastic clatter of cassettes from the front seat, and in a minute there's metal blaring from the stereo. "Jesus, Sticky, I got more than that one goddamn tape, you know?" and "Bite me," Sticky says. "You want to hear something different, then you can find it yourself."

In the backseat, Rabbit shivers and hugs himself tight, wishing he'd worn his good coat instead of just a sweater. He watches the rain battering itself against the window, the procession of side streets and decay, his own dim reflection laid over everything, and the melancholy growl and thrash from the ghouls' tape deck sounds like the color of the sky.

All the way down Tchoupitoulas to Napoleon, the river like a crooked black leviathan on their left, and the ghoul named Harper pulls into an abandoned Texaco station. he kills the Ford's headlights and rolls to a stop beside an old Chevy van that's more bondo than paint, more rust than metal, sloppy silver-gray duct-tape bandages over the back windows. Both vehicles parked beneath the sagging steel awning, between concrete islands long since stripped of their pumps and hoses, sharing this shelter, something against the rain.

"I thought we were going to Lafayette. I thought you guys were taking me to the cemetery," Rabbit says, sounding as anxious as he feels.

"We'll get you to the boneyard soon enough, *petit lapin*," Sticky replies, lighting a cigarette, smoky words, and "Don't fret about that. Just sit tight. This is business."

Harper gets out, then, steps out of the car, and the van's driver's-side door swings open. The big man who climbs down onto the tarmac has skin the color of muddy water or roasted almonds, mulatto skin and the biggest fucking knife Rabbit's ever seen strapped into a leather sheath on his belt; there's a ragged scar across the bridge of his nose, cheek-to-cheek scar like someone tried to saw the top of his head off and damn near succeeded.

"Who's he?" Rabbit asks Sticky, and she takes another drag off her cigarette and shakes her head.

"You don't really want to know *his* name. He works for the voodoo lady. He buys most of our stuff. That's already *more* than you need to know."

"Well, I don't believe in all that shit," and Rabbit knows that he's lying, saying this out loud to piss off Sticky, and just maybe it'll make him feel a little less afraid in the bargain. "I don't believe all that voodoo shit."

"I don't remember asking if you did," Sticky says.

Rabbit leans back in his seat and watches Harper and the mulatto, trying to hear whatever they're saying, but the rain's too loud on the awning, the sour wind coming off the river, and they've turned away besides. *You could kill an alligator with a knife like that*, Rabbit thinks. *You could kill a bear.* He shivers again and buttons his navy-blue cardigan all the way up to the collar, rubs his hands together and notices how much of the cheap red nail polish he's chewed off since the ghouls picked him up. He learned a long time ago not to chew his nails because some of the johns like the way they feel, come on, little girl, dig 'em into me, make me *bleed*, and you can never tell when one of those artificial things might pop right off halfway through a trick. But now there are uneven patches of red gnawed away, and so he jams his hands deep into the pockets of his sweater; warmer that way, anyhow.

"What's your real name?" he asks Sticky, first clumsy thing that comes into his head, never mind that he's spent enough time at JoJo Franklin's to know that sort of question's none of his business, but the sizzle and drumbeat rhythm of the rain is almost worse than no sound at all, and "What's yours?" she asks him right back.

"Rabbit," he says. "My real name's Rabbit. It's even on my birth certificate."

"Well *that's* fucked up. What kinda sick, sadistic bitch names her little boy Rabbit?" and he doesn't know what to say to that, doesn't know the answer, and maybe it's better if he settles for the rain and keeps his fat mouth shut; this girl in her smudgy eyeliner, her patchwork shreds of lace and velvet, too sharp for him. Nothing that she can't shrug off, that she can't make him wish he hadn't said.

"She liked rabbits," he whispers.

And then the ghoul and the mulatto turn around again, and Harper's face looks even worse than before, paler, a blanched and seasick face, and he's rubbing hard at his pocked and stubbly chin. The voodoo man has a big arm around Harper's skinny shoulders, and he's smiling a hungry wolf-wide smile that makes Rabbit want to crawl down into the floorboard behind Sticky's seat where the man can't see him.

"God, Harper, you're such a pussy," Sticky mutters and crushes her cigarette out in the ashtray.

"Is something wrong?" Rabbit asks her, and this time Sticky doesn't answer, just stares silently through the streaky windshield at the two men standing there between the station wagon and the van. The mulatto pats his knife with one huge hand, pats it like a gunslinger in a black-and-white western movie, and then he leans close to Harper and whispers something in the ghoul's left ear. Harper nods his head, and now he's looking straight at Sticky, helpless dark eyes, shadows where his eyes should be, the puffy red flesh underneath the shadows, and Sticky lights another cigarette. The voodoo man kisses Harper on the cheek and shoves him roughly towards the Ford, shoves him so hard he stumbles, almost falls, but he catches himself on the hood.

"Shit," Sticky hisses, angry-loud cottonmouth hiss, and she's motioning for Harper to get back in the car. But he stands there in front of them, straightening his shabby clothes, and Rabbit knows that expression on his face, familiar because it's stared back at him from so many mirrors: the face you wear to make the monsters think you're not afraid of them, even when you're ready to piss your pants. *Especially* when you're ready to piss yourself. "Tell Miss Charbonnet it won't happen again," Harper says. "It was a mix-up, that's all," his voice muffled by the storm, muffled because he's out there and they're in here.

"Yeah," the big man replies. "I tell her that. But you remember, Monsieur Vautour, or she gon' be pickin' *your* bones for her gris-gris."

Rabbit staring down at his feet while the mulatto talks, counting the holes in his ratty high-top sneakers, anything so he won't have to see that look on Harper's face, and then someone's rapping hard on his window, knuckles hard against the glass, and he almost screams. When he looks up, the voodoo man is staring in; that scarred, coffee-brown face pressed against the glass, wolf smile and ivory teeth, eyes like bloodshot eggs, and "This *your* pretty boy?" he asks. "What *you* need with such a pretty boy? Maybe he come back with me."

The Ford coughs to life, dry wheeze and oil-burn hack from consumptive piston lungs, and Harper's back behind the steering wheel, spitting curses under his breath. The voodoo man grins and licks Rabbit's window, dragging his pink tongue slowly across the glass, glistening trail of saliva like something a slug would leave behind.

But then the car's moving again, pulling away from the awning and the laughing man and his Bowie knife, bald tires spinning, squealing, and in a moment they're swallowed by the night and the rain. Back on Napoleon and heading north, Rabbit's frantic heart trapped behind his ribs and trying to tear its way out, and neither Sticky nor Harper says a word, and the car doesn't slow down until they're almost all the way to Prytania Street.

Past stately Garden District homes, Corinthian and Ionic columns, wrought-iron balcony rails, a thousand hollow dreams of stolen nobility. And then this crumbling, white-walled city of the dead, walls of marble and whitewashed brick to hold in the moldering citizens of the necropolis, to divide now from then. Harper parks the Ford under the limbs of an enormous oak, great tree almost as old as the cemetery itself, age-crooked limbs draped with Spanish moss, crowned with parasitic epiphyte ferns, the massive, scabrous trunk that ends in intestine-twisted roots that have buckled and finally shattered the sidewalk. Rabbit looks out his window, up at the tree, and it makes him feel small, a tiny flame to flare and gutter, and one day soon this will all still be here without him.

"How are we supposed to get in?" he asks the ghouls, and they ignore him; Sticky's murmuring into a cell phone, and Harper's busy checking the batteries in his flashlight. Rabbit notices that the rain has almost stopped, hardly a trickle now, and he sees or imagines a cold glimpse of stars somewhere far above the tattered clouds and city lights. Twinkling fire to make even this tree feel small and young, and then Sticky's off the phone.

"It better be open this time," she says. "That's all I've got to say. Sarah says the groundskeeper took a hundred from her this afternoon, so it better not be fucking locked."

"This is gonna go *fine*," Harper tells her, screwing the head back on his flashlight. "So, *please*, see if you can stop bitching for just five minutes," but Rabbit can tell that Harper's still scared, trying to *sound* tough, trying not to think about the voodoo man and his big-ass knife.

"It's almost stopped raining," Rabbit says, and Sticky glances up at the sky through the limbs of the oak.

"Lucky fuckin' us," she mumbles and gets out of the station wagon.

Harper's already out and raising the hatch, lowering the tailgate, and he keeps looking over his shoulder to be sure that no one's watching them, no curious, prying eyes from the wide front porches along Prytania, no one braving the rain to walk their fucking dog. He takes a pickaxe and a sledgehammer from the back of the car, a crowbar, leans them all against the fender. Then an empty burlap sack like the kind Rabbit's seen filled with Vidalia onions and roasted peanuts in the French Market, but he's pretty sure this particular bag hasn't held vegetables in a very long time.

"Get the chisels," Harper whispers to Sticky, and she leans into the open hatch, removes an antique leather satchel, undoes the clasps, and then stares at whatever's inside.

"You want me to get out now?" Rabbit asks, and Harper nods, absentminded, indifferent nod, other things on his mind right now besides their passenger, besides worrisome Rabbit, and he wonders if JoJo's paid the ghouls to take him along tonight or if it's all to square some debt they owe, some "favor" to wipe the slate clean because they're into JoJo Franklin for money or drugs or worse.

Rabbit opens his door, half out into the clammy, cool night before he sees the gun Harper's holding, sleek black pistol that glints dull in the watery yellow streetlight; the ghoul pops in a fresh clip and flips off the safety before he tucks the gun into the waistband of his jeans. Rabbit closes the car door, steps over rainwater gurgling fast through the gutter, little river caught between the curb and the street, and "What do you need with that?" he asks and points at the gun. "What do you need with a gun when you're robbing dead people?"

"You ask a whole goddamn lot of questions, whore," Harper says, that last word like a slap that's supposed to sting, supposed to leave his ears ringing and his eyes watering, but Rabbit's heard it so many times, so many different ways, and by now it might as well be his middle name.

"And *you* never answer any of them," he says, and Sticky scowls bitterly up at him from her silent catalog of the satchel's contents. Then she smiles, and it's not the sad-pretty smile from before, this smile mean, cold-blooded, a smile that makes Rabbit think of the white alligators at the aquarium, the way they always seem to smile so soft and sweet when you're nothing but warm meat to them.

"People can be sentimental, *petit lapin*, and sometimes they get in the way. Tonight, we ain't got time to argue," and she closes the satchel, flips the tarnished brass clasps closed, and Harper's easing the tailgate up, the hatch down. Careful, cat-slow moves but every sound magnified in the still after the rain, and he checks again to be sure that no one's noticed them.

"You just stay close," Sticky tells Rabbit. "Don't go wandering off in there. I'd hate to think you were a ghost and shoot you by mistake." And then she hands him the pickaxe.

"Yeah, sure," Rabbit says. "Whatever," and he follows the two ghouls past the ancient oak, past the high cemetery walls, and the wind rustles wet leaves overhead, like jealous, secret voices.

Down the sidewalk and around the corner onto Washington, Rabbit always hanging back at least two or three steps behind Sticky and Harper, and the tall brick wall has turned to marble here. He knows this side isn't *just* a wall, that it doubles as the rear of a long row of vaults, the bodies laid four deep like a giant's gruesome building blocks.

All his nineteen years lived in the city, but Rabbit's never actually been inside Lafayette, this place he associates with gaudy tours of "haunted New Orleans," with the paperback Anne Rice novels he read before he dropped out of high school and ended up turning tricks for JoJo Franklin. Not that he's ever had anything against graveyards; sometimes he still slips away on long nights when it's too muggy to sleep and business is slow enough that he probably won't be missed, only a couple of blocks from the old house on Burgundy and it's easy enough to clamber over the walls into St. Louis No. 1. Sometimes he spends hours alone there, not so bad if you keep out of the way of the crack dealers and the muggers from the Iberville projects, the weir-does sneaking in for a midnight peek at Marie Laveau's tomb; a good place to get stoned and pretend he never has to go back to JoJo and the huffing, sweaty men who pay for pretty boys dressed up like prettier girls.

"See? I told you," Harper says to Sticky. "This one's gonna go smooth as duck shit," and there's smug, certain relief in his voice. Rabbit puts one hand against the ornamental iron gate, sharp staves and Victorian scrolls, the high arch that reads LAFAYETTE CEMETERY NO 1 in steel-black letters a foot high. There's a smaller gate on their left, and Harper's already swinging it slowly, carefully, open, but the hinges groan and squeak anyway. Noise like someone stomping a box of field mice, and he curses quietly under his breath and looks up and down the street before opening the gate the rest of the way.

Past the gate and down the patchy, tree-lined asphalt and cement lane that leads them towards the death-still heart of the cemetery, under low branches to form a canopy over Rabbit and the ghouls; more oaks here, and tall magnolias, too, their dry brown leaves scattered in drifts about the ground. And the weathered, stone-pale crypts on either side, the vaulted and gabled roofs, domed roofs with cornices engraved with the names of forgotten families, the forgotten dead. Marble crosses crowning some of the tombs, and others flanked by spires like the fronts of miniature cathedrals. Harper switches on his flashlight and plays it erratically along the path in front of them.

"So what's wrong with *these*?" Rabbit whispers to Sticky and points at the night-shrouded tombs along the lane, thinking she'll only ignore him again, getting used to it, anyway, but "Our clients are picky folks," she whispers back. "They have very specific needs." Then Harper shushes them both, and Rabbit sees that they've come to a sort of crossroads; they turn right, north, back towards Prytania Street. The air smells like the oily New Orleans rain and the close-cropped grass growing between the plots, growing along the path, and maybe also the faintest whiff of decay, but Rabbit suspects that's probably only in his head. Smelling the stink of rotting things only because he's nervous, because he *expects* that odor, and then he remembers the way the inside of the station wagon smelled, so maybe it's coming from the burlap sack that Harper's carrying slung over his right shoulder.

Harper turns again, then, leaving the wide main path, and Rabbit pauses, not so eager to follow the ghouls into the cluttered maze of crypts, the narrow trails between them paved with cracked and irregular flagstones, not so eager for the deeper shadows cringing between the low and close-packed houses of the dead. He thinks about getting lost in there, getting turned around in the dark and not being able to find his way out again.

"You waiting for an engraved invitation?" Sticky asks him from the dark, her annoyed, impatient hiss, and he grips the pickaxe a little tighter and steps off the path towards her, can't actually see her anymore so walking slowly towards the spot he *thinks* her voice was coming from.

Why can't I see the flashlight? Rabbit wonders and bumps one knee hard on the corner of a tomb, bites his tongue so he won't yell. The pain bright and dizzying, bright, but no light there either, and why the hell is he getting so freaked out, just a goddamned cemetery, most of these bodies gone to dust a hundred years ago. He leans against a wall, limestone weathered sandpaper rough, and waits for his leg to stop hurting, thinking about what he said back at the gas station, how he didn't believe any of this voodoo shit. No ghosts here but the ones in his head, the ones they keep around for the tourists. Rabbit closes his eyes and breathes deep, breathes slow, and the pain in his knee is already fading.

"Right here," Harper says. "This is the one," his voice not so far away, and when Rabbit opens his eyes he can see the white beam of the ghoul's flashlight again. *Just get this shit over with*, he thinks and pictures JoJo Franklin back in his house on Burgundy, laughing it up because he knows that Rabbit's out here in the rain and the cold, stumbling around in the dark with creepy Sticky and creepier Harper.

"I didn't steal anything, you stupid motherfucker," he says very, very quietly.

"Are you sure?" Sticky whispers, and "Yeah, I'm fuckin' *sure*, okay?" Harper replies, angry, indignant, raising his voice a little now. "Doesn't it say Brennan right fuckin' there?"

Rabbit follows their voices, bickering trail of bitter bread crumbs, following the unsteady flashlight, and in a moment he's standing behind the ghouls, standing behind Sticky, reading the words chiseled into the marble slab that seals the tiny mausoleum, words just beginning to wear from time and rain and all the shit in the air. Mary Elaine Brennan. Born 1896. Died 1947. May she find peace at last. *Right*, Rabbit thinks. *May she find peace until these two freaks steal her body*, and Sticky turns and glares at him like he said it out loud or maybe she can read his mind or something.

"How do you want to open it?" she asks, speaking to Harper, but she's still looking at Rabbit.

"He said we had to do it without waking her up. He said that was very important. That we do it without waking her up."

"Fine," Sticky says through a mocking, humorless smile, "We shan't wake up the poor, old dead lady," and she turns away from Rabbit, finally, and he realizes that he's sweating; never mind the cold, the dank night air, sweating from that knowing, feral look in her eyes, those irises the same translucent green as an old Coke bottle. He watches as she leans into the beam of the flashlight, searching until she finds the small bolt set near the top of the marble slab. The callused pad of one thumb rubbed slow and gentle back and forth across the rust-ruined head of the bolt, and then she glances over her shoulder at Harper, squinting at the light. "Quiet as a little pink worm," she says.

"Yeah, well, just don't take all goddamn night long doing it," Harper grumbles, and now Sticky's setting her leather satchel down on the wet grass, opening it, digging about for something inside.

"You want it done fast or you want it done right?" she asks, and Rabbit realizes that he's praying, words he thought he forgot years and years ago, forgotten like shame and dignity, like contrition, but now his lips shape them, mouthing a desperate and soundless appeal to whatever down-and-out saint watches over whores. Sticky takes her hand out of the satchel, and she's holding a T-shaped piece of steel, a small hexagonal socket welded onto one end, and Rabbit stops praying. "What's that?" he asks her.

"Just a tool of the trade," she replies, standing up again, and she fits the socket end over the bolt that holds the marble slab in place, that's held it that way for almost fifty years. Her ashen fists wrapped firm around the handles, white knuckles and wrist-taut ligaments, and Sticky takes a deep breath, exhales, and gives the steel thing a single, violent counterclockwise turn. For a second it resists her, two seconds, and then there's an ugly scrunching sound, metal grinding against old mortar, against stone, and the ghoul laughs softly to herself as she winds the strange tool around and around, drawing the bolt out, drawing it free. Rabbit glances at Harper, and his eyes are very wide, pit-dark eyes that glisten, that watch his companion's every move, and the look on his face makes Rabbit think of the men who pay however much JoJo asks for half an hour alone with one of his boys.

"Good girl," Harper whispers, breathless, lascivious whisper, and far away, off towards the north and Lake Pontchartrain, Rabbit hears a low and cracking sound from the sky, like thunder.

Fifteen minutes later, and the ghouls have opened the tomb of Mary Brennan, the thin marble slab laid to one side, deposited on a velvet-soft bed of damp cemetery grass until later, and the long bolt sitting there on top so it won't get lost. Bricks and mortar behind the marble, but Harper wrapped the head of his sledge hammer in a towel so it hardly made a sound and only took three or four good swings to punch out a hole as big around as Rabbit's fist. Then Sticky handed the flashlight to Rabbit and went to work with a mallet and a big chisel from her leather satchel, chipping away at the hole until it wasn't so small anymore, and "There," she says, "that ought to do the trick."

She puts her hammer and chisel back into the satchel, closes the bag, and turns to Rabbit; he hasn't moved, is still shining the flashlight at the hole the ghouls have made in the wall of the dead woman's crypt. Black hole in red-brown bricks and punky mortar the color of raw oysters; *Like a mouth*, he thinks and immediately shoves the unpleasant image away.

Sticky takes the flashlight from his hands, and he looks at her a moment, no need for her to tell him what comes next because he can see it on her face. Her hard white face that seems just a little sorry now, dingy shred of pity for him, and "You want me to crawl through there, don't you?" he asks her. "You want me to crawl through there and steal that lady's bones."

"That's the deal, squirt," she says. "Saves us having to make that hole any bigger, and you'll be square with your boss man. You'll be in and out of there before you know it."

"I swear I didn't steal anything from him," Rabbit says, useless mantra that doesn't even make him feel better anymore, just something that might be true; he shuts his eyes for a moment and listens to his heart beating too fast, too hard. Then there's something cold and heavy in his hands, and when he opens his eyes again he's holding a pair of pliers, red latex handles, and "All we need are her wisdom teeth," Harper says. "There are four. Two lowers, two uppers. Just work them back and forth a bit, and they should pop right out."

Rabbit takes a breath, catching the rotten smell leaking from the open tomb, and this time he's pretty sure it isn't his imagination. "You want me to pull out her teeth?" and before Harper can answer, "Jesus. Why don't I just take her whole goddamn head, and then—"

"No," Sticky says, schoolteacher firm, mothervoice, and "It can *only* be her teeth. *Nothing* else, okay? And when you're done, put these in her mouth so she won't know that you've taken anything."

And now Sticky's holding four teeth in her left palm, four ivory molars, their sharp and ginger-yellow roots, and Rabbit shakes his head, confused, tired of this crazy, morbid game. "If you've already got those, what do you want with more?"

"Those are just pig teeth," Harper says. "They're no good to us, but she won't know the difference."

"This is really twisted shit. You two know that, right?" but Rabbit takes the teeth from Sticky anyway, and they feel like dice in his hand.

"Just the wisdom teeth," Harper says again. "And do it fast. Don't fuck around in there," and this time Rabbit laughs at him, ugly hollow-dry laugh, but honest enough that it makes the tall, craggy-faced ghoul wince, that it gets Rabbit moving. "Give me the damn flashlight," he says, and before Harper can argue, Sticky hands it to Rabbit and he laughs again, for Harper, and turns his back on the ghouls.

Rabbit holds the pliers in his teeth as he wriggles and pulls himself through the rough, uneven hole in the masonry, the four pig molars and flashlight already laid inside so at least he's not crawling into pitch blackness. Crawling into glare and shadows instead, the stark and disorienting wash of light across the chilly concrete floor of the tomb, and he can see that Mary Brennan's coffin is nothing fancy; a narrow black-lacquered pine box chewed by decades of mold and the bugs, and he knows if it's locked he's probably going to have to get Sticky to pass her mallet and chisel through the hole to him. He slips, then, lets the pliers fall from his mouth, and the shattered edge of a brick bites into his ass, ripping straight through the seat of his jeans. Rabbit curses and loses his grip, loses his balance, and tumbles the rest of the way into the tomb.

He lands on top of the flashlight, and there's a tiny, brittle sound as the bulb breaks and the greedy, thick darkness rushes back to claim the inside of this fetid box, this stinking pool of midnight that hasn't been touched by the sun or fresh air for half a century. This place that was meant to stay dark forever, and for a second Rabbit thinks he'll scream, that he's finally had too much and it doesn't really matter what the ghouls will do to him, doesn't matter if someone hears and calls the cops, because he's lying on the floor of a crypt next to a dead woman's coffin, next to the dead woman *inside* the coffin, and he isn't going to be able to stop himself from screaming.

But then there's a sound outside that does stop him, a man's voice that isn't Harper, and he sees that there's enough light coming in through the hole in the masonry to find his way back. So screw playing dentist for corpses, screw all this shit, and Rabbit's scrambling across the floor on his hands and knees towards the hole when he hears the voice again. And this time he recognizes it, this time he can make out exactly what it's saying, and that's all he needs to be reminded that there are worse things in the world than rotten old ladies, worse things even than ghosts.

"Madame Charbonnet don't *give* dumb white motherfuckers no second chances," the voodoo man says, bellowing like something starving and locked inside a cage. "Madame Charbonnet got *plenty* folks what know the difference 'tween a shin bone and a short rib. She got all she ever gon' need *without* you, *vautour.*"

"*Please,*" Harper begs the man, blubbering like a beaten and terrified child. "It was a *mistake*, goddammit," he says. "It was a honest goddamn mistake."

And now Rabbit's reached the hole again, too scared to look, but peering over the edge of the bricks, anyway, worse not to know, worse to sit here waiting for *his* turn, for the big man and his knife to come looking for *him*.

"Give me a chance to make it right—"

"Yeah, Madame Charbonnet, she say you understand," the voodoo man snarls, and Rabbit's staring at the spot where his voice is coming from, but there's only Sticky, hard to see clearly in the gloom, but he's sure there's no one outside the crypt but Sticky and Harper. And then he sees the gun in her hands, Harper's gun pressed hard against his own temple, and Rabbit blinks and squints, but nothing changes. Harper on his knees in the wet grass and Sticky's holding the pistol against his head. And then she opens her mouth, and Rabbit knows where the voodoo man's voice is coming from.

"She even gon' say some prayers for you," Sticky says, but it isn't really Sticky at all, and Rabbit can see the way her eyes have rolled all the way back in her head so there's nothing showing but the whites, can see the way the muscles in her face writhe and twitch, and that makes him think of a dead cat he found once behind JoJo Franklin's, the mindless dance of maggots beneath its matted calico fur.

"Please, Jodie, *please* god don't do this to me—"

And then she squeezes the trigger, and the gunpowder roar is loud enough to wake every soul asleep in Lafayette, solid wall of sound that rolls like drowning water across the cemetery and out into the world beyond its high and chalk-white walls. Harper slumps over sideways, lies in a silent heap at her feet, and Sticky's arm jerks, marionette-stiff lurch, and then the gun's pointing at her own head. A sudden, wrenching spasm washes across her face, and Rabbit can see the black spray of blood from her nostrils.

"You shut your eyes, now, *petit lapin*," she says, and this time it's her voice, the wilted memory of her voice. "It's almost over."

In the crypt, Rabbit does what she tells him, and a second later the pistol roars again, and in the shocked silence it leaves behind he can hear sirens, and his heart, and the soft sound of rain falling on the roof of Mary Brennan's grave.

…BETWEEN THE GARGOYLE TREES

THE OLD THEATER, AND ONCE IT MUST HAVE BEEN something grand, something glitzy for the stars, maybe fifty years ago, maybe sixty. Once the ragged screen was a silver window, a magic portal to wide and Technicolor daydreams, projected delusions of heroism and happy endings while the real world went to shit outside. Never quite so ostentatious as Grauman's or the Egyptian, but nothing shoddy, either; gold paint and Art-Deco plaster, Arabian façades and miles of crushed velvet the color of a fresh cut. But then television and disillusions too deep to be brushed aside with celluloid balms, and by the seventies, the Vista was showing midnight double features for hippies and kids more interested in each other than the B-grade science fiction and horror flicks on the screen. A few more years, Reagan in the White House and a new owner up from Tijuana, and the place turned a profit screening porn and selling stroke mags and sex toys in the lobby. Finally, the Northridge quake in '94 to put the old whore out of business, to crumple her foundations and weaken the disintegrating walls, and the man from Tijuana took his settlement from the insurance company and hung a red sign out front, condemned—no trespassing. And no one has, except the rats and desert bugs, the swifts that found a broken window, the ashgray mold that grows wherever the rain gets in.

Jimmy DeSade sits alone in the darkened theater, and he does not know and he does not care about these facts, this trivial chronology of decay. It doesn't concern him, except that the Vista has stood abandoned since the earthquake, unsafe, and if anyone noticed when he and the Gristle Twins forced their way in with crowbars and bolt cutters, they haven't bothered to call the police.

Jimmy takes the last drag off his cigarette and drops it to the stained and threadbare carpet, crushes out the butt with the sharp and silver toe of his left boot. He exhales smoke and breathes in the deadstill air that smells like any place that's been shut away too long, dust and spiderwebs, mausoleum air, but there's a ranker, sweetsick smell just underneath, as well. A smell that could be rot, the rot of flesh instead of architecture, familiar smell to his nostrils, but he knows it's nothing more sinister than the ghosts of spilled soft drinks and melted Ju-Ju Bees, dried semen and the acrid reek of popcorn butter. Nothing more. He lights another cigarette and glances over his shoulder at all the dark crouched there behind him listening to the sounds of the Gristle Twins busy in the projection booth, setting up the generator, jerry-rigging wires and fuses, and the big, antique projector they got off a man named Spivey in Chinatown. Socket-wrench and ball-peen racket, bang and scrape, and one or another of them cursing. The dull yellow glow from their big flashlights, and Jimmy turns around again and stares into the blackness, towards the screen he cannot see. Almost nothing down here to break the tangible, always-night pooled inside the Vista—not trapped, but hiding—just the dull hint of sunlight filtered down from somewhere a hundred feet overhead.

Like being at the bottom of the ocean, he thinks. *The bottom of a well*, and he pulls on his cigarette so it glows brightly for a moment, like the deadly lure of some deep-sea fish.

Only a few hours earlier, in the place that he sleeps by the

Pacific, the corrugated-tin hovel at the edge of a continent where the air smells like salt and smog and dying fish—on the bed that is really only mattresses, but softer than the bare concrete underneath. Opening his eyes and sunlight through the cracks where the sheets of metal meet unevenly or don't meet at all, where maybe he stuffed newspaper once, but he hasn't done that in a long, long time. Sunlight the same hot color as the beach outside, and he squinted his pale eyes, thought about going back to sleep, the shabby old dream of a thin woman with gray wings and ball-bearing eyes, and he told Salmagundi about her once and she stared at him, silently, until he had to look away. After that, he never mentioned the dream to anyone else, or any other dream, either.

Lying there in the not quite dark, thinking about closing his eyes again, and there was music, then, from a radio, piano-key and hoarse-voice snatch of words and melody. And Jimmy DeSade sat up and listened, listening hard past the surf and the sound of cars passing on the narrow, winding road through the broken, yellow-brown cliffs. Listening hard for more, but there was no more; a subtle shift in the wind to carry the sound in another direction, maybe, or it had only been someone walking by with a boom box and now they were too far away. *Once I built a railroad, now it's done, brother can you spare a dime,* and he could think of no reason that should have frightened him. But it had. Cold sweat on his palms and upper lip, chill bumps, and the next line of that damned song right there on the tip of his tongue like a scalding coffee burn. He stared, squinting, across the shack towards the crooked table and the crooked chair, something shiny over there; he really had forgotten all about the film until he saw the listless aluminum glint of the 16mm canister where he'd left it the night before. The reel still safe inside its can, and he'd only looked at it once, just to be sure Spivey hadn't been trying to stiff him.

He honestly hadn't intended to kill Mr. Louis Spivey, had gone down to the basement beneath the Chinese apothecary with the five thousand dollars that the greasy little man had asked for on the telephone, just Jimmy and the Gristle Twins, and it was going to be a clean transaction. But first all those nervous, hungry men pouring over cardboard boxes of video-cassettes, whatever you want and it's in there somewhere, the smut and snuff and those things there were no names for. And then Spivey had tried to get an extra thousand out of him at the last minute. Jimmy already holding the canister, holding *her*, and Spivey mumbling some bullshit lie about a Dutch customs agent and bribes, and Jimmy had pulled out his big Smith and Wesson .45 and put a cap through the motherfucker's left eye. The gun loud as bottled thunder in the smoky basement and everyone had turned to see, everyone had looked, and then they'd all looked away again, satisfied that this had nothing to do with them, and Jimmy had taken the film and the Gristle Twins had followed him back up into the ginger- and gasoline-scented night.

But later it all seemed inevitable, sitting there in his shack by the ocean, the midday sun cutting through the walls and the thing in the canister reminding him what a dream might have tried to save him from, had tried to make him forget. He was going to see her again, and surely some sacrifice had been necessary, a little blood and brains for that miracle not too much to ask, surely. Jimmy thought about the bottle of Scotch sitting by the film canister, and he realized that he had to piss. Outside, the sun was as bright as the arc of an acetylene torch, and Jimmy DeSade could not remember where he'd left his shades.

Excerpt from "Salmagundi Desvernine," *Industrial Culture Handbook* (Re/Search Publications, 1983), p. 92.

SAL: No. I wanted to make a film, that's all.
R/S: I haven't seen all of it. Only about ten minutes, last November in Montreal.
SAL: Well, it was all bullshit. It was a mistake. A lumbering, pretentious mistake. I'm just glad I figured that much out

before I wasted any more time or money on the damned thing.

R/S: I truly thought it captured something very bleak, lost, I was never sure if I was seeing—

SAL: I tried to find all the copies and destroy them last year. There were only a few, but some of them got away from me. I burned the three I had. I think a man in Munich is supposed to have one. A friend in San Francisco told me that. But I wish I could get them all back. I wish I could burn them all. I don't like knowing that they're out there.

R/S: Maybe you should look at it again. The little bit I saw, a shipyard, a machine shop, and I kept thinking of Piranesi.

SAL: Yeah?

R/S: All that light and space and still the suffocating sense of enclosure, like a Piranesi etching.

SAL: Jesus, it was worse than my poems. I thought maybe I could explain these ideas with film, explain them *visually*, since they've killed poetry, made emotion almost completely inaccessible through language.

R/S: Who's killed poetry?

SAL: *They*. They. Everyone after fucking William Butler Yeats...

Five minutes since the projector finally flickered to life, its white, unsteady beam to divide the darkness down the middle, to spill its burden of images across the old movie screen. Only a distant glimpse of her so far, someone that must have been her moving pale and spidersilent along a filthy Hudson River shore, rust and mud and the Palisades rising gray and unyielding in the distance. He leans forward, trying to see her face, and then clearly hears the faint staccato *pop* before the screen goes black again, the whole *world* goes black again, swallowed alive by the greedy, violated gloom of the Vista, and he's out of his seat in an instant, screaming up at the Gristle Twins.

"The fuckin' *bulb* blew, okay!" Manny shouts back. "It wasn't our goddamn fault!"

And Jimmy stands very still, breathing too hard, too fast, watching the indistinct purple spots floating before his face, weightless afterimages writhing in the dark, and of course they're all still there when he closes his eyes and puts a hand across his face. His head already too full of the ten thousand shades of gray sealed up tight inside Salmagundi's film, the never simply black and white moments captured more than twenty years ago. That last year before he met her, and, remembering, Jimmy DeSade opens his eyes and sits down again.

A party in some SoHo shithole, discrepant mix of punk rockers and gallery mavens, needle freaks and slumming socialites, and him there to make sure that everyone stayed happy (or unhappy, as the case may be), to see that the flow of white powder and blue pills never ran dry. He was sitting in a corner near the door to the toilet, patiently listening while a drunken transvestite tried to explain a book by Aleister Crowley. Light the color of a slaughterhouse floor from the single naked bulb screwed into a socket on the wall, and the transvestite's face was red as uncooked hamburger in the sickly crimson wash; almost ready to tell the freak to fuck the hell off, go find someone else to annoy, and then he saw her, porcelain frail and hair like strands of the day, like thread spun from sunlight, the tall girl in silk and velvet and pearls. "Who is she?" he whispered, pointing, and so the skinny, sexless boy strained to see through the restless curtain of marijuana and cigarette smoke.

"Oh, *her*," the transvestite said and made a face like he'd bitten into a piece of rotten fruit. "I think she's some kind of artist. I heard she made a film once. She's supposed to have a lot of money."

"What's her *name?*" and the boy sighed loudly, exasperated, leaking-balloon sound, and sat down on the floor, back against the door to the crapper.

"Why don't you go *ask* her?" he sneered. But Jimmy DeSade didn't move, sat silent beneath the red light and watched her for half an hour: the elegant, long fingers that held her glass of burgundy, the soft wrinkle at the corners of her rouged mouth when she laughed, every move and expression something entirely unexpected. And then she turned, and he knew she saw him, that her bright eyes had caught him staring, and she tipped her head slightly to one side, like a cat, curious, and raised her chin just a little, and smiled.

Almost two before Manny finally showed up at the shack by the sea, one knock hard and the corrugated door shivered on its rust-stiff hinges. "Yeah," Jimmy said and the Gristle Twins slipped in with the afternoon light, Mr. DeSade's pit bulls; you only need two soldiers when they're sick assholes like these two. These two that crawled out of the ruin and dust burn of East L.A. years ago, and they were still just puppies back then, mean, alley-hard pups but puppies, nonetheless. Wild things that had to be tied a few times, left in the sun without water or food, and if they'd been hungry to start with, Jimmy taught them to starve, taught them to be empty of anything but fury and appetite. You don't turn your back too long on dogs like that, and Jimmy blinked, pupils too big and lazy for all that light; "Shut the goddamn door, motherfuckers," and one of them did. The hinges made a sound like a dying rat.

"So, we good to go?" he asked, and Manny glanced uneasily at his brother, and then they both looked at Jimmy. "What?" he asked them. "What is it now?"

"Spivey," Manny said, "He was in with a buncha them Chinese sonsabitches. They figure you didn't have no right to go whacking him like that."

And for a minute Jimmy DeSade sat listening to the wind and the busy sound of cars, thinking about the empty Cutty Sark bottle on the table in front of him, little picture in his head of Spivey's face when he saw the gun. The gutless little piggy trying to backpedal at the last second, "Hey, *look*, man. Forget that shit, okay? I'm even gonna throw in the projector for free, right?" Jimmy realized how thirsty he was, and maybe he needed something besides whiskey.

"So what's it gonna cost us to clear things with the Chinese," he asked the Gristle Twins, and one of them sighed loudly, and he knew this time it wasn't about money or dope, this time it was going to be about the pretty Asian boys in their neat suits and shiny shoes and shinier guns. The way they laughed, and his head hurt, his eyes hurt behind his black, plastic sunglasses.

"And we got that delivery to make at three-thirty," Manny said. "It's in the trunk. Ain't gonna keep long in this fuckin' heat."

Just silence from Jimmy, tall, pale man and his wobbly, dry-rot chair, wobblier dry-rot table, all leather and gaudy silver, and he ran the gaunt fingers of one hand through his spiky, tar-black hair. Manny reluctant to say another word, but "That homo motherfucker in Palo Verdes," he whispered "The scorpion guy," and there was just enough light to see Jimmy DeSade nod his head.

"Well, Jesus, let's not keep the bastard waiting," he said, and picked up the dented film canister and left the empty Scotch bottle sitting there alone on the table.

From his seat in the Vista, he stares up at the things on the screen, the scrapsharp angles of steel, the concrete shadows, and the camera moves smoothly from a window to a door and back again. Broken glass like crystal teeth, and past them he can see the river, the dead, mercurial river, and Jimmy DeSade *knows* dead; the difference between metaphor and a corpse, and the wet gray expanse of water sliding past the shipyard is the real McCoy. Never mind the eels, the crabs, the scaly fish hidden away in the muddy water, never mind the gulls. He's seen the life inside the dead enough to know, the maggoty riches beneath skin the wasteland color of chalk. The camera loses focus for a moment, and then there's someone standing outside the broken window, back to the lens and her hair is almost white on the screen. The camera lingers as she watches the river, the poisoned Hudson rolling south towards the harbor and the sea.

"Turn around," he whispers. "Please turn around," but she doesn't, and in another moment the camera leaves her, pans left and it's just the door again, the ugly door and the cloud-dulled sun coming in through the hole where the doorknob used to be. But now there's writing on the door, sloppy words scrawled in something black; runny black words, and if he hadn't spent so many years with Salmagundi he might have thought it was only paint.

He doesn't read the three lines of poetry, reaches instead for the bottle of whiskey sitting on the floor and takes a big swallow, and when he looks at the screen again, there's nothing but a flat plain of shattered glass and weathered cement, discarded machine bits, something that resembles the ribcage of a great animal. But it's only rebar, and then he sees her lying inside, naked hatchling inside an iron-twig nest, and her fingers have rubbed themselves raw against the corrosion, against the metal, and she leaves drops of herself on the drab cement.

They dumped the olive-green body bag on the floor of the fat man's garage. "The gift wrapping's extra, you know," Jimmy said, one thumb jabbed at the plastic bag while the fat man in his mustard-colored house coat and matching slippers counted out the money, one thousand, two, three, and Manny lit another cigarette, stinking sweet Salem menthol, but nothing would have covered up the smell. The man was sweating despite the air conditioning, at least twenty-five degrees cooler in there than outside, but the fat man was sweating, anyway. Anxious sweat because he always was afraid of the ribsy ghoul that sold him the toys he needed, sweat because he wanted to be alone, alone with his secrets and desire, and "That makes five," he stuttered. "Just like we agreed."

Jimmy DeSade counted the bills before he folded them and stuffed them into a pocket inside his leather jacket.

"Always a pleasure doin' business with an honest man," he said, and the fat man led them back to the door. Jimmy walked silently past the fat man's rose garden, the Gristle Twins following close behind, walking back to the old Lincoln parked by the curb, the big, paint-scabbed car baking underneath the white and merciless California sun. Jimmy was already behind the wheel and turning the key in the ignition when he noticed the slip of paper folded and tucked beneath one of the windshield wipers.

"What the hell is that?" and Manny didn't answer him, passed the stiff piece of rice paper to Jimmy, and there was nothing on it but a single Chinese character, brush-careful ideogram, and the Gristle Twin in the backseat grunted nervously and looked away, staring out the window at a solitary cloud, lost and drifting across the high summer sky.

"What's that supposed to mean?" Manny asked, and Jimmy wadded the sheet of paper into a tiny crumpled ball and tossed it out his window onto the sizzling asphalt, then watched as the chaparral-parched and ocean-salt wind rolled it away down the street.

"It don't mean jack shit," Jimmy DeSade lied and started the car.

Excerpt from "Salmagundi Desvernine," *Industrial Culture Handbook* (Re/Search Publications, 1983), pp. 94-95.

R/S: That title, …*Between the Gargoyle Trees*, someone told me it was borrowed from Kafka, or that it was a reference to Kafka, or something like that.
SAL: It wasn't either. When I was a child, there were these two trees where I grew up, just two old dead trees. My sister called them the gargoyle trees because they sort of seemed to loom over you, and loom towards each other, almost like the gargoyles at Chartres or Notre Dame. Gargoyles are supposed to be guardians, the physical embodiment of our worst night-

mares, visions of Hell to frighten away the monsters, and so I always thought of those two old trees as protecting us, as keeping all the bad things out.

R/S: So how were they relevant to the film then, significant enough that you named it after them?

SAL: Have you ever noticed that modern architecture has no gargoyles? The Victorians, I mean the late Victorians, who prided themselves on their rationalism, on their scientific thought and practicality, even they had gargoyles. When I was in London, I was on Cromwell Road and walked by the natural history museum one afternoon, and, well, it's like seeing a medieval cathedral erected to honor Victorian geology. There are hundreds of stone pterodactyls and prehistoric fish and things like that, trilobites and things, decorating the place. It was built in 1862, I think. And even the goddamn Chrysler Building has those eight eagle heads way up there at the base of the spire, you know? That was done about 1930, but those are some of the very last gargoyles. And Van Alen, who was Chrysler's architect, studied at the École des Beaux Arts in Paris. Anyway, then we get into the International Style, functionalism, minimalism, post-modernism, whatever you want to call it, and so it's all these ugly, sterile people boxes of glass and steel and concrete, all glossy, smooth surfaces and sharp corners. No gargoyles.

R/S: What do you think that means?

SAL: Well... wait, think of it this way. What do you see when you stop and look at one of those minimalist skyscrapers? You see a mirror, right? You see a reflection of the city around whatever building you're looking at, or, if you're standing close enough, you might even see yourself...

Sudden chiaroscuro, grainy rush of wet and dark across dust and pale sheet metal, oil or blood or shadow, all the same now, and Jimmy DeSade can hear the Gristle Twins arguing in the projection booth.

"What the fuck was that?"

"I didn't hear anything."

"Well then *listen*, asshole. *There*. You tellin' me you didn't hear that?"

Jimmy doesn't take his eyes off the screen to tell them to shut the fuck up or wait outside. Already halfway through the film, and there have only been glimpses of her, fleeting glimpses less tangible than his uncertain memories; another swallow from the bottle of Cutty Sark, and he realizes that his hands are shaking. Realizes that he can't hold them steady anymore, and there's Scotch dribbling down his chin, soaking through the front of his T-shirt. He reaches beneath the theater seat, bends and reaches but doesn't dare take his eyes off the screen, because there's no telling where any of this is leading, that shifting and colorless collage, and if there's any logic to this bleak progression of images he hasn't figured it out. His left hand groping under the seat, and the antique candy tin is exactly where he put it.

Onscreen, that indefinite, viscous liquid coming to an edge and then pouring over it, syrup-smooth cataract at the end of some flat and alien world; dark amoeba sea spilling away into an abyss, and the camera slowly moves down and down and down, until it finds her upturned face, eyes squeezed shut and mouth gaping open wide, drowning, gagging on the stuff, her skin and hair slicked and glistening with it, and finally, the camera pulls back so he can see that she's kneeling, naked and filthy on a jagged carpet of rusted nails and shattered glass. Her arms outstretched wide to receive, to welcome the flood, and Jimmy De-Sade doesn't move, doesn't fucking breathe, the old tin box sitting forgotten in his lap, his eyes too full of her, of the terrible, wasted beauty of her.

So far the soundtrack has been little more than the inconstant Hudson wind; raw, flensing cadence, and, occasionally, clumsy footsteps or the scrape or brittle clatter of metal dragged across metal. But now her voice, Salmagundi Desvernine's silken crystal-shard voice-over speaking to him across two ruined decades, speaking across the ten dead years since she lay down in an abandoned New Jersey shipyard and slipped unnoticed from the world, leaving him alive and alone. And "The Sea of Faith," she says. "Was once too, at the full, and round earth's shore lay like the folds of a bright girdle furl'd..."

"Well, go *see*, motherfucker," Manny growls from the projection booth, and Jimmy's straining not to lose a single word as the camera pans past Salmagundi and back towards the river again.

"But now I only hear its melancholy, long, withdrawing roar, retreating..."

He leans forward, quick and careless move, and the tin box tumbles noisily from his lap to the hard floor, but he does not move to retrieve it, doesn't check to see that the tiny vials of cocaine haven't broken, that the sundry handful of remembrances of her are all still safe inside their dinged and dented reliquary. Because now he's seen what distracted the camera's eye from Salmagundi, the lurching, rough shape like an impossible living tangle of scrap and wire, as it slips along the muddy shore towards the river.

"...retreating, to the breath of the night wind..."

And Jimmy DeSade wants to turn away, something wrong about that shuffling heap, the way it moves or the uneven angles of its jackstraw symmetry, just one of her goddamn puppets, sure, something else that should have stayed locked away in her imagination, and then the camera looks away for him, and now Salmagundi's sprawled in the sticky mess, lies writhing like a poisoned dog as the nails and glass bite at her body. And he *does* close his eyes, finally, and one hand up to cover them like a child.

"...down the vast edges drear," she says. "And naked shingles of the world."

Halfway from Palos Verdes to Hollywood and the Vista, the last hour wedged there in between, and the old Mexican woman coughed into her checkered handkerchief and shuffled the cards again. No one in the stuffy little back room but her and Jimmy DeSade, both the Gristle Twins waiting for him in the laundromat out front. Her walls lined with coyote skulls and plaster saints, votive candles that smelled like cinnamon and pears, and she glanced at him as she placed the deck in front of her, waited as he reached across the table and cut the cards, and then she shuffled them again.

"You do not look well today, Jimmy," she said softly and selected a single card from the deck, a pentacle for his dark hair, his eyes, the King of Pentacles for his sex, and the old woman laid the significator face up in front of her. The cards passed to Jimmy DeSade, then, and he shuffled them again, shuffled fast and hard like they were about to play a game of poker, and then he used his left hand to cut the deck into three equal stacks. With her left hand, the old woman retrieved the cards, made them one neat, dogeared stack again before turning up the topmost card.

"*This* card covers you," she said and hid the significator beneath the Lightning-struck Tower. Another card, the Nine of Swords laid at right angles to and across the Tower, and she said, "*This* one crosses you, Jimmy."

The room too small, too hot, and he wiped the oily sweat from his forehead before it could run into his eyes or drip to the table, breathed in the stale, wax-scented air. "What is it that scares the boogeyman?" she asked, smiled her crooked, tobacco-yellow smile and turned up the third card, the King of Swords, reversed, and "This is beneath you," she said. That card slipped expertly under the significator, and Jimmy wanted a cigarette, wanted to breathe anything besides the stink of the candles and dusty bones, but no one smoked in this room, or drank, or cursed, except the old Mexican woman.

"This card, this is *behind* you," she said, and laid the High Priestess, the fourth card, to the left of the significator. And Jimmy stared silently down at the beautiful woman, the rind of a crescent moon at her feet, the crown on her head, and from somewhere beyond the stifling, skulldressed room, somewhere up or down the street, the scalding screech of spinning tires and someone shouting in Spanish. The old woman had already turned over the fifth card, and she placed it above the significator, tapped it once with the long, red-lacquered nail of her right index finger; "This card crowns you, Jimmy DeSade," she said, and he looked through his sunglasses at the young boy with his burden of ten flowering staves, struggling towards the sanctuary of a distant city.

"That's enough," Jimmy whispered before she could turn the sixth card, his voice too dry to speak any louder, and so she paused, glaring at him with her brown eyes.

"It makes no difference to me," she said. "I get paid, either way."

And Jimmy reached for his gun then, the same big Smith and Wesson that he'd used to kill Louis Spivey, and he pointed the snubby barrel at the old woman's head. Sweat-slicked fingers tight around the trigger and his hand trembling like a dying wino, but she only smiled for him again, her wry and knowing smile, and looked down at the undealt cards in her hand.

"Will you kill *me* now, Jimmy?" and she crossed herself and laughed. "*¿Está el monstruo asustado de una vieja mujer?*"

Excerpt from "Salmagundi Desvernine," *Industrial Culture Handbook* (Re/Search Publications, 1983), p. 95.

R/S: There are some pretty bizarre rumors, you have to admit. Like your cameraman, Mascetti, killing himself after seeing the final cut—
SAL: Christ, that's total bullshit. There never was a final cut. We never finished editing the thing.
R/S: But he killed himself—
SAL: He was a junky. He drank when he wasn't shooting up. Yes, Tony Mascetti OD'd, and yes, we had stopped working on the film by then. I don't see the connection.
R/S: Belgium actually banned the film, did you know that?

They said it was "depraved and injurious."
SAL: Yeah? Well, good for Belgium. I'm not going to talk about the goddamn film anymore, okay?

Jimmy has picked the tin box up from the place where it lay on the theater floor, holds it close, all these mean and disparate fragments of her life: a lock of blonde hair, a pearl and opal ring, the Polaroid photograph of two little girls standing in front of a crumbling stone wall, her needle and her spoon. Onscreen, she sits in a room, empty charcoal place with wallpaper peeling walls and a porcelain vase of white lilies on the floor near her bare feet. A moth-gnawed Oriental rug and the old chair she's sitting in and nothing else; Salmagundi in one of her antique gowns, one of her great grandmother's dresses, and she isn't looking at the camera. She holds her head high and a little to one side, this demeanor that might seem haughty on anyone else, might seem haughty to him, if he didn't understand, if Jimmy DeSade hadn't walked with the ghost trapped inside her flesh, the Gilded-Age spirit grounded in soot and lifeless, oil-starved machineries.

A shadow washing across the scene, then, right to left, abrupt and formless intimation of form that passed like a swiftly-moving cloud between the earth and sun, and Salmagundi doesn't move, doesn't blink, and he thinks that in another moment his heart will stop beating. All these years gone by, and he has forgotten so much of her, has buried so much of himself so he would not have to remember. Losing himself inside the nightskin of a monster that could never have known such an awful, undeniable light, and so cannot suffer in its absence.

Onscreen, she bends over, and now there's a close-up of her hand, her short and ragged nails, always chewed down past the quick, bloody cuticles, and she draws one of the flowers slowly from the vase.

Both Gristle Twins have begun shouting from somewhere in the darkness behind him—angry, surprised shouts from the Vista's lobby—and they're answered immediately by the unmistakable roar of automatic gunfire. Guns and other less familiar voices that aren't speaking English, the discordant crash and tinkle of breaking glass, and then there's just the musty-cool silence again, perfect except for the gentle purr of the projector, the film moving between its hungry steel sprockets. Jimmy DeSade smells kerosene, a sudden, acrid reek that burns his nostrils, burns his wet eyes, and he reaches for his gun. But the camera has pulled back again, and now she holds the flower out like she's trying to give it to someone, passing the lily to the cameraman, maybe, and Jimmy's hand stops halfway to his leather shoulder holster.

Way up there, her ashen lips move silently, and she smiles and it's over, ending as abruptly, as bluntly, as it began; the screen gone blinding white in an instant, and he can hear the fluttering of the unattended pickup reel from the empty projection booth. The air is thick with the sour stink of kerosene, and the insistent Mandarin voices that have come to punish him for killing Mr. Louis Spivey. Jimmy DeSade thinks of the old Mexican woman, and he opens the antique tin candy box and takes out the lock of Salmagundi's hair. In a few more minutes, the air is hot and filled with smoke and the insatiable sounds that fire makes.

Salammbô Redux
(2007)

MOST DAYS, THE BOY NAMED SEBASTIAN PRETENDS that he is writing a book about the woman who lives in the cottage by the sea. Most days, since his unheralded and un-invited arrival at Watch Hill almost a year ago, she allows him to pretend that he is writing a book about her. But the truth is that he merely has nowhere else to go, and she has found that having him around is usually better than being alone, so the woman and the boy have arrived at a sort of *accord silencieux*. On good days, the woman imagines that the relationship is some-how mutually beneficial, but there are bad days, too, when it seems at best mutually parasitic. Those are the honest days, the sober days, the days when every wall seems to contain a mirror and every thought a regret. The days when it is not enough to walk down the sandy road to the narrow beach or along the winding lane to the lighthouse, when the sea air and the sound of the breakers are not sufficient to soothe her nerves. And on those days she hates the boy and wishes that he would go away and leave her alone again. She even offers to pay his train fare back to Brooklyn or New Haven or Boston or wherever it is he's supposed to have come from this week. That changes, too—his place of origin—like her unpredictable moods, like his gender, like the inconstant New England weather, and she wonders if she will ever learn the truth of his provenance.

LL ME ONE OF YOUR DREAMS
THE SALTON SEA THE DAY IT RAINED BLOOD
I'LL ANSWER A QUESTION
WHY?
THE DAY YOU RAN AWAY
WICKED
YOU WERE TELLING ME A
I WISH IT WERE

She is not quite yet a crone, and he is a chameleon, and they sit together, but completely apart, listening to the waves and waiting for the sun to set, because the nights are almost always easier to bear than the daylight.

He has a silver-grey RadioShack microcassette recorder and a box full of tapes, each one thirty minutes long, fifteen minutes to a side. Most are filled up with some conversation or another, this afternoon or that morning or an evening fossilized on frail strips of magnetic tape, their words captured in thin coatings of cobalt and ferric oxide, by take-up and supply reels and technology neither pretends to understand. The tape recorder is only a prop, of course, an obligatory piece of evidence that he really has come to write a book about her, or (depending on the day) a Ph. D. dissertation, or a magazine article, or an interview for a website. She supposes it is necessary, that he must have something tangible to bolster his story, and most times it doesn't bother her, being recorded. When it does, she simply tells him to turn it off. On those occasions, he rarely argues, which is one way that Salammbô Desvernine knows that she and the boy who calls himself Sebastian have an understanding.

And here it is, a sweltering August afternoon, and they sit together on the small veranda facing Block Island Sound, with his tape recorder lying on the table between them. There are also two sweating tumblers, because he made them ice tea with lemon and sprigs of fresh mint, and they sit facing the sea and watch the dazzling white sun shimmering off the blue-green water.

"You were telling me about Salmagundi," Sebastian says, his clumsy attempt at being sly, but she laughs and shakes her head, because she never talks to anyone about her dead sister, not even the boy and his tape recorder. He often wishes that she would, but there are secrets that will stay secret if she can help it, and usually she can. He doesn't say anything else for a few minutes, sips his tea and watches her watching the sound.

"No, okay, but you *were* telling me about the Salton Sea, about the yellow birds and the dead fish and—"

"That was twenty-two years ago," she says, then closes her eyes and changes the subject. "I wish it were October," she tells the boy. "I wish it were October, and this goddamn heat was done with for another year. I used to love the summer, but I find that every year I love it a little less than the year before."

Sebastian waits a moment, waiting to see if she's finished, then returns to the matter of the Salton Sea. "You were telling me about the day you saw it rain—"

"It is a goddamned wicked place," says Salammbô, interrupting him again.

"I don't believe that places are wicked," the boy replies, not interested in this argument they've had more than once before, though never about the Salton Sea. "People, maybe—but places are just places."

She opens her eyes, and it seems to her the waters of the sound truly have caught fire, that the waves are washed in a quicksilver sheen of white flame, and any moment the wind will shift direction. Then she and the boy who calls himself Sebastian will be seared to a crisp, reduced to lifeless husks of charcoal, and she'll never have to hear another of his questions.

"The Salton Sea," he says again. "The day it rained blood."

She takes a deep breath of the still summer air trapped beneath the veranda's low roof, and is disappointed when her lungs are not instantly immolated. "1985," she sighs, realizing this is one of the days she wishes that the boy had never shown up on her doorstep. "June 1985. I was still with the museum in LA back then. I'd been collecting gopher snakes in the San Jacinto and San Bernardino mountains, because I was interested in interbreeding between the San Diego and Sonora subspecies. By the way, I presented a paper on that, a couple of years later, at the annual meeting of the American Society of Ichthyologists and Herpetologists."

"I wasn't asking you about the snakes," Sebastian tells her and makes a show of picking a mint leaf out of his glass. Salammbô turns her head and stares at him a moment before continuing; he just flicks away the soggy bit of mint and then watches the shore and the quicksilver sun shining off the waves and doesn't look at her.

"The meeting was held in Veracruz, and it was actually my first time in Mexico," she says, if only because she knows perfectly well he doesn't care. "As I recall, the paper was entitled 'Instances of interbreeding between adjacent populations of the colubrid *Pituophis melanoleucus* in southern California.'"

"What did I do to piss you off this time?" he asks, then reaches for the recorder and presses the button marked stop.

Salammbô shrugs and shakes her head, drinking her glass of tea, because it's not one thing that she could name for him, that she could put her finger on, and maybe it's not even him at all. Maybe it's only the heat and her aching back, the sun and the fact that it's August instead of October.

"It's a wicked place," she says again. "Trust me. I don't care whether you believe that or not. I was there."

Sebastian switches his tape recorder on again.

"One day, I swear I'm going to hide that thing," she says and glances at the machine. "Maybe I could bury it on the god-damned beach."

"Sal, you already know I've read the article you wrote about that day for *Fate* magazine. I have it upstairs in my suitcase, so why the hell won't you talk about what happened?" And that's true; the boy found the tattered magazine in a used bookstore in Connecticut and bought it for fifty cents. "True Tales of the Strange and Unknown," promised right there on the cover, and sandwiched between "Ghost of the 14th Tunnel" and "The Wisdom of Snails," is "Blood from the Sky" by Dr. Salammbô Desvernine, formerly of the Los Angeles County Museum of Natural History.

"Maybe it's none of your business," she says and goes back to watching the sound. "Maybe it's nothing I want to talk about."

"Then why'd you write it?"

"Maybe I thought it would help," she replies. "If other people knew, if I wasn't the only one."

"But it didn't help?" he asks, and when she doesn't answer,

when a full minute has come and gone, he adds, "You'd already read Charles Fort, before you wrote the article?"

"Of course, I'd already read Charles Fort."

"So you knew it was something that had happened to lots of other people, something that had been reported over and over again."

Salammbô sets her half-empty glass back down on the table and rubs at her eyes. "Words on paper," she says. "That's one thing. Some crazy old fuck sitting in a library, collecting and cataloging seemingly inexplicable anecdotes because he has a beef with science, that's one thing. Having it happen to you, that's another goddamn thing entirely."

"It didn't help, publishing that article?" he asks. "It didn't help at all?"

"Why do you keep at me with these questions, when you already know the answers?" and then she switches off the tape recorder herself. Down on the beach, there's a lanky black dog chasing gulls, and Salammbô shuts her eyes and tries to pretend it's autumn and there's no one on the veranda but her.

At dinner, the boy shows up in drag, as he very often does, and tonight he's wearing a slinky black negligée that hardly comes down to the tops of his thighs, a gaudy strand of cheap plastic pearls, lipstick and nail polish the same iridescent shade of red, and silk stockings. He isn't wearing shoes, though, or a wig, and no makeup besides the lipstick. He sits across the table from Salammbô, and they both pick disinterestedly at the cold meal—pasta salad with artichokes and black olives and lumps of feta cheese. The wine is more interesting, and less intimidating, than the food, and Salammbô pours her third glass of the California Merlot and then sits watching Sebastian as he repeatedly spears the same olive on his fork. The tape recorder is lying on the table near his plate, because he hardly ever goes anywhere without it. Salammbô has found he is always easier to take in the evenings than in the afternoons, but then she finds that most things are. He spears the olive for the fourth time and realizes that she's looking at him.

"A shame you were not actually born a girl," she says.

"Why is it a shame?" he asks indignantly and frowns.

Salammbô squints at him over the rim of her wineglass, wishing that she hadn't left her bifocals somewhere else in the cottage. And because she is a little drunk, she keeps talking, when she knows she would be better off shutting up. "Because," she says, "it's a shame to see so much beauty wasted on a man."

"Why is it a shame, Sal?" he replies, and pulls the olive off his fork. "Jesus. And why is it a waste? You sound like my mother. I've never wanted to be a girl. I just like dressing this way. It doesn't mean I want to be a woman."

She wishes that she'd not started this, but had instead let the silence between them lie undisturbed, because now he's at least pretending to be offended, and she'd only meant it as a compliment. But alcohol always loosens her tongue. Another glass or two of the Merlot, and she might even find the courage to tell Sebastian that he's the only thing with a penis she's ever found attractive. Never mind that she sounds like his mother, because she's easily old enough to *be* his mother, his twenty-four years to her fifty three, her a product of the Baby Boom and him not even born until she'd already begun making a mess of her own life.

And she knows it's not just the crossdressing, though she would be lying if she claimed she didn't enjoy seeing him all tarted up like this. Truthfully, she finds Sebastian at his most beautiful in tattered jeans and a T-shirt, his dirty-blond hair pulled back in a short ponytail and his unshaven cheeks rough with a day or two worth of stubble so pale that it's almost translucent. Salammbô Desvernine has been a lesbian all her life, and yet, again and again, she has found her eyes making love to this strange boy, this uninvited guest, even though she knows that his glamour must surely be some vital part of his guile, just another angle to his con. It's not enough to flatter her with his constant interest and questions and the goddamn fifteen-minute tapes; there must also be infatuation, this uneasy, unlikely seduction.

She notices that the tape recorder's running, but she can't remember having seen him switch it on.

"When was the last time you got laid, anyway?" he asks, stabbing the olive again, and she tells herself that the blood rushing into her face is only the wine, and that she is neither angry nor embarrassed. Sebastian chews, and already he has begun toying with a bit of artichoke.

"I fail to see how that's any concern of yours," she says and takes another swallow of wine.

"Oh, but you're free to question the appropriateness of my sex?"

"That's not what I was doing, Sebastian."

"That's what it sounded like to me."

Salammbô sighs and pushes her plate away, wanting a cigarette and something stronger than the Merlot, wanting to unspeak words spoken barely a minute or two before, wanting to be alone and away from Sebastian's tape recorder and his pretty, taunting face.

"Why the hell don't you smoke, anyway?" she asks him, and at least she can see it wasn't what he was expecting.

"It's a nasty habit," he tells her. "Why the hell did you quit?"

"My fucking blood pressure," she says, "and it's an expensive habit. I didn't mean to insult you, Sebastian. I didn't mean to question your manhood."

"Sure," he shrugs. "Whatever. It's honestly nothing I haven't heard before. Anyway, is that also why you stopped having sex?"

She stares at him a moment, lost in the convoluted folds of dialogue, wondering if there's any way out but straight ahead, desiring desperately to backpedal. "I don't know what you're asking me," she says, finally.

"Your fucking blood pressure," he says, glancing up at Salammbô and then back to the pasta salad. "Is that why you stopped having sex?"

"Sebastian, I want you to please turn that thing off," she says and points at the tape recorder.

"Why? What difference does it make to you?"

She sees that her glass is empty and sets it down beside her plate, resisting the urge to refill it. There's a strong wind blowing off the sound, whispering around the weathered edges of the cottage, and farther off, she can hear the surf and the bell buoy anchored at Watch Hill lighthouse, clanging to itself in the darkness.

"How do you know I didn't just make it all up?" she asks him, and now the boy bites his lip and leans back in his chair.

"Did you? Is that what you're telling me?"

"No, but I'm asking why you assume that I didn't. An awful lot of other people certainly did."

"The article says you submitted samples to—" he begins, but then she's laughing, and he doesn't finish.

"Maybe I stuck my own thumb," she says and wipes at her mouth with her napkin. "You must have thought of that. The others did. Maybe I paid some Mexican boy I met on the beach to let me prick *his* thumb. Maybe I paid him a few dollars for his trouble."

"And maybe you just want to mess with my head," Sebastian says, and she can tell he's thinking about switching the recorder off.

"Maybe that's all I ever wanted, dear," she replies and forces a wry sort of smile. Then Salammbô Desvernine excuses herself, leaving him alone at the table. She takes the bottle and whatever's left inside and retreats to the veranda to smell the sea and to try to think about anything at all but the boy and his tapes and all his questions about 1985.

Salammbô cannot recall the last time that she slept well, though she knows it has been many, many years now, more years than it takes to make two decades. She dislikes taking pills to sleep, but has been using sedatives of one sort or another so long that she cannot recall what sleep was like without them. She takes whatever is most in vogue with whomever happens to be her physician, and lately that means Ambien and Klonopin, and sometimes the pills help, and sometimes they don't. It isn't so much the insomnia as the dreams she has when she finally falls asleep, and there's no point trying to distinguish between the dreams that are nightmares and the dreams that *aren't* nightmares. They are all unwelcome things, all invasions of alternate consciousnesses wherein she is not her waking self and cannot ever even *recall* her waking self. If the psychiatrists have thought up a label for this condition, she has not yet heard it. In all her life, she has never had a "lucid" dream, and, indeed, she cannot quite comprehend what it would be like, that awareness that one is only asleep and dreaming, and perhaps the ability to *shape* the dream. In truth, she is not entirely convinced lucid dreaming is anything more than a lie told by boastful, insecure men and women inventing tales to impress others and thereby make themselves seem more important and less helpless.

Sometimes, while she is waiting for the dreams to begin, waiting to forget herself and live bits of other lives that may or may not bear some resemblance to her own, the boy named Sebastian comes into her bedroom and sits with her, at the foot of the bed or cross-legged on the floor beside it. Sometimes he reads to her, and other times they talk. He is suspicious of both the pills Salammbô takes and of her fear of her own dreams. He is a great admirer, or so he says, of the work of Carl Jung and Fritz Purls, and so some nights he talks about Gestalt Therapy and the language of dreams and the unconscious suppression of aspects of personality. Mostly, she just listens, but there are times she cannot resist arguing with him.

This night, she lies listening to the wind and the ocean, and he's leaning against her side of the bed, facing the open closet. Salammbô never sleeps with the closet doors shut. He is wearing a gray sweatshirt at least two sizes too large for him and green boxer shorts decorated with some Japanese cartoon character or another. The little lamp on the bedside table is on, and the room is filled with shadows.

"The Ambien helps me to forget them, usually," she tells him, "so I don't spend half the day wandering about like a zombie."

He sighs and shakes his head. "Me, I'm always *trying* to remember my dreams. I have a journal that I write them down in whenever they seem important enough that I don't want to forget. Any detail might be important, you know, and you never can tell which one, so I try to remember them all. I just can't understand why anyone takes pills that help them *forget* their dreams. Why would you ever choose to close yourself off like that, intentionally ignoring what your unconscious mind is trying to tell you?"

"I assure you, I have more than enough problems with my *conscious* mind," she replies, wishing Sebastian would stop talking about dreams and read to her from the hardback copy of Virginia Woolf's *Orlando: A Biography* lying open in his lap. The night before, he left off halfway through Chapter Three, when Salammbô became too sleepy to listen anymore.

"Maybe you wouldn't, Sal, if you'd actually listen to what your dreams are trying to tell you."

She rolls over, then, setting her back to him. If he isn't going to read, she'll just have to settle for listening to him talk, but that usually works just as well. His voice and the night sounds outside her cottage and the pills. And she tries to recall if she's ever told him that it is not so much falling asleep she minds, as the waking up again, the disorientation and regret and exhaustion she feels almost every morning.

"Then tell me one of your dreams," she says. "Tell one dream that put your conscious mind at ease."

"I don't have to prove anything to you," he says, and she hears him close the book.

"I was not aware that I was asking you to, Sebastian. I just wanted to listen to your voice. And you're not reading—"

"I don't think I like this book. It's really awfully obvious. I mean, I know it's a *roman à clef*, and all the stuff about Woolf and Vita Sackville-West."

"It's a sort of love letter," Salammbô says, beginning to feel the Ambien taking effect, the edges of her perception starting to fade and fray and then fold back upon themselves.

"So why didn't she just write what she meant, instead of hiding it inside all this tiresome fantasy?"

"Dear, it was 1928, the same year *The Well of Loneliness* was banned in England. Besides, you just complained a moment ago it's too obvious."

"Well, it is. But if Virginia Woolf wanted to write a love letter to another woman, I don't see why she didn't just *do* it, instead of being so oblique."

"How can a novel be both obvious *and* oblique?"

He doesn't answer her, but instead tells her about a dream he had not long before he first came to Watch Hill. He was riding a Greyhound Bus, he says, and it was late at night or early in the morning, and raining. It was also raining in his dream, and he was a little boy again, watching the rain from the living-room window of his parent's house. Not *his* house, he says, because it never did feel like his home, just the place he lived until he was eighteen and his mother told him it was time to get a job or go to college. He hadn't wanted to do either one, so he cashed out a Treasury Bond his grandmother had left him and started traveling, trying not to think about what would happen when the money ran out.

"It was raining," Salammbô says groggily, only inches away from sleep now. "In your dream."

"Yeah," he replies. "And there was thunder and lightning, and the air smelled like diesel exhaust, because I was really on the bus. In a flash of lightning, I saw something watching me from beneath a tree. It was tall, and it was black, but I don't think it was a man."

And then he realizes that Salammbô is asleep, her breath wheezing softly in and out, regular as the pulse of a metronome. He sits a while on the floor, staring at the cover of the Virginia

Woolf novel and thinking about the dream and about the black thing beneath the tree watching him.

"Close your eyes," the boy says to Salammbô, and so she obediently closes her eyes. She's seen too much of the summer sun, anyway, hung so high and bright and white. God punched a hole through the blue, and now all this hot is pouring in, bleaching the sky until it is all but colorless, burning the tourists crowding Bay Street the sticky, glazed brown of a pork roast. They aren't nearly so bad here as over in Misquamicut, mostly families instead of drunken, rowdy college students pretending Rhode Island is Florida. But they're bad enough, and she wouldn't even be here if Sebastian hadn't insisted. She's sitting on a stone bench facing Watch Hill Cove, all the boats moored there and bobbing idly on the blistered water, and there are swans, and the noisy gray gulls stalk bits of garbage along the seawall.

"Don't open them," Sebastian says. "You have to promise me, Sal, that you won't open them."

And of course she promises. She will promise him almost anything. So much of her life spent paying off one debt or another, seeking this or that odd snippet of absolution, and on days like this, she has begun to understand that the boy is one of those debts.

"This will be in my book," he tells her. "This day, when you said it was too hot to go out and your feet hurt too badly. But I wanted to look for old postcards at Book and Tackle and get a frozen lemonade and see the gypsies' carousel." And behind her eyelids, Salammbô can still see the brightly painted wooden horses swinging round and round, flying even though they've all been weighted down with fat, sunburned children. "The scene before we find the dead jellyfish stranded on the sand."

"You're just making this up as you go along, aren't you?" she asks.

"Maybe it's a sort of *roman à clef*," he replies, and she can hear the brush of his bare feet against the grass in the stingy rind of park between the street and the bay. "All the names have been changed to protect the innocent. Well, they will be changed. No one will ever know it's you in the book, and no one will ever know that it's me, either. What the lawyers don't know won't hurt them."

"Can I please open my eyes now?"

"Only if you want to spoil the surprise," he says, and now she can hear the way he's frowning as clearly as she can hear his feet crushing and bending all those blades of grass. "Besides, the scene will read better if you keep them closed."

"It's my life," she says. "I haven't given you permission to write about my life."

"It's my life, too. And no one will ever know."

Salammbô's about to tell him that *she* will know, when the boy leans forward and kisses her. His lips are as full and smooth as those of any girl she has ever kissed, and there is only the faintest prickle of razor stubble as their cheeks graze. She could almost believe she was kissing a girl, if she didn't know better. His hair smells like the patchouli-scented shampoo he uses, and his tongue flicks quickly past her teeth before she pulls away.

"Sebastian!" she says, scolding him, finally opening her eyes, but only because she knows this is the way the scene in his book should read. *And then she opened her eyes, this woman old enough to have been the boy's mother, and he's standing there in front of her, smiling and looking very pleased with himself.*

"There's someone here to see you," Sebastian says, and when he steps aside, Salammbô has to squint and shield her eyes because of the afternoon glare flashing off the bay. And still, there is only the featureless silhouette of a woman, sitting on the concrete seawall, ten or fifteen feet away.

"She's feeding the swans popcorn," Sebastian says. "But she'll come over in a moment." And then he sits down on the stone bench beside Salammbô.

"Why did you do that? Why did you kiss me?" she asks, when

she really wants to ask who the woman is, because no one ever comes to visit her anymore, no one but the boy with his tape recorder and suitcase full of dresses.

"I thought you wanted me to," he answers. "It's been so long since you've kissed anyone. So long since you've *let* anyone kiss you."

"I don't think you're supposed to feed them," Salammbô says, still squinting out from beneath the shade of her palm at the woman-shaped eclipse standing at the edge of the sea. "I don't think it's good for them. And certainly not popcorn."

"I believe," says Sebastian, "that this is the chapter that will most confuse the reviewers and critics. This is the part they will almost certainly call oblique and obvious. But, then, they'll like the next one, when you show me the ruined fort out on Napatree Point, and tell me that if it were autumn I could see the Monarch butterflies."

"You can't write about her," Salammbô tells him, standing up and taking a step nearer the woman feeding popcorn to the swans. "You can write about me and that silly goddamned magazine article, but you *can't* write about Salmagundi."

"Oh, it isn't *her*," Sebastian assures her. "This isn't going to be that sort of a ghost story, Sal."

"This isn't going to be a ghost story at all."

"Whatever you say, but it's going to be *my* book. It's only your life."

And the woman turns towards her then, her face shining with a light all its own, and Salammbô Desvernine sees that Sebastian was telling the truth, and this is not her dead sister. And this is not anyone else she has ever known alive. No one she has ever kissed. No one she has ever made love to. So, maybe it will be that sort of ghost story, after all.

"I believe that I may even have my epigraph," he says, but now the boy's voice is much harder to hear, half drowned by the slopping noise of the salty water against the wall and the roar of Salammbô's racing thoughts and the flutter of the wide and snowy wings of the swans, spreading out and starting to melt beneath the August sun. The eclipse is breaking apart—that silhouette, her guest, Sebastian's surprise, the woman he said had come to see her, when almost no one ever comes to see her. In another moment, nothing will remain, not even a shadow to stain the grass, and somewhere behind Salammbô, Sebastian is still talking, as though she might still be listening.

"Something from Lewis Carroll," he says. "Even though he was sort of a pedophile."

"He was not," she whispers, hardly loud enough for Sebastian to have heard. And then the dream ends, and this time when Salammbô opens her eyes, she opens them to morning sun shining in through the curtains, falling in butter-yellow shafts against her bedroom wall. Disoriented by abrupt familiarity, by the waking shock of remembering herself, she sits up and finds Sebastian sleeping on the floor beside her bed, the copy of *Orlando: A Biography* lying next to him.

A couple of minutes past midnight, and the boy is lying on the sofa in his black negligée and a blacker wig that doesn't really work with his complexion, and Salammbô is seated on a cushion on the floor, the big cardboard box open in front of her. The boy is lying on his stomach, his head hanging over the edge, watching her the way a cat watches something that has managed to catch it's attention, but isn't actually all that interesting. And she realizes that she often thinks of him as a cat, something feline in his gaze, which so often manages to be simultaneously intense and disinterested, like a cat's gaze. And also something cat-like in his androgyny, perhaps, and then again, maybe it's just easier to dismiss the way he makes her feel if she takes away his humanity completely. If he is not a pretty cross-dressing young man, but only some fay invader to her home, something dressed up just so to confuse her libido. And when she thinks of him as a cat, those are the moments when she almost glimpses his true face shining through the glamour.

His tape recorder is lying on the coffee table; he's flipped the tape to Side 2, and the reels are spinning again, taking down everything she says.

She reaches into the cardboard box, which has begun to seem almost bottomless, and takes out a salt-and-pepper flecked pebble, and she holds it up for the boy to see.

"Yeah? It's a rock," he says, magnificently unimpressed.

Salammbô frowns and holds the pebble nearer the lamp. "The day I left the island, I found it on the little beach below the castle, while I was waiting for Mr. Cotswold—the ferryman."

"The day you ran away," Sebastian says.

"The day I *left*," she replies. "The day I saved my life. July 30th, 1968." And she stares at the small, rounded lump of granite, this souvenir she's carried about with her the last thirty-nine years.

"And you just left your sister there to fend for herself, while you ran off to California to be a hippie," Sebastian says, and looks expectantly at the box, because maybe the next thing Salammbô pulls out it will be more interesting than a pebble.

"She was still just a kid," Salammbô replies. "Jesus, it's not like I could have taken her with me." And then she adds, for the benefit of the tape recorder, "And I was never a goddamn hippie," before returning the pebble to its place in the clutter of the cardboard box.

"So, you never dropped acid?"

"No, I never dropped acid."

"Did you ever go back? To the island, I mean."

No," she tells him, "I never went back," and she knows that she answered the question too quickly, and that the boy's bright enough to hear the lie. The half lie, because it's true that she's never stepped foot on Pollepel Island after she left, but she has driven north on Route 9D and south on Interstate 9W, has parked and stood there on the bank of the river, in the windy gap between Storm King and Breakneck mountains, and stared through binoculars at the crumbling ruins of Silas Desvernine's castle and the ruins of the house where she was born.

"I read somewhere that Salmagundi's buried there, on the island," Sebastian says, and Salammbô shakes her head.

"Then you read wrong," she says, and reaches into the cardboard box again. She takes out a red, white, and blue "McGovern for President in '72" campaign pin, and hands it to Sebastian, who hands it right back to her.

"You could probably get something for that on eBay," he says, and Salammbô sighs and shakes her head again. She sets the presidential button face-up on the edge of the coffee table, and the next thing she pulls out is a spiral-bound notebook with a worn and slightly sun-faded cover the color of canned peaches. She opens it and flips through the pages, makes a face, and then returns it to the box without having shown it to the boy.

"No fair," he protests. "What was that? You said I could see it all."

"I never told you any such thing," she says, peering at Sebastian over the tops of her spectacles. "Let's just say it's a good thing that I decided to become a herpetologist, instead of a folk singer or a poet."

"It's not fair," he says again. "You could at *least* let me read it. It's not like I'm asking to make photocopies or anything."

"It's fair if I say it's fair. These are my memories, for better or worse. I show you what I want you to see."

"Fucking gyp, that's what it is," he mutters and rolls over onto his back, watching the ceiling now instead of Salammbô and her tatty box of keepsakes. "Don't suppose there's anything in there from the Salton Sea. Of course, if there were, you wouldn't let me see it."

"There's nothing in here from the Salton Sea," she says. "By the time I got there, I'm afraid there wasn't much of a market left for tourist gewgaws and trinkets."

"We should drive out the Point Judith and look at the lighthouse," the boy says, abruptly changing the subject.

"It's after midnight."

"So?" he replies. "I'm bored. I'm tired of watching you *ooh* and *ah* over all this crap. I'd rather go look at the lighthouse."

Salammbô folds the four cardboard flaps shut again and pushes the box aside. "I should just throw it out with the trash," she says. "All of it. There's nothing in there I need anymore."

"But they're your memories," Sebastian says, making the last word sound like something shameful, something profane. "Your memories, Sal, for better or worse. You don't toss your memories out with the trash."

"Don't be a cunt," she tells him, then removes her bifocals and rubs her eyes.

"Why not? Maybe if I *were* a cunt, you'd trust me. If I were a girl. Or if I *wanted* to be a girl—"

"Drop it, Sebastian. Acting like a petulant child—of either sex—isn't going to guilt trip me into showing you that stupid notebook or talking about the Salton Sea. And if you want me to drive you to Point Judith now or any other time, you're going to have to put something on besides that nightie."

"Fine," he says. "I'll go get my fucking sweater," and then Sebastian is up off the couch, and Salammbô sits staring at the dusty old cardboard box and trying to remember why she ever imagined it would be a good idea to drag all that stuff out and parade it before the scowling boy. Like she thought there was something there to impress him, some other secret that might satisfy his curiosity. The clock on the mantle chimes a quarter after twelve, and Salammbô switches off the tape recorder.

Salammbô does not often dream of her dead sister, and sometimes, when she lets herself think about her nightmares, she believes that it's simply because she never knew Salmagundi Desvernine as a grown woman. In Salammbô's waking mind's eye, her sister is always the same frail, flaxen-haired ten year old she was the day that Salammbô left the island and began the long journey of her life that led first to San Francisco, then Los Angeles, then later to the shore of the Salton Sea, and eventually to this cottage in Watch Hill and the pretty boy with all his questions. Her sister's journey proved somewhat shorter,

ending in the derelict sprawl of an abandoned New Jersey shipyard that had once made their family rich. Salammbô might
never have learned even this much of her sister's death, but for
an anonymous phone call to the Weehawken Police Department, the call that led them to the ruined shipyard and to
Salmagundi's corpse.

And that's something in the cardboard box of memories that
Salammbô did *not* show the boy, her scrapbook of clippings,
the last several pages devoted to the discovery of her sister's
body sealed inside a bizarre coffin of glass and steel, as if her
death had been the final installation in an artistic career too
outré and esoteric to have ever garnered much interest beyond
the pages of obscure art magazines and a now largely extinct
clique of industrial-culture fanatics. But in death, Salmagundi
found a celebrity that she'd neither received nor courted in
life, and she was labeled the "Scrapyard Cinderella" and the
"Sleeping Beauty of Weekawken" by the papers and CNN and
Newsweek. It only took the detectives and reporters a few weeks
to find the enigma's older sister, and before the affair was over
and done with—those posthumous fifteen minutes—
Salammbô had to threaten lawsuits and move from Providence
to the cottage in Watch Hill to regain her privacy. But the mass
media has a mercifully short attention span, and all these years
later the "Scrapyard Cinderella" is little more than an urban
legend and one of the raggedy ghosts in the retinue of
Salammbô's private hauntings.

And this night, after she's driven herself and the boy east to
the Point Judith lighthouse and land's end at the mouth of Nar-
ragansett Bay, driving there and back again and not returning
home until almost three a.m., this night Salammbô *does* dream
of her dead sister. At first, it is only one of her more frequent,
less remarkable nightmares—her old laboratory space in the
LA County museum's herpetology department and something
venomous missing from its locked tank, her trapped there in
the lab alone and searching beneath every table, behind every
cabinet for the fugitive viper or elapid, the copperhead or

cobra, and only ever catching the briefest glimpses of dry iridescent scales. But then the dream shifts, as dreams do, and fluorescent lighting and black epoxy tabletops dissolve around her, replaced by a freezing winter day and a muddy riverbank. The sky above her is heavy with gray-blue clouds and snow that has not yet fallen, and only the bleary recollection of sunlight can find its way to earth.

If she turns to look behind her, there will be the crumbling façade of the castle on Pollepel Island, or there will be the crumbling skeletons of the shipyard's towering iron dinosaurs. Or there will be both, for she may well be standing at the shore of the Hudson and looking across the river at the bleak Manhattan skyline, and yet also standing on that other shore, forty miles or so north as the crow flies. And if she were only a crow, she would spread dusky wings and fly away and not be part of whatever's coming next. But she is only Salammbô, watching the dark water rush and swirl past two places at once.

Her sister's body floats not far away, caught behind a jam of waterlogged limbs and roots, and so held back from the relentless river flowing down to the sea. Salmagundi drifts on her back, eyes open and seeming to watch the clouds, swaddled by a gentle eddy. She might merely be some grim re-imagining of Millais' *Ophelia*, buoyed up not by the green and placid waters of a Danish stream, no bouquet of herbs held limply in her upturned palms, no dress of bright fabrics to bear her up. Instead of the painter's fair-complexioned drowning, Salmagundi's hands are empty, and her belly is distended slightly with the inevitable gases of decomposition. But her flesh is not that of a corpse consigned to the water and insect larvae and the gnawing teeth of fish, but has taken on all the innumerable hues and textures of rust and verdigris and every form of metallic oxidation. Here, she is only another sort of vessel forged and welded and finally launched from the steamy, bustling docks, left to drift for however long eternity might prove to be. Salammbô takes a step towards the body, the cold Hudson and colder mud closing hungrily about her ankles.

"You would not show me this," the boy says from somewhere nearby, but she can't see him.

"I wouldn't show this to anyone," she replies. "I wouldn't see it myself, if I had any say in the matter."

"She's a right yar little boat," the boy says. "She'll sail far and wide, round the Horn and back again, her holds filled to bursting with treasure and oil."

"Shut up," Salmagundi tells him, and she takes another step into the river.

Blue were her eyes as the fairy flax,
Her cheeks like the dawn of day,
And her bosom white as the hawthorn buds,
That ope in the month of May.

"What did you come here to find?" the boy asks. "Do you even know anymore? Did you ever."

The salt sea was frozen on her breast,
The salt tears in her eyes;
And he saw her hair, like the brown sea-weed,
On the billows fall and rise.

"Why have *you* come here, Sebastian? Why the fuck won't you go away and leave me alone?"

"Is that what you want? To be alone?"

And there's an angry, warning sound then from the low-slung sky, and Salammbô has already begun trying to untangle her sister's wet blonde hair from the branches when she finally notices the enormous autumn-colored serpent coiled between Salmagundi's breasts. Its eyes are rubies, and it flicks a forked lavender tongue, tasting the air. The rain begins a moment later.

They are alone on Moonstone Beach, days and days later, and many miles east of the cottage at Watch Hill. It's sunset, and for almost two hours they've been hunting for the wave-polished nuggets of grey-white orthoclase feldspar from which the beach takes its name, smooth and rounded pebbles of potassium aluminum silicate washed free of a submarine vein of igneous rock exposed somewhere not far offshore. And because he has no interest in such things, Salammbô has been lecturing the boy on local geology, explaining how this part of South County records a time of volcanism and mountain building dating back even before the dinosaurs, all the way to the Permian Age. She has also shown him shriveled black mermaid's purses, taking care to point out that they are actually only the egg cases of various sorts of skates, stingrays, and sharks. Near the place where the sand changes over to a dense tangle of beach roses, green briars, and poison ivy, back towards the dark, briny waters of Card and Trustom ponds, she found a number of baby Fowler's toads, and watching them hop and crawl across the sand, he thought he recognized something almost like excitement in her eyes.

"Do you even see the beach?" he asks, and for a moment she doesn't understand the question. "Do you see the *beach*, Salammbô," he continues, "the beauty of it as a whole, or are you too busy picking it apart and worrying over the innards and the skeleton and such."

She sits down, facing the ocean and the coming night, and Salammbô digs her bare toes into the sand. "I see the beach," she replies. "I see it as the sum of all its parts, all of which I try to understand, and this makes it that much more wondrous."

"That's not how it seems to me," says Sebastian, and he tosses one of the larger moonstones into the sea before sitting down beside her. "I don't see how can you be so clinical, so analytical and reductionist, and still manage to comprehend the whole. I think it's unknowable, in the end. This beach and every other beach in the world. You're only fooling yourself if you think otherwise."

She picks up a piece of driftwood and begins using it to draw circles between them. "So, this evening you have your thinking cap on. This evening, my pretty boy is feeling all philosophical."

"God, that's condescending. And I'm not yours," he tells her brusquely, pushing the sleeves of his summer sweater back up to his elbows. Linen yarn the color of oatmeal and brown sugar, a gift from Salammbô not long after he arrived, because he had nothing suitable for the cool Rhode Island evenings. "I won't ever be yours. Frankly, I doubt I'll ever be anyone's."

"Forgive the conceit," she says. "Indulge me just a little, now and then."

"It feels like all I ever do lately is indulge you," he says, and for a moment she wants to slap him, wants to slap him hard enough that his ears will ring and he'll taste copper. But the moment passes, and she goes back to drawing circles in the sand.

"Scientists," continues Sebastian, "are always too busy picking apart and asking questions, too busy chasing secrets to be bothered with what's right there in front of them."

"I'm not a scientist, not anymore," she replies, not taking her eyes off the sand and the things she's traced there. "I haven't been a scientist for a long, long time now. I'm quite sure I'll never be a scientist again."

"You still act like one."

"How's that, Sebastian?"

"I don't need to know unpronounceable Latin names or radiometric dates or what the fuck ever to appreciate a beach. I just need to open my eyes, and to listen, to smell and taste the salt on the air. I don't need someone telling me there's no such thing as mermaids, or that I won't really hear the ocean when I hold a shell to my ear. Maybe the mysteries are more important than all the answers you could ever think up."

"So, here I've gone and spoiled it for you?"

"No," he growls and kicks at the sand, raising a fine spray of grit and dried scraps of seaweed. "You couldn't ever spoil it for me. Christ, Salammbô, I'm not a child, and I didn't come here so you could tell me what's what and change the way I see the fucking world."

"Why *did* you come here?" she asks, and it's not like she's never asked him that before. She's asked him more times than she can now recall, and usually the boy has some answer or another at the ready, usually something about the old issue of *Fate* and what she might have seen that day twenty-two years ago on the parched shores of the Salton Sea. But this time he only sighs and shakes his head, as though he's never thought about it, or as if perhaps he once knew perfectly well, but has now forgotten his reason for seeking her out and moving in and becoming her second shadow.

"Then I'll tell you something," she says and wipes her right palm across the sand, erasing all the circles drawn there. "I'll answer a question."

"That figures," he mutters. "I don't have my tape recorder, so now you'll talk."

"Oh, I think you'll remember. You can write it all down later. Hell, I'll even sign it, if you want, like an affidavit or a deposition or something."

"What happened at Bombay Beach?" he asks hopefully.

"No, not that," and Salammbô Desvernine ignores the sour look of disappoint and the way it spoils his face and dims his bright eyes. "Not that. But another question you've asked me."

The boy lifts his head and stares out at Block Island Sound, at the darkening sea and the sky washed indigo and pink, purple and all manner of ashy grays. "The tides coming in," he says.

"You want to hear this or not?" she asks, and he tosses another pebble at the waves. "Or have you had some sort of sudden epiphany? Have you decided it's too much like a scientist, what you're doing, too busy chasing all these secrets to be bothered with what's right there in front of you? Maybe missing the forest for the trees?"

"Fuck you," he says. "It's not the same thing, and you know it's not the same thing. Don't you dare try to use my own words against me."

"Sebastian, you'd best learn something right now, something you should have learned long ago. Your own words are your worst enemy and will almost always be used against you. That's what it usually comes down to, sooner or later. You open your mouth and someone hears, and they take note. And they wait for just the right moment."

"You're so goddamned cynical," he sighs.

"Be that as it may, I'm telling you the truth. Now, dear, do you want to have one of your questions answered, or would you rather preserve the mystery a little longer, whole and intact? The choice is yours, and I wouldn't dare presume to make it for you."

Sebastian takes a deep breath and lets it out slowly, keeping his eyes on the lights of a fishing boat bobbing about a few hundred yards out into the sound. "You'll tell me, Salammbô, because that's what you want or need to do. It's not about the choices I make, so don't pretend it is."

"Very well," she says, and now she's also watching the little boat, the yellow-orange incandescent flicker from its wheelhouse and the Christmas-tree sparkle of running lights—green to starboard, red to port, and white at the stern. And Salammbô tells the boy why she lives alone in the cottage at Watch Hill, why she has no friends to speak of, which was one of the first questions he ever asked her. In the end, it's only a story of having had her words and secrets, her confidences, turned against her by someone she once believed entirely beyond any acts of betrayal. A story of pettiness and cruelty and of the lies friends will tell when a friendship has ceased to be profitable or convenient. It is a very simple and inexpressibly complex story of cowardice, of a woman who forsook herself and Salammbô and hid behind a man, the low and brutal sort of man who can be used as a battering ram and yet still think himself chivalrous, a knight-errant who really has no more honor or fidelity than a sledgehammer. And by the time she's done, the waxing moon is up and the beach is dark, and Sebastian sits there on the sand, shivering and hugging himself as the tide rises quickly, inexorably, towards them.

"Rivers of blood that vein albuminous seas, or an egg-like composition, in the incubation of which this earth is a local center of development—that there are super-arteries of blood in Genesistrine: that sunsets are consciousness of them: that they flush the skies with northern lights sometimes: super-embry-onic reservoirs from which life-forms emanate—

"Or that our whole solar system is a living thing: that show-ers of blood upon this earth are its internal hemorrhages—

"Or vast living things in the sky, as there are vast living things in the oceans—

"Or some one especial thing: an especial time: an especial place. A thing the size of the Brooklyn Bridge. It's alive in outer space—something the size of Central Park kills it—

"It drips.

"We think of ice fields above this earth: which do not, them-selves, fall to this earth, but from which water does fall—"

—Charles Fort, *The Book of the Damned* (1919)

And because it was inevitable from the day she let the boy cross her threshold and take up residence in her home, the night fi-nally arrives when she tells him what he's come all the way from Hartford or Providence or Albany to hear. It is another dinner, near the end of August, where the summer has begun to lose its grip on New England, and he sits across from her in an emer-ald-green, floor-length evening gown and a wig that doesn't look the least bit like a wig. His face is painted perfect as a run-way model's, and he drinks the Madeira she has poured for him.

"Don't expect to hear exactly what you read in that article," she says, and Sebastian tells her that he would be disappointed if he did. "For starters," she adds, "I wrote that thing in 1988. Also, it's full of lies, not to mention changes that the editor made for reasons known only to himself and maybe a few of the lesser Assyrian deities."

Salammbô is drunk, and she knows it. Otherwise, she never would have found the courage to say the things she's about to say. The boy is sober as a judge, and he watches her the way a cat watches a mouse that has not yet stopped twitching, and his RadioShack tape recorder sits on the table between them, taking down every word.

"Bombay Beach," he says.

"Bombay Beach," she nods, and then describes the neat rows of desolation at the edge of the Salton Sea, five streets north to south, eight east to west. The power poles like humming crucifixions lined up beneath the blue-white desert sky and the scrubby brown land at the base of the San Bernardino Mountains, two-hundred and twenty-eight feet below sea level. Shacks and RVs, mobile homes and crumbling cinderblock, rusting tin roofs, someplace that may as well be the very edge of the world, and perhaps it is. She tells him that Bombay Beach was founded in 1929 by a man named R. E. Gilligan, and once upon a time it was a mecca for vacationers and retirees, back when the inland sea was not so salty, when there were still plenty of fish, and before floods submerged a sizable portion of the town below Fifth Street.

"I wanted to see the Salton, that's all," she says, and so she took the only exit into Bombay off California 111 and followed A Street to Avenue A where the road veered left, becoming 5th Street. She parked her car and walked the three hundred or so feet to the water's edge, and for a while Salammbô dwells on the details—an abandoned motel, wooden pilings encrusted with salt, a school bus sunk into the rime almost up to its roof, the gulls and pelicans, the water so still and flat it might well be made of polished glass. "Those science-fiction movies set in wastelands after nuclear wars," she says, "that's what it was like standing there on the shore of the Salton Sea."

And then Salammbô turns and watches the open dining room window leading out to that other, living sea while she talks about coming upon the naked brown-skinned girl kneeling in the mud, the girl whose throat had been cut from ear to ear, but there she was anyway, kneeling like any good Catholic, her coral rosary beads still clutched tightly in her folded hands.

"There wasn't anything like that in the article," Sebastian protests, and Salammbô asks him to please not interrupt her, not if he has any desire to hear the rest.

"The birds had already taken her eyes," she says, "but her face was turned upwards—towards Heaven, I suppose. She must still have believed, even as the murderer's knife or razor was drawn across her skin, even as her life sprayed from severed arteries onto the dust and sand and the evaporite rind of that poisonous fucking lake. She must have been waiting for the bloody fucking Virgin Mary or Jesus or some saint to come down on rays of pure, blazing light and bear her safely up into a place where children are not raped and killed and left to rot and feed the gulls and maggots.

"I am not ashamed to say that I was sick then. It must have been quite a picture, if anyone was looking, the girl's kneeling corpse and me beside her on hands and knees, puking up my breakfast."

Sebastian sips the dry Madeira squeezed from white Cerceal grapes and bottled five years earlier, and he doesn't look at Salammbô, and he doesn't say a word.

"I sat there with her for, I don't know, maybe an hour, maybe an hour and a half, thinking surely someone would come along, you know, and then I could tell them to go for the police. But nobody ever came. I didn't want to leave her by herself like that, but that's exactly what I finally did. I got up and walked back to my car and drove away to the goddamn interstate and didn't stop driving until I was all the way in fucking Palm Springs. And that's what happened, my dear Sebastian. That's the day I saw blood rain from the sky above the Salton Sea. That's the day I began to..." but she trails off and sits staring silently at the window, listening to the soothing canticle of chilly wind and the breakers and the clang of the bell buoy anchored at Watch Hill Point.

And the boy shuts off the tape recorder, and then he sits quietly, finishing his wine and waiting for Salammbô Desvernine to say anything else at all.

Epilogue:

Zelda Fitzgerald in Ballet Attire

1

In this absence of others
There is not the peace we're led
To believe in like Sunday school

I cannot hear for the roar This wind
Has me half-deaf Good as that
Or more
Nothing has been restored Things fall apart and
That's the way
They stay
Nothing to be learned except edges slice and
Children take apart because
They can and cry at the mess
They've made   Oh

Look to Father for the glue (which is Heaven)
To mother for licking wounds (which is this
Brooding shade with crystal wrists)   Oh

2

Ugly lines of paper houses
The sky is never dark
And the stars forget themselves
We are pink eyes in cages

3

Our lives are not innocent
Any more than they can be romantic;
The long red century has laid dull stone
Between us and any finer attribute.

We have buried what we might have known of
Such things,
Sewn the graves with salt and indifference
That nothing might grow there ever again
Except dim and orphaned memory.

There are words we cannot even write,
Or speak, for the forgetting of their sincerity.

Eggshell and no
Royal restoration.
These fragments shored
For you, and I finally see for you alone.

October 12, 1995 — July 20, 1999

Afterword
by Peter Straub

1

CAITLÍN R. KIERNAN STRIDES INTO A ROOM WITH A look in her eye that says you had better come up to the mark, because you won't get much slack from *this* quarter. Her shoulders are back, her spine is straight, and she projects the charismatic confident self-sufficiency seen only in tall people who learned long ago that the only way to carry off their height is not to slouch—as weaker souls do—but to suggest by their posture that they are even taller. (I don't know how tall Caitlín actually is, but I'm 6′2″, and I'm pretty sure she looks at me straight-on, face-to-face. In fact, there are times when Caitlín appears to gaze down at me from a position located several inches above eye-level, even under conditions that render it physically impossible, as, for example, when I am seated comfortably but inelegantly in a chair and she has deployed herself on the floor.) Let's go back to the moment Caitlín enters our hypothetical room—she is wearing attractive gear layered with a kind of stylish bohemian panache that suits her down to the ground, party clothes for a party a bit more *louche* than those to which you are accustomed, especially if you are over forty. She moves from person to person, making the sort of remarks that are called "asides," her manner modulating from the confidential to the disengaged to the amused as she progresses, all the while ignoring the rude fact that most of the other people in the room, in varying degrees of obviousness, happen to be looking at her.

The word "striking" has been applied to Caitlín Kiernan so often that it has ceased to be anything but irritating, and with good reason. "Striking," an otherwise harmless pat on the back, implies the refusal to articulate any definition more nuanced; it's a cop-out. Caitlín *is* striking; she's the sort of person who instantly compels attention, but so are Madonna, George Hamilton, Dennis Rodman, Placido Domingo, RuPaul, Sandra Bernhart, Iggy Pop, and the late Duke Ellington. We need, and Caitlín deserves, more specificity.

Caitlín Kiernan is first of all a writer distinguished by certain unique gifts; from that everything else flows. Like all worthwhile writers of fiction, she is in urgent possession of a vision, a point of view communicable only through representation in an ongoing series of short stories and novels. For those who find themselves under this obligation, fiction presents itself as a kind of aperture. The aperture provides a means of both expression and focus, but it is narrow and infinitely difficult to negotiate. Supple, exploratory access to its resources is given only to those whose internal structures render such access crucial to psychic survival, and in most cases the discovery of how best to use it arrives after years of unrewarding slog. No one unaffected by this weird process could be expected to understand it, a matter which results in a widespread delusion amongst the civilian populace.

If you happen to be a writer, during the course of almost every social situation some vainglorious, well-meaning idiot is going to plant himself before you and explain that had he not gone into brain surgery, real estate sales, pork belly futures, or the importation of black-market domestic servants, he'd be a writer, too, because he is a creative-type person, just like you, only he never had the time to put his ideas on paper. (The best response to this kind of thing is, "You know, that's interesting.

I always knew I could be a brain surgeon, but I was too busy writing to get around to it.") A good part of Caitlín's presence is grounded in the awareness of having successfully evolved a distinctive voice and manner all her own, which, with unerring instinct, she turned to the investigation of a fictional territory ideally suited to their particular resonances.

That landscape haunts the stories in *Tales of Pain and Wonder*, a perfect title for this collection. The setting changes from Athens, Georgia, to Los Angeles, New York City, New Orleans, Atlanta, San Francisco, and a Hudson River island near Storm King mountain, but the nature of the territory, the essential landscape, remains the same. Kiernan's characters inhabit a worn-out, exhausted world long since degraded by pollution and neglect into a uniformly oppressive bleakness.

... the asphalt ended in sticky red mud and pine trees, pothole alley behind the shopping center. Much darker back there, tree shadows, whispering needles and dumpster shadows, wet garbage stink.

("Superheroes")

Salmagundi Desvernine ... stares through broken panes across the corrugated rooftops towards front gates padlocked and chained against the world outside ... strains to steal a glimpse beyond the road that winds through other abandoned industries, disappears, finally, between high gneiss and granite bluffs, boulders pollution-scarred and spray-paint tagged, wrapped in fog the color of rust.

("Glass Coffin")

Stinking maze of loading docks and wholesale butchers: diesel fumes, fresh blood; knives and meat hooks for everything down here. Past concrete and greasy plastic drums marked INEDIBLE—DO NOT EAT ...

("The Last Child of Lir")

The interiors of the rooms, clubs and theaters where the characters sleep, eat, have sex and pursue their obsessions, and through which they drift in search of amusement or enlightenment, offer an only slightly domesticated version of the devastation outside. Broken glass litters the concrete floors; the windows are either filthy or cracked; the furniture is junk; elevators reek of urine, and staircases threaten. Rubbish accumulates. We are located well below the poverty line, and all living arrangements are temporary. Hopeless squalor has become a common condition, as if in the wake of some apocalyptic catastrophe.

Lost and passive, the affectless boys and girls who populate these stories, too childish to be called men and women even when they are approaching thirty, unquestioningly accept the hopelessness of their surroundings and live within its paralyzing terms. All but three of these characters seem to have entered the world unburdened by the presence of mothers and fathers, and for an excellent reason: Were we to be introduced to their parents, the larger, more explanatory psychological framework in which we would instantly begin to locate Deacon, Magwitch, Rabbit, Glitch, Erica, Lark and Crispin is utterly irrelevant to Kiernan's concerns. Psychological insight, which permits a kind of description in fact detached from judgment, is none the less often experienced as judgmental, as are other neutral forms of description. Even the hint of conventional judgment, however misapplied, would interfere with our appreciation of these stories. We must take Kiernan's disenfranchised protagonists on their own terms, as her fiction presents them to us. Once we have done so, we are free to notice what matters, what is important about them.

These lost children know they have the life expectancy of moths, and that predators, human and otherwise, lurk and hover, yet an instinctive gallantry prohibits them from feeling anything like self-pity. They seldom whine. In the absence of other structures, they have chosen their own elective families, to which they are deeply loyal. These people are fellow-travel-ers, they're in it together, and for all their mutual bitching they care for the well-being of their companions. They stick up for and defend each other, sometimes at tremendous cost. Marginalization, poverty and precarious health have not stripped them of a kind of valor, a kind of courageous readiness. Although by conventional standards nearly everything about their circumstances conspires to make them seem dismissible—their aimlessness, squalor, drug usage, crazy sexual tropisms and pathetic ambitions, if they have ambitions—they are in no way to be dismissed. Kiernan's characters have adapted to their surroundings so thoroughly that they might as well have been produced by them, and are not so much without ambition as beyond it. In the most basic way, they are *getting on*. For all their fragility, they are open to the extraordinary experiences lying in wait for them. Their receptivity to the extraordinary, a category which here involves horror, monstrosity, mystery, enigma, ecstasy, revulsion, and the sense of the sacred, depends upon their vulnerability.

A symbiotic connection between revelation and alienated protagonists in ill health resonates throughout the Romantic tradition. (More about this later. Kiernan's attachment to the essentially Romantic, early-Modernist poets William Butler Yeats and T. S. Eliot adds another, extremely interesting, layer to these stories.) This connection, long ago become so thematic as to be nearly reflexive, can these days be found in the work of M. John Harrison, Ramsey Campbell, Thomas Tessier, Poppy Z. Brite, and plenty of others, including me. For writers, who always feel marginalized, the notion that wounded outcasts are uniquely equipped to receive deep-level transmissions cannot help but be seductive. (There's some truth in it, as the lives of many gifted writers, musicians and other artists indicate. Think of Hart Crane and Poe, think of Charlie Parker.) Kiernan's remarkable contribution to our literature has been to mold this theme into an expressive vehicle by embedding it within her narrative technique, thereby creating the aesthetic which gives these stories their expressive and individual form.

The most significant characters in *Tales Pain And Wonder* appear and reappear throughout the collection, surfacing in one location or another over time. Deacon "Deke" Silvey moves to Birmingham, Alabama, from Atlanta; the twins Crispin and Lark drift from Los Angeles to Seattle and San Francisco, then back to L.A.; Jenny Haniver finds her way from a derelict New Jersey shipyard, inherited by Salmagundi and Salammbô Desvernine, to a basement apartment in Greenwich Village; a homicidal drug dealer extravagantly named Jimmy DeSade pilots an old Lincoln from Georgia to Mexico, New Orleans, Los Angeles and New York; but no matter where they travel none of them ever change or grow. Moving around is merely a literalization of the aimlessness and passivity that render them suitable for their essential task. They are to serve as witnesses. In story after story, Kiernan's protagonists are led into variations on the theme of a shattering encounter with profound Otherness, a revelation of hideous and seductive powers which enforce an increased helplessness and passivity upon those with whom they come into contact.

In their obdurate purity of means, their dream-like refusal to yield any more information than is necessary for the creation of the central effect, the stories themselves echo the condition of the characters within them. Only a handful—"Breakfast in the House of the Rising Sun," "In the Water Works," "San Andreas" and perhaps "Estate"—unfold in the manner common to short stories from Chekhov to Flannery O'Connor, by suspending details and events along a narrative arc like that of a novel in miniature. Kiernan can martial her material into that kind of form whenever she feels like loosening up and getting expansive, but the nature of her vision customarily demands a more compressed, elided and enigmatic narrative technique. Cinematic pans and jump-cuts from character to character are cut to the bone, along with back-story explanations; plot has been distilled down to movement towards encounter and encounter; in the absence of familiar narrative comforts, details take on a surreal glow, and the trappings of rationality evaporate; a fetishistic, entranced eroticism prevails; meaning is devoured by mystery, and coherence can be glimpsed only in terrifying, myth-like fragments.

The fragmentation of coherence and the disappearance of meaning reduce value, as generally understood, to loyalty to one's companions and the awareness of exhaustion and despair. The world is dying, and faith is dead. Human behavior is seen to be parodic and empty. The human body, formerly an emblem of value, has become deeply distasteful, a revulsion, an object best treated with mutilation, injury, deliberate wounding.

Yet fractured coherence speaks of a larger, genuine coherence existing either in memory or immediately beyond human apprehension. Uniquely qualified for the role, Kiernan's characters are led to their moment of witness—their perception of alien Otherness—and find in it an enigmatic but persuasive transcendence. Certain scholarly or scientifically-disposed characters, collectors of oddities preserved in glass jars and fishtanks, have devoted themselves to research into explanatory Otherness; the rest, aided or not by the efforts of the former, stumble upon it. In both cases, revelation typically occurs in the rich psychic terrain invoked by journey *downward* and *inward*, movement beneath the earth's crust, movement into secret passages, mineshafts, hidden realms.

~ 2 ~

"They were keeping her in a subbasement, Deke."

Abandoned warehouses, basements, subbasements, crypts, sewers, underground rivers, subterranean caves...the ultimately authoritative lurks underground, often in a cavern with access to water. Water-creatures of all kinds, being cold-blooded and inhuman, imply its presence, for There is a wavering yellow-green light beneath the water, the gaudy drab light of things which will never see the sun and have learned to make their own ("Tears Seven Times Salt"). In "Paedomorphosis," Annie, a halfheartedly aspiring musician disaffected with her "baby dyke" bandmates, encounters goth Elise, a paleontologist's daughter who seduces her on a "shimmering carpet like all the colors of autumn lying beneath still and murky waters," then entices her through underground vaults to an black lake inhabited by "fetal" salamanders "the pinkwhite of an old scar," and provides the most humane, intimate revelation of an underlying Otherness in these stories by raising her arms to expose the presence of gills, "crimson slits where her armpits should be, the feathered edges bright with oxygen-rich blood, gasping slits like twin and puckered mouths." Ever after, Annie is haunted by a vision of "vast and empty spaces."

Vastness, emptiness, and coldness are the touchstones of the mysterious and alien set of forces to which the disenfranchised elect are given access. "Postcards From the King of Tides," one of this collection's most effective stories, moves like a series of snapshots depicting the progress of hapless Lark and Crispin, twins marked with "the stain of protracted innocence," from a stalled car across a stream to signs advertising mermaids and miracles! and into a seedy trailer smelling of saltwater and rot, where a sinister caretaker offers, what else, ranks of pickled curiosities floating in jars and at last thrusts aside a curtain and displays his final exhibit. Arctic cold pours from the opened space. The old man recites Tennyson on the Kraken:

There hath he lain for ages, and will lie
Battening upon huge sea worms in his sleep,
Until the latter fire shall heat the deep...

Lark yields to a swooning sense of immanence that threatens to engulf her within "this perfect, absolute cold and darkness...and the thing swimming through the black." When Crispin wrenches her away, a "sudden emptyhollow feeling... like waking from a dream of heaven or someone dead alive again" pierces her—she has been given a vision of a destructive purity.

"The Long Hall on the Top Floor" extends the moment of revelation into an account of its emotional consequences.

Sadie, a zombie-like young woman with "boiled fish eyes," brings the wasted psychic Deacon Silvey to an old warehouse and leads him upstairs to a hallway. Again, the visionary encounter begins with an immersion into coldness that "isn't *just* cold, it's indifference, the freezing temperature of an apathy so absolute, so perfect." Undone, Silvey collapses, keeping his eyes helplessly on the tiny window at the corridor's end, where a "dim shadow," a "fluid stain," resembles wings "or long, jointed legs moving fast through some deep and secret ocean." These images are mere approximations, he understands; what he has glimpsed is beyond his comprehension and neither wishes nor is meant to be seen. Sadie refuses to play along. Awed recognition has shocked her out of zombie-hood, and she insists on putting into words the stages, one by one, of her recognition. We can paraphrase the steps of her recognition in this way:

1) *Whatever I saw was beautiful.*

2) *The power of its beauty forced me to find out if that thing was real, and I did find out. It was real, all right.*

3) *Even though it was horrible and frightening, I am grateful for its reality. Everything else is so empty of meaning that only fear reminds me I am   still alive.*

Transcendence, in this world the single escape from a pervasive death-in-life, has become inextricably dependent upon the shock of fear.

～ 3 ～

And now there's writing there, sloppy words scrawled in something black; runny, black words . . .

We have arrived at a point not far from Rilke and the visionary insights at the beginning of the first Duino Elegy:

Denn das Schöne is nichts / als des Schrecklichen Anfang, den wir noch grade ertragen,

("For beauty is nothing / but the beginning of terror, which we are still just able to endure,")

and

Ein jeder Engel ist schrecklich.

("Every angel is terrifying.")

Nothing could be further from the reassuring New Age oatmeal ladled out by beloved "uplift" merchants like Marianne Williamson, Deepak Chopra, and their myriad clones, who want us to know that if only we were to cast off our negativity we would wake up mystically fulfilled in a paradisal garden. A search for "Angels" in any on-line bookstore turns up an endless list of books about personal encounters with warm-hearted celestial beings always prepared to step in and offer assistance, as Della Reese does every Sunday evening, right after *60 Minutes.* (Ms. Reese and her fellow-angels are terrifying, all right, but not in the way Rilke meant. Television angels, and the ones in cuddly best-sellers, behave like the know-it-all relatives you dread seeing at Thanksgiving.) The kind of people who benignly think of themselves as "spiritual" never understand this, but sublimity incorporates a substantial quantity of terror, and mystery, being by definition inhuman, ruthlessly violates rational order. Violence shares a border with the sacred. Mystery accommodates awe and fear, emotional majesty and emotional devastation. Kiernan's title, *Tales of Pain and Wonder,* instantly locates us within an educated point of view, one which has been defined by her responses to both personal experience and the experience of literature.

The idea of literature, representing art in general as our most accurate and comprehensive means of expression, haunts this collection like a despairing ghost. Matthew Arnold's "Dover Beach," Eliot's "The Waste Land," and the poetry of Yeats float beneath the surface of the prose, their resonant summations of lost faith, lost coherence, lost innocence in a fragmented, brutally degraded world with "neither joy, nor love, nor light,/ Nor certitude, nor peace" invoking the painful recognition of their own lost usefulness. Only a very few of the characters in these stories call upon the resources of art, and those that do meet with frustration. Here, a deeply literary sensibility seems to turn against itself and declare its own central touchstones no longer valid. Salmagundi Desvernine, who escapes the self-imprisonment of the typical Kiernan protagonist by fleeing from ruined Pollepel to San Francisco and becoming an avant-garde artist, laments the death of poetry—and, by extension, all of literature—in two of the collection's most finely developed stories, "Salmagundi" and "…Between the Gargoyle Trees." On both occasions, she uses the same words, condemns the same villain, and refers to the same iconic figure of now-unattainable verbal authenticity, William Butler Yeats.

Poetry isn't just dead, it was *killed*, done away with by contemporary poets who "eviscerated" poetry by making "emotion almost completely inaccessible through language." Salmagundi disdainfully calls these murderers *they*, thereby turning them into a faceless crowd, a kind of lynch mob. *They* consist of "Everyone after [or since] fucking Yeats and T. S. Eliot [or fucking William Yeats]." "Salmagundi" gives us a little more specificity by referring to "The 'poet-citizens,'" but it's still difficult to identify the villains. The category "everyone after Eliot and Yeats" includes an enormous number of poets of wildly differing techniques, approaches, value-systems, and poetics. Was Wallace Stevens a "poet-citizen"? (Yes, probably.) Were Robert Lowell, John Berryman, and Elizabeth Bishop? (Dubious.) Or Anne Sexton and Sylvia Plath? (Even more dubious.) Frank O'Hara, John Ashbery, and James Schuyler? (Not at all, although Salmagundi Desvernine might find them guilty of having done a gene-splice on the traditional relationship between words and feelings. In 1922, a lot of people accused T. S. Eliot of the same offense.)

Of course, in the end these quibbles mean nothing—I bring

them up only because Kiernan is using her artist-*savant* to express a blanket condemnation she herself knows better than to share. Salmagundi Desvernine, that extraordinary character, progresses towards immaculate failure and abandonment of the human realm; her creator is shoring fragments against the widespread ruin, bringing into being a condemned universe shot through with golden threads.

Nothing is ever the same as they said it was.
It's what I've never seen before that I recognize.

—Diane Arbus (1971)

I shake,
For the reeking flesh
Is as romantic as hell.
The need to have seen it all,
The voyeur of utter destruction as beauty.
I shake.

—David Bowie (1995)

ALTERNATIVE TABLE OF CONTENTS

THE TWENTY-TWO STORIES that comprise this edition of *Tales of Pain and Wonder* have been arranged according to the date that they were written, regardless of the very loose narrative that connects many of the pieces. Below is an alternative Table of Contents with the stories arranged by their narrative chronology, for those wishing to read them in that order.

About the Author

THE NEW YORK TIMES recently called Caitlín R. Kiernan "one of our essential writers of dark fiction" and S. T. Joshi has declared "...hers is now the voice of weird fiction." Her novels include *Silk, Threshold, Low Red Moon, Daughter of Hounds, The Red Tree* (nominated for the Shirley Jackson and World Fantasy awards), and *The Drowning Girl: A Memoir* (winner of the James Tiptree, Jr. and Bram Stoker awards, nominated for the Nebula, World Fantasy, British Fantasy, Mythopoeic, Locus, and Shirley Jackson awards). To date, her short fiction has been collected in thirteen volumes, including *Tales of Pain and Wonder, From Weird and Distant Shores, Alabaster, A is for Alien, The Ammonite Violin & Others, Confessions of a Five-Chambered Heart, Two Worlds and In Between: The Best of Caitlín R. Kiernan (Volume One)*, and the World Fantasy Award winning *The Ape's Wife and Other Stories.* She has also won a World Fantasy Award for Best Short Fiction for "The Prayer of Ninety Cats." During the 1990s, she wrote *The Dreaming* for DC Comics' Vertigo imprint and has recently completed *Alabaster* for Dark Horse Comics. The first volume, *Alabaster: Wolves*, received the Bram Stoker Award. She lives in Providence, Rhode Island with her partner, Kathryn Pollnac.

But all she ever *wanted* was to be a paleontologist...

About the Artist

RICHARD A. KIRK was born in Hull, England in 1962. He lives and works in Canada. In addition to illustrating works by Caitlin R. Kiernan, Richard has illustrated numerous books for authors such as Clive Barker, China Mieville, Thomas Ligotti, and Christopher Golden. Most recently, Richard created the artwork for eighth the studio release by the band Korn.

Richard is an active gallery artist, showing internationally with the Strychnin Gallery in New York, Berlin, London and many other cities. His works can be found in many private collections throughout the world.

For further information, visit Richard's online gallery at www.richardakirk.com.